NOMAD

James Swallow is an veteran author and scriptwriter with over fifteen years of experience in fiction, television, radio, journalism, new media and video games.

He is a three-time New York Times bestselling author of thirty-eight novels with over 750,000 books currently in print, in nine different worldwide territories.

He was nominated by the British Academy of Film and Television Arts (BAFTA) for his writing on the critically acclaimed DEUS EX: HUMAN REVOLUTION, 2013's blockbuster videogame with over 2.18 million copies sold.

قف

NOMAD

JAMES SWALLOW

ZAFFRE

First published in Great Britain in 2016 by
ZAFFRE PUBLISHING
80-81 Wimpole St, London W1G 9RE
www.zaffrebooks.co.uk

A CIP catalogue record for this book is available from the British Library.

Hardback ISBN: 978-1-78576-041-9
Trade Paperback ISBN: 978-1-78576-183-6
Ebook ISBN: 978-1-78576-042-6

1 3 5 7 9 10 8 6 4 2

Typeset by IDSUK (Data Connection) Ltd

Printed and bound by Clays Ltd, St Ives Plc

Zaffre Publishing is an imprint of Bonnier Zaffre,
a Bonnier Publishing company
www.bonnierzaffre.co.uk
www.bonnierpublishing.co.uk

For Mum and Dad,
who drew the map,
and for Mandy,
who had the compass.

This book is dedicated to the memory of Darren Mills.

ONE

The day was coming to an end, but still the heat fell like hammers.

Barcelona shimmered as if it were a mirage, the air lensed by the warmth of the day escaping from the narrow streets, back into the cloudless sky. As he walked, Pasco patted his shoulder with a rolled-up copy of *El Periodico*, tapping out an aimless rhythm across the top of his *sergent*'s chevrons. His uniform shirt was sticking to his barrel chest, but he didn't notice it. Pasco was a son of this city, fourth-generation, and he'd grown up in the Balearic sunshine. His old face attested to that, careworn like good calf-skin leather.

He navigated around the knots of tourists and locals without really being aware of it. The uniform did most of the work for him, the pale blue of the Mossos d'Esquadra and the red-banded cap on his head cutting a path through people on the busy street. Now that the sun had dropped below the rooftops, the first wave of revellers were shaking off their siesta and coming out to play. Joining them were pale Germans and paler British, yet to build up a tolerance to the heat and grateful for the cooling atmosphere and the open-air cafes in this part of the old town. Minor criminals – pickpockets and opportunist thieves – would already be among them.

But few would be found near this corner of the Ciutat Vella district, thanks to the imposing, slab-sided shape of the main police station on the Nou de la Rambla. It was a charmless building, all heavy white stone and blue-tinted glass, built with the modernist ethic that had swept over the city in the last few decades.

He crossed the station's courtyard, passing Enrique going the other way, and the two policemen exchanged nods. Enrique pointed at the newspaper. 'Hey, Abello. Finish it today?' He smiled, showing tobacco-stained teeth.

Pasco snapped open the paper with a flourish. It was a little ritual that they shared once a week, when the cryptic crossword was published. He offered it to Enrique to show him that every clue had been filled in, the letters written in a careful hand.

The younger man scowled. Pasco knew the other *sergent* hadn't completed the puzzle himself, which meant that Enrique would be required to buy him a packet of the good cigarillos, as their regular competition demanded.

'You've got better all of a sudden,' Enrique asked, with no little suspicion.

Pasco gave a shrug. 'The warm air. Makes me smarter.'

Enrique's scowl deepened. 'If I catch you cheating, I will fill your desk with cat shit.' He gave a rueful smile of defeat and walked on.

Pasco snorted. Soon, perhaps in a week or two, after he had made up enough wins to redress the lead Enrique had on him, he would reveal his secret. A birthday gift from his grandson, an electronic gadget that kept all his names and address, birthdates and phone numbers. It was a clever thing, packed with a huge library of words and phrases in different languages, and it had come in useful more than once when Pasco had found himself dealing with foreign tourists. It also had a dictionary in it that was excellent at suggesting whole words when you only had a few letters to go on.

Thinking about the boy made him think about his son, and guilt stirred in his chest. He was supposed to call him yesterday, but after work a few of the men went to the local bar and he had lost the rest of the evening with his colleagues and their rough good humour.

Pasco sighed. His son worried about him now that his mother was with the angels. *Papa, a man like you should not be walking the streets*, he would say. *Policeman is a job for men of my age, not yours. Let them give you a desk.*

A desk; the very idea made Pasco's heart shrink in his chest. He loved this city like it was his own private property, and to see it from behind a desk, day in and day out . . . His son didn't understand that it would be a slow death for him, slow and hard, like the cancer that had taken his beautiful Rosa.

Through the glass doors into the precinct hall, a steady mutter of conversation and office noise washed over him. Stepping through the arches of the metal detectors, he nodded absently to the man on duty there as the scanner bleated. The other police officer waved him through with a distracted nod.

Pasco doffed his cap and he tried to push his thoughts of family aside. There were bigger problems for Pasco to deal with. Sometimes, his son seemed like he had come from another planet, with all his talk of things like the global warming that made the summer heat murderous, the scandals of the impossibly rich, and the men of other countries who seemed to kill each other for reasons Pasco couldn't begin to fathom.

He sighed. It was because of those things that he didn't buy the paper for the news anymore. All too depressing. It was just the crossword now, and nothing else.

Pasco noticed the boy then, and chided himself for being too deep in his own head. It was no reason not to remain observant.

The youth was in his late teens, but the pallor of his face made it difficult to be certain exactly how old he was. He had a heavy brow and dark eyes, filled with worry. The ends of black curls peeked out from under a tan painter's cap, the rest of him hidden inside a nondescript tracksuit the colour of tilled earth. He walked like his training shoes were too tight for him, stepping awkwardly as he made his way toward the big desk where Tomás the duty officer was growling something at a junior mosso.

The youth became aware of Pasco looking directly at him and flinched as if he had been struck. The *sergent* got a good look at him then, head on. He was washed out, filmed with sweat, and there was a line of bruising on his neck.

His eyes, though, were what caught Pasco. The teenager's eyes were so very serious, in that way that only the young were capable of. He saw his son and his grandson in them.

The youth in the tracksuit gave him an owlish blink, as if he was going to say something, and then his legs bent under him. He landed hard on the tiled floor and skidded. People heard the impact, the heavy noise of it echoing in the hall, and they turned to stare.

Pasco was immediately at the teenager's side, kneeling down to look him over. He looked ill; not like a junkie dragged through withdrawal, but someone afflicted with the sort of bone-deep sickness that ate away at a person. 'Are you all right, boy?' asked the *sergent*. 'What's the matter? Do you need a doctor?'

The look Pasco got in return told him that the youth didn't understand a word of Spanish. Part of his mind – the trained, focused part of him that was pure police – was already evaluating the boy, thinking of him in terms of how he would be logged and reported in the day's paperwork. 'Where are you from?' He asked the question without thinking about it. The silent youth looked back with his serious eyes.

The *sergent* cast around and found a familiar face in the yellow and orange of a paramedic's jacket. 'Noya!' He shouted the girl's name, but she was already on her way to him, the toolbox-shape of an emergency kit in her gloved hand.

Noya was a regular at the precinct. The petite Catalan girl was part of an ambulance crew from the local hospital, and more often than not, when a medical crisis arose at the station, her team was the one that answered the call. Pasco liked her even though a lot of the other men didn't. She was brisk and severe, but fiercely competent.

'Help me get him over to a bench,' she demanded. Between them, they helped the youth stagger to a wooden seat in the waiting area, the paramedic yelling at the people sat upon it to vacate. They scattered and Pasco laid the boy down.

His breathing changed, coming in short gasps like a frightened animal.

The level of noise in the entrance hall dropped as people began to notice what was going on, pausing in the middle of their own little dramas to watch the unfolding of this one. Some were coming closer to get a better look.

Noya snapped her fingers to attract the youth's attention. 'Hey. Can you hear me?'

'I don't think he understands,' Pasco told her.

She had her fingers at his neck, checking his pulse. 'It's not heat-stroke,' Noya replied. She reached for the zipper on his tracksuit jacket and the boy snatched at it, preventing the paramedic from opening it. A new emotion crept into his eyes; *fear*. He tried to speak, but all that came out was a dry gasp.

'I need to open your shirt.' Noya said sternly. She waggled a stethoscope at him. 'To listen.' She was speaking loudly and over-enunciating each word, as if talking to a slow child.

The youth looked past her to Pasco, and again he tried to say something. Licking dry lips, he forced out a word, and the effort seemed to cost him.

The *sergent* only caught part of it and he leaned in. The boy tried again, and this time Pasco heard the whisper clearly.

'*Shahiden*.'

The word meant nothing to him. He frowned.

'Get back,' Noya snapped at Pasco. 'Don't crowd me.' She tried to grab the zipper, and again the youth resisted her. She scowled. 'I don't have time for this.' The paramedic pulled an ingot of bright orange plastic from her pocket. A rescue tool, it was typically used for cutting the seatbelts off victims of traffic accidents, but Noya could wield it like a surgeon, and with a single swift motion she hooked it in the tracksuit collar and sliced it open.

Pasco did as he was told, falling back a step or two, giving Noya room to work. Her partner, a skinny Portuguese lad, came across the hall with a folding stretcher in one hand. The youth said the word again, and without thinking about it, Pasco pulled out his birthday gift and thumbed the tab marked *Translator*. As best he could, he repeated what he had heard into the device's pinhole microphone.

It would not have been an exaggeration to say that Jadeed's room was the most expensive space he had ever been in. The executive suite on the upper floor of the Hilton was alien to him in a way he found difficult to articulate. It wasn't something he would have spoken about to the other men, for fear that they might be amused by it and consider him parochial and unworldly. He didn't like to be thought of as inferior.

But the suite could quite easily have encompassed the entire footprint of the slum apartment in Jeddah where he had grown up. The first night, he had not been able to sleep in the huge, soft bed, interrupted by dreams of being swamped in a vast, empty space. He took sheets and made a place instead in the living room, arranged in the lee of a long sofa where he wouldn't be seen by someone entering through the doorway. It served him much better.

Jadeed sipped from a tumbler of water as he crossed the room toward one of the floor-to-ceiling windows. It seemed wrong to him that so much space should account for the needs of a single person. He felt that in his bones, as if it were a violation of some kind of law. It was wasteful. But then, it was *Western*.

At the open window, he felt more comfortable. A low moon was already visible in the sky, and lights were coming on across Barcelona, all along the Diagonal Mar and out toward the city centre. Sounds reached up to him from sixteen floors below, where restaurant terraces in the shopping mall across the street were taking in their early evening business.

He sat before a low table and lit one of the Czech cigarettes that were his sole vice, taking a long draw. He tossed the match into a glass ashtray before exhaling a cloud of blue smoke.

Next to the ashtray were a pair of compact but powerful Bushnell binoculars, a wireless headset and the flat, glassy tile of a smartphone. Jadeed nudged the phone with his finger, turning it idly in a circle where it lay. Although the device outwardly resembled any one of a number of next-generation handsets, it had been heavily modified. Beneath the brushed aluminium surface, there was barely a single component still in place from the original design. Jadeed remained suspicious of the technology, but more intelligent men than he had told him it was safe to use, and he knew enough not to question.

The smartphone buzzed and he blinked in surprise. Stubbing out the cigarette, he hooked the lozenge-shaped headset's loop over his right ear and tapped the phone's screen. The panel immediately illuminated with a number of coloured icons and an oscillating display showing the rise and fall of a signal waveform.

He heard a resonant voice in his ear. '*I am watching*.' Khadir's words were strong and clear, almost as if he were standing at Jadeed's shoulder. Only the ghostly whisper of static beneath them betrayed the fact that the man on the other end of the line was thousands of miles away. There was a fractional delay, doubtless some artefact of the complex course taken by the call's clandestine routing around the globe and back via satellite relay, through encryption filters at both ends.

Jadeed nodded. 'Very soon now.' He reached for the binoculars and scanned the rooftops. He quickly found his sightline. After a moment, he looked away to the smartphone, carefully tapping one of the application icons. It grew into a window containing a countdown clock, and Jadeed watched the numbers tumble toward zero. Khadir would be looking at the exact same display.

The clock reached the two minute mark and blinked red. '*One hundred and twenty seconds*,' murmured the voice. '*We are committed*.'

Jadeed smiled slightly. 'Has there ever been a moment when that was not so?'

Khadir didn't rise to the comment. '*Were there any issues with the sample before deployment?*'

He glanced down at the fingers of his right hand. They were still a little red and inflamed from where he had been forced to use them to inflict a moment of discipline, wrapping the steel spheres of his *misbaha* prayer beads in a tight loop like a knuckleduster. 'No,' he lied. Silence answered him, and he reluctantly amended his reply. 'Nothing of note.'

If Khadir heard the pause in his voice, he didn't comment on it. '*I appreciate you handling this personally*,' he said. '*You understand that I need eyes I trust to witness this?*'

'Of course.' The fact was, there were many men that Khadir could have given this assignment to, men they would have been more than willing to leave to take the blame after the fact; but this was too important to be left to inferiors. 'I have my departure arranged.' Jadeed had paid for the room for another day, but he would be leaving it in little more than . . .

He glanced at the smartphone. Only sixty seconds now. The binoculars came up again and found their mark. 'This is what the Americans would call the moment of truth,' said Jadeed, almost to himself.

'*How apt*,' offered Khadir.

The boy tried to stop Noya, but his effort was weak and half-hearted, as if he couldn't muster the energy to do it. He moaned as Noya pressed the disc of the stethoscope to his chest. Her other hand moved lightly over the youth's torso, stubby fingers clad in blue latex probing at his flesh. Each touch got another pained reaction.

The paramedic swore under her breath and bunched a handful of the boy's t-shirt in her fist, and she bared his chest with another slice of the cutter.

Pasco heard her partner gasp. He actually heard the sound of the Portuguese recoiling in that sharp breath, the man's face twisting. He knew that expression too, of disgust and horror being swiftly shut away beneath a professional façade of detachment. One of the tourists watching the scene unfold made a gagging noise and went ashen.

Pasco was compelled to take a look at the boy and he regretted it immediately, crossing himself as he realized what had been done to him. '*Santa Maria . . .*'

Suddenly he felt his age, right there in the marrow of his bones, heavy like lead. It disappointed him to think that someone could inflict such horrors as the young man had suffered.

A soft digital *ping* brought his attention back to the electronic gadget in his hand. Pasco had forgotten he was holding it in his thick fingers. The device offered a translation of the word he had given, and his blood ran cold.

Shahiden (Arabic, Noun), it read. *Martyr.*

Noya began to speak. 'I think there's something–'

The wet gasp the boy gave was the last thing Pasco Abello heard.

One moment there was nothing but a sea of red-tiled rooftops, and the next a grey-black blossom of haze and debris filled the optics of the binoculars. Jadeed let them drop just as the sound-shock of the explosion crossed the two mile distance to the balcony, buffeting him as it passed, rattling the tall windows.

He closed his eyes and visualised the effect of the weapon, almost basking in the thought of it. The first blinding flash of the detonation itself and the ring of compacted air radiating out through the interior of the police station, glass and plastic shattering under the catastrophic overpressure. The bodies of those closest to the ignition point would have been destroyed utterly. Blood would atomise into vapour, flesh becoming cinders. Supporting pillars and walls would distend and crack, ballooned outward by forces they were never meant to contain. In a few microseconds, the building would break apart and begin to die. The structure would collapse under its own weight, the discharge churning outward in thunderous torrents, channelling destruction into the surrounding streets.

He opened his eyes. Behind the rush of the blast noise came a shrieking machine chorus of honking horns and bleating sirens as every car alarm within a mile radius went off at once. In the cool evening air there was no breeze to stir the motion of the pillar of smoke that spiralled upward. It hung like a great black dagger pointing into the heart of the ruin.

He waited, straining to hear, and was rewarded by a long, low rumble that resonated in his chest, blotting out the chatter of the people on the avenue below, as they struggled to understand what had just happened. A second, larger dust cloud projected itself into the air as the stricken building collapsed. Jadeed couldn't see the station house from where he sat, but he could see the mark its demise left behind.

'*Broad dispersal,*' noted Khadir, with clinical focus. '*There are fires.*'

Jadeed wondered exactly how his superior was seeing that. *A spy satellite or a drone, perhaps*? He absently looked up into the darkening sky. 'The gas lines will–' he began, but before he could fully voice his thought, the dull concussion of a secondary detonation joined the unfolding chaos. New streamers of smoke rose with the main plume, illuminated from within by gas-fuelled fires.

Jadeed rose from the chair, gathering up the phone and binoculars.

'*I am satisfied,*' said the voice in his ear. '*The sample meets with my approval.*' The last words sounded like they were being directed at someone else.

'I am leaving now,' Jadeed replied, but when he looked down at the smartphone, the display was static, the waveform signal a flat line, the countdown frozen at zero. The phone went into his pocket, clattering against his prayer beads.

He took the small case containing everything he needed from where it lay on the bed, securing the compact Beretta 84F pistol sitting next to it in a hip holster, which was concealed by the cut of his clothes.

In all the noise and confusion, the sound of the Hilton's fire alarm shrilled away unnoticed as he left the hotel through the emergency exit, and threaded away between the people pointing and gawping at the column of smoke.

TWO

The interior of the warehouse was filled with sharp-edged shadows cast by skeletal yellow work lamps, surrounding a line of collapsible benches at the rear of a Renault truck. The vehicle was painted forest green, and it sat inert with the rear doors hanging open. Figures in black clothing moved around it, a ready sense of urgency in their motions.

Marc Dane blew out a breath and turned away from watching them, shoving his hands into the pockets of his jacket, walking in a slow circle in the semi-darkness. The pre-dawn air was cold and damp, and he could smell the salt and rust of the nearby seaport. Through the grimy windows it was possible to make out the sodium-bright glow of the Dunkirk docks and the square hills of cargo containers along the lines of the wharves.

Marc was wound tight with energy, already regretting the cocktail of coarse instant coffee and Red Bull that had been his morning eye-opener. Inside the jacket, his fingers drummed as he tried to find a quiet spot in his thoughts. It took effort.

It was like this on every sortie, and every time he thought that the *next* time he would be free of the unease. But it hadn't happened yet, and the corner of his lip pulled up in a crooked smile as he considered that it probably never would. Marc's left hand went to his unruly shock of dishwater blond hair and ran through it. He had a face that was young for a man in his late thirties, pale with it, and the dark clothes he wore made him seem rail-thin.

He took another long breath and spotted Leon climbing into the back of the truck. Leon Taub was old enough to be Marc's father, but he was still fit and sharp-witted. Behind a pair of thick glasses perched on an unlovely nose, there was an intelligence that had not been dulled by forty years of covert operations in darkened buildings, wet alleyways and harm's way. Taub saw him looking and gave a wan salute with the plastic coffee cup in his hand, disappearing inside the vehicle. Owen Davis followed the older man up into the truck; Davis's face was set in the continual grimace that was his default expression. Marc watched the dour Welshman survey the preparation area around the truck with a sour, judgemental air, and looked away.

The remainder of the team – the tactical element – were gathered together near the benches, and Marc picked up their dry laughter and the metallic sounds of weapons being made ready. Like Marc, Leon and Owen, the others were all dressed in dark colours, but unlike his military-surplus jacket and nondescript jeans, they wore black outfits of heavy rip-stop materials and leather tactical boots. They sported vests studded with gear pouches, armour inserts, encrypted radio rigs and holsters. The group resembled an armed response team from some law enforcement bureau, but none of their kit sported agency sigils, rank patches or any kind of identification. Their equipment was an eclectic mix sourced from manufacturers all over the world, nothing bearing a tell-tale serial number that could be traced if it were to fall into the wrong hands.

None of them carried the same primary weapon; the members of the group were variously armed with Heckler & Koch submachine guns, Mossberg tactical shotguns or carbine variants of the workhorse Colt M4 assault rifle. The only common denominator was the cylindrical suppressor fitted to every firearm, enough to smother any muzzle flash and reduce the sound of gunshots to a gruff cough.

Marc's own duty sidearm – a Glock 17 semi-automatic – was lying unloaded in the back of the truck, along with a custom-built laptop computer, remote surveillance console and the rest of the tools of his trade. His operational role, a job that headquarters euphemistically designated as 'forward mission specialist', meant that he wasn't expected to use a gun – but it was a requirement for all field-rated personnel to have some form of protection. Still, carrying the pistol on a mission always made Marc feel as if he was inviting trouble.

Out in the real world, where normal people lived and worked, the group assembled in this vacant French warehouse did not exist. Marc Dane's world, with its guns and its secrets, was a dark parallel reality existing alongside it, hidden in the long shadows.

It was nearly two years since he had joined Operations Team Seven, call sign 'Nomad', one of ten rapid-reaction units run under the covert aegis of the British Secret Intelligence Service. Long months since the head-hunters had come, after his tour ended with the Royal Navy's Fleet Air Arm. Months of intensive training, and counter-terrorism and counter-espionage operations. Months of being a ghost to the real world. Marc Dane had dropped off the face of the earth, and this was where he found himself.

He pulled at the cuff of his jacket to peer at the battered Cabot dive watch on his wrist, Marc's sole remaining connection to his naval service. An hour at most before sunrise. He nodded to himself and tried without success to shake off the last of the tension, which despite his best efforts had gathered in a tense knot at the base of his neck.

'Told you to switch to decaf,' said a voice from the shadows.

He turned as she approached. Samantha Green was a head shorter than Marc's six foot two inches, but she had a way about her that made it seem like it was you that had to look up to her. She grinned at him from under the peak of a dark ballistic mesh baseball cap. Even with streaks of night camo on her face, her looks were striking. 'I'm cool,' he told her.

'Oh, you wish that was true,' Sam replied, not unkindly. She let her hands rest on the MP7A1 submachine gun hanging at her waist, sizing him up. 'Don't sweat it. We've done this a hundred times before.' She nodded toward the rest of the tactical squad. 'Boss knows what he's doing.'

The man she indicated caught her look and nodded back. Gavin Rix was Nomad's mission commander on the ground, a decorated former Special Air Service sergeant, a stocky and well-muscled soldier with a boxer's craggy features and a shaven head. He gave them both a thumbs up and a smile that was almost fatherly.

'Yeah.' Marc meant that to sound convincing, but failed. 'Just, y'know . . . Be careful.'

Sam gave a mock-pout. 'Oh, that's sweet.' She cocked her head. 'Would you feel better if I gave you a cuddle?'

'I don't know.' Despite himself, Marc laughed. Sam could always bring that out of him. 'Do you want to see?'

Her brown eyes flashed. 'Keep it professional.' She started to walk away.

'I think we're past that point,' Marc added, in a low voice.

Sam stopped and looked back at him. She had that expression again, the one he could never read. 'Job on,' she said. 'Job off. Don't mix them up.'

'Sam . . .' Marc frowned, groping for the right thing to say. 'I get it, but–'

'Job on,' she repeated, all the warmth suddenly gone from her expression.

The long night in Tunisia that had found them alone the first time had been months ago, but Marc still didn't know where he stood with her. Fraternising within a unit wasn't supposed to happen, but if Rix or the others knew something was going on, they didn't say.

Sam was all about the moment, the rush of the now, and that was attractive to him. He knew that in the army she had served two tours as an explosives ordinance and demolitions specialist. She liked the taste of adrenaline.

But Marc had no map with her. Sometimes he thought he had a read on the woman, in those moments when she was almost like a normal person, like someone with a real life. But then that cavalier streak of hers kicked in and he was left wondering. It seemed like the only thing Sam was ever honest about, ever serious about, was the mission.

Part of him knew he should let it drop, but Marc was stubborn, even as he could see her manner cooling toward him. 'Sam–' he began.

'*Sammy!*' The moment snapped as one of the men from the tactical squad strode over, calling out her name. Iain Nash was the unit's second-in-command, and he had the kind of swagger in his walk that Marc always connected with the tough kids he'd avoided as a teenager, growing up on a council housing estate in South London. Nash gave him a dismissive nod. He had a gaunt face framed by dark hair and a stubbled chin. There was a whipcord look to him, a manner that seemed coiled too tight for a covert operations specialist. But Nash was an accomplished operator, drawn, like Sam, from the British Army, cherry-picked by men in the upper echelons of the security services.

Along with Rob Bell, who had been a copper with the Metropolitan Police's CO19 firearms division, and a former Royal Marine named Bill Marshall, Nash filled out the part of OpTeam Seven that dealt with the sharp end of their assignments. Marc, Leon and Owen were their information and on-site support crew, what Rix called the *blokes in the van* as opposed to the *blokes with the guns*.

'Need a word,' Nash told Sam, and raised an eyebrow in Marc's direction. 'Tick tock,' he added, watching him. 'Better get your toy box working, yeah? Almost kick-off.'

'Right,' Marc nodded after a moment, accepting the implied dismissal, and he began a slow walk back toward the truck. He heard the mutter of a low, guarded conversation strike up between Nash and Sam the moment his back was turned, and frowned.

Marc wasn't a fool, and so far he wasn't allowing his feelings for Sam – *whatever the hell those were* – to get in the way of the job, no matter what she might have thought. But there was something going on with the tactical operators that was being kept from the rest of the unit. This wasn't the first time Marc had seen Sam or Nash or Rix take a moment for a conversation away from prying ears, and none of them appeared to have any intention of explaining why.

He thought about Rix's definitions. The *blokes in the van* and the *blokes with the guns*. There was always going to be a gap between the support team and the strike element, that was a fact of life in this kind of group dynamic. They didn't tend to drink with each other after the fact, didn't cross over that much beyond the needs of the job, but Marc felt the distance more keenly than he wanted to admit.

He could have been one of them. The MI6 recruiters had offered him the chance to apply for field officer status in the OpTeam program, but he had let it pass. All this time afterward, and still he wasn't sure what had stopped him. He had said no, chosen to play it safe and not to take the risk.

Marc looked back at Sam as he climbed into the truck. She was nodding intently at something Nash was saying, and didn't seem to notice him.

Talia Patel had not slept in the past sixteen hours, but she would be damned if she was going to let that show on her face. Stealing a yawn inside the confines of the empty elevator, she pulled at the rumpled silk blouse under her Prada jacket, standing straight as the door opened.

Exiting on the operations floor, she crossed through the security checkpoint, touching the smartcard in her hand on the RFID scanner in the wall. The armed guard at the monitor waved her through and she walked as quickly as decorum would allow toward the room designated as Hub White.

Branching off every fifty feet along the length of the corridor were doors with digital displays hanging at eye level. Some were dark, others lit with text showing that the rooms beyond were *Secured* or *Standby*, and in some cases in a state of *Lockdown*. If you ignored the guard with the gun, the unremarkable look of the place resembled the same kind of business space that existed in dozens of office blocks all across the city of London; but this corridor was two hundred feet beneath those streets, deep in the sublevels below Albert Embankment and the glass and stone of Number 85, Vauxhall Cross. This was the factory floor of MI6, Great Britain's Secret Intelligence Service, where the task of ensuring a nation's security went on around the clock.

Despite the early hour, the building was busy. The work at the MI6 did not follow the usual rules, something that Talia had come to learn the hard way as senior intelligence analyst for K Section, the command-and-control division in charge of field actions for the OpTeam program. She hesitated, discreetly checking her reflection on the surface of the book-sized digital pad she was carrying. Her sharp, but not unattractive features were framed by straight black hair hanging to shoulder-length, hazel eyes in a tawny face. Talia was satisfied; she looked professional, and above all, *awake*.

At the door to Hub White she gestured once more with the smartcard, this time following up with a four-digit day code on an input keypad, and the magnetic locks opened with a quiet thud. Talia entered, passing through a second sound-deadening door before she found herself on the raised gallery that ringed the busy operations centre. In a nod toward the classic design of a theatre, the gallery was nicknamed 'the circle' while the level three steps down was 'the stalls', an open space lined with digital map desks, communications panels and computer monitors. Above it hung large screens layered with signal feeds from dozens of data sources. The size of a tennis court, from this small nerve centre, K Section were equipped to run an active mission anywhere in the world.

At present, every system in Hub White was directed towards the Port of Dunkirk across the English Channel, all monitor stations filled, all screens active. Talia stepped down into the stalls, catching sight of a weather map of the French coastline. It had been a cold, moonless night, and the nearest front of rain clouds wouldn't arrive over the coast until at least mid-morning.

She found Donald Royce at the map table, the flat display resembling a desk strewn with documents – only here, the 'papers' were actually virtual panels that could be moved around and manipulated by touch. Royce was engrossed in one of the panes of data. Her superior was average height and slight with it, soft in his features but possessed of a focus that could be directed like a laser when circumstances demanded. He was Eton-educated, betrayed as such by his meticulous Middle-English manners, and there was a dogged kind of intensity to him that Talia found intimidating at times.

He looked up, peering across his frameless spectacles. 'You're cutting it fine.'

'Sorry, sir,' she replied. 'I wanted to make sure we had the most recent hourly reports from Signals.' Talia handed him the data tablet.

'Thorough as ever,' he said, paging through the report with sweeps of his index finger, skimming the content with a practised eye. The reports from the all-seeing information specialists at the GCHQ facility in Cheltenham were as thorough as ever. 'Anything here we need to worry about?'

She shook her head. 'Not a peep. Nomad's presence remains unnoticed, as far as we can tell.'

'Good to know.' He handed the tablet back and peered at the map screen.

Talia glanced at the mission clock on the wall, two displays showing Greenwich Mean Time and the local hour in Dunkirk. They were less than ten minutes away from the point where OpTeam Seven would be given their final go or no-go command.

Royce steepled his fingers, studying a still of the *Palomino*, a freighter of Turkish origins, flying a Dutch flag. It had been docked at the port for the last twelve hours, and the picture showed it lying high against its moorings. Nothing of any bulk had been loaded on or off the vessel in that time, not even fuel and provisions.

'We are certain, aren't we?' Royce asked, in a subdued voice that only Talia heard.

'You saw the capture from GCHQ yourself, sir,' she reminded him. 'Cellular trace from a known arms dealer. Along with signals intelligence from the web and our other sources, we have probable cause to commit.' She was business-like about her reply, but both of them understood the import of what was about to happen. This would not be bloodless. Those sort of missions were not what the OpTeams were used for.

'We have to be sure,' he continued. 'Because if . . . Because *when* the French get wind of this, we will truly be knee deep in the *merde*.'

'The DCRI are being monitored,' she noted, indicating a junior analyst working a keyboard. The analyst had one job only – to continually sift the communications feeds of France's domestic security service in real-time, looking for any indication that the Direction Centrale du Renseignement Intérieur were aware of the covert operation taking place in their backyard.

It had not been an easy sell for the senior mission director, getting the Prime Minister, the Joint Intelligence Committee and the Foreign Office to sign off on a red-rated assignment that would take place on the soil of an allied government, all without the DCRI's knowledge. Cutting the French out of the operational loop was a calculated but necessary risk.

The data did not lie. There was a strong possibility that the DCRI had been penetrated by assets connected to the mission targets, and the plain fact was, this operation was too important to jeopardize. Royce suggested that it would be better to seek forgiveness rather than ask permission, and so the tasking orders for Nomad had been drawn up in deep secrecy. They would deal with any repercussions if they happened, but the hope was that OpTeam Seven would complete the mission under the radar and the French would never even know they had been there.

Talia was confident that they could do the job. Nomad were a highly proficient unit. With their proactive mission mandate from the PM, Nomad and the other OpTeams had been instrumental in seeking out and neutralising several Category A dangers to British national security interests, and tonight the *Palomino* was at the centre of just such a threat.

Talia had known from the moment she had seen the news footage of the Barcelona explosion that this atrocity would come into the orbit of K Section. Terrorism in Europe was a cancer spreading without concern for borders or nation-states, and among the extremist cadres who claimed responsibility for the deaths in Spain, a name that rang a warning rose above all the others.

They called themselves Al Sayf. *The Sword.* Outwardly, the face they showed to the world was of radical Islamic origins, men sifted from the dregs of Al Qaeda, the Soldiers of God and other splinter groups, but inwardly they were a far more complex organisation that MI6 were only beginning to understand, that extremist religion was only one part of. In their manifesto, they had threatened to kill a British city before the end of the year; not *attack*, but *kill.* They had used that exact word.

And they were ghosts. Al Sayf had learned well the lessons of their fellow radicals, killed running to ground in the Afghan hills or destroyed from within through subversion. These were men equally at home building improvised explosive devices in Kandahar hovels or directing cyber-attack sorties from million-dollar corporate enclaves in Dubai. The development of the MI6's OpTeam program was a direct reaction to such terrorist threats.

British Intelligence couldn't follow the men, so they followed the weapons. Al Sayf were agile and dangerous, but they were small and scattered. They needed a support mechanism, one large enough that it would not be able to exist without showing up somewhere.

Royce was poring over the Combine file, his thoughts doubtless paralleling those of Patel. That was the name they went by inside Vauxhall Cross. Just the vaguest outline, the faint shadow of a power group on the edges of the global stage. Moving outside of issues like ideology and creed. Independent of national identity. Motivated not just by money, but by some larger design that had yet to become clear.

The weapon Al Sayf deployed in Barcelona was suspected as having come from Combine sources. They were in the business of brokering weapons technology and support capacity to terrorist and para-military groups around the planet. They were the armourers and quartermasters of desperate and ruthless men, and if Al Sayf were like ghosts, then the Combine were less than breath on the wind.

'We've been tracking these slippery buggers for years,' Royce said, almost to himself. 'Tonight we've got a good scent.' He stared at the image of the *Palomino* again, as if he was willing it to give up some new piece of information through the strength of his scrutiny.

It represented a rare conjunction of events. The possibility of gathering new intelligence that would lead both ways along the chain of connection, to Al Sayf and to their Combine partners.

A fragmentary intercept of cell phone traffic had led them to this, the suggestion that the freighter's cargo was a weapon in transit from the Combine to a terrorist buyer. In the wake of the Barcelona attack, the Spanish Centro Nacional de Inteligencia were still picking up the pieces and had provided precious little results from their investigation to their European partners – a sure indicator that they had nothing to give.

Somehow, an extremely powerful explosive device had been smuggled into a police station through a gauntlet of trained officers and state-of-the art metal detectors without setting off a single alarm, and a hundred people had died in the ensuing blast. If the *Palomino* was carrying a similar device, something invisible to conventional security methods . . .

Talia felt a dull chill run through her. There were a dozen major cities within hours of Dunkirk, any one of which could be an intended target. Brussels. Paris. Amsterdam. *London*.

She glanced at the mission clock. 'Sir? They're in position. It's time.'

Royce didn't look up. 'Nomad is green for go.'

THREE

'Rules of engagement,' said Rix, scanning the faces of everyone in the back of the truck. 'Silent kit. Weapons free, but zero local collateral if anyone comes looking. Some live captures would be useful, but that's secondary to the main event. Find the device and secure it.'

'It would help if we knew what we were looking for,' said Bell. The dark face of the taciturn ex-copper was tense with concentration.

'If it was easy, they'd have the Yanks do it for us,' muttered Marshall, his rough Black Country accent rising. 'Let me guess, we'll know it when we see it, right boss?'

'You read my mind,' Rix replied.

Marc listened with half an ear, most of his attention on the screen in front of him. Cameras embedded in the bodywork of the truck provided him with a full three hundred and sixty degree view of the exterior, and he scanned them for movement.

Nothing. The port security patrol would not pass back this way again for at least another twenty minutes.

Owen had brought the truck up to the docks, concealing it behind a low stack of freight containers. The *Palomino* was moored across the nearby wharf, lit by a few deck lamps.

'It's quiet,' he announced.

'Can you send up the flying saucer, maybe?' Leon threw him a look.

'I'll give it a go.' He glanced back at Rix, who nodded.

Marc's slender fingers danced over the keypad of a compact portable console next to his laptop, and in answer there was a low thud above their heads.

On the roof of the Renault truck was a plastic box that resembled an air-conditioning unit typical for this kind of cargo vehicle. It opened and a motorised arm silently threw a discus-shaped device into the air, which spun into the low breeze coming in off the water.

The 'saucer' was a small remote drone, the little brother to the unmanned aerial combat vehicles in use by most of the world's larger military forces. Built from super-light polymers and aerogel compounds, it could loiter over targets of interest for up to twenty minutes. A wireless transmitter sent the live feed from a micro-camera directly back to Marc's panel. Using a repurposed controller from a videogame console, he flew the tiny aircraft over the dock in a long loop.

'*Nomad is green for go*,' said a voice over the general radio channel, crackling with the hiss of a signal scrambler.

'Green light,' Rix announced, pressing his finger to the headphone at his right ear. 'Soon as we're ready, we go in.'

Marc became aware that Nash was at his shoulder. He could almost feel the man straining to be let off the leash. 'Nothing out there?' he demanded.

'Nothing–' Marc began, but Nash was gone before he could finish, pulling up a mesh mask to conceal his face.

'Deploy,' snapped Rix, and he and Marshall pushed open the truck's rear doors. In less than two seconds, the tactical squad were gone and the doors closed behind them. Sam was the last one out.

'Game on, eh?' Owen made a show of cracking his knuckles and bent forward over his panel, losing himself in the lines of frequency strength across the monitors that listened in on radio signals and electromagnetic transmissions. Leon said nothing, the images from the screens reflecting in his glasses.

Marc watched the group appear at the bottom of the drone's video display and his lips thinned. He nudged the tiny thumb-stick forward and flew the disc out toward the *Palomino*, scouting the route.

Sam snapped open the MP7's fore grip and collapsible stock, and pulled the SMG tight to her shoulder as she moved low and fast around a wall of blue cargo containers. Halting at the corner, she crouched and peered out at the *Palomino*. A single gangway led up to the ship, and on the deck she could see an indistinct shadow moving.

A pinprick of red light glowed and faded. 'Nomad Three,' she whispered, her voice picked up by the microphone pad pressing against her throat. 'Got a smoker on the weather deck. Mobile, any others?'

'*This is Mobile Three. We see two men on the bridge*,' reported Marc. Sam looked up in the night sky, trying to find the drone, but she saw nothing. For a moment she thought she could hear the faint buzz of the micro-UAV's rotors, but she couldn't be sure. '*No line of sight between targets*,' he added. '*Clear to engage*.'

'Copy that,' Rix was behind her. 'Marsh, he's yours.'

'*Copy*.' Bill Marshall growled in Sam's ear, and she saw him emerge from behind one of the other containers a short distance away. The wiry ex-Marine was fast, coming up to the foot of the gangway in a loping run. With a delicacy and grace surprising for a man of his stature, Marshall moved up the gantry in total silence.

Sam flicked off the safety on her weapon and took aim as the red glow of the cigarette tip flared again, ready to open fire if Marshall didn't take out the guard.

She needn't have worried. Marshall melted into the shadows just as the smoker leaned into the light to toss his cigarette butt into the water. There was the glint of light off an anodized blade and the guard went down without a sound, swallowed by the dark.

A moment later Marshall's voice was on the comm again. '*All aboard the Skylark*.'

Rix patted Sam on the shoulder and she threaded around the corner, moving swiftly toward the gantry. Nash was there a step before her, his M4 raised, and he led the way up. Rix was at her back, and the last man on to the ship was Bell. She glimpsed an untidy shape in the shadows under the flying bridge.

'Get rid of that, will ya?' said Rix, and Marshall gave a grave nod, gathering up the corpse.

'*Mobile Three, advisory. We have a single target emerging on the foredeck*,' Marc reported. '*Armed, assault rifle*.'

Rix didn't need to give the order. All the members of the tactical team found cover immediately, going silent. Sam dropped into the shadow of a lifeboat and chanced a look forward. 'No visual,' she whispered.

'Same here,' said Nash from close by. He was leaning over an oil drum, the carbine extended before him. 'Mobile Three, this is Nomad Two. Need a better steer than that, yeah? Do your job.'

'*Wait one.*' Marc's channel cut for a moment, and Nash turned toward where he knew she was hiding.

'What's your boyfriend playing at?' he asked, isolating the mike so his words wouldn't be broadcast to the rest of the team.

Sam did the same thing. 'He's not my boyfriend. What is this, junior school? Grow up, Nasher.'

There was a crackle and Marc's voice returned. '*Nomad Two, he's coming to you. Three seconds.*'

Nash nodded to himself and flicked a switch on the side of the M4. A diffuse blob of shadow moved at the edge of Sam's vision, lost in the gloom. She watched him track in the approaching guard and pull the trigger. The M4 chugged and a spray of dark liquid haloed the air for a brief instant.

'Target neutralized.'

'Nomad One confirms,' said Rix, emerging from his cover. 'Any more for any more?'

'Nobody else up here, boss,' said Bell. 'Could be below, watching the package.'

'Yeah, well,' said the mission commander. 'Gift horse and all that, right?' Rix shot a look toward the woman. 'Sammy, you keep this deck secure–'

'I'll back her up,' Nash broke in.

Rix accepted this with a nod. 'Right. Marsh, Robby. You're with me. We'll sweep the cargo bays first.' He beckoned them toward him. 'Quick and clever, ladies. I'd like to be home in time for a Full English.'

'*Do your job*,' snorted Owen, in a passable imitation of Nash's gruff tones. 'A thank you might be nice.' He had the transmitter on mute so only Marc and Leon could heard him.

'He's a little busy, you think?' offered Leon.

Owen's eternal grimace deepened. 'Some respect is due.' He stabbed a finger toward Marc. 'You could have just let that creep with the AK-47 walk up on them, and then what?' He mimed a pistol, his thumb the falling hammer. Without pausing for breath, Davies went on. 'You know what Nash says. All that shit about our kit being 'the toy box', talking about us like we're in here playing *Call of Duty* all the time instead of, you know, contributing. They need us.'

'Who's saying that they don't?' asked Leon.

'You know what I mean.' Owen's brogue always grew thicker when he was annoyed about something, and that tended to be almost all of the time. Marc couldn't remember when he'd seen the Welshman actually smile.

'Owen,' said Marc, tapping his monitor. 'Focus, mate.'

That got him an acid look. 'Look, you may not mind, but I'm not the kind of man who tolerates that sort of thing, see?' The other man looked away. 'Nash keeps it up, I'll have to sort him out.'

Leon gave Marc a wan look over the top of his glasses, and the two men shared a moment of silent agreement. Owen liked to talk about being a tough guy, making a big deal about his *tae kwon do* classes and how he wasn't one to be easily cowed, but he always seemed to quieten down in the company of the tactical team. He was an excellent mission technician, but in everything else he could only talk a good game.

'You want I should open a private channel for you?' Leon asked mildly, reaching for the radio console. 'Just you and Nash, for a nice chat?'

'He's not worth it,' Owen replied, after a while.

'You let it bother you too much,' Marc told him. 'It's just typical 'alpha dog' bullshit.'

Leon and Marc had heard Owen's complaints on many occasions. The three of them had sat in similar vehicles under similar circumstances countless times before. Taub liked to joke that their workplace was just like any other kind of office environment, only with the added detail of changing scenery and all the people with guns. Marc wished he could duplicate the older man's casual attitude. Leon had a seemingly bottomless well of stories that stretched back to MI6's glory days in the cold war and a laid-back, old-school skill set to match.

Owen muttered something under his breath and glared at his screen, a schematic of the *Palomino* copied from the vessel's insurance files held by Lloyds of London. Overlaid across the image were blue dots, each designating the location of an OpTeam member. Two were static, while three were moving swiftly toward the bow of the ship.

The Welshman leaned in, suddenly all-business. 'Nomad One, Mobile Two. Be advised. Satellite reads low-level thermal bloom on the deck below you. Could be a generator or a crew compartment.'

'*Nomad One copies, Mobile Two. Proceeding.*'

Bell dragged the second dead guard to the gunwale and slipped him over the side with barely a splash. The assault rifle went next, as Marshall levered open the hatch in the foredeck with Rix covering him, the black shape of his tactical shotgun aiming down into the hull spaces below.

'Clear,' said Rix.

Bell stepped past, taking the ladder down with his MP5 SD3 submachine gun in his grip. Beneath the weapon's integral silencer was a flashlight, and he panned it around the dim interior of the corridor. Without looking up he beckoned the others, and they joined him in short order.

Bell aimed his torch beam at the walls, highlighting patches of rust and other signs of general neglect. 'Doesn't look like up-keep is a big deal on this tub.'

Rix pointed ahead. 'Move,' he told them.

The three men began a swift exploration of the deck, moving aft down the narrow corridors, staying in a loose cluster. The close confines of the ship's spaces could turn any compartment into a death trap if a firefight broke out. All it would take was one alert crewman with an AK-47, and the mission would go loud and bad very fast.

The corridor split into a T-junction, one branch leading to a closed hatch, the other to one that hung open. The low mutter of a television reached them and Bell dropped into a crouch, signalling for Rix and Marshall to halt.

He sniffed the air like a hunting dog. Bell smelled cigarettes and the odour of cooked meat. He peered around the lip of the hatch and saw an open door in the corridor beyond. Blue light reflected from a screen, and as he considered the situation, the TV's speaker gave off a rush of laugh-track noise. Voices inside the room joined in.

'Maybe they want to share the joke?' whispered Marshall.

Rix threw Bell the nod, and he was at the door in three quick steps. He went in high, panning the MP5 across the makeshift common room. He didn't need to look back to know that Rix was covering him with the silenced Mossberg.

There were three men in there, all of them swarthy and unkempt, all in dirty bluish overalls that suggested they were part of the maintenance crew. But the pair of assault rifles propped up against the wall seemed to give the lie to that. Two were seated on a decrepit old sofa before a blurry portable television, the other was on his feet at a small stove.

'All right, lads?' said Rix, in a conversational tone.

The man at the stove reacted first, dropping the pan of soup in his hand and snatching at the butt of a heavy-framed revolver in his belt. Rix's shotgun made a sound like a can of stones thrown against a wall, and the errant cook was blown back into the bulkhead, a bright blossom of red across his chest.

The others were shocked into movement and Bell's lip twisted as he fired a three-round burst that opened up a sucking chest wound in the closest of the men. The last of the crewmen made it to the rifles and then thought better of it, his survival instinct catching up to him just in time.

Rix stepped over the soup cook – still alive, although not long for it – and prodded the uninjured man in the side of the head with the Mossberg's barrel. 'How many on the ship?' he asked.

'No,' said the man, raising his hands. 'No.'

Bell checked the man he had shot. 'This one's done.'

Marshall was at the door, glancing this way and that, his M4 slung and a Browning Hi-Power pistol in his thick-fingered fist. 'No-one coming.'

Rix poked their prisoner with his gun again, reaching out to silence the television. 'How many men?' he repeated. 'Where is the weapon?'

'No English,' said the man, raising his hands to lace them together at the back of his head.

'You talk or you die,' Rix went on. 'Last chance.'

Bell held up a hand before the man, fingers spread. 'Five? This many?' He opened and closed it twice. 'Ten?'

That got him a nod. 'Ten. Yes. Ten.'

Marshall gave a grunt. 'Skeleton crew?'

Rix had an answer to that, but it was lost as the prisoner's hands blurred and came away from his neck with the bright arrowhead of the push-dagger he had concealed in the back of his collar. The blade came down in a fast slash that cut open the mission commander's right sleeve, biting into him even as he dodged away.

The man screamed as he lunged at Rix, intent on burying the dagger in his neck, but Bell was too quick and the MP5 rattled off another burst. He let the weapon's recoil rise on its own and the gun marched 9mm rounds up the stomach and ribs of the attacker.

Rix kicked him away and the other man collapsed across the sofa, twitching as he began to bleed out. 'Fuck.' He let the Mossberg hang free on its sling and clutched at his arm.

Bell tore a bandage pack from his gear vest and handed it to his commander. 'That'll leave a mark.'

'Piss off,' Rix spat, tending to his injury. 'So much for a live one, then.'

A voice crackled in their ears. '*This is Nomad Two. Do you have contact?*'

'Three targets down,' Marshall reported. 'Proceeding.'

'*Copy*,' said Nash. '*Be advised. We're not seeing any movement up here. Where the bloody hell is everyone?*'

'Where indeed?' grated Rix. 'All right, moving on. If the boat's empty, this should make our job easier.'

Marshall jerked his thumb in the direction of the branching corridor. 'The other hatch. Leads into the cargo bay, boss.'

'That way, then.'

'Mobile Three,' said Sam. 'Marc, do you read me?' She pressed flat against the side of a support girder, looking toward the aft of the *Palomino*.

'*I'm here*,' said Marc.

'Can you orbit the drone around the ship? Give us a read on the number of tangos? Something's not kosher about this.'

'*Mobile One agrees*,' said the voice in her headset. '*Winds are picking up, so we're down on loiter duration. I don't think we can keep the saucer airborne for more than a couple more minutes.*'

She nodded absently. The breeze across the deck of the freighter was growing colder and more insistent. 'Do what you can.'

Something fast and low blurred past overhead, framed against the grey haze of the oncoming dawn.

'He got anything?' Nash called out, pitching his voice softly. He was crouched several feet away with the carbine at his shoulder, panning back and forth in a fruitless search for a target.

'*Still no reads,*' Marc replied. '*No targets on deck, I repeat, no targets.*'

Nash made a sour face. 'Two guards patrolling, and not another soul? That don't make sense.'

'No,' admitted Sam, 'It doesn't.'

'You hold here,' Nash told her, rising to his feet. 'I'm gonna scope out the seaward side of the ship for myself, see if they missed something.'

'The drone–'

He shot her a look. 'Is a gimmick. I don't trust a kid's toy to give me intel.' Nash moved away, melting into the shadows.

Bell dropped back to the rear-guard position and Marshall took point, leading with his M4, steering himself along the suspended catwalks over the empty cargo holds of the ship. He panned the gun right and left, stepping carefully with his NVG goggles snapped down over his eyes. The white-on-green images gave everything a surreal, detached air, as if he was peering at some virtual world.

'Unless they're shipping dead air and rust, there's nothing here,' noted Bell.

Passing through the first two freight compartments, there were only echoing metallic voids and the stink of stale seawater and corrosion; but then Marshall had to remind himself that the weapon they were searching for did not have to be huge. The reports shown to the team during their briefing made it clear that the device used in Barcelona was portable, and Bill knew well enough that someone smart enough could fit a nuclear bomb inside a medium-sized suitcase, or a bio-weapon in a vial the size of a fountain pen. Size did not automatically equal lethality.

'We'll know it when we see it,' he muttered to himself.

'You what?' said Rix from behind, as they reached the hatch leading into the next compartment.

'Nothing, boss.' Marshall leaned into the lever and the door clacked open. 'Thinking out loud . . .'

He trailed off as the hatch swung wide and presented the main cargo space. This one was a good three times the size of the first two, filling up the rest of the *Palomino*'s hull forward of the bridge.

What made him go silent was the unmistakable scent of human odours above the wet and the rust. Down below, in an area that normally would have been filled by hundreds of cargo containers, there was just one. A single green rectangle of corrugated steel, resting along the line of the keel. Arranged around the front of it was a makeshift porch built out of scaffold rods, rope and tarpaulins. He spotted a few camp beds and a big plastic drum like the kind used to store rainwater for irrigating gardens.

And there were people. Kids, really. Teenagers by the look of them, maybe four or five, peering up at them with dirty faces. Their uniformly dishevelled appearance made it hard to tell if they were boys or girls.

They all looked utterly terrified, and small wonder, considering they were staring up at three intruders with guns, men rendered faceless and alien behind the bug-eye masks of night vision gear.

'What we got here?' Bell broke the silence. 'People trafficking?'

'Not nearly enough of them for that,' Marshall noted, thinking it through. 'Recreational supplies, maybe? For the crew.'

Rix cursed softly under his breath, flipping up his NVGs, and the other men followed suit. Marshall had been to Gavin Rix's house for dinner once or twice, and he had seen the man's pride and joy – Callie and June, his daughters, sweet girls the pair of them, and the absolute apples of their dad's eye. The youngest ones down there on the deck had to be the same age as Rix's daughters, and Marshall only had to look at his mission commander to know the man was thinking the same thing.

'Careful,' said Rix, finding the steep access steps that led down to the makeshift camp. 'Don't spook them.'

'I'm calling this in,' said Bell, pressing his throat mike. 'Mobile? Nomad Five. We have civilian contact on board.'

Marc's brow creased and he leaned across the keyboard before him. Inside the hull of the ship, the radio comms were heavy with static interference. 'Nomad Five, clarify. You mean the crew?'

'*Negative*,' Bell's deep voice was firm. '*Could be prisoners. We're in the main hold. They've got them living down here.*'

He shot Owen a look, but the other man shook his head. 'Satellite infra-red isn't picking up anything.'

'Under some kind of cover, maybe?' suggested Leon. 'The Russian mafia use military-spec diffusion material to line the boats they have for shipping in girls for the sex trade. Could be the same thing.'

Rix's words cut through the stale air in the back of the truck and the mix of horror and genuine disgust in his tone gave Marc pause. '*They're just kids . . .*' he said.

'*All call signs, attention*.' A new voice sounded, and Marc looked up to see a 'master transmit' message on the communications panel. '*This is Hub White. Primary objective remains the priority. Locate and isolate the device. All other concerns are secondary*.'

Marc's throat went dry. 'Mobile . . . copies.'

'*Copy*,' said Bell, after a moment, and Marc could almost see the grim twist of the man's lips as he said the word.

'Boss,' hissed Bell from the gantry. 'We gotta come back for them later.'

Rix didn't look up as Marshall followed him on to the lower level. 'I heard,' he said. 'Just give me a bloody second.'

'Boss–' Marshall ventured, uncertain what to say.

Rix cut him off with a stern look. 'They might know where the package is, Bill. We can't just walk on by.' Then, very deliberately, Rix reached for his headset jack and disconnected it from the radio rig.

Taking care to approach without any sudden movements, Rix slung his shotgun over his shoulder and held up his hands, palms out. The youngsters gathered in a knot, almost as if they were trying to protect one another, and the sad, pitiful nature of the act made Marshall feel sick inside. Closer now, he could see the hollowness in their cheeks and the scars on them. Somebody had made a point of hurting these kids, and his grip tightened on the butt of his carbine in anger.

The tallest of them was a girl. She had pale brown skin that made Marshall peg her as Indian, but he was lousy with that kind of thing and for all he knew he could have been a continent or two off her point of origin. She brushed lank black hair back from her eyes and came out of the group to meet Rix.

'You understand me?' he asked her. 'We've come to help you.' Rix smiled warmly, speaking in a gentle, friendly tone.

There was a voice in Marshall's ear asking for a status update, but he ignored it, watching the girl and the other kids for any sign of threat. As horrified as he was by the conditions here, he was still a professional soldier, and he wasn't about to let his guard down.

The girl reached out and took Rix's hand. She was crying, tears cutting wet streaks through the dirt smeared across her cheeks.

'We'll take you somewhere safe,' Rix was saying. 'We're looking for something here. You understand?'

She nodded, and pulled on Rix's arm, pointing at the container. The girl said something in a language Marshall didn't recognise.

'Boss!' Bell called out from the catwalk. 'This is not the time.'

'She wants us to see in there,' Rix replied. He nodded at the girl, encouraging her. 'It's all right, love. Don't cry. It'll be fine.'

Marshall tensed as the kid went to the doors at the back of the lone container and pulled at the latch, her effort making it swing open. He had a sudden vision of what might be inside – More children? Stacks of little corpses?

Before Rix could stop her, the girl disappeared inside, lost in the blackness. Marshall raised his carbine and thumbed the touchpad to switch on the torch slung beneath the muzzle. Rix had a flashlight in his hand and was doing the same.

Rods of light probed the dark interior, sweeping over a mesh of cables strung from the roof and the sides of the container walls, connecting back and forth like the work of a mad spider. The cables ended in blocky lumps of plastic that resembled engine parts.

Rix picked one and zeroed in on it. The box was glued to the interior wall with a fat plug of orange epoxy glue. It was the uniform khaki-green of military technology, lined with a string of text in Chinese, and a stencil of the international symbol for explosives. There were dozens of identical components all around them.

Marshall's torch beam found the girl, where she stood at the heart of the wire-web, a black plastic firing box in her shaking hand.

A lead snaked away from the box and into the mess of cables.

'Bomb!' he barked, his mind catching up with what he was seeing.

'*Shahiden*,' said the sobbing girl, pressing down on the trigger button.

The micro-UAV's battery meter fell into the red, and Marc grimaced as the shuddering view from the on board camera became unwatchable. He sent the saucer drone up high over the ship, hoping that he could squeeze the last few drops of power out of it before it gave up the ghost. The wind had worked the little prop engines harder than he had expected, and it had taken a lot of juice just to stay on station. Marc stabbed the auto-return key that would set the drone on a direct course back to the mobile operations vehicle, but he knew that he had left it too late. The drone would fall out of the air into the harbour channel and be lost forever.

'*Boss!*' He heard Bell say over the open channel, '*this is not the time*.'

The drone's line of sight spun lazily as it spiralled down over the deck of the *Palomino*, catching the water, the deck, the sky – and for a split second Marc glimpsed the very definite shape of a human being moving at the bow. 'Someone there?'

He shot a look at Owen's screen, but the schematic showed no targets. The locator markers for Sam and Nash were both in static positions on either side of the ship, in cover and standing sentinel.

'I think we have movement on the–' he began

Bill Marshall's cry of alarm broke over him. '*Bomb*!'

A crash of howling static screamed through the headsets of everyone in the truck, and a heartbeat later the blast wave hit them.

The explosive charges inside the container detonated as one, forming a perfect sphere of white fire that blossomed like a miniature sun. The detonation filled the cargo compartment, expanding in milliseconds to throw a firestorm into the ship's corridors. Everything flammable combusted immediately, walls of lethal heat-buckling steel. Streamers of fire spurted into the air, taking the path of least resistance.

The *Palomino* was fatally holed at the waterline, the blast punching outward through the inner and outer hulls. Years of neglect heaped upon the old freighter, combined with the careful positioning of the device, broke open flaws in the fatigued frames. Cracking along her starboard side, *Palomino* immediately began a steep list toward the dock, spilling out fire and splinters of metal. Everything not lashed down juddered and slid across the weather deck as the fires from below took hold, spreading through the interior spaces to boil out of hatches and doorways.

On the seaward side, a slick of burning oil was already spreading in a black halo, and acrid, heavy smoke turned in the air above. The depth of the dock was shallow, but still deep enough to swamp the freighter all the way to the flying bridge. *Palomino*'s bow dropped as the ship sank into the grey water, dying by the second.

Marc's heart hammered against his ribs and he felt dizzy, his blood singing in his ears. The interior of the mobile unit was a mess, panels hanging askew and monitor screens filled with rains of bright static. A wet mess of spilled coffee was everywhere, drooling from a cracked thermal carafe. Owen was kneeling, his face sporting a gruesome cut above his eye and Leon lay on the floor, cursing a blue streak in Hebrew as he tried to right himself.

Marc lurched toward his console and grabbed at it to steady himself. The UAV controls were dead, the monitor showing nothing but the words NO SIGNAL flashing red.

The external cameras looked into a vision of hell. The blast had knocked down some of the stacked containers – one of which had broadsided the truck as it tumbled – but the view was framed by a wall of orange flames and black haze boiling up from the deck of the sinking *Palomino*.

Panic and fear surged through him. Marc pulled at the twisted cord of his headset and dragged it back over his head, jamming the earpiece into place. 'Mobile Three to all Nomad call signs,' He was shaking with the shock and he pressed down on the sensation, forcing it away. 'This is Mobile Three, all Nomad designates respond immediately!'

A hissing chorus of static answered him.

FOUR

Marc sat heavily in his chair in front of the screens, staring at them but not really seeing the slow death of the freighter. Numbly, he paged through the communications protocols, skipping frequencies, going through the OpTeam's primary and secondary radio channels, repeating his call for any response. He felt dead. Disconnected.

It had all been over in an instant, the flash and shock of an explosion. His thoughts twisted in on themselves. He could only see Sam, Sam's face and nothing else. All the lies he had told himself about being able to compartmentalize his feelings toward her crumbled in that moment. *Was she dead?* It seemed too big an idea to hold in his head.

'What the hell did they do?' Owen grunted, probing gingerly at the oozing cut on his head as he rose. 'Some kind of booby-trap . . . ?'

One lens of Leon's glasses was broken, but he didn't seem to notice. 'I can't raise Hub White,' he reported. The older man's voice was cold and devoid of emotion. The comradely manner he usually exhibited was gone, suddenly locked away. His hands flew over the keyboard in front of him. 'We've lost all our comms.'

'This . . . ' Owen was trying to put it all together. 'This has never happened before.' He swallowed hard. 'The tactical team were on the boat . . . The boat's *gone*.'

Marc shook his head. 'There could be survivors, we have to make sure–'

'What we have to do is go, *now*.' Leon's reply was hard. He jerked his thumb at the panel leading to the truck's cab. 'Owen, get up there, take the wheel.'

'Yes . . .' said the other man. 'Right.'

'*No!*' Marc shouted, surging to his feet, the headset falling away. 'We can't just leave!'

'They are dead, Marc. The mission is blown.' Leon said the words in a flat, toneless voice. 'You know the fall-back routine as well as I do. In the event of critical mission failure, extract to primary rendezvous and await further instructions.'

He was shaking his head. 'We can't,' he repeated.

Owen rounded on him. 'Think, man! The whole town probably heard that explosion! Fire and police will be here in minutes, and if we get caught . . . ' He let the statement hang.

Marc blinked, feeling things spiralling away from him, out of his control. Owen was right. He had a brief vision of the three of them locked up in DCRI custody, trying to explain away why MI6 were at the site of a terrorist attack. If they were arrested, no help from Vauxhall Cross would be forthcoming.

'Get us out of here,' ordered Leon.

Marc looked away, still struggling to process the chain of events. 'No,' he repeated. 'We can't leave them behind.'

'Leave *who*?' Leon grabbed Marc's arm, and the old man's bony fingers were like iron rods. 'We are all that is left. Get a grip, boy.' He frowned, a moment of emotion returning to his face. 'Look, I know you care about Samantha, but–'

The sound of her name was like a shock to his system, and Marc savagely tore himself from Leon's grip. 'We have to be sure!' he shouted, shoving the other man away from him. Pushed on by anger and fear, Marc threw himself at the rear doors and shouldered them open, leaping down to the wharf. He sprinted away, vanishing into the smoke.

'What the hell does he think doing?' called Owen. '*Never leave the van*, that's the only fucking rule we never break!'

Leon sagged against the console, and pulled his glasses from his face. 'Two minutes. Just give him two minutes.'

The gunman rose slowly from behind the cover of the ventilator unit on the roof of the warehouse, coming up from a crouch as falling fragments of hull metal clattered down around him. The hot stink of burning diesel washed across the fading night and he advanced warily, pulling down the bulky gun bag on his shoulder.

Reaching the edge of the roof, he crouched and tugged at the heavy zippers on the bag. The gunman paused, sparing a glance over at the burning ship.

His orders had been very specific. Allow the targets to board; wait for the trap to be triggered; clean up any stragglers.

The weapon in the bag resembled a thickset assault rifle with a muzzle like a drain pipe and a broad ammunition carousel. Colombian Army-issue, the RBG-6 was a multiple grenade launcher, capable of firing off 40mm grenade shells like bullets from a six-shooter. The gunman snapped open the carousel and fed high explosive rounds into the empty chambers, before bringing the weapon to his shoulder. Against the shimmers from the fires, he caught sight of something moving and turned to track it.

A wall of heat assailed Marc as he sprinted out across the dock, and he gulped in a lungful of smoky, thick air that made him cough. The inferno from the *Palomino*'s death throes hurled coils of flame into the pre-dawn sky, blanketing the area with low, black cloud.

He was halfway to the edge of the dock before the heat ripped the speed right out of him, beating him back from the blazing ruin. Marc slowed, belatedly realising that in his headlong rush he had left the truck without a radio or a weapon.

'Stupid,' he muttered, shielding his face with his arm. 'What the hell am I doing?' Marc staggered to a halt.

Leon's words were tolling in his thoughts like a bell, over and over. *They are dead. They are dead. They are dead.*

A pall of grim certainty settled over him, robbing him of all momentum. The old man was right. He had to go back to the vehicle.

They had to get away – but he couldn't make his legs move, couldn't turn around. It didn't seem real. She couldn't just be *gone*. Marc could not make himself believe it.

'*Sam!*' All the anger and fear and panic exploded out of him in a single cry.

Across the span of the dock, he saw the remnants of the metal gangway strewn nearby, and on the concrete, a ragged heap in the shape of a body.

For a moment, Marc thought it was just the dance of the fires making the shadows jump, but he saw movement.

Then he was running again, ignoring the stinging in his throat and lungs.

All the cloying, punishing heat from the fires went away when he found her. For a split-second, it was as if he had been swallowed up by a wave of frigid, polar cold. The colour drained from his cheeks as she struggled to look up at him, the whites of her eyes stained red where the capillaries had ruptured. Her pretty face was covered with a mask of blood and dirt.

He remembered the tracker display; she had been on the side of the *Palomino* closest to the dock. When the explosion was triggered, she might have had tried to make it to the gangway, hoping to flee the conflagration only to be picked up by the shockwave and hurled brutally down to the dock.

Sam resembled a shop window dummy after a fire, blackened and smouldering. He bent and gathered her up in his arms, shouldering her weight. She gave a weak, hollow moan of agony and her head lolled forward.

'I've got you,' Marc told her. 'Come on!'

She could barely walk, and he half-carried, half-dragged her across the dock, through the mess of debris. Sam felt strangely light against him, as if she had been hollowed out. Marc had the stink of burnt hair and plastic in his nostrils, and she cried with every step, pulling on his jacket with her one uninjured hand. Her other arm hung limp and useless at her side.

Sam gasped something and stumbled. Marc couldn't keep his balance and she slipped away, dragging him down with her. The two of them collapsed against an overturned cargo container. He landed badly on his haunches and looked down. Marc's hands were wet with dark arterial blood.

'Oh no,' His throat went dry. 'Sam. Sam, please, we have to get you to a doctor.'

Without warning, she grabbed his collar in her fist and savagely pulled herself toward him. 'Stop,' she said thickly. A foam of pink spittle gathered at the corner of her mouth. Something inside her was broken and bleeding. 'Listen.' It took all her effort to focus on him. 'Listen to me.'

'Sam . . .'

'They are dead,' she gasped, the effort of the words costing her. 'Set-up. Killed us, Marc. Must have . . . Known we were getting close.'

He didn't understand what she meant. 'Close to what?'

'Traitor. At the Cross.'

'In the service?' said Marc, aghast at the suggestion.

'In bed with . . .' Sam choked. 'With those Combine bastards.' She stiffened and bit down on the pain, glaring at him. 'You listen to me. Nash, Rix . . . We were on to something. Off-grid. We were . . . putting it together.'

'You never said anything . . .' He trailed off.

'Rix wanted . . . played close.' She took an agonized breath. 'I trust you. Wasn't that, Marc. I'm sorry.'

'Who is it?' he demanded.

'Not sure. But got . . . some proof.' Marc felt her hand slackening. 'Camden Market. Remember?' Unbidden, a pained smile split Sam's features, her eyes brimming with tears. 'I loved it in Camden.'

'I remember,' he told her, and a jagged dart of regret twisted in his gut. Marc pulled her closer. 'Come on! This isn't done yet . . .'

He fell silent as he touched her stomach. Her clothes were soaked through with crimson.

'Careful,' Sam gasped. 'Careful who you trust.' She shuddered against him. 'Sorry. Sorry.'

With a surge of effort, Marc pulled Sam on to his shoulder, raising her into a fireman's carry. 'Stay with me!' he barked.

His legs felt like they were made of lead, but Marc forced himself forward. In the distance there were the sounds of police sirens approaching.

Ahead of him, an empty cargo container threw out fat orange sparks as it skidded sideways across the concrete, bulldozed aside by the flat prow of the truck. He glimpsed Owen at the wheel, the Welshman's face filled with near-panic as he flashed the headlights and stamped on the brakes.

The boxy Renault juddered into a turn, the rear end skidding out toward Marc. The back doors flapped open, promising escape and safety.

'We're going, Sam!' he told her.

Marc couldn't be certain, but it sounded like she said something back to him. In that moment he paused and caught the sound of a hollow double report on the wind, from somewhere overhead.

He looked up to see a pair of fist-sized shells describing downward arcs from the roof of the nearest warehouse. The first hit the ground on the far side of the vehicle, exploding on impact, and the second smashed through the thin roof of the cargo bed, detonating inside the Renault.

The truck left the ground and flipped over, coming apart from within in a secondary firestorm. Leon and Owen were consumed in the fireball, but Marc never saw it happen. The blast tore Sam's limp body from his grasp and threw the pair of them back across the dock, both spinning wildly into the oil-choked water below.

Marc caught a glimpse of a figure silhouetted atop the warehouse roof as he tumbled away, but the fire lashed at him, blotting it out; and then he was striking the churn of the Bassin de Mardyck canal.

The stinging impact of the water ripped the breath from his lungs and Marc twisted, a froth of bubbles wreathing his head. Patches of burning oil on the surface of the channel gave the murk an infernal cast. He saw Sam drifting in the dimness, her body falling away from him. Blood swirled around her in a black haze, like slow smoke.

He reached for her, their fingertips meeting briefly, but she didn't respond. Her face turned in the wake of the motion and Sam's eyes stared blankly back at him.

He screamed out in defiance and grief, the last breath in his lungs lost in the act. His chest burning, Marc desperately tried to swim after her, but she was fading into the gloom, receding faster than he could follow.

The currents took Sam from him and dragged her down.

Dull daylight attenuated by smoke cast long pools of shadow around the edges of the warehouse as the sun slowly advanced up from the horizon. In the cold illumination of the morning, the building looked empty and menacing.

Part of the shadows in the alley before the entrance broke off and moved swiftly across to the heavy wooden doors, there resolving into a figure that followed the wall to the lock mechanism, which was concealed inside a welded steel security box.

Marc reached inside for the combination padlock that had been there the night before and found it gone. He pawed at it blankly, for a moment not understanding what he was looking at.

He blinked, frowning. Ever since he had dragged himself out of the harbour channel, it had been as if he had surrendered control of his actions, as if some internal autopilot was driving him. He was running on pure reaction now, barely thinking, his mind ceded to instinct.

The missing lock didn't make sense. The post-operation schedule was that Nomad would regroup and return to the warehouse. Once there, the unit would secure their gear, then disperse and exfiltrate from France along individual transit routes set up by Hub White. Succeed or fail, that was how the procedure went. Even if it was only one man coming back, even if the mission had been blown wide open . . .

Marc halted, breathing hard. The grim nature of his circumstance pressed down on him like a great weight, and it threatened to crush him. He sensed raw panic out there on the edges of his thoughts, ready to come in and engulf all reason if he let it. All his training, from the Navy to the OpTeams and everything in between, none of it had prepared him for this, to be *a sole survivor*. Marc Dane had been part of a team for so long, it was almost impossible to imagine himself outside of that metric.

But now everything had been torn away. His safe zone, his squad mates, all gone. Marc looked up as the first few drops of rain began to fall around him, and a sense of isolation chilled him.

The missing lock . . . That was a warning sign. *Someone had been here.* He knew that he should keep on walking, find a route away from the docks and out of Dunkirk – but to where?

Inside, the collapsible benches, work lamps and generator were where they had been left, but with only the weak, watery sunshine the warehouse interior was steeped in shadow. Motes of dust kicked up by his arrival drifted through shafts of daylight, reminding him of the play of the murk in the dock canal. He pushed the thought away, still feeling the cold and damp of his clothes against his flesh.

Marc threaded his way through the lines of tall support pillars holding up the iron roof and approached the benches warily, looking for the cases the OpTeam had left in place before departing for the sortie. The cases were exfiltration kits. Inside were new number plates for the Renault and rolls of plastic film sporting massive self-adhesive logos that could be applied to the truck's bodywork to change its appearance. There were also kits for each of Nomad's team members, fresh clothes and temporary identity packs – so-called 'snap covers', made up of passports, credit cards, even pocket litter like ticket stubs and gum wrappers. Once the mission was over, they would slip into these short-term legends, blend in and vanish.

All the cases were open, their contents missing.

That made no sense. *Who could have known that we were here*? Marc glanced at his wrist. The dial of his dive watch was smeared with dirt, but the works were undamaged. No more than two hours had passed since the explosion at the docks.

In the event of a catastrophic mission failure, there were plans in place to sanitize all traces of an operation – especially in a situation like the *Palomino* raid, where discovery could instigate a major diplomatic incident – but Marc could not believe that the security services had put such things into motion so swiftly.

If not them, then who?

A metal folding chair lay on its side next to the benches and Marc stooped to right it. He fell into the seat and ran his hands over his face and through his hair. He felt cold deep in his core, a holdover from the shock and the water still seeping through his clothes, his shoes.

The panic was there again, coming close, darkening everything like the passage of a storm cloud before the sun. Marc shook his head, pushing the sensation back with a physical action. It would have been easy to give in to it, to release – but he had been trained for this. He was the last one left, and it could not end with him.

I need answers.

He opened his eyes, and saw something in the depths of the shadows, out by the vehicle doors. He blinked and looked again, for a moment certain that the fatigue and the stress of the last few hours were playing tricks on him.

There was a dark-coloured four-door Fiat parked close to the wall, tucked in so that it wouldn't be immediately apparent to anyone entering the warehouse. The car had most definitely *not* been there when the OpTeam had left.

Marc rose slowly to his feet, and now the chill running through him was of a different stripe. Every muscle in his body was screaming at him to run, to *get the hell out of there*. He could hear Leon and Owen in his thoughts, both of them chiding him for ignoring operational rules. *You should have run. You should have run and not looked back.*

He walked to the car, slow and careful, breathing through an open mouth to keep his silence, straining hard to hear the sounds of the derelict space around him. The warehouse gave up nothing, and peering into the shadows was fruitless.

On the bonnet of the black Fiat was a heavy gear bag made of dark nylon, lying there as if it had been discarded by someone with more important issues to address. The bag was military spec, the same style as the kit carried by Sam, Rix and the rest. Marc threw a wary glance over his shoulder and reached for it, drawing open the zipper. Held inside under folding Velcro straps was a grenade launcher. He remembered the sound–

A hollow double report on the wind, from somewhere overhead.

As his fingers touched the frame of the weapon, from behind him Marc heard the very clear, very distinct sound of a footstep.

'Do not be stupid.' The words came with the hard edges of German-taught English. 'Raise your hands.'

The gunman stepped out from behind the pillar, aiming the Sig Sauer semi-automatic at a spot directly between the British agent's shoulder blades. The lengthy silencer attached to the muzzle of the weapon doubled its length, and it did not waver.

With exaggerated care, the agent put up his arms. He could see him staring into the windscreen of the Fiat, attempting to get a view of the gunman though the reflection in the glass.

'Hey, I didn't steal anything,' he said, playing dumb in passable French. 'I was just looking for a place to crash.'

The gunman advanced until he was a few feet from the other man. 'Do not lie to me. I will ask the questions. If you move, I will kill you. If you lie, I will kill you.' There was a faint line of damp footmarks across the dusty concrete of the warehouse floor, left by the agent's ruined shoes. He gave off a musky, stale odour, like a wet dog. 'You escaped from the canal. Who is with you?' asked the gunman.

'I can't help you,' came the reply, in English this time. He seemed too tired to keep up the pretence.

The gunman paused, considering how best to proceed. After the destruction of the ship and the obliteration of the vehicle, he had believed his job to be complete. The surveillance of the staging area was little more than a formality, something a less thorough operative might not have bothered with; but the gunman had a methodical manner that bordered on the pathological.

Escaping the scrutiny of the Sûreté through the chaotic arrival of the emergency services had been simple. Police cars were the first on site at the wharf, and in those precious few minutes while they were still evaluating the situation, he had reversed the non-reflective jacket he wore to reveal a passable copy of a midnight blue Police Nationale coat. In the turmoil it was enough. He wasn't challenged as he made his way out to where the Fiat was hidden.

The safe point was exactly where he had been told to find it, and once he had made certain the warehouse was sanitized, the gunman took up a position to wait.

His estimate was four hours. Long enough to be considered thorough, long enough that any stragglers would make themselves known. But he hadn't expected any survivors. It went against his ordered view of the world. The 40mm high explosive shells he had fired into the truck were enough to hobble a military APC. He had not seriously considered that any members of the British support team would be resilient enough to live this long.

He kept his careful aim with the Sig Sauer. The gunman did not like extraneous details. They irritated him.

'I will ask you again,' he told the agent. 'Who is with you?' If there were others, it would be necessary to deal with them as well.

The reply came after a long moment. 'I'm alone,' said the other man. 'You did your job,' he added bitterly. 'You killed them all.'

There was anger and desperation in those words. They did not sound like a lie. Despite himself, the gunman allowed a small smile. 'Move to the rear of the car. Open the trunk with your right hand.'

The other man obeyed cautiously, and the gunman followed him, staying at his back. The Fiat's hatchback rose to reveal the empty boot. As a matter of course, the gunman had lined it with thick sheets of polypropylene.

The agent baulked at the sight of it, understanding immediately. The plastic worked admirably in insulating a vehicle from blood traces. The gunman already had a location sighted and prepared for dumping any bodies, a spot just off one of the service canals near the harbour. The agent's corpse would be found within a day or so.

'Turn around,' he demanded. The gunman moved slightly. He wanted to improve the angle of the kill shot and lessen the risk of a messy through-and-through trajectory.

'What, so you can look me in the eye when you do it?' The agent's voice was tight with tension. The gunman had heard the same thing a hundred times before.

'Yes,' he said mildly. 'Turn and face me.'

Everything around Marc seemed to narrow in that moment, his focus drawing close until there was nothing else but the thunder of his heart in his chest. He had seen the steel-black shape of the suppressed pistol, distorted by the windscreen reflection into a hooked talon emerging from the German's fist.

In his mind's eye he saw the moment unfold. The cough of the silencer, the impact of the bullet cutting into him, slamming him back into the car. Falling into darkness, spinning and turning . . .

And suddenly Marc was remembering another moment like this one, a point of balance on the edge of death.

Two years earlier, low over the South China Sea on a night exercise, the Lynx's rotors howling against a vicious storm front that had rolled in from out of nowhere. A blinding flash of white searing his eyes as a lightning bolt cut the air, the smoky crash as the helicopter took the hit, power dying across all the boards. The pilot lolling semi-conscious at his controls, Marc straining from the observer's station to reach the stick. The inexorable pull as the Lynx turned in toward the wave tops, spinning through auto-rotate, falling toward death and darkness . . .

He remembered what he had felt in that moment; it wasn't fear. There was no panic then, no paralysis by dread. No, what Marc Dane recalled most clearly from the crash that almost killed him was his *anger*.

His fury peaked in that moment. He refused to die because of something so random, without cause or purpose. He had to know the reason. There had to be an answer to it.

He would not die now, ended by a bullet from a nameless assassin.

He saw the killer shift his stance, moving to line up his shot. He was heavy-set and broad across the shoulders, easily Marc's superior in terms of muscle and power, even without the matter of the semi-automatic pistol in his hand.

He didn't have a plan. There wasn't any training he had gone through for a scenario such as this one. But he had no other choice.

Marc turned, putting his left foot out to push off the Fiat's rear bumper. He pressed all his strength into the motion and used it to propel him up and backward toward the gunman.

The other man grunted and got off a single shot, but the action did the trick, catching the gunman by surprise. A line of fire ripped across Marc's left forearm, but he was already colliding with the assassin, and the two of them went down hard, crashing to the ground in an untidy heap.

Marc brought up his arm and then drove the elbow into whatever was beneath him. He felt something buckle and heard a faraway noise, like the snap of a stick of damp wood. The gunman's hand spasmed and the pistol was gone, spinning away across the concrete.

Marc's forearm felt like it had been dipped in acid, the stinging, burning pain making his fingers tremble. He tried to roll away, but the gunman was too quick to recover. With a grunt of effort, the other man threw him off and Marc tumbled, bouncing off a support pillar. Constellations of pain exploded behind his eyes and he gasped in a breath of dusty air.

The gunman did not hurry. He picked himself up and walked over to where the pistol had fallen, gathering it in his hand. Marc was back on his feet as the gun tracked toward him.

He broke into a headlong sprint as the other man held his position and fired after him, pivoting to follow Marc between the pillars. The gunman emptied the rest of the Sig Sauer's magazine, seven more rounds snapping at the crumbling brickwork as he ran for the line of benches. Marc vaulted over the worktables and vanished from sight.

The gunman muttered under his breath in terse German, and came after him. As he walked, slow and careful, favouring his right side, he thumbed the ammunition release and the magazine fell away with a hollow rattle. He fished a fresh one from a pocket in his jacket and slammed it home, cocking the slide in a single motion.

At the benches, the gunman reached out with his free hand to the closest of the collapsible tables and yanked it upward. The plastic trestle spun and tumbled, knocking down the others either side of it. 'Do not prolong this,' he warned, searching for his target. 'I will make you regret it.'

Marc's attack came from his blind side, in a wild and clumsy rush. From out of the shadows, the British agent swung the yellow-and-black pole of a work light rig like a two-handed sword, striking the gunman squarely in the chest with the cluster of lamps at the upper end. Glass and plastic shattered against him, hardened halogen bulbs popping and sparking, disconnected power cables snapping through the air like whips. The gunman staggered backward, his balance failing, and Marc swung back the other way, this time catching the assassin across the face with the splayed metal legs of the work light tripod.

The gun went away again, and the killer fell against one of the collapsed benches. Marc tried to pin him with the rig, but he shouldered it aside, using his body mass to deflect the blow. He was coming back up, his face and chest a mess of tiny, bloody scratches, and the cool detachment of before was melting away, replaced by icy ferocity.

Marc threw punches, first to the jaw, then a hard double to the gut, but it was like hitting a wall of leather, dense and heavy. The gunman shook it off and came at him with surprising speed. He barely got his hands up before the gunman's thick, meaty fingers found their way to his throat and gripped tight.

Hot chugs of breath gusted from the assassin's mouth as he applied pressure to Marc's trachea. The gunman's eyes were a striking cornflower blue, and utterly dead. Marc could not break the assassin's gaze as the air in his lungs soured, the inexorable pressure around his neck increasing even as he fought against the other man's grasp.

He flailed and punched at the gunman's chest, trying to find the place where he had heard the rib snap before.

The colour began to drain from his vision, his head swimming as the interior of the warehouse turned into shifting lines of shade. Dull sparkles gathered at the edges of his vision, closing in on him. The ceaseless hissing of blood pressure became the only sound in his ears. The gunman was inching it out. He would end Marc with his own hands to be absolutely certain of the kill.

Dizzy and unfocused, Marc managed to bring his fingers up. He clawed at the assassin's cheeks, tearing blindly at the deep cuts that were already there, trying to draw some kind of reaction from him, anything at all, anything that would for one brief moment ease the relentless constriction about his throat.

He found the soft tissues around the gunman's right eye and with all the force he could muster, Marc pressed his thumb into the socket and twisted it. A growl built in the killer's throat as Marc pushed and pushed, compressing the organ into the back of the skull cavity. The gunman pressed harder, trying the end the contest before it could slip out of his favour.

Marc's head swam, his skull aching and throbbing as if it were filled with a slick of slow oil laced with needles. He was aware of blood streaming from one of his nostrils, but still he pressed on, pushing and pushing, losing himself in the action until there was no conscious thought behind it.

Something soft and wet gave beneath Marc's thumb, a sudden hot spurt of fluid, and the gunman released an animal scream. He threw his victim away and staggered forward, clutching at his face, dragging trails of sticky liquid from his ruined eye. Marc saw all this down a tunnel of grey, heard it through a woolly filter of blunted sound. He gasped and choked as his empty lungs seized in his chest, hungry for oxygen.

The gunman stumbled against the fallen work lamp Marc had struck him with and collapsed into the mess of cables dangling from the splayed tripod feet.

What Marc did next came from nowhere; later he would think back to this moment and search his recollection for the impulse that made him do it.

Marc threw himself at the gunman and snatched at the bunch of cables, curling them about his wrist with a savage tug. The power lines drooping over the assassin's chest went taut and snapped up about the gunman's throat before he could push them away. Marc shouted wordlessly and put all his weight into the motion. The cables tightened into a noose, biting into the other man's bull-neck.

The gunman gasped, his face flushing cherry-red, his legs kicking as he tried to get free. All at once, hate and fury boiled over in Marc. Every iota of emotion that had been churning around inside him, the anger and the grief, the shock and the confusion, all manifested itself in a final, violent action as he jerked the cable as tight as it would go.

A drawn-out, sickly crackle emerged from the gunman's lips as his neck twisted. The bigger man's body went slack and dropped to the concrete floor.

Eventually, Marc let the cable go and rose unsteadily to his feet. His hands sang with abrasion burns and his joints ached with the release of tension. He took two wary steps away. The shiver of an adrenaline crash moved through him for the second time that day. It was hard to breathe normally.

He found an iron pillar and slumped down against it, glaring at the dead man among the mess of cables and debris. The gun was lying nearby, just out of arm's reach, but he ached too much to stretch out to snag it.

Marc Dane was no stranger to death. He had been in the thick of combat, he had fired weapons that he knew had to have taken lives – missiles fired off a helicopter's launch rail, submachine guns shot from the back of moving vehicles – but he had never been this close. Not hand to hand, face to face. Breath to final breath.

He had never looked a man in the eye and then ended him, until now.

Marc stared down at his hands, watched them as the tremors eased away into nothing. The sun marched slowly up the grimy windows of the warehouse and he sat there, watching the morning move on, his thoughts empty, the pain across his body slowly easing from a strident throbbing to a dull ache. He kept waiting for the moment to come, for some fraction of understanding to strike him, for some new insight to rise from the life he had taken.

But there was nothing, only a faint, enduring echo. A strange new kind of anger that didn't ebb or wane, a drive that kept pushing at him to rise to his feet, to start walking. To find the people who had betrayed Nomad and murdered them.

Traitor. At the Cross. Sam's voice sounded in his thoughts, so sudden and so clear that it was almost as if she were standing there next to him. He didn't want to accept that she could be right, but the dead man lying across from him was all the proof he needed.

The *Palomino* had been one gigantic trap, laid to draw in MI6 and OpTeam Seven. The gunman, there to deal with any loose ends. They planned for the bomb on the ship to kill the tactical team, and the assassin was there to destroy the support element. Marc had broken that chain of events by going after Sam, by doing something foolish and human and outside the rules.

The gunman hadn't tracked Marc, he had come here and waited for him. *How could he have known where to find me?* Marc finally rose to his feet, gathered up the gun and walked back to the dead man.

'You knew where to go,' he said aloud. 'You were *told*.'

It made a chilling kind of sense. A traitor explained the looted kits, the reason why Nomad had been assigned to this operation when some of their number had been conducting an eyes-only investigation into . . . *what*?

This was more than just Al Sayf and their terrorist ambitions – this represented a penetration of MI6 at levels way over Marc's pay grade. The enormity of it robbed him of his breath and he wiped beads of sweat from his brow.

Careful who you trust, Sam had told him, just before she said she was sorry.

Was she sorry because she had kept this from him, or sorry because she had been a part of it?

Marc waited out the day, using the time to clean up the disorder in the warehouse as much as possible. He stripped the gunman for what money he had on him, taking the Sig Sauer P220 pistol. The unwieldy MGL he dismantled and left in the car boot with the dead man's corpse.

The last thing he did was to set a strip of rag alight and throw it into the Fiat's passenger seat. The car was catching well as he left the warehouse, and Marc found his way out through the alleys of the industrial area. He made it to the main road as the first of the fire engines sped past in the opposite direction, and when he was sure no-one was looking, he pulled the detonators from the remainder of the 40mm grenade shells, throwing the lot over the sea wall and into the Channel.

Marc walked south along the highway, out of Dunkirk, losing himself in the shadows at the road's edge.

FIVE

From a distance, the collection of buildings appeared to be lying derelict. Concrete slabs were arranged in low blocks that huddled at the end of a dirt track, standing up against a forbidding, stony hillside. In the heat of the day they baked under skies sparse with clouds, and at night, when the temperature fell, they were traps for the cold winds.

The razor wire and the men with guns were what set it apart from other homesteads and farms out in the mountainous wilds. Anyone who came too close to the compound would be run off – or worse. Not that there was much cause for anyone to be out this far.

Halil wondered why anyone would ever want to come here of their own volition in the first place, out over the scrubland and the endless miles of sand and rock. It was nothing like the town where he had grown up, with the thronging masses of people and the constant pulse of life.

But that place was gone now, if he were to believe what the teachers had told him. Gone into rubble and fire, destroyed. Wiped out, as his father and mother had been, in the rain of bombs from the sky.

The sun was going down behind the mountains, and he judged the moment good enough to move out from the barracks to the shower block. Halil did it quickly, without looking back to see if his compatriot was keeping up.

Sometimes, Halil tried to remember the life he had lived before this one. It was hard, and it only came back to him in fragments. There were some days when he wondered if that old life had ever really existed. Was it a just a story he had read in a book? The life of some other boy who went to school, who laughed and played until the day it all went away in screaming and fire.

Perhaps he had always been here. He didn't know how old he was now – seventeen or eighteen? How could he tell without someone to show him?

He remembered many winters in this place, the frost crunching underfoot in the courtyard. It didn't seem to make a difference to the teachers, though. Whatever the weather, they made them run the drills and do their chores, whether it was cleaning out the latrines, carrying packs of stones back and forth across the quad, or learning to dismantle a rifle. If they were not outdoors in the courtyard or running the track around the fence, they were in the classrooms learning from dusty textbooks or reading passages from the Qu'ran. But the cold-eyed men who led the prayers looked like no Imam Halil had ever known, and this place was no madrassa.

He was one of the older boys now. Halil was tall and wiry, and sometimes the others made fun of him because of it. That was part of the reason that he had made friends with Tarki. Tarki's size was a mystery; stocky and thickset, maybe a year younger than Halil, the other teenager seemed able to maintain his weight despite the meagre diet they were fed. He endured the mocking catcalls about his girth, and one time Halil had grown tired of hearing them, and stood up for him. So they were friends, after a fashion.

Tarki arrived next to him, and puffed out a breath, his moon face flushed with anxiety. 'We should go back,' he muttered, in his peculiar accent.

Halil looked at him and shook his head. Tarki's story was much like his. But where Halil had gone to a good school and lived a life of reasonable comfort, with books and television and food enough for his family, Tarki had come from a goat farm where running water was a luxury and reading was a skill out of his reach. Tarki had told him the name of the village he was born in, but it was meaningless to Halil. They spoke the same language, but they might have been from nations a world apart.

All they had in common – all *any* of them had in common – was that they had no-one to miss them out beyond the razor wire. This place, this 'orphanage', as the teachers called it, was home to strays left behind by warfare.

Every boy had suffered a variation on the same theme; family taken away by conflict. Each one rendered alone by bombs and guns, by conflicts they didn't understand.

'Come on.' Halil moved quickly toward the main building, while the guard on the roof turned out of the wind. He heard a match strike, caught the scent of cheap tobacco. Speeding up to a sprint, he made it to a broken wall and Tarki came after him. Halil pushed the other youth in through a hole in the shabby concrete, under a curtain of fragmented blocks clinging to a grid of exposed rebar. He followed him through and froze, listening.

The guard's boots echoed over their heads, but there was no urgency to the steps. 'He didn't see us,' Tarki whispered, incredulous.

'Told you,' said Halil, with a smug grin. 'Now, slow and quiet, okay?'

'What are we looking for?' Tarki dithered, and Halil glared at him.

'Whatever we find,' he retorted, and picked his way across the room.

Unless they were there with a teacher, the boys were banned from the main blockhouse. The central building was taller than all the rest of the structures in the orphanage, and the men lived in there. Halil suspected that things other than the instruction of youths went on inside.

The other boys were content enough to accept that. Most of them seemed willing to accept the lot they had been given. If they followed the rules and did as they were told, then the teachers showed them fairness. Halil could not help but wonder if this was because it made the youths do as they were told, not because the teachers really believed they were due it. But he kept his questions to himself, even from Tarki. His father had once told him that the truly clever man remains silent until the most important moment.

The men in this place called themselves teachers, but they were not. It made him angry in a small, silent way to hear them take that title. Halil's father had been a *real* teacher. An educated man who had travelled to a great university in England when he was just a few years older than his son was now, who knew facts about everything and made it all seem fascinating. Halil's father had spoken many languages, taught them in schools. He had been a clever man.

The teachers here were cunning, but that was not the same thing. They were thuggish, they were hard and unyielding. Halil kept quiet and did nothing to raise attention. He did not excel, he did not fail. Instead, he watched.

The two youths moved gingerly though the empty outer rooms, into corridors choked with discarded chairs, winding inbetween walls that had been crudely knocked through with sledgehammers.

There were many decaying rooms like this on the edges of the compound, and Halil was beginning to understand that they had been left this way deliberately. The men in charge of the orphanage wanted it to appear tumbledown and neglected, to make anyone looking think it was a worthless place.

He wanted to know why that was. He wanted to know about the helicopters they heard in the hills but never glimpsed, or who was in the black jeeps that came and went in the night every few weeks.

And he wanted to know about what happened to the youths who had been here when he arrived, the older teenagers. People went away in the orphanage, and when they did it was as if they had never existed. The ones who left never came back.

There were only two faces from outside that Halil had seen more than once. There was the dark-skinned man with the cruel gaze who would watch from the edges of the quad, and the taller one who sometimes came to talk to them. The one with the cruel eyes was like a hawk, always looking for weakness. Halil made sure he never met his sight, for fear he might see right through him.

The tall man was different. When he came, it was an event. The teachers were reverential to him, seeking his favour. He wore no insignia or badges of rank, but in his thoughts Halil imagined him as a general, the leader of some vast army. He was handsome and aloof, like a mythic hero, and when he spoke his words made everything else turn to silence. Sometimes he brought films for the youths to watch, full of fire and action. The films were about battles and enemies, wars that were going on in countries that were just names on a map to Halil. Once, the films showed places that he thought he recognized from the pictures of England his father had in their old house.

Sometimes, one of the other youths would slacken and perform poorly; the regimens of training and education were strict and inflexible, and those who fell behind were soon isolated. A moment would come and the ones who did not keep up would not be at dinner that evening. If anyone asked, they would be told that the missing youth had been 'sent back'.

Halil wondered exactly *where* they had been sent back *to*.

His curiosity was cracking the edges of the silent mask he wore. Something in the tempo of the lessons and the mood of the orphanage was changing, and Halil could sense it, like a clock ticking down.

And so he was here. Halil had convinced Tarki to come with him, to dare to enter the main buildings, just to sate the gnawing questions pulling at him. 'Maybe we can find out some things . . .' He spoke without thinking. 'About our families.'

'My parents died,' Tarki said automatically. 'This my home now.'

'That's what the teachers tell us,' he retorted. 'Don't you want to get away from here one day?'

'We will,' Tarki insisted. 'Once we've learned enough.' He gave a sheepish grin. 'I've learned my words, almost all of them. I'll be done soon.'

Halil wandered to one of the walls, picking at the peeling paint. A strip came off between his fingers. 'Where are we going to go? Where *they* decide to send us?'

'I suppose so. Is that so bad? The teachers–'

A sudden jolt of annoyance cut through Halil. 'Don't you even care?' he demanded. 'They are not teachers, they are soldiers! Teachers don't have guns!'

Tarki glanced around nervously. 'You're too loud. Be quiet.'

'I am sick of being quiet!' Halil snapped, with a heat that surprised him. 'I–'

His angry words died in his throat as he heard the low mutter of conversation nearby, and the grind of boots on the tiled floor, coming closer.

It was starting to rain as Marc reached Calais, and he skirted the port town, working his way around the edges in search of the Jungle.

It was the name the locals gave to a shanty town created out of trash and old tents, accreted by the slow trickle of illegal migrants working their way across Europe toward the French border and Great Britain. The police and customs officers had bulldozed the original Jungle a few years back, but the illegals kept coming and they kept rebuilding it somewhere else, in hopes of staying off the government radar. As an active clandestine pipeline into the UK, it was very much an ongoing concern for the security services, but the route was managed by Albanian organised crime groups and they were hard to penetrate. It didn't help that jurisdictional conflicts between MI6 and the DCRI got in the way of every attempt to shut down the route for good.

He stole a pair of tracksuit trousers from a neglected washing line, grabbing them before the rain soaked them through. He found a petrol station with an all-night mini-market attached, and used some of the money he had stolen from the gunman's corpse to get a couple of tasteless microwave burgers and a deep cup of dark, tarry coffee. The meat was grey and mushy, but it was edible, and he found a corner away from the security cameras where he could eat. A few more euros went on a packet of disposable razors, a khaki baseball cap with an embroidered tricolour and a cheap black hoodie with the letters F-R-A-N-C-E sewn across the chest.

For a long moment he looked up at a disposable cell phone in a pack above the counter, and thought about buying it; but what would be the point? He couldn't exactly call the front desk at Vauxhall Cross and ask them to send a car for him.

On some level, Marc was still operating on instinct, and that told him that his trust was now a commodity not to be spent at random. He was in the wind, with no idea who was after him. Sooner or later, the man he had killed would fail to report in and the people running the assassin would know something was wrong. His window of opportunity to find out who was responsible for the deaths of his team was closing, and if Marc was going to do this himself, he had to do it now.

He cracked open the razors and used the blades to cut off the letters on the hoodie, discarding the shreds to make the thing more nondescript. His jeans and jacket were filthy and they stank of oil, smoke and cordite. Marc ditched them in a waste bin, but not before slicing out the jacket's thick inner zip pocket to become a makeshift bag for the Sig Sauer.

On the road near the Jungle there was a cluster of figures, crouched low on the grass verge near a parked car. Young men mostly, some sharing cigarettes or peering warily into the dark. Marc heard snatches of what sounded like Arabic and Polish. Like the new kid at school, he shuffled up to the group and looked for a place on the edge, keeping his hat down, trying not to draw attention.

That lasted all of two minutes before a pair of heavy-set men in cold weather coats exited the car and came striding out towards them. Before Marc could get up, the largest of the pair grabbed him by the scruff of his hood and pulled him off balance.

'Who the fuck are you?' demanded the other man in growled, mangled French. 'Think you can roll up here and sneak on to the line, asshole?'

Marc played submissive. 'Need a ride,' he replied.

'Is that so? Why should I accommodate you?' The man peered at him. 'You a criminal? A terrorist?'

'As if!' Marc managed a weak grin and a Gallic shrug. 'I can pay . . .'

'You will,' grunted the one holding him up. He went for the pocket of the hoodie where the gun was hidden, but Marc held up a hand.

'Not there. Here.' He indicated his hat, and the first man tore it off his head. A fold of notes fluttered out from where he had hidden them in the lining, and the thug caught them with a dexterity surprising for a man of his bulk. He fingered the money.

'Congratulations, my friend.' The other man smiled, showing yellowed tombstone teeth. 'You paid the fine for pissing me off. Now where's the cash for the trip?'

Marc played along, reaching into his shoe for the last of the euros. He kept his other hand near the pocket with the pistol. If the extra money wasn't enough, his only remaining option was to improvise something at gunpoint, and that would not end well.

'Much better,' said the thug, and pressed his cap back into his chest. '*Bon voyage*.'

Men were coming, making their way along the corridor. There was a rough laugh as they rounded the corner, and Halil froze. He caught one of them complaining about a poor performance, a pathetic score . . . They were discussing the results of a football match.

The colour drained from Tarki's face and he threw a nervous look in the direction they had come. 'We have to run!' he rasped. 'I don't want a beating!'

Halil held his breath. The two youths were out of sight. If they maintained their silence, if they just kept their cool, they would not be discovered.

One look at Tarki told Halil that all rational thought had fled from the other teenager. He saw the flash of abject panic in Tarki's eyes and raised a hand to try and stop him, but it was too late. Tarki bolted, running back through the broken walls and away toward the breach in the concrete.

The rattle and creak of motion was like a switch being tripped, and the casual conversation between the two men in the corridor changed instantly. Their voices went low and serious. Halil heard the snap of holsters being released.

His every instinct was to sprint headlong after his friend and pray that he would get away before he was seen. The teachers hit the boys with batons when they broke the rules, and the bigger the infraction, the bigger the stick.

He wanted to run, but the men were at the door. Slowly, quietly, he dropped down and shrank behind a broken cabinet resting against one of the walls.

The door opened, framing a figure. He peered inside, sniffing the air. Halil was suddenly very aware of the odour of his own sweat. The moment stretched to breaking point, and Halil was certain the man was looking directly at him, penetrating the darkness. But the door closed and the pace of the previous conversation returned. The goalkeeper, the men decided, was worthless. They shared a laugh and walked on.

Halil became aware that he had been holding his breath tightly in his chest, and with a shudder, he released it. He sat there in the dark for a while, waiting for the men to come back, for it to be revealed that they *had* seen him, that they were tricking him.

But they did not return, and neither did Tarki. Halil got to his feet and took a few experimental steps over the creaking floor. Each one he took emboldened him a little more, and presently a smile broke on his lips.

This was a little victory for him, and the fear of being caught made it all the more sweet. He was learning a new lesson here – that the teachers were *not* all-seeing.

Defiant pride rose in his chest. For so long the teachers had made him feel inferior, as if his life was only allowed to go on at their sufferance, but now here he was, breaking their rules and doing it under their noses.

Halil wanted a memorial for the moment, a keepsake. A way to prove to the other boys that he had done this thing and come back unharmed.

Halil cast around, looking for something he could take back to the barracks to mark his adventure, but there was nothing, only bits of broken glass and scraps of wood. He picked one up and toyed with it. Then, without stopping to think, he went to the walls and used the stick to draw lines in the peeling paint. Down low by the door, where it wasn't immediately apparent, he wrote his name in little scratches. He marked the place, making it his territory, and grinned.

Somewhere deep in the building, a door slammed. Before, that sound would have sent his heart racing, it would have pushed him to run away like Tarki. Now he stood and listened, excited by the prospect. 'I am sick of being quiet,' he repeated to himself.

Halil crept to the door, easing it open. The ill-lit corridor ranged away from him, back in the direction the two men had come from. He decided that he wanted to know what was on other side of the door at the far end.

A truck pulling a soft-sided trailer growled down the road and juddered to a halt with a hiss of air brakes. Marc was slow off the line as the rest of the illegals bolted to their feet and sprinted toward the back of the vehicle. He came up at the rear of the group, watching carefully.

The Albanians moved up to the cab and the driver stepped out. He was in his fifties, dour and balding, dressed in a heavy lumberjack shirt. Marc caught sight of an envelope passing between the thug and the driver, and the other man went to the latches on the side of the trailer and snapped them open. The vinyl wall of the container slid open on squeaking runners like a thick curtain, revealing shrink-wrapped pallets loaded with cardboard boxes. Some of the men were already climbing up, moving loose boxes aside to reveal a hidden space where the group would be able to hide.

Marc glanced at the name on the side of the trailer, seeing the logo of a Yorkshire-based haulage firm. He caught the driver asking for a light and heard a matching accent. The man was looking at his envelope. 'This is a bit light.'

'Less today.' The Albanian gave a noncommittal nod. 'Lot of *les flics* around tonight. The police.'

'Oh yeah?'

The other man nodded gravely. 'You didn't hear what happen, down the road? At Dunkirk?'

The driver shook his head. 'I listen to Johnny Cash in this country, not the bloody radio.'

'Ah. Well.' He mimed an explosion. 'The police, they see mad bombers everywhere. Bad for business. People keep low profile.'

'I was promised–'

'Take or leave it.' All the false warmth drained out of the Albanian's tone.

The driver didn't press his luck. 'Aye, right then,' he replied, after a moment.

Hands beckoned Marc from within the cave of boxes and he scrambled up into it. The dislodged cargo came back into place, piece by piece, and they were walled in.

Someone cracked a chemical light stick and the eerie green glow bathed a sea of silent faces. Marc counted nine others in there with him. Glancing around, he tried to read the names on the boxes, wondering what kind of load the driver was hauling. He caught sight of a bill of lading; they were bound for Manchester, via Dover and Calais.

Marc shifted, avoiding the pit where a urine-stained plastic bucket had been left for their use, and found a corner where he could sit back and wait.

Outside, the cab door slammed and the muffled strains of 'I Walk the Line' filtered back to them. Then the truck's engine coughed into life and they were moving. Marc stole a glance at the Cabot and logged the time in his thoughts. England was a few hours away, and soon he would be one step closer to safety.

Or something, he thought grimly.

The corridor was lit every few feet by a light bulb inside a metal cage. Doors led away to other rooms, and Halil could sense other people beyond them, with the occasional murmur of a distant voice or the rattle of a tea glass.

The brimming confidence he had felt after he escaped detection was starting to wane, and he tried to hold on to it, but it was like a sea tide. The wave of daring had come in and filled him up, but now it was pulling back again and there was nothing Halil could do to stop it. Questioning voices in his head – all of which sounded like Tarki at his most nasal and whiny – eroded his defiance second by second. He felt tremors in his legs, as if he had been running too fast.

He had to turn back. One single wrong move, one mistake and he would be caught. Halil had never heard of any of the teenagers doing what he was doing now – did that mean that those who dared to come here would be 'sent back'?

Wood scraped on the floor in a nearby room – someone moving a chair – and Halil almost cried out in surprise. He ducked away, snaking through the gap between two doors into the first room he came to.

It was a large space, with shuttered windows looking out into the evening. The room was dominated by a long, wide table of old pine cluttered with papers, cups and pieces of equipment that Halil couldn't identify. At one end, a bulky portable computer sat, making quiet ticking sounds. There was a telephone handset nearby, connected by wires to the computer. More cables went to a curious pole made of scuffed steel, which stood on splayed tripod feet near one of the windows. The pole ended in a bowl made of metal mesh that reminded Halil of an inverted umbrella, or the television aerials that sprouted from the roofs of the houses where his family had lived.

He touched it and almost knocked it over, a spike of fright stabbing into his gut. Halil backed away from the device, almost tripping over the cables snaking from it across the floor.

What was he doing? What did he hope to prove? Suddenly Halil felt foolish and afraid. He was almost a man and yet here he was, playing games of dare like some little child. Tarki had been right to leave him behind. Perhaps even now, the other youth was telling one of the teachers what they had been doing. Perhaps they were looking for him at this very moment.

His cheeks flushed red with embarrassment. Halil was supposed to be smart, but he was behaving like an idiot! Dread was building in him, welling up to consume his last remaining measures of courage. He would be caught, and a beating would be the *best* that he could expect, it would be what he begged them for.

How could he have thought he would get away with this? Halil saw his own actions as if from a distance, watching himself. *He had written his name on the wall!* How many boys named Halil were there at the orphanage? His idiotic, impulsive bravado would be his undoing.

He had to get out. He had to go back, scratch out the words on the wall, get away and hope, hope to heaven that Tarki had not talked to Adad or any of the other youths in their dormitory.

But the door in the corridor opened and closed, and there were men coming. Halil turned in a frantic circle, looking for a place to hide. The table was too high; there would be no cover below it. The windows were secured with iron bars.

There was a side room with a broken door in the far corner, and he ran to it. Inside, old chairs stood piled up among torn rolls of carpet. The little space stank of mildew and mouse shit, but it was some kind of concealment, and Halil hid inside. He drew up his knees and made himself small, flinching back from the chink of light that spilled in through the door. He felt the flutter of his racing pulse.

Out in the main room, the doors opened and the first to enter was the cruel-eyed man. Halil's stomach twisted in fear as the man turned to address the person following him.

It was the tall man, the warrior, the general. *Of course* it was him. Where there was one, there would be the other. A teacher joined them, continuing the conversation they had been having in the other room.

'It's a strong crop,' the teacher said. 'You'll be pleased, Khadir.'

The general threw the teacher a sideways look, as if he was disappointed with the other man's presumption. 'We will see,' he intoned. The warrior had a deep growl in his voice that made Halil think of a lion. His face was rough with a wiry black beard and a full head of hair that made that impression even stronger. He turned away. 'Jadeed. Is it ready?'

The cruel-eyed one was at the computer, and the keys chattered under his fingertips. 'Almost time,' he noted.

Somehow, knowing the names of the two men frightened Halil more than anything else. He remembered the stories his father had told him about demons and djinn from ancient history, of how those who knew the name of a beast gained a terrible insight into its soul. Khadir loomed large as he crossed the room, and for one brief moment Halil could not be sure if the man was a terrible angel or a devil in earthly incarnation.

The teacher looked at his watch. 'This must be done now?' he asked.

Jadeed didn't look up as he went to the metal pole, frowning at it. 'It is important to our mission.' He reached out and adjusted the device. 'Did one of your men touch this?'

'Of course not,' the teacher replied hotly. 'You were very clear about the . . . The equipment.'

'See to it,' Khadir ordered. 'I will not let the Combine condescend to us because we kept them waiting.'

Halil saw Jadeed's head bob in agreement. He altered the angle of the aerial slightly and an answering warble sounded from the portable computer. A stab of pain tightened around Halil's ankles, and he tensed. His legs were starting to cramp.

The teacher gestured toward the door. 'I can wait outside if you require privacy?'

'That won't be necessary,' Jadeed cut him off. 'Wait there and do not speak.' He picked up the handset and Halil heard a distant string of electronic chirps. In return, Jadeed spoke a series of numbers, one after another. It was only a moment later that Halil realized that the numbers were in English.

Khadir settled into a seat with his back to the youth's hiding place and poured himself a glass of tea from a carafe on the table. He gave Jadeed a languid nod and tapped his earlobe.

The other man did something to the computer and suddenly a speaker box on the table was alive, crackling with static like a poorly-tuned radio. '*Secured?*' said a gruff, guttural voice with a heavy British accent.

'Of course,' replied Khadir. He glanced at the teacher, who looked back at him with a blank, slightly nervous expression. 'Who is this? You are not familiar to me.'

'*I am the man you're gonna be talking to from now on.*'

Halil closed his eyes and concentrated. Seamlessly, the general had shifted into speaking English. It seemed peculiar to hear it, the same resonant tone gliding over words with a different cadence from Halil's native tongue.

It was difficult for him to do, but the boy listened and translated the words in his head. His father and mother had taught him the language of the British and the Americans when he had been young. It was a skill he prized, but one he kept secret. No-one in the orphanage had anything but antipathy for the Westerners, and to admit he could speak like them would have made him a pariah. Concentrating on the words helped him block out the tremors in his legs.

The teacher clearly didn't understand a word of what was being said, but Khadir and Jadeed were fluent.

'*Let's get straight to the point,*' said the foreigner. He seemed irritable and terse. '*I've seen your work and it's all well and good. But we're going to be taking a more, what do you wanna call it – pro-active – role.*'

Halil didn't see Khadir's face, but he heard the chill in his voice. 'Is that so?'

'*I've been brought on by our mutual friends as a . . . A contractor. So, I'll be your point of contact. Everything goes through me. You follow?*'

'Your predecessor–'

'*He's out of the picture. Have we got an understanding here?*'

A long moment passed before Khadir answered. 'We have.'

'*That's good. Where are we on the big job?*'

Jadeed moved around the table, and Halil caught sight of a simmering annoyance in his gaze.

'The crop is almost ready to harvest. What is the status of the delivery?'

The man on the radio gave a grunt of amusement. '*Don't you worry. You'll get your gear when you need it. That's what we do.*'

Khadir leaned forward. 'We kept our part of the agreement. We cannot proceed–'

'*You* can *proceed*,' the voice corrected. '*Next contact will be as scheduled. Out.*' The line dissolved into static.

Jadeed's hands tightened into fists. 'Arrogant goat-shit!' He slipped out of English with an explosive snarl.

Before he could say any more, Khadir had raised a finger to silence him. 'Our needs make us allies,' he went on, switching back. 'But only for the moment.'

He kept talking, but Halil wasn't listening any more. The slow burn of pain in his legs was building by the second into agony. He felt as if he were kneeling in a furnace, the cramped angle of his stoop making his calf muscles twitch with the effort. Tears in his eyes, the youth tried to hunch forward, tried to shift slightly to ease the pain, but nothing worked. If only they would leave . . .

And then without warning, Halil's right leg spasmed and kicked at one of the chairs. Wood scraped on the floor, the sound as loud as a gunshot.

The broken door was torn open and Jadeed was suddenly there, filling the doorway. His face twisted with anger. 'What is this?'

Before Halil could raise a hand to protect himself, Jadeed's arm shot out and grabbed a bunch of the youth's hair. He pulled him up and out of the side room. Halil tripped on his numbed legs, falling to the floor in front of Khadir.

The other man observed, his eyes narrowing. The teacher at the door came forward, drawing a short baton from his belt, but Khadir shook his head and he halted.

For a second, Halil thought his beating had been postponed, but then a whipping sting of new pain seared his face as Jadeed flicked his wrist and struck him across the cheek with a loop of *misbaha* beads in his fist.

'What is this?' Jadeed shouted again, this time directing the question to the teacher. The other man shrank back a step, his face a muddle of worry and annoyance.

Halil looked up and Khadir's dark eyes were burning into his. The man radiated a stony, fearsome magnetism, and he could not break his gaze. 'What is your name, boy?'

He failed to keep the tremor from his voice. 'Huh-Halil,' he managed. 'I wasn't . . . I didn't want to . . .' He couldn't frame an excuse, the new welt on his face throbbing.

Khadir nodded toward the side room. 'What were you doing in there? Stealing?'

'No!' Halil insisted. 'Hiding, sir.'

'Hiding.' Khadir repeated. 'And listening?'

'Commander,' ventured the teacher, 'Let me deal with the little rat. I will make sure it doesn't get in the way again.'

Khadir ignored him. 'You must be a clever one. Clever or lucky.' He glanced up at Jadeed, who hovered over Halil with his fists bunched.

Halil could sense the cruel-eyed man humming with the power to end his life, straining at the leash like a snarling dog. He shrank toward the floor, willing it to open up and swallow him whole, cursing his own idiocy.

Khadir gave the teacher a withering look. 'To come this far into the compound without getting caught by the guards, you must be a good recruit, Halil. You clearly have ability, even if you lack discipline . . .'

'You know you are not supposed to be here!' shouted the teacher, pointing at Halil with the baton. 'You should be beaten bloody for this as an example to the others!'

'Be quiet,' snarled Jadeed. The other man coloured, but did as he was told.

'I was j-just looking,' Halil stammered. 'It was a . . . A dare.'

'What did you hear?' Khadir asked, almost kindly. 'Tell me.'

'Nothing!' insisted the teenager. 'Just talking. Voices.'

Khadir nodded absently. 'Tell me what you heard.'

Halil almost answered the question before he realised Khadir had asked it in English. It took a physical effort for him to clamp down on his reply. He blinked away tears and shook his head. 'I . . . I don't understand.' Halil's blood ran cold. Khadir was testing him to see if he had followed any of the conversation with the Britisher.

He heard the jangle of the steel prayer beads by his ear as Jadeed let the length of them drop, and the sound made him jump.

Khadir topped up his tea glass and shifted in his seat, his actions unhurried. When he spoke again, it was in English once more, and the tone was mild and conversational. 'Jadeed? If I take a drink from this tea, you will break the boy's neck.'

Everything in Halil wanted to flinch, to shy away, to try to run from the killer standing behind him, but he knew that the slightest reaction he gave, even the very smallest inkling of understanding, would see him killed.

Khadir brought the glass to his lips, swirled it under his hawkish nose. 'You didn't mean to hear, did you? I know that. Just admit it and we will move on. There will be no punishment.' He paused, taking in the aroma of the hot black tea. 'Do not lie to me.'

Halil's fears screamed in his head, telling him to come clean, to beg forgiveness and hope that Khadir would be merciful. Very carefully, the youth schooled his features, keeping his expression blank and fearful.

'I don't understand what you are saying,' he offered, praying that his lie would be strong enough.

Halil saw a brief flash of emotion cross Khadir's face, but it was gone so quickly he could barely read it. Was it annoyance, disappointment, or something else? 'Very well,' he said, switching back to their common dialect. 'You can go.'

The teenager rose shakily to his feet, blinking, scarcely able to believe that he might have deceived the general.

Khadir continued, nodding to the teacher. 'Take him back to the barracks. But rebuke him first.'

Halil turned and threw up his hands again, but he was too late to stop the other man coming in and striking him repeatedly with the wooden baton. He felt back to the floor, taking hit after hit on his arms, his ribs, his head.

The pain blurred into one long cascade of hurt until finally the beating ended and Halil shivered on the floor, unable even to cry.

Dimly, he heard Jadeed ask a question. 'We have plenty more, commander. Why keep this one?' The voice seemed to come from a great distance away.

'Young pups must be trained,' Khadir replied, his words coming closer. 'And it is an affront to me to see potential put to waste.'

Halil blinked and through his haze of pain, saw the hawkish face of the tall man loom over him as the teacher dragged him back to his feet.

'This is your lesson for today,' Khadir told the youth. 'Learn it well. Do as you are told, obey the rules and soon . . . Very soon, you will be gifted with a great purpose.'

SIX

Donald Royce cupped his hands in the washbasin's icy water and splashed it over his face, letting the chill hit his skin. He blinked and shook away the fatigue pulling on him, looking up to study his reflection in the washroom's mirror. Cool, steady eyes stared back.

It was important for him to maintain composure, to project the right aspect to his staff. The situation was at a critical point, and any mistake now could make things spiral out of control.

There was a discreet knock on the door. 'Sir? I have the updates.'

'I'll be out in a moment.' Royce crossed to the hanger where a freshly-pressed Russell & Hodge shirt was waiting. He dressed, took a breath, and walked back into his office.

Talia Patel was there, the data pad in her hand like it was welded to her. Royce couldn't think of a time when he had seen her without it. She was efficient that way, and that was the reason she was his senior analyst; but she was also circumspect, and didn't ask too many questions. He liked that about her.

'Have you slept?' he asked. 'How did you find the time?'

'I cat-nap,' she told him. 'Growing up in a big family, you learn to snatch sleep where you can.'

'Teach me that sometime,' he replied. 'I'm running on cups of coffee and angst.' Royce blew out a breath. 'How is it on the floor?'

Talia paused, and that was an answer in itself. She was trying to frame a palatable reply. 'I've rotated in another team. Everyone else I sent home after they passed off to the new shift.'

'I want every person who was in Hub White when it happened to be monitored. Standard thing, you know the drill.' He sighed. 'Have to be thorough.'

She offered him the data tablet. Royce gave it a sour look. 'Already done,' Talia noted.

The updates made for grim reading. A secondary team out of the Paris field office had been deployed, but by the time they had reached Dunkirk the explosion site had been fully cordoned off. According to TV5 and Sky News, the local authorities had announced that the blast from the *Palomino* was caused by a fuel fire on board the ship, which meant that the DCRI had already thrown a curtain over the facts behind the matter.

'Ground team reports that bodies have been recovered and taken to the morgue at a nearby army base.' Talia frowned slightly. 'French intelligence have sent up a few flares, pulled some of their analysts in, but so far they're not talking to anyone else.'

'What a sodding mess,' Royce said grimly. He put down the data pad and walked to the window.

The explosion at the docks had lit up every monitor in Hub White, and a second later the lines of communication into the area went dead. Royce and Patel and the rest of the command centre team had been cut off, with only the satellite link still open for them to watch what was taking place. Helpless and unable to intervene, they could only glimpse fractions of events through the plume of fire rising from the burning freighter.

Emergency lockdown protocols were now in effect, regarding the *Palomino* operation, and unit Nomad. Talia's reports only underlined what Royce already knew; every member of OpTeam Seven was now missing presumed dead, and the focus was on damage control and disavowal. Along with the team on site, at MI6 there were technicians working to ensure that any possible connections between the incident and the British security services were cut. One error, one missed link, could bring the DCRI to the front door of Vauxhall Cross – and that was something that Donald Royce could not allow to happen.

'It's galling that our first action has to be this,' said Talia, thinking along the same lines. 'Firewalling our allies, instead of concentrating on our own people.'

'One thing at a time. We need to have deniability in place,' he said, thinking aloud. 'Something we can afford to burn if it comes down to it.'

Talia gave a nod. 'Farrier has that in hand.'

'John Farrier?' She nodded again. 'I thought he was already overseas.'

'I held him over.'

'Good. Sensible choice. He's got experience with this sort of thing.' Royce grabbed his jacket and drew himself up. All at once, the energy seemed to ebb out of him. He leaned forward and steadied himself on his desk.

'Sir?' Talia asked, with genuine concern.

He waved her away and stood up straight. 'Some days I hate this bloody job.' Royce straightened his tie. 'Right. Let's go and walk the room, then.'

'There's something else,' she told him, frowning. 'We have a visitor from the ninth floor.'

He was outside the operations centre. Sandy-haired, hansome and poised, the man looked as if he had just stepped off the cover of *GQ* magazine – but he had a sneer that gave every expression a little cruelty to it. The mission director shot him a brisk nod by way of greeting. 'Welles.'

'Royce,' came the reply. The man fell in step with him. 'It seems that you have-'

Royce stopped dead in the corridor and turned on his heel to stare the other man in the eye. 'Victor,' he began, in a low, steady voice, 'if you are about to say something asinine about whatever 'mess' I have myself in, I warn you that I will smack that smug Oxbridge attitude of yours right off your bloody face. This is not the time. Are we clear?'

Welles narrowed his eyes. 'When did you sleep last, Donald? You should get some rest. It's making you bad-tempered.' He folded his arms. 'Despite whatever personal disagreements you and I have had, I would never denigrate the loss of officers in order to do something as crass as score points. Don't put words in my mouth.'

Royce turned away. 'Why are you even here? Isn't there enough for you to do up on nine, sniffing out drunkards and honey traps?' But the mission director knew exactly why Victor Welles was there. The ninth floor of the MI6 building was home to MI6's internal investigations department. *The spies who watched the spies.*

'A catastrophic mission failure took place on your watch,' replied Welles, matter-of-fact. 'Eight officers are dead, Royce.'

'Hasn't been confirmed . . .' he said, grimacing.

'That's more than enough reason. Control and the JIC agree. The Foreign Secretary has ordered an investigation to start immediately.'

'We're still picking up the pieces!' Royce fumed.

'I'll stay out from under your feet,' Welles told him. 'You do your job and I will do mine.'

'And what exactly does that mean?'

The other man pushed past him toward the command centre door. 'I'm here to determine if Nomad was lost due to enemy action . . . or other causes.'

The truck lurched and Marc blinked awake. He had a momentary flash of disorientation, then remembered where he was.

The chem-light was almost dead, a feeble green ember burning cold in the middle of the hide. He scanned the faces of the illegals crowded in there with him. Most of them were dozing. The still air was dull and thick with human smells, enough to make anyone drowsy. Marc shook it off and ran his hands over his pockets. The Sig Sauer was still there.

He rubbed his eyes. Marc had no recollection of dropping off, not of the truck boarding the ferry and the passage over the channel. It was as if some part of his body had seized the moment and shut him down for the duration, trying to rest where it could.

The truck was moving, and by the sound of the wheels on asphalt, he could tell they were no longer on the cross-channel ferry. There was a lot of stopping and starting, and all around Marc could hear the grumble of other vehicle engines. He moved a box away and listened hard. Voices reached him, and although he couldn't parse the words, the rhythm of the words was English, not French. They were in Dover, most likely somewhere still inside the port.

The vehicle moved out of a queue and drove slowly, the ambient noise around them dropping. Something hit a wrong note with Marc. If they had passed through customs, they should have been on the exit road, picking up speed, making for the motorway.

The truck halted. Again he strained to listen, picking up a muffled, indistinct voice. It was the driver, and it took a moment for Marc to realise he was hearing one end of a telephone conversation. Then the cab door opened and closed and everything fell silent.

He looked back into the hide. The other passengers were watching him now, picking up on the urgency of his actions. They knew something was wrong.

Marc pushed aside more of the boxes and wormed his way to the side of the trailer. He found a loop of the flexible curtain barrier hanging slack and pulled at it, making a gap.

Peering outside, he saw lines of other trucks. The driver had left his load on a parking apron, a short distance from the main cargo terminal.

As quickly as he could, Marc squeezed out and dragged himself up and over, on to the roof of the trailer. He dropped flat on his belly and slid toward the rear, in the direction of the driver's retreating footsteps.

The man in the lumberjack shirt was approaching a group of people coming the other way, men and women with torches and blue jackets. The driver gave them a wave and Marc understood. The man was playing both sides of the people-smuggling game. He had his money, but now he was calling in customs officers to arrest the illegals he had brought from Calais, pretending he was the good citizen.

Marc swore. If he was caught, arrested with a gun on him . . . His face would be all over the criminal database within the hour.

He needed to get away, *now*. And to do that, he needed a distraction.

Marc swarmed along the top of the trailer, staying low. The cab was locked, but there was a sunroof over the driver's seat that broke cleanly when he stamped on it. Inside, the cab was a mess of overfilled ashtrays and fast-food wrappers. He pawed through the glove compartment and storage bins, hoping to find the envelope of money the driver had taken for his work, but it wasn't there.

'He's not that stupid, then,' Marc muttered. He needed a plan, and something began to form in his thoughts as he caught sight of a crumpled high-visibility vest lying in the foot well.

Marc exited the cab, chancing a look back. The driver was returning with the customs officers in tow. There was less than a minute to make this happen.

The latches holding the curtain along the side of the trailer opened with a double fastener, one after another. Marc grabbed a fistful of the vinyl and pulled as hard as he could, opening it up to reveal the nervous faces of the people gathered inside.

'Out!' he snapped. 'Run!' He repeated it in French and they caught on, spilling out on to the asphalt. Bright flashlight beams swept up beneath the axles of the truck and Marc heard the rush of boots, strident calls to stop.

The migrants needed no other encouragement, and they bolted away from the parked vehicle in different directions, scattering before the customs officers. Marc broke into a full-tilt sprint, following a Somalian youth around a high-sided container on a flatbed. The instant he was out of the line of sight of the customs team, he threw away his baseball cap and shrugged into the fluorescent yellow hi-vis jacket he had concealed inside the hoodie, immediately altering his outline. Marc took a deep breath to normalize his breathing and wandered back the way he came, feigning a look of surprise.

He almost collided with a pair of customs officers coming the other way. Marc pointed. 'Over there, mate! Two of them, running like hell!'

If he had thought about it twice, the ruse might have seemed like idiocy, but it worked. The customs men were focused on the pursuit, reacting first instead of thinking. They were used to seeing dark-haired, dark-skinned men trying to jump the fence, not scruffy blond blokes with London accents. But it was the hi-vis vest that sold the lie for him, the standard uniform for any working stiff, the colours that subconsciously communicated that guy wearing it was *supposed to be there*. The customs officers ran on and left him behind, disappearing into the lines of parked trailers.

The next part was the hardest. Slowing his stride to a casual, unhurried pace, Marc walked right past the nonplussed driver and the officer angrily giving him the third degree. The key was to walk, not to run.

He made his way up to the main gate, and the vest did its work again.

Ten minutes later he was on the main road leading into Dover. The fluorescent jacket went into a waste bin, and Mark hunched forward, pulling his hood up against the biting morning wind coming in off the English Channel.

At Dover Priory station, the earliest train was preparing to depart and a small but dogged crowd of commuters bound for London were in well before the start of the rush hour. They stood in a loose knot before the departure board, peering at folded newspapers or sipping at steaming extra-shot coffees. They had the morose silence of the not-quite-awake about them, and Marc could empathise.

Wary of the security cameras studding the walls of the station concourse, Marc carefully navigated to the far side where a line of dispensers offered snacks and cans of soda.

He had a few euro coins, but nothing close to the cost of the rail fare. Outside in the car park there were a dozen vehicles he could have hotwired, given time. But he was running on empty now, and he knew it. All the fatigue, all the effort of the past few days was trying to drag him down into its depths. He was in no state to drive, and his thoughts were becoming sluggish. Without rest Marc would start making mistakes, and that would get him caught.

He frowned. *When did I start thinking like a fugitive?*

He walked down the line of the drink machines until he found the older model he was looking for. Taking care to position his back to block the line of sight of the nearest camera, Marc held down the coin return switch and pushed the six dispensing buttons in a numerical order he'd learned as a swabbie on liberty nights in Plymouth. He did it wrong twice, miscounting and swearing under his breath, but on the third attempt the vending machine's hard-wired operator code kicked in and it dutifully spat out every last coin in the change hopper, until Marc's pocket jangled with fistfuls of loose change.

In a stall in the men's toilets he counted out enough to buy a single to Charing Cross, plus a little extra for a cup of tea and a sandwich. The rest he dumped in the hat of a homeless man selling copies of *The Big Issue.*

He took the first train out. The tea remained untouched as sleep took hold and pulled him under.

Marc dreamed of Samantha Green.

'Camden Market,' she said. *'I loved it in Camden.'*

Perhaps he had loved it too, just for a while. Back then, in the summer.

The safe house was a three-storey mid-terrace a few streets back from Chalk Farm Road, and it had a set of those walk-up stairs and stone porticos that trendy estate agents always crowed about, along with a windowed basement peering out through black iron railings.

Sam threw him a sly look over her shoulder as she opened the door, holding a hand to keep him on the stoop while she deftly typed a disarm code into the electronic alarm pad right inside the entrance. 'Gimme a sec,' she said. In a moment it was done, and she pulled him inside, giving the street a last check before shutting the door.

Marc noted the retrofitted layer of metal on the back of the door, thick enough to absorb small-arms fire. The house was one of dozens of safe points located all over the city, ordinary homes that were deliberately nondescript, set up as bolt-holes for MI6 officers or cover addresses to bolster active legends. Many of them lay idle for months at a time, with the Service quietly paying the bills.

Sam knew the locations of a bunch of places like this, and she knew when they were in downtime, when they were unoccupied. Marc assumed that there was someone in logistics who owed her a favour, but he didn't push it, and Sam made it clear that was how she wanted things.

Don't push it. The words had never been said, but by some unspoken process, they had come to an understanding about this *thing* they had going on. Or at least, Sam had. Whenever Marc tried to shine a light on his place in the dynamics of this relationship, he couldn't look at it square-on. For now, it was a case of if *it ain't broke, don't fix it.*

He followed her through the narrow hall and into a galley kitchen. 'I like this place,' she told him, miraculously finding a bottle of wine in the humming refrigerator.

Marc washed up glasses in the grubby sink and looked around. 'How often have you come here?'

'A lot,' she admitted. 'It's a good place to crash. The Stables are just down the road.' Sam pointed with the wine bottle. 'Good eats over there. Nightlife.' She smiled. 'Maybe I'll come live here when I retire.'

'You won't retire,' Marc said it without thinking, with more edge than he expected.

'Don't be so sure,' she chided, working the cork. 'Royce finds out that I've been using these places as my own private crash-pads, I'll be retired right out the door.' She poured a generous amount of wine into each glass, then drained hers halfway. 'Still. I'll burn that bridge when I come to it.'

In spite of himself, Marc grinned. She did that to him, her cheeky smile daring him to stay serious, challenging him with every look. It was hard to break away from.

'What are we doing here?' he asked her.

She came closer to him, her arm snaking around his back. 'I know what *I'm* doing.'

'That's not what I meant–' he began, but Sam shook her head.

'Shut up,' she told him. 'Some things you don't have to think about so much.'

He tasted the rich, burnt caramel flavour of the wine when they kissed, and the tip of her tongue pushed at his lips. Sam pressed the curve of herself into him, and he resisted for a moment before he bent into the motion.

There was a bedroom upstairs, but it seemed like it was too damn far to go, so they slipped into the living room where chinks of evening sunset threw honey-gold light over the walls and the threadbare furnishings. Sam pushed him back on to the sofa with a steady, firm pressure, the heel of her hand on his chest and he fell back with a bump. They had more wine between Marc pulling off his jacket and shirt and Sam discarding her blouse. There was something coy in her eyes as she unclipped her bra and rolled it up off her chest and away. Marc traced a line up from her waist, following the edges of her ribs, coming up under her small breasts and matching the curve where they merged with her strong, spare torso. Sam had a build that was part-athlete, part-dancer, and smooth skin that most women her age would have killed for. In the sunset light, her eyes glittered and she laughed softly as Marc gently stroked her nipple with his thumb.

'I've got an idea,' she told him. 'Let me drive.'

With dexterity, she used one hand to unbutton her jeans and the other to work on the buckle and zip of Marc's cargo trousers. It took some shifting, but soon they were naked. Sam straddled his erection, pressing into him, her body relaxed and blood-warm.

He cupped her backside, made Sam gasp and give a soft giggle as his long fingers stroked the flesh between her legs. She bent forward, pushing her breasts toward his mouth and slowly rocking her hips forward and back, forward and back.

They both gasped as she let him enter her, and the pace of their motions changed, picking up speed. Marc felt sweat beading his back, his arms, as Sam ground against him. He let himself fall into it.

She rose up and her back arched, supported by the line of his legs, his knees behind her shoulders. He guided her hips as she ran her hands up along her stomach, her breasts and around her neck. Strobe lights blinked and ranged across the walls in bars of cold blue as an ambulance raced past along the street outside. Sam was framed in the light for a split-second, her dark eyes shining. She became a silhouette lined in icy colour, and a low moan escaped her lips as she came closer to climax.

Marc tensed, teeth set, unwilling to release before she did. He slipped his fingers between her thighs and stroked her there, building the tempo. Sam tensed and pushed back, and finally it was enough for them both. She gave out a sound that was sharp, like the bark of a vixen, dragging it into a drawn-out sigh. In turn his head lolled forward as a shudder ran through him, a low hiss escaping from his teeth.

All the strength in Marc's arms, his muscles vanished and he sagged back, his sweat-slick skin suddenly itchy against the cotton covers of the sofa. 'Oh. *Fuck*,' he managed. He was dry-throated and hoarse.

'That's the word, yeah.' Sam whispered, bending down to kiss his chest. She let her weight settle on him and they lay there as the room turned darker, the shadows lengthening.

It seemed like hours had passed before either of them spoke again. 'Is this what they call an assignation?' Marc gave voice to the random thought.

'You tell me,' Sam replied lazily. 'You're the one who reads all the books.'

He smiled again. 'I am entranced by you.' He meant it.

'More fancy words?' She turned away, staring at the ceiling, and Marc felt a barrier drop between them. She was right there in his arms, but there was a sense of distance that had swept in from nowhere.

He frowned. Even when they were here, she was never really *here*. She was too reckless, too rootless to ever come to rest, not for a second. It was only on the missions where Sam seemed to draw in, to be full and whole and in focus.

Marc knew that. *He knew it.* That was who Samantha Green was, and she had never hidden it from him. But still, each time he realised it again, it seemed like a kind of betrayal.

Sam got up and went to the downstairs bathroom, showering quickly with just like they had taught her in the military. When she came back, she had more wine and gave him a careful, measuring stare.

'You've never met a girl like me before, have you?'

He shook his head. 'And then some.'

'That's a good thing.' Her voice turned distant. 'This life . . . The job.' She nodded to herself. 'It's not made for relationships. It's hard on that.' Sam looked back at him, a questioning look in her eyes. 'Job on. Job off.' She swilled the wine around. 'You get that, right?'

'I get that,' he lied.

They made love again that night, and afterward Marc dropped into a light sleep. He remembered waking around two in the morning, alone in the silent house, the heat of the day lingering in the empty rooms.

He was still dreaming of her as the train rolled across the Thames and into the terminus.

The telephone rang and the strident noise shocked Royce out of a doze. He jerked, almost upending a cup of coffee on his desk, and swore. The mission director took a deep breath and then snatched up the handset from the cradle.

'What?' he demanded, his voice toneless. Hours in Hub White, sifting through the same after-action footage, had worn his frayed nerves down to nothing. Royce gave the grey morning light peeking in through his windows a narrow-eyed stare as he waited for the reply.

'*Good morning to you, too.*' Irritatingly, Victor Welles sounded as if he was rested and fully focused. '*I'm glad you're here. I would have hated to drag you back in from Sussex.*'

Royce glared accusingly at the clock on his desk. He had a vague recollection of somebody – Talia, most likely – suggesting that he have one of the pool drivers take him home, get him off-site for some rest. That hadn't happened. That *couldn't* happen. The situation had too many variables. He had to be close, to keep an eye on things until they approached something like stability.

'I repeat,' he said, fishing in a desk drawer for a tube of caffeine tablets, '*what*?' He swallowed a couple of the red pills with a swig from the stale coffee and grimaced at the foul taste.

'There's been a development on the Nomad incident.' Royce's expression darkened. Welles was already using that term for the events in Dunkirk, *'the Nomad incident'*, as if it was a pithy headline he had pulled from one of the tabloids. *'I'm in the main atrium. You need to get out here, now. And bring Patel with you.'*

'Despite your charming manner and boyish good looks, Welles, I don't feel motivated to jump at your word of command.'

'You may want to reconsider. We've had a walk in. And you really should be here to see it.'

The line went dead and Royce sat there for a moment, re-arranging Welles's words in his mind.

A walk in. It was tradecraft slang for a person of interest, an officer or enemy operative who broke protocol by taking the most direct route possible to bring themselves to the attention of an agency – the front door.

Royce's fingers prickled as he gripped the telephone handset tightly, his thoughts churning over what he could expect to find downstairs.

He swallowed and tapped a speed-dial button. 'Talia,' he said, at the moment she picked up, not waiting for her to answer. 'Drop everything and meet me at the atrium, *this very minute*.'

They rode the elevator to the ground floor in silence, and Talia Patel chanced a look across at her boss. Royce was straightening his tie and smoothing his hair, doing his best to make himself look like anything but a man who hadn't slept in two days. He was good at it, she reflected. Royce stiffened and squared his shoulders, and with a blink he seemed to make all that fatigue go away.

Talia was certain that she was the only one who saw his weaker moments; certainly not his subordinates, the OpTeams, or even his wife. She wondered what that meant.

The lift doors opened and they emerged into the main reception area of the Vauxhall Cross building, the green glass doors beyond facing out toward the street.

There was a man standing in the middle of the circular space. He wore a hoodie that was dark and dirty, and tracksuit trousers a size too large for him. At first glance he resembled the kind of disaffected urban troublemaker that was a favoured target of the reactionary press.

Victor Welles was standing nearby, and two men from his security detail had positioned themselves on either side of the hooded figure. Welles's men were armed with snub-nosed MP5K submachine guns, holding them low but with obvious threat.

The hooded man raised his hands slowly. 'Just so you know, I have a gun in my pocket,' he said. His voice was familiar, but thick with exhaustion.

Welles gave Royce a sideways look. 'Ghost at the window, Donald.' He stepped forward. 'You. Take the hood off, hands on your head.'

'I'm not . . .' He turned toward them.

'Do it!' barked one of the security officers.

Slowly, he pulled the hood down and for a moment Talia couldn't place the drawn, sallow face. Eyes full of anger and frustration scanned her, then found Royce.

'Dane.' Royce blinked and his hand went to his chin. 'Good lord. You're alive.'

'Came right in off the street, bold as brass,' offered Welles. He gave a sharp gesture and his men came in. One aimed his gun while the other frisked Marc roughly, recovering a silenced pistol from the hoodie's belly pocket.

Talia saw the weapon and wasn't sure what to think.

'Marc Dane,' Welles continued, taking on a hard, formal tone, 'as of now you're under detention pending investigation into the events of the past forty-eight hours.'

'I came in on my own!' Marc retorted, pulling against the man holding his arm. Dane's cheeks coloured and he snarled at Royce. 'You left me behind in France! Why the hell did you do that?'

'Marc,' Royce began, struggling to find the right words. 'I don't–'

'You'll get your chance to talk to him soon enough,' Welles broke in. He lowered his voice for a moment. 'I wanted you to see this, Donald, so that there is no misunderstanding between us at a later time.' He didn't wait for a reply, and turned away. 'Dane. You're being held under internal security regulations, section thirty. There will be an immediate debriefing.'

Marc hissed as the security officer snapped a set of handcuffs around his wrists, and Talia found her voice. 'Is that actually necessary?' she demanded. 'This man is one of ours, he's not a criminal. I think we can keep this cordial, don't you?'

'That doesn't work for me,' Welles replied, shooting her a dismissive look. 'What works for me are *answers*. And seeing as how there have been precious few of those forthcoming from Hub White, I'm going to take the opportunity to debrief someone who was actually on site when the *Palomino* exploded.' He nodded to his men. 'Clean him up and take him to one of the secure conference rooms.'

Royce regained some momentum as Dane was led away toward one of the secure elevators. 'Marc! For god's sake, what happened over there?'

'They're all dead,' he retorted, his anger boiling over. 'Sam. Nash. Rix. Every single one of them.'

SEVEN

Across the dark wood of the conference room table, Welles asked the questions, every once in a while sparing the data pad in front of him a quick look. Marc had no idea what he was checking, but the camera in the corner of the far wall had him fixed in its sights and there was no way to know what other devices were in the room as well, watching him for any tells.

The room looked ordinary enough, but when no-one spoke, the flat way the silence lay there showed the falseness of it. The walls were sound-proofed, the windows inch-thick armoured polymer. The reproduction of a Turner painting on the wall was probably studded with listening devices, and the speckled foam tiles in the ceiling could be hiding a myriad of scanners looking at skin temperature, voice stressors, eye-blink ratios, the lot. The room was an interrogation space hiding behind the veneer of civility. No bare concrete walls and steel chairs bolted to the floor here, no harsh spotlights and cell doors – although MI6 had those kind of rooms as well, if you went deep enough. This place was supposed to make Marc feel like he wasn't a prisoner, but even though they had dressed the wound on his arm and done away with the cuffs, he didn't buy it.

Welles made him go through it all a third time. It was a classic interrogation technique, forcing repetition out of a suspect in order to find the places where the story didn't match up. Welles was looking for the breaks in Marc's narrative – but all he had was the truth.

Most of it, anyhow.

Careful who you trust. Marc remembered Sam's words at the dockside, and he kept that tiny fragment of events to himself. Welles had a reputation throughout the Service as a man who looked for notches to put on his belt, for expedient choices that weren't necessarily the right ones. Marc had no intention of placing his faith in a man like that. He had to get through this, find someone he could confide in.

His reverie broke with a start as Welles tossed something metallic and heavy on to the desk, where it landed with a solid thud. It was the gunman's Sig Sauer semi-automatic, now wrapped in a plastic evidence bag. 'I'd appreciate it if you paid attention,' Welles was saying. He nodded at the pistol. 'Where did you get this?'

'I told you,' he said wearily. 'I took it from the man who tried to kill me.'

Welles glanced at his pad, consulting his notes. 'But you left the grenade launcher, though? Why? Too conspicuous?'

'Don't take the piss,' Marc growled, and immediately regretted it.

The other man smiled slightly, as if he had scored a minor victory. Then the smile went away. 'Technical are chasing down the details as we speak, but this weapon appears to be part of a shipment sold by a Lithuanian arms dealer. It's not the kind of thing a British intelligence officer should have on him.'

'Needs must,' Marc shot back. 'I was running for my life. I had to defend myself.'

Welles checked his notes again. 'Which is why you killed this mystery man, and then made sure his body and his vehicle were set alight, so there would be little evidence left behind?'

'We had our orders . . .' Marc muttered. 'The French police were in the area . . . Hub White wanted zero traces.'

'Zero traces. Is that what you call setting fire to a car with a corpse in the boot? And of course, now we can't get anyone near the remains to verify what you're telling me.'

Marc showed teeth. 'I didn't have a lot of choice in the matter!'

That got him a slow, considered nod. 'It must have been difficult for you. The kill, I mean. Your first time, hand to hand, like that.'

'What?' The reply wrong-footed him. 'Uh. Yes. It was.'

Welles went on as if he hadn't spoken. 'I mean, you're not a field officer. You're not rated to go directly in harm's way, are you?'

'What . . . do you mean?'

'Just making an observation. Because you had the opportunity to take on that role, and you turned it down. Am I right?'

Despite his weariness, Marc felt his hands tense into fists. 'How is that relevant?'

'It's relevant because to understand these events, I have to understand you.' The other man's manner shifted, the faux-conversational tone dropping away to reveal a flinty edge beneath. 'You were there, and you came through it alive when seven other officers did not. Officers who were much better trained than you. That automatically makes you very, very relevant, Dane.'

A fist of icy cold was forming in Marc's stomach. 'I'm alive and here and talking to you because of blind, stupid luck.'

'Don't sell yourself short.' The casual manner returned for a moment. 'You showed real initiative. We confirmed your illegal crossing at Dover with the Border Agency. Very smart move.'

Marc went on. 'You're talking to me like . . .'

'Like you're responsible?' Welles snapped. 'At best, you let something slip by you, and OpTeam Seven paid for that laxity with their lives. At worst, you're to blame for what happened.'

'No!' Marc pushed away from the desk, shaking his head, confused and angry at what he was hearing. 'That's not it.' He looked up. 'This mission was a set-up, man! They were waiting for us on the *Palomino*, they had that guy with the grenade launcher positioned to mop up any survivors . . . It was an ambush, plain and simple!'

'It does look that way, doesn't it? Conveniently, there's no way for us to access the remains of the truck for any data recordings.' Welles shot back. 'So if someone warned the targets, we need to start looking for a penetration here at MI6.'

'Yes,' said Marc, and he was thinking of Sam again, of her warning.

'I'm glad we're on the same page.'

Marc's thoughts suddenly caught up to Welles's implication and he glared at him. 'You're accusing *me*?'

'I never said that.'

He leaned across the table, staring defiantly at the other man, and in that moment all he wanted to do was punch Welles in the face. 'I came back, damn it! Why would I come back if I was part of this?'

'That's a good question. Considering how you went silent for over twenty-four hours, how you covertly re-entered the country, without any Service oversight–'

'I told you!' he shouted. 'I had no choice!'

'So you keep saying,' Welles matched him, speaking over his words. 'But come on, Dane. If you really wanted to, you could have phoned the front desk! But you didn't! Instead, you went dark for an entire day!' He let that hang in the air for a moment. 'You're not a fool. I mean, you appreciate how that looks, don't you?'

'I . . .' Marc felt sick inside as the understanding washed over him. 'You weren't there. You don't understand.' He forced the wellspring of fear in him down and away, working hard to keep his voice level. 'If I betrayed my team to Al Sayf, or the Combine . . .' He bit out every word. 'If I did that, why the hell would I walk back into the Cross and surrender to you?'

'I can think of some reasons.' Welles looked away, musing. 'Maybe the people you sold out to double-crossed you, and you've come crying back to us. Maybe you screwed up so badly you thought you would cut your losses. Maybe you're not as clever as the psych file says you are.'

Marc shook his head, incredulous. 'Where are you getting all this? Don't you want to know who was behind the explosion? Why they chose to hit Nomad? Doesn't any of that matter to you?'

Annoyance flashed briefly in Welles's eyes. 'Don't tell me how to do my job. We have people working on those things right now.

Those questions will be answered. All elements of this misadventure will be fully analysed.'

'*Misadventure*?' he spat the word back across the table. 'Don't talk about it like it's a bad fucking football result! I saw them all die over there! My team-mates, my–'

'Your *what*?' Welles seized on his outburst. He manipulated something on the data pad's screen and from the corner of his eye Marc saw Sam's face appear on the display. 'Did you think that we didn't know, Dane? About you and Green?'

Marc stiffened, and suddenly he could find nothing to say.

'We knew,' Welles continued. 'That's our job, up on nine. To know about that sort of thing.' He leaned in. 'Did you get close to her because she was one of OpTeam Seven's senior field officers? Did you think that would . . . help you somehow?'

Welles's cell phone bleated and he pulled it out of his pocket. His expression soured and he shot a glance at the security camera before dismissing the call.

'You're way out of line,' Marc told him, low and cold.

'I don't know what you thought was going on there,' said the other man, 'but you were not the first . . . *liaison* . . . Green had within the Service. She was quite the free spirit.'

The phone rang again, and this time Welles switched it off, but Marc wasn't seeing him anymore. He was thinking of the dream, of a night in Camden. Of fire and smoke and blood on a bleak French dockside.

'I don't know anything about that,' said Marc, in a dead voice.

Welles was going to say something else, but then the magnetic lock on the door buzzed, snapping open, and one of the security guards was standing there. 'Sir?' he said. 'You need to step outside for a minute.'

Marc's interrogator frowned. 'All right. Let's take a break, as I see I won't get any peace until I deal with this.' He stood up and leaned in to gather up his pad. 'We're just having a warm-up chat, anyway.'

he told him. 'I'll come back in twenty minutes. Take the time to have a think about your situation while I'm gone.'

The door slammed and Marc was suddenly surrounded by silence.

'What the hell do you think you are doing in there?' Royce's voice cracked like a whip, and Talia found herself glancing along the corridor outside the conference room, afraid that someone of higher rank would happen on the confrontation.

'My job,' Welles replied, without apology. He strode away, forcing them to keep up.

Talia and Royce had been allowed to watch the so-called 'interview' from an observation room down the hall, but the mission director's tolerance for Welles' style of questioning soon ran thin. When he ignored his calls, Royce stormed out and demanded an explanation.

'I won't have you trying to bully a confession from one of my officers,' said Royce.

Welles raised an eyebrow. 'I haven't even got the thumbscrews out yet.'

'How does some suspected relationship between two consenting adults have anything to do with the *Palomino* explosion?' Royce demanded.

'Oh, believe me, there's nothing *suspected* about it,' said Welles. 'And you know full well the regulations about office romances.'

'As if you don't have enough dirty pictures on file already,' Royce shot back. 'My operatives are all professionals. They're not compromised by the kind of sordid insinuations you're making.'

'What exactly does that mean, Donald? That you turn a blind eye to shagging in the ranks as long as it doesn't impact on mission performance?' They reached the elevator bank and Welles turned to stare at him.

'Pretty much, yes.' Royce gave the other man a challenging glare in return. 'The OpTeams keep their own houses in order. I keep a loose rein on my crews because they are bloody good at what they do. I *trust* them, and I don't like you playing games with one of my men for your own amusement! If you have proof of misconduct, show it to me.'

'I really don't care what you like,' Welles replied, with a sniff. 'Your . . . what did you call it? Your *loose rein* may have compromised an entire mission! Dane belongs to me now, and I will question him any way I want to. If I want to mess with his head by bringing up his dead girlfriend, I'll do it.' He pointed a finger in Royce's face. 'I don't answer to you, Donald. I answer to Control, and Control wants facts.' He nodded back in the direction of the conference room. 'I'm going to get the facts, the *proof*, and you are going to stay out of my way. I paid you the courtesy of letting you know your man was still alive, but now we're done. If he's innocent, you'll get him back. If not . . .' He let the sentence hang.

The elevator arrived and he turned to walk in, but Royce pushed past Talia and stepped into Welles's path. 'Victor,' he said firmly. 'Don't take your personal dislike of me out on one of my operatives.'

'Perish the thought.'

Talia could stay silent no longer, and spoke up. 'Marc Dane is a good asset. He's risked his life for this country on dozens of occasions, and as a naval officer before he came to the Service. He's not a traitor, he doesn't . . .' She halted, floundering to find the right words. 'He just doesn't have that in him.'

'I'm sure they said that about Philby, too.' Welles spared her a look. 'All this impassioned support for your man is very touching, but it doesn't change anything. There's an undeniable truth here that the committee and I both agree on, which you have to accept.'

'Which is?' asked Talia, dreading the answer.

'Marc Dane survived an attack that blew up half the Dunkirk docks, when by rights he should have been killed along with the rest of the Nomad team. That fact *alone* means that he should be treated with suspicion.' He stepped around Royce and into the lift. 'Green, Rix, Nash, Taub, Davies, Bell and Marshall.' Welles reeled off the names like a litany. 'We owe it to all of them to be certain where the blame for their deaths lies.'

I'm a fool, Marc told himself.

Of everything he had expected to occur when he returned to London, somehow it had never occurred to him that he would be blamed for all of this. He was just one of the *blokes in the van*, watching screens and working the tech. This kind of thing didn't happen to him.

His thoughts were churning, pulling him in different directions. The events of the past day were repeating, merging with flashes of memory, questions Marc had never wanted to answer now pushing themselves to the front of his mind. He felt afraid and alone, and it was a new kind of dread that was totally alien to him.

Once upon a time, I was so fearless . . . Where the hell did that go?

That was the past, when there had been nothing to lose. But then there was the helicopter crash, and then the Service . . . and Sam. His perspective had changed.

And now all that was slipping away from him.

The door opened, and he jerked upright in the chair, startled.

'Hey, Marc. Welcome back to Legoland.'

The last thing he expected to see was a friendly face. John Farrier stepped into the room and sat in the chair that Welles had vacated. He gave him a wan smile.

The other man was six years Marc's senior, and he wore all his experience in the lines around his eyes and the hawkish cast of his face. One of the very first OpTeam crew leaders, Farrier had been a mentor for the younger man during Marc's training. He had a solid reputation as a veteran non-official cover officer, one of MI6's lone wolf operatives. It was Farrier who had recruited Marc, back at the start.

'Mate,' he told him gravely, 'you look like shit.'

Marc gave a dry chuckle. 'Nice to see you too.'

Farrier frowned. 'I know all about it, Marc. Patel brought me in to run top cover for the clean-up.' He shook his head. 'What the hell happened?'

'Did Welles send you?' Marc asked, hesitating as the thought occurred to him. 'Are you gonna be the good cop?'

'That oily little prick?' Farrier snorted. 'He'd have kittens if he knew I was in here.' He nodded at the door. 'I'm not supposed to be within a mile of you. But I've got pull.' Farrier pointed at the camera eye; the red 'active' light above it was dark. 'I called in a marker with someone in monitoring. That's going to stay off for a while.' He leaned forward. 'I wanted to talk to you, let you know you're not being cut adrift by everyone.'

'It feels that way,' said Marc. 'I had nothing, John. And they had shooters out after me . . .' He ran out of breath. 'They killed them. Sam . . . She died right in my arms.'

'Who's *they*?' asked Farrier, as that sank in.

'The tangos. Al Sayf. Or whoever they were working with. The one that came for me was German, I think.'

Farrier shook his head. 'If it was Al Sayf, they'd have told the whole world by now. Get us into shit with the French for operating on their turf. Not a peep yet, though.'

'The Combine, then,' Marc went on. 'The ones supplying their weapons.' He looked up and saw Farrier watching him. 'What?'

The other man's frown deepened. 'Welles has got a serious hard-on for you, Marc. You know he has an axe to grind with Royce and he's never liked the OpTeam program, right from day one. You might have been better off staying dark than coming in like you did.'

'What else could I have done?'

Farrier didn't answer that. 'He's gearing up to put the frame around your neck for this.'

Marc nodded once, feeling hollow inside. 'I guessed that much.' He hated the way his next words made him sound weak and powerless. 'Can you help me?'

Farrier looked away. 'I shouldn't even be here. I'm jumping the fence, supposed to be going to diplomatic official cover at the embassy in Rome. Security deployment.' He straightened his jacket, his voice turning distant. 'I'm already a day late.'

'Right. I get it.' Marc's throat went dry. 'I'm not part of it, John. You believe me when I say that, don't you?'

Farrier nodded without hesitation. 'Of course I do. I wouldn't be here if I didn't. But I wanted to warn you. Welles is going to press hard. Harder than you've ever had to deal with before.'

'I'm not afraid of him.' He said the words without conviction, and the other man saw it.

'You should be,' Farrier told Marc. 'He's not stupid, and he's got a lot of clout.' He fell silent, as if he had said more than he meant to.

'What are you not telling me?' Marc demanded. Farrier's sudden, uncharacteristic reticence was ringing alarm bells in his head.

'Welles put in for JIC authorisation to move you to a secure location. A country house.'

'Where?'

'Don't know. He's playing it close to his chest. But they gave it to him.'

Country House was a typically mocking Service euphemism for what was more commonly known as a 'black site'. Undisclosed detention facilities, some of them in allied countries with markedly less interest in human rights than the United Kingdom, others hidden in plain sight at military facilities across the rural counties.

If Marc vanished into one of those sites, it would be as if he had fallen off the face of the world. Welles had him as the chief suspect of an investigation into the suspected breach of the OpTeam hierarchy, and once he was off-grid, Marc would be 'processed' – another bland term with a darker meaning. The kinds of forceful interrogation utilised in a black site were not bound by any but the most cursory rules of conduct.

'Someone very high up the ladder is extremely pissed off about what happened in France,' Farrier was saying. 'They want a swift resolution and a body to swing from the gallows.'

'That's not me,' Marc insisted. 'I'm not to blame for this!'

'Then who is?'

Careful who you trust, Sam had told him; but if not Farrier, then who? He was running out of options. 'Welles is right,' he began, the words spilling out of him. 'There's been a penetration, someone inside the security services with connections to the Combine. I think it has to be someone at operational level or above. That must be why Nomad was targeted, that's why–'

Sam's name was on his lips, but before he could say more, the door buzzed angrily and Welles's security officer pushed into the room. 'That's enough,' he said, eyes darting back toward the corridor. 'You're done here, Farrier. Get out.'

'No, wait!' Marc's voice caught. 'Not yet, damn it!'

Farrier gave him a look. 'Give me two more minutes.'

'No minutes, no waiting.' The guard's voice became a snarl, as he pressed a hand to his head where a coil of cable led to the black comma of a radio earpiece. 'Welles finds out you were here, and no amount of favours I owe you will be enough. *Out*!'

Farrier stood up, turning back to give Marc a look that he couldn't read. 'Stay strong. Be smart,' he told him. 'That's what you're good at.' And then, very deliberately, the other man tapped the back of the chair twice with his index finger.

'Come on!' snapped the security officer, and shoved Farrier through the door, slamming it closed.

On an impulse he couldn't be sure of, Marc leaned forward and looked at the seat cushion where Farrier had been sitting, catching a glint of metal. He reached down and his hand came back with a silver ring the diameter of a large coin. Hanging from it was a black plastic fob that resembled the kind of electronic keys used on the majority of modern cars. On one side was a small solar panel, on the other a square button. Three white LED emitters protruded from the opposite face.

Was this Farrier's way of trying to help him? Marc quickly concealed the key fob inside the elastic cuff of his hoodie and leaned back into his chair. He glanced up at the security camera just as the red light winked on and he looked away, turning over Farrier's words in his mind.

'I'm on my own.' He said the words aloud to fix them in his thoughts, and for a moment the panic rose a little inside him, coming up like a slow, inexorable floodtide.

But then he thought about Sam, and the nameless gunman who had tried to choke the life from him. He thought about the *Palomino*, and the people who were already dead. And slowly, he pushed the cold sense of dread away.

They came for him soon after, three men in black suits and identical glowers, the look of ex-police officers about them. Marc knew the type well enough, and didn't give them any resistance as they secured his wrists in front of him with a pair of rigid cuffs.

Welles watched, his expression neutral. 'I think it's better for everybody if we continue our discussion somewhere else. These gentlemen will take you to a secure location. I'll be along later, and we'll resume.'

'What's wrong with this place?' Marc returned, never breaking the other man's gaze.

'Emotions are running a little high here, don't you think?' Welles shrugged. 'Might be better to get some distance. No chance of interruptions, that sort of thing.'

Marc studied his interrogator, trying to get a read on him. He decided to take a chance. 'There's something I didn't tell you.'

That got Welles's attention. 'Oh?' He threw the security men a look and they hesitated, waiting for a word of command. 'Do go on.'

'Sam Green knew there was a penetration of MI6 *before* the mission began. She told me she was investigating it.'

'There's no record of anything like that,' Welles replied dismissively. 'And OpTeam field officers don't look for leaks. That's my job.'

'This was off-book. Don't you get it? That's why we were ambushed. Someone knew Sam was sniffing around, so they took action!'

'Was this her female intuition, or did Green have any actual evidence?'

Marc's lips thinned. 'I honestly don't know.' That was almost the truth. 'But she had suspicions. I think I could–'

Welles folded his arms. 'That's your best play, is it? Throw out some vague comments from a woman too dead to confirm them?' He turned to one of the men. 'Please, give me the keys. I'm so convinced, I'm going to release Mister Dane here right away.'

'Welles, listen to me–'

Suddenly the other man was prodding Marc in his chest, his face tight with annoyance. 'No, *you* listen to *me*. I don't like anything you have said since you rolled up. Don't you think we've already got men sifting through everything Green and Rix and the rest of Nomad left behind? I know what you and Royce think of my department. Now you're going to watch it in action.'

'You've got it all wrong.'

'We'll see.' Welles sneered and stepped back. 'I'm going to put you in a deep, dark hole, and lean on you until I get what I want.'

'Even if I don't *have* what you want?' Marc shot back.

Welles gestured to the security officers. 'Get him out of here. Make sure he doesn't talk to anyone.'

The three men formed up around Marc and marched him to the elevator bank, where a lift was waiting. He saw Welles's face vanish from sight as the doors slid closed and then they were on their way down toward the building's secure parking garage on the sub-levels.

When the elevator doors opened he was marched out toward a glossy black Range Rover. The vehicle sat low on its shocks, a clear sign that it was reinforced with bullet-proof glass and sidewall armour. But even with the car's opaque windows, it would blend easily into city traffic, just one more 'Chelsea Tractor'.

The back door was opened for him and he took the centre seat, pressed in on both sides by two of his minders. The third man climbed in behind the wheel and the Range Rover rumbled into life, rolling away from the kerb toward a ramp leading to street level. Through the windscreen, Marc glimpsed a widening chink of daylight up ahead, as a heavy security gate began to slide open.

Welles had been right, after a fashion. Mentioning Sam and her suspicions had been the last card Marc had, and the investigator's reaction had told him all he needed to know.

Working in the Service made you suspicious – it came with the job, where conviction was a rare coin, when the people you met out in the world could easily be there to burn you – but now Marc was seeing deceit on the faces of everyone around him. The people he could trust, the people he *had* trusted . . . all of them were now dead and gone.

Maybe Welles was the one responsible for that, or maybe he was doing just what he was supposed to, searching for the weak link inside the Service. Either way, the man would never give Marc the benefit of the doubt. He looked down at the black metal encircling his wrists.

If Sam and the others had been right, if there really *was* a traitor in the ranks at MI6 who had cold-bloodedly sent them off to perish, then Marc Dane was a clear and present danger to that person. A potentially *lethal* threat to their safety.

Marc had come back to headquarters because he believed he would be safe, following some sort of blind animal instinct to run for the lair; but now his life was narrowing toward two equally unpalatable conclusions. He would either be made to take the fall for what had taken place in Dunkirk, or he would be silently erased, before anything he knew could have an impact on the plans of the Combine and their insider.

There was a third path, but he had no idea of where it would lead him, or how far it would go.

EIGHT

The Range Rover's engine growled as the car sped out on to Albert Embankment, turning tightly into the nearside lane.

Marc watched the buildings flash past as they headed northwards along the line of the Thames. He tried to build a mental picture of the route they would take, out of the city to the London Orbital motorway and then . . . *Where*?

They were less than an hour away from the nearest airfield, where a courier jet could pick him up for a discreet cross-border rendition, but Marc had his doubts about that. Welles wanted to interrogate him in person, and Marc didn't think that he would go to the trouble of following a detainee to a secret prison in another nation – not when there were facilities within the UK where he could do as much and still be able to make it back to Mayfair for drinks at his club.

No. They would take Marc to a holding location, some hole in the ground built during the Cold War to resist a barrage of Soviet nukes, just a door in a hillside at the end of a footpath. There were more of those places than people knew, repurposed after the fact.

They passed Lambeth Palace and the car slowed as the traffic started to thicken. Marc looked up across the river and saw the tower of Big Ben through the dull afternoon. He didn't make it obvious, but with his peripheral vision he took the measure of the guards.

The driver was bull-necked and he had the nose of a pub brawler, broken more than once and unevenly reset. He wore a pair of glasses that rested awkwardly on his face. On Marc's right was the man who had let Farrier in to talk. He had a heavy brow, deep-set eyes and the smell of cologne about him. He caught Marc's eye and gave him a loaded look, a silent warning not to mention his earlier indiscretion. Marc considered that for a moment, wondering if he could use it to his advantage, but nothing sprang to mind and he discarded the thought. The third man was dark-skinned with a shaven head and a well-maintained beard, and he kept a wary eye on the lines of vehicles around them. Marc was certain that they were armed.

All of the security officers had more body mass than Marc's spare, wiry frame, each built heavy to intimidate and project threat. But they were different kinds of men to the operatives that usually Marc worked with. They were reactive, just on the right side of thuggery to be considered professionals instead of common heavies.

He thought hard about the third path. This was it, right here and right now. Marc was at the fulcrum of a point of no return, the tension of it turning around him, and what he did in the next few minutes would be critical.

He could wait until they were out on the motorway and look for an opportunity there. But that felt wrong, it felt like the weak choice. London was the better option. In the city, he could blend in and fade, at least for a little while. And there was something he still needed to do here.

He began to regulate his breathing as the Range Rover drove by St. Thomas's Hospital, the engine note falling as the vehicle continued to decelerate. Up ahead, traffic threaded around the Plaza Hotel roundabout leading on to Westminster Bridge. The approaches to the junction were full of double-decker buses, delivery vans and cars, steady but sluggish, picked up from the feed roads and let off to cross the river, or pass under the rail bridge out of Waterloo station.

Marc angled his hands so his right thumb hooked on the edge of his pocket where the key fob was concealed. Through the fabric of the tracksuit trousers, he pressed the small device up into his fingers, and palmed it.

The Range Rover halted, joining a line of cars ready to cross the roundabout, hemmed in on one side by the high flank of a bus. Marc let his hand slip toward the press-button release for the seatbelt.

He counted to three, head down, just barely able to see the glow of the traffic lights from the corner of his eye.

Red. Red-Amber.

Green for go.

The car rocked as the driver pressed on the accelerator pedal, and Marc made a sudden turn of his head, as if he had seen something out of the left side of the Range Rover. The first guard reacted without conscious thought, turning to look in the same direction, wary of danger.

In the same second, Marc hit the seatbelt release, screwed his eyes tightly shut and pointed the key fob at the face of the guard on his right, mashing the button on the device with his thumb. The triple LEDs gave off a sudden, dazzling flash of light, a million candlepower strobe that instantly blinded the man.

The light was so harsh it was like needles in his head, even through Marc's eyelids, but he ignored the pain and the dancing blobs of purple across his vision. Blinking away the afterimages on his retina, Marc surged forward toward the driver's seat and grabbed at the edge of the steering wheel, jerking it savagely to the right.

The driver was too slow to fight him and the margin was too narrow to matter. The Range Rover's tyres screeched as it suddenly veered across the road and broadsided the bus with a grinding crash. The impact blew out the emergency airbag in a cloud of dust, battering the driver into his seat. Marc rocked backward as the Range Rover's speed bled away. The other guard was scrambling to grab him, but he was a big guy and even the back seat of the SUV was a tight fit for the three of them. Marc propelled his elbow down at the man's throat and hit him hard. He lolled forward, choking.

Marc turned into a wild punch thrown by the blinded guard, and it rang bells inside his skull. The blow was just a glancing shot, the other man still dizzy, and Marc realized that if the heavy haymaker had connected full-on, it would have been all over for him. Scrambling, he threw himself against the dark-skinned man. He connected with the guard's nose and felt bone snap. Blood gushed from the other man's nostrils in a crimson fan.

The Range Rover rocked and stopped abruptly, a dull thud vibrating through the framework as it collided with a concrete bollard on the far side of the street. Outside, a chorus of shouts, car horns, crunches of glass and the sounds of shunted metal began to build as the traffic knotted and clogged.

The driver was dazed, dusted with white powder from the airbag ejection system, blinking owlishly. Marc's joints lit with pain from the impact he had taken, but he swallowed it down and lunged a second time, tearing at the man's jacket, ripping open the inside pocket. He found the stubby metal key rod that would open the mag-lock of the handcuffs, and a leather wallet. He wanted to look for a weapon, too, but he hesitated and lost the chance.

'You piece of shit . . .' Marc felt a tug as one of the guards in the back grabbed at him, catching the hood of his top and pulling hard on it. 'Come here!'

He still had the key fob in his fingers, and he pointed it under his arm, pressing the button again. The second time around, the flash-burst wasn't nearly as powerful, the internal capacitor of the device barely recharged – but it was still enough to get a snarl of pain from the man he had already near-blinded once.

Marc scrambled over the empty front passenger seat and shouldered open the door, falling forward out of the Range Rover and into a heap on the asphalt. He heard cloth rip as the hood was torn away, flaps of it hanging ragged over his shoulders.

An arena of stalled cars and trucks were all around, the path to the bridge blocked by the bus the car had collided with. Marc sprinted toward the road that passed under the railway bridge, into the shadows beneath. Bus passengers meant people with cell phone cameras, and he didn't want them splashing his face across a hundred social networking sites before he even took a step.

He knew the security men were coming after him, so he didn't waste time chancing a look over his shoulder. Instead, he fled around the curve of the road and followed it up toward the taxi ranks outside Waterloo station. As he ran, he released the cuffs and tossed them away along with the remnants of the hoodie.

He slowed as he crossed the road, weaving around a black cab whose driver showed his displeasure with a loud combination of horn and expletives. Marc looked at the windows of the taxi and in the reflection he saw figures a few hundred metres behind him, racing to catch up on his lead.

Up the stone stairs and through the Victory Arch across the main entrance, Marc moved into the station proper, forcing himself to slow to a walking pace. If he ran, he would stand out like a flare on a dark night, and Waterloo was heavy with coppers. The rail terminal was close to a police station, so there was always a blue uniform somewhere in his sightline.

He ducked into a booking office and stood before a ticket machine, using the moment to search the wallet he had stolen from the driver. He took the money – fifty pounds in crumpled tens and fives – and left the wallet on top of the machine.

When he came out, two security officers were already on the concourse, sweeping slowly through the pre-rush hour crowd in his direction. He cursed when he saw the third, the man whose nose he had broken. With one hand the guard was holding a red-stained handkerchief to his nostrils, and with the other he was showing a police officer the screen of his smartphone.

And my picture.

Marc needed an exit vector, and he needed it quickly. A cluster of noisy teenagers carrying sports bags passed in front of him and Marc fell in step with them. Behind their cover he made it all the way to the entrance of the pharmacy on the far side of the concourse.

A risky solution was taking shape in his thoughts, but he went with the impulse. Marc knew he had only moments to find a way out. He didn't have time to second-guess himself.

Inside the pharmacy, he bought a bottle of water, a pack of lithium batteries, a stubby travel-size can of aerosol deodorant and some condoms. From there, he slipped across to a coffee stand and deftly snatched a stainless steel travel mug from a souvenir display.

He had to misdirect his pursuers, and as quickly as possible. It had worked for him in Dover and it could work now. It was a basic rule of tradecraft – *vary the pattern, deceive the watchers.*

Holding his purchases close to his hip, he walked on. Marc willed himself to blend in, to stay unremarkable and unseen as he counted down the seconds before he was through the door, and into a nearby gastropub that faced out on to the train platforms.

A sign told him the toilets were tucked behind the bar. He threaded between the tables, pausing to grab a metal knife off an uncleaned food plate. He vanished into the Gents, locking himself in a stall.

If they came at him in the next few minutes, he would have no way out. He was taking a big risk, but it was all a calculated gamble now. Given how near they were to Vauxhall Cross, given what Marc knew about the response times of the security services . . . They would have a net thrown over Waterloo less than fifteen minutes after the initial alert call went out.

Acting quickly, Marc filled one of the condoms with water and suspended it inside the cap of the travel mug. The knife was blunt, but it had enough of an edge to cut into the casing of the batteries, and he sawed at them until he had exposed the grey lithium within. The broken batteries went into the mug along with the little aerosol can, and he carefully clamped the modified cap back in place.

He hesitated, holding his breath to listen. He was still alone. On impulse, he chugged the rest of the water and tossed the plastic bottle aside, before giving his improvised device a sharp shake and setting it atop the toilet cistern. A thin wisp of white smoke emerged from an air hole in the top of the travel cup.

Then Marc was walking away, out of the men's room, crossing the bar, forcing his stride to stay casual and unhurried as he made for the exit.

Speed and confidence were key. If you were fast enough, if you seemed assured about it, you could get a long way before someone looking right at you had caught what you were doing.

He was at the door when the exothermic reaction between the water and the lithium become hot enough to burn through the pressurised aerosol canister. There was a loud, flat bang of combustion from the toilets and the sudden acrid stink of burning chemicals; a second later the shrill clarion of the pub's smoke alarm sounded. Everyone in the room was on their feet, moving, at the edge of panic. Londoners had seen enough bombs on their streets over the decades, enough that the fear of more was an excellent motivator.

Marc allowed himself to be carried out with the pub patrons, and he crossed the eye line of a policeman and kept on going. Hurried but utterly normal, he turned and walked down to the escalators leading to Waterloo's Underground station.

Still nothing. No cry of alarm, no shouts of *Stop Him!*

Two minutes later he was on a northbound tube. As the doors closed and they began to roll away, Marc was certain he glimpsed the guard with the busted nose on the platform, but then the tunnel blacked out the sight of the man and he was away, free and clear.

For now.

At the committee level, the décor of Vauxhall Cross abruptly shifted from the modernist-minimalist style of the lower floors to something closer to the halls of a gentleman's club. The carpets were richer, the walls panelled with polished wood, the chairs upholstered with oxblood leather.

Royce self-consciously straightened his tie as he crossed the small anteroom outside the office of the deputy director, slowing to a halt. The director's secretary, a bullish woman with the face of a sour old aunt, peered over the top of her monitor and nodded once. 'Go right in,' she told him. 'You're expected.'

He took a breath and turned the brass handles, stepping into the room beyond. Tall windows with a greenish-gold tint filled one wall of the office, looking out over the Thames towards Millbank. They framed a massive regency desk the size of a small car, hemmed in on both sides by floor-to-ceiling bookshelves.

Behind the desk, the deputy director looked up from a sheaf of papers bearing the 'UK Eyes Alpha' imprint, and inclined his head toward a chair. 'Sit,' he commanded.

Royce did as he was told. 'Sir Oliver–' He began, but the other man waggled a finger at him, and he fell silent.

Sir Oliver Finch-Shortland was one of the most powerful men in the British intelligence community, a scion of a family that had served the crown since the Wars of the Roses, up through the formation of the SOE during the Second World War and on into the new millennium. Of average height, he was well past the back end of his fifties. Finch-Shortland had a narrow aspect that was all sharp angles, and in his younger years it had lent him a wolfish quality. These days, he didn't show his fangs so often, but when he did, it was clear he had lost little of the strength that had made him. Behind his back, they called the deputy director 'the Old Dog', and that was as much a joke as it was a warning about his bite.

He put down the files – Sir Oliver refused to read anything that wasn't presented to him on paper – and turned a leaden glare on the Royce. 'I really don't enjoy interfering on a departmental level, Donald. I try to find people who can do the job without me looking over their shoulders. That's you.'

'Thank you, Sir Oliver.'

He ignored the reply. 'That's you,' he continued, 'if you don't make a right balls-up of the whole thing.' The deputy director prodded the papers on his desk with a thin, well-manicured finger. 'Dear god, man. A dozen suspects and an entire team of officers blown to pieces? This sort of thing does not happen to us!' His lips thinned. 'All this sound and fury, that not how we operate. That's not how I *want* my subordinates to operate.'

'Sir–'

The finger came up again. 'And then I'm told you have a man, a survivor of this catastrophe, a potential turncoat, no less, who slips the net no more than a mile or so down the street from this very building!' Finch-Shortland's voice shifted as he spoke, becoming a harsh snarl. 'I relish the moment when I will have to relay that little detail to the PM and the rest of the cabinet office.' When Royce didn't say anything, the deputy director gave him a terse flick of the wrist. 'You can speak now. And what I want to hear are answers, and not excuses.'

Royce took a breath and launched in. 'The officer in question is Marc Dane, a mission support specialist from OpTeam Seven, the group compromised in France. He got away from three of Welles' men, setting off a small, improvised firebomb to cover his escape. Our colleagues at MI5 are assisting, they've seized all closed-circuit camera footage, and are sifting it now for leads.'

'Much to their amusement, no doubt. Have you given Five the full story? They do so enjoy seeing their sister agency being made to look foolish.'

'I'm not about to tell our friends at Thames House any more than they need to know, sir. Dane's identity has been flagged at all borders and the Met have him on a watch list. We've given them the standard cover. Anti-terror investigations, that sort of thing.'

The other man brought his hands together, the fingers forming a steeple. 'This fellow. His escape from custody represents a serious failure on the part of your staff, you and Welles.'

'With all due respect, Sir Oliver, I didn't want Dane taken off the premises for debriefing in the first place. We could have done that here.'

Finch-Shortland's grey eyes flashed. 'I hope that wasn't a veiled 'I told you so', Donald. I tire easily of any inter-departmental politicking in the Service. We leave that kind of game-playing to the Americans, do you understand?'

'I'm just stating a fact,' Royce replied smoothly.

The deputy director gave a soft grunt and leaned back in his chair, the leather creaking. 'Don't sweeten the pill. How serious is this?'

Royce let out a slow breath. He had been dreading this moment. 'It would seem that the concerns we had about the possibility of a penetration of the OpTeam structure were not unfounded. I'm afraid we have to consider that MI6 may have a Combine asset within it.'

'Those damned gunrunners? How can we be certain?'

'That question is ongoing, sir. Right now, all we have is circumstantial evidence.'

'I wouldn't call a man instigating a road accident and assaulting three security staff 'circumstantial'.'

'We don't have a full picture of Dane's mind-set,' Royce went on. 'He was at the centre of a very traumatic incident, there's a possibility–'

'I know he's one of yours,' said the deputy director, 'but be clear-eyed about this. He ran.' He paused. 'How exactly did he do that, by the way? Dane's a button-pusher.'

Royce bristled. 'Not exactly. That's the mistake that Welles and his men made, considering him nothing more than a field technician. But Dane has training, aptitude. He's former Royal Navy.'

'Perhaps he had outside help.'

'I don't think so, sir.' Royce paused, considering. 'Frankly, I think his escape proves Marc is more resourceful than any of us gave him credit for.'

'Well, do remember to give the lad a gold star after we clap him in irons.' Finch-Shortland shook his head, glancing down at the papers. 'It says here he blinded one of the men guarding him . . .'

Royce reached into his pocket and placed a black key fob on the desk. 'He used one of these. It's part of our covert devices suite, a less-than-lethal flash unit. At close quarters, it can give off a burst of extremely high-intensity light, strong enough to overload the human optic nerve for a short period.'

The other man eyed the key fob warily. 'Where did he get it?'

'I don't know,' Royce admitted. 'There's no record of Dane being issued one for the Dunkirk mission.'

'But what he did . . . Well, that shows forethought, doesn't it? He planned and executed an escape on the fly, from right under our noses. We trained him, after all. He must have had an idea about our protocols . . . Where he was going.'

'Maybe that's why he ran?' offered Royce.

Finch-Shortland gave a low sigh. 'I know you will be reluctant to admit there was a weak link in your department, but I've read Welles's report. Dane was under the shadow of suspicion the moment he came through the door. If he didn't have anything to fear, he had no reason to flee.'

'Again, with respect, I hope you're wrong, Sir Oliver. Dane is intelligent but he's not experienced. This could just be . . . An extreme reaction to an extreme situation.'

'We can judge his state of mind once he's under lock and key. The last thing we need is a rogue officer on the loose.'

Royce had more to say, but the intercom on Finch-Shortland's desk gave a strident buzz. '*Sir Oliver*?' said the secretary's voice.

'What is it, Judith?'

'*Mister Royce's aide is here. She says it's urgent.*'

'Send her in.'

Royce stood up as Talia entered. She looked stressed and shot him a concerned look. 'I'm so sorry to interrupt.' She offered

Royce her data pad. 'A preliminary report just came in from the information surveillance desk at Five. I thought you would want to see it immediately.'

Sir Oliver got up and came around the desk. 'This is about the errant Mister Dane, I take it?'

She nodded. 'MI5's hackers have already set up monitoring of his email accounts and on-line presence. They found something.'

Royce's expression hardened. 'There are details of a deposit here in a bank account keyed to Dane's biometric signature. A holding trust in the Cayman Islands.'

'A new account, totalling six hundred thousand US dollars,' Talia explained. 'We've tracked the wire transfer to a bank in Beijing. It's a known shell company.'

'There's more,' said Royce. 'Notification of flight bookings under a different name.' He handed back the pad to Talia. 'London to Riyadh. One way.'

'Saudi Arabia,' offered Finch-Shortland. 'Among other things, a nation that has no extradition treaty with the United Kingdom.' He gave Royce a level look. 'Tell me, Donald, do you still think Dane is just looking for a bit of breathing room?' He turned away. 'Get him back.'

At first Marc thought the message was another one of those fake Nigerian bank scams, the so-called 'phishing' stings that swelled the inboxes of millions of email accounts worldwide. But the message passed through his junk-mail filters and it addressed him personally. It didn't ask him for any personal information – it had that already. The BrightStar Cayman Trust was welcoming Marc Dane to their exclusive client list, and asking him if he wanted some advice on where he could invest the six-figure sum with his name on it, which had materialised in their bank.

He checked the exact time of the deposit. According to the receipt, the money had changed hands several days before the operation in France. A cold prickle of anxiety crept along the length of his spine.

The next message in his unanswered stack just made things worse. It was an e-ticket from Qatar Airways, for a business class flight from Heathrow to King Khalid International under the name of Thom Halle. The Halle identity was a standby snap cover Marc had been issued several months ago, an airtight Belgian passport forged to the usual high standards of the security services.

For a moment, he blinked at the text on the little screen before him. He had picked the Blackberry from the suit pocket of a dozing businessman on the Underground, and here in a dingy coffee bar with free wi-fi access, Marc had dared to chance a look online to gather information. He regretted that now.

It had taken a while to get here. First, Marc had doubled back on himself. It was a trick that Leon had told him about, something the old school spies called 'washing the route', the act of running in a loop in order to make sure you didn't have a follower. At Euston station, Marc jumped off the train just as the doors were hissing shut, and made his way down to the Victoria Line platform. He rode south, back one stop to Warren Street, and then did the same in reverse, crossing to the Northern Line again and deliberately taking a route through the passages that went against the flow of the commuters. Then he rode two stops past his destination, crossed platforms and finally emerged from Camden Town station as evening began to draw in.

He was as clean as he could hope to be, but that didn't mean he could relax. Feeling edgy and with a headache threatening to bloom behind his eyes, he bought himself another jacket – a dark, weather proof SuperDry knock-off – and followed the street toward the nearby canal.

The narrow coffee bar was sandwiched between a store specializing in leather wear and a brightly-lit frontage that was all glass cabinets full of jewelled mobile phone cases. Finding a table at the back, Marc got himself a cup of strong, mud-coloured Kenyan and attacked a thick sandwich, working the stolen Blackberry's tiny keys with greasy fingers.

First he looked for any traces of his escape on news websites. The improvised bomb had rated a mention on some of the social networks, a line of hashtag conversations rising briefly in the aftermath as commuters complained about the police ordering a temporary evacuation of Waterloo. He sifted the web and social messaging sites using '*accident car bus westminster bridge*' as a search string but there was only a cursory mention on a traffic report page.

Standard Service protocol, he considered. They were keeping things quiet for the moment.

He finished the sandwich and then ate another. It hadn't registered with Marc how hungry he had been, how empty inside, not until the smell of fresh-cooked food from one of the street vendors had washed over him. He had to remind himself to slow down and not bolt it.

But his appetite was dead now, the half-chewed ham and cheese losing all taste in his mouth.

The money, the ticket . . . They were coming out of the shadows to build a case against him. Someone was stacking evidence against Marc that would prove he was the traitor Welles had accused him of being.

But as objectionable as the man was, he couldn't believe that Welles would fit him up like this. It had to be the Combine, moving in to deal with him as swiftly as they could. Marc put down the Blackberry and took a careful sip of the coffee. It was an effort to think straight, to reason it through and not just *react*.

Dunkirk, the *Palomino* . . . The people who destroyed the freighter, the ones who hired the gunman . . . They wanted bodies, not a survivor.

I broke their plan, Marc told himself. *I left the van.*

If he had stayed, the grenade that murdered Leon and Owen would have killed him as well. They wanted them all dead, every member of Nomad wiped out, and the gunman had been there to make sure it ended that way.

The deaths of OpTeam Seven would have cut off the undisclosed investigation going on inside the Service, at least for a while. Enough time for the asset within the organisation to cover themselves, to get away, or do something else . . .

What did that mean? He asked himself the question, trying to think like the enemy.

It meant that Marc was as much an opportunity for the Combine as he was a problem. He studied the emails again. Both were authentic, but the money and the airline ticket were quick-and-dirty plays. They lacked subtlety. Whoever was building this frame was taking advantage of an unforeseen situation, scrambling to make him look guilty, putting it all together on the fly. Marc imagined that this was just the start. If he dug deeper, he would probably find a drop somewhere, a lock-up or a safe deposit box in his name packed with more incriminating material. It would be easy enough for a group like the Combine to set up something like that. They had money and a long reach.

If someone had already decided he was guilty – someone like Victor Welles – then all this would tip the needle further into the red. Welles wouldn't look too hard at the evidence. *Why the hell would he want to?*

Anything Marc said to defend himself would sound like a vague conspiracy theory – because that was *exactly* what it was.

'I am so fucked.' It was a second or two before he realized that he had vocalised the thought. A couple of teenagers at a nearby table gave him an arch look, then went back to ignoring him.

He didn't notice their attention. All he could focus on was the rising thunder of the blood in his ears, the slow twisting of his gut like a claw reaching into him, tightening with every passing moment. The tide of dread was building, acidic like bile. The food he had eaten was like lumps of lead in his belly.

The flood of panic threatened to overwhelm him. He wasn't trained for this. He wasn't an agent, he was a tech guy, a back-seater who had a gun but never fired it in anger. This escape, all of it, had been on blind luck and happenstance! They were going to catch him. He was going to be found and disappeared . . .

Marc put his hands on the table and laid them flat to stop them shaking. With effort, he metered his breathing, staring fixedly at the space in front of him. Inside him, there was chaos, and Marc Dane looked right into it.

In the car, at the crash, he had felt himself at a moment of change. And now, here in this unassuming, ordinary café, he was feeling that again, but stronger now, far more potent. Fear raced through him, and it wanted to take hold. If he let that happen, he would lose everything. If he let that happen, *they* would win.

In that moment, Marc found what he needed. He reached inward and strangled the panic before it could grow. He thought about the people who wanted him dead, who had killed and lied.

By inches, his fear made the slow, inexorable change into resentment.

Someone out there – perhaps even someone he knew – had played the members of OpTeam Seven as if they were pawns on a chessboard, sacrificing them in a game so big that Marc could only see the edges of it.

Questions came to him in a torrent. *What had Sam, Rix and Nash uncovered? What had they come close to? Who did this?*

He held his fury for a long moment, examining it. This was not just about his pain at losing Sam, or his anger at the deaths of his teammates, not any more. *I need to know,* he told himself. *I need to find the truth and prove I wasn't a part of it.*

And at last, Marc found an understanding that made it all snap cleanly into focus. The Combine and their associates in Al Sayf had done this because they were *afraid*. They feared what Nomad would discover, perhaps what had already been discovered.

The others were dead, and now Nomad was only one man. Nomad was Marc Dane, and they were afraid of *him*. He nodded to himself. There was nowhere he could go but deeper into the labyrinth. There was no safe path anymore. This was the moment to commit to the risk of it all.

I'm going to find out what Sam knew. A slow, glacial calm descended on him. *And then I'm going to drag those secrets into the light for the whole bloody world to see.*

NINE

In the dark the house looked different. Sullen, somehow, robbed of all the warmth and life that he'd known in there with Sam.

Marc crossed the road and made his way up the stairs to the front door. Picking the lock was the easy part, the trick was getting inside fast enough to secure the alarm before it activated.

He slammed the door shut and pulled open the security panel. In the dimness of the hallway he was working off nothing but the soft glow of the illuminated buttons and the display. As he punched in the code, Marc tensed. If they had changed the alarm setting for the safe house, he wouldn't know about it until it was too late. No shrilling, screaming sirens would be set off; instead, a warning would be fed straight back to MI6 and someone would come looking.

The alarm setting went from red and ARMED to green and SAFE, and Marc blew out the breath he'd been holding in. This would be the last place Welles would think to come looking for him, but that didn't give Marc any excuse to breathe easy.

In the shoe caddy by the door there was a false bottom, and beneath it, the same model of Glock pistol he had been issued in OpTeam Seven. Marc slid down the wall and sat there on the floor, checking the gun, cocking it.

Waiting.

Two hours later he woke up with a jerk and reflexively pointed the gun at the door, blinking sleep from his eyes.

'*Shit*.' His voice echoed in the empty hallway. Gingerly, he clicked the Glock's safety catch into place and stuffed the pistol in a jacket pocket. The fatigue had come out of nowhere, swept up over him before he even knew it. Angry at his own weakness, he climbed up, wincing at fresh aches in his back.

Like an explorer moving through the chambers of a tomb, Marc walked a path from room to room, turning on every light, looking in every corner, switching them off again as he left. His initial impression didn't change. The house seemed like a dead space, still and old. He found the empty wine bottle in the kitchen where they had left it weeks earlier. The safe house had remained idle all that time, but somehow Marc could sense the ghost of Samantha Green in its spaces. She had come back here since the day they had spent together, he was certain of it.

When he found the bag, he knew his instincts were correct. Concealed in a cupboard under the staircase, lost among brooms and a vacuum cleaner, it lacked the layer of dust on everything else.

The bag was a black daypack that would not look out of place on an airport luggage carousel. Inside, it had inset panels made of a dense plastic that could smother the terahertz-wave signals from metal detectors. Buried among a few changes of shapeless unisex clothes and some toiletries were boxes of ammunition, zip lock packs of money in pounds, dollars and euros, a survival knife and a heavy-duty flashlight. He took the bag into the living room and emptied it methodically, taking inventory of everything in there. In tradecraft, they called this a 'go-bag', a prepared kit of gear that an operative could gather up and take at a moment's notice if circumstances were turning against them.

The clothes were hers, and so were the fake IDs secreted in one of the side compartments. Marc leafed through passports from four different countries, each under a different name, each bearing a different picture of Sam looking back at him. Her hair cut short in one, wearing glasses in another or peering out from under a long wig. The eyes didn't change, though; her laughing, daring eyes.

He sat across from the sofa where they had made love and listened for the echo of her. This was all he had now, a collection of pieces that were not the real Sam. Marc divided up what he could use from what he would discard, and in the process something slipped from the folds of a shirt. A metal bar, the length and thickness of his thumb.

He recognised it immediately, turning it over in his fingers. It was an IronKey solid-state memory stick, a secure flash drive unit that could hold several gigabytes of data. What made it special was the construction of the stick and the built-in encryption software. Any attempt to crack the casing or break the password protecting the contents through a brute force hack would cause it to permanently erase its contents.

He held it in the palm of his hand and studied it. *Is this worth killing for?*

Very carefully, he placed the memory stick on the table in front of him, and reached for the packets of money. There were a few credit cards in there as well, and those Marc could make immediate use of. He turned on the stolen Blackberry one last time. It was a risk using the device again, but he had few options.

Marc found an unprotected wi-fi connection, and started to gather what he was going to need.

The drizzle from the showerhead slowed to a trickle. She took a slow breath and held it, running her long-fingered hands up over her scalp and across the dark fuzz of her close-cropped hair. With military precision, Lucy Keyes let her breath back out in a slow, silent exhale and reached for the thick towel hanging on the rail near the tub. She didn't bother to rub off the water still clinging to her, coiling the cloth around and over her like a toga.

From the corner of her eye she caught sight of her own face in the wide mirror. Dark as ochre, she was stark against the brilliant white tile of the walls. A boyish face that the short hair accented, sharp-chinned with eyes that looked sleepy, if you didn't pay attention. The towel concealed a body that was athletic and spare, and it hid other things too. A shallow burn mark on her waist. The pucker of the healed wound from a 9mm bullet. Other scars went deeper, forever out of sight.

She gave herself a languid wink and wandered into the bedroom. Lucy was met by a panoramic view of London, dimming now as night made its approach, lights coming on all across the streets below. The window looked down to Hyde Park, and she could pick out the shimmer of the snake-shaped lake that ran the length of the greensward. She made coffee and orbited the suite, thinking over her assignment.

Soft carpeting gave under her feet and she enjoyed the simplicity of the sensation. Sometimes it was important to take a moment for the small things like that, she reflected. When Lucy was growing up in a sparsely furnished apartment in Queens with her mother and brother, she'd been ten years old before they had anything other than threadbare rugs on the uneven floor. She remembered what seemed like a lifetime of splinters, and soles of feet made tough.

A suite in the iconic Park Tower hotel on Knightsbridge was a hell of a long way from those backstreets, but Lucy's course through the world had taken a lot of detours like this one, some high but a lot more low.

She was pouring the coffee when she saw that the laptop on the desk was showing a blinking amber light. Biting back a curse, she reached for it and flipped up the screen.

The computer had a thickset, rugged look to it, like it was designed to be dropped out of a transport plane without a parachute. It was military specification hardware, crammed with encryption software and sheathed in a layer of ballistic shell that would stop grenade fragments and low-calibre rounds. Lucy didn't care for all the tech-specs, though. It worked when she told it to, and she liked that just fine. Once, in a Brazilian favela, she'd used a similar machine to replace a ceramic armour plate in a combat vest, but that had been a bad day. She'd made it back in one piece. The laptop, not so much.

The screen asked her for an access code and she swiped her finger over an infrared print reader. It took two attempts because her hands were still wet, but then the display blinked into a video image. It looked like a small but expensive office, panelled in light wood and brushed steel. Only the oval windows gave it away. She was looking into a room on board a private jetliner, and by the tone of the light through the portals she guessed it was somewhere over the ocean.

A familiar face slid into view. '*Ah. Keyes. You grace me with your presence at last.*' The man on the screen was tall and pale. He wore fashionable spectacles and an expression that was perpetually arch. His accent was French-Canadian.

'Delancort,' she replied, deliberately sounding out the name in her New Yorker drawl. 'What's going on?' The blinking light meant that he had been trying to contact her; the noise of the leisurely shower she had taken must have smothered the sound of the alert chime.

He raised an eyebrow, studying her. '*That's an interesting look for you.*'

Lucy scowled back at the dot-sized camera in crown of the laptop. 'Like what you see?' she dared him.

Delancort gave a shrug and demurred. '*You're not my type, you know that.*'

She folded her arms over her chest. 'So, what? We're going early? I'm not due to meet the contact for another three hours.'

'*That assignment has been scrubbed,*' he told her. '*You're being re-tasked.*'

Lucy felt the first tingle of anticipation. 'Can I put something on first?'

'*Make it quick. He wants to talk to you.*' The screen blinked and showed a holding panel, and Lucy walked out of range of the camera, fishing her clothes from the armchair where they lay.

She was pulling down a blouse when the display flickered and Ekko Solomon stared back out at her. Lucy stiffened and drew into something that was almost but not quite the parade ground attention that had been drilled into her in basic training.

Solomon did that to her. Something about the man made her automatically respond with a soldier's deference to a commander. He gave her a shallow nod. '*Lucy. There's been a change of plans.*' His voice was careful and resonant, with the clipped diction typical of African-educated English. In person, he was an imposing man, but suave with it. Lucy had never known a moment when he didn't look impeccably dressed or seem perfectly focused. Ekko Solomon was one of the richest men in the world, a billionaire with assets across a dozen third world nations and beyond. His business empire – the Rubicon Group – covered coltan and diamond mines, oil interests, technology and aviation. But it was a very different element of Rubicon that employed Lucy Keyes. On her passport – the real one, that rarely saw the light of day – Lucy's job was listed as 'security consultant', part of the Rubicon corporation's Special Conditions Division. That was a pretty way to say she was a private military contractor. What people in the bad old days used to call a mercenary.

Once upon a time, Lucy Keyes had been First Lieutenant Keyes of the United States Army, a Tier One recon/sniper specialist, part of Delta Force's clandestine all-female F Squad. But that had been a very different time in her life, and when she dwelled upon it now, she saw a different person back there. Another Lucy, far distant from the one standing barefoot in a five-star hotel room.

Solomon was the reason she was here, and she owed him for that. She owed him for a lot of things.

'You wanted me to meet with Hong.' She found her voice, becoming business-like. 'That's off?'

He gave another nod. '*I've passed Mr. Hong to another member of staff to deal with. To be honest, it was probably overkill to send you.*'

'Right.' In a way, she had been looking forward to the rendezvous in Chinatown. A quiet meeting with a compliant asset, a low-to-zero threat environment. It would almost have been a vacation. 'But the information he has–'

'It can wait. I received an urgent call an hour ago from one of our contacts in the British ministry. An MI6 operation is taking place in London as we speak, an operation relevant to Rubicon's interests.' He smiled slightly. *'You are in the right place at the right time, Lucy.'*

'In my experience, there's no such thing, boss.' She sat on the edge of the bed and turned the laptop to face her, double-checking the active status of the scrambler built into the computer. 'MI6 aren't supposed to operate inside the UK. They're external security.'

'Yes. That gives you an idea of the exigency of the situation.'

'What's the protocol here?' Lucy gestured absently toward a Walther P99 semi-automatic lying on a bedside table. 'Is this a wet job? Do I need my tools?'

'Henri has made the arrangements,' said Solomon, nodding in the direction of his assistant, who hovered in the background. *'Expect a delivery.'*

'Okay,' she replied. 'Got a target for me?'

'You misunderstand,' he told her. *'This will be surveillance, not tactical.'*

Lucy frowned. 'That's not exactly my speciality . . .'

'I know.' Solomon gave her a smile. *'But I need someone I trust to do this. I need to keep the chain of information as short as possible.'*

She accepted this with a nod. 'Copy that.'

Solomon did something out of sight of the camera and the laptop screen changed to a set of data windows, the video relay shrinking into the corner of the display. The first thing that caught her eye was a picture of a white guy in his thirties, a grainy still pulled from a security camera feed. He was wearing a grubby hoodie and he looked strung-out, tense.

Delancort's voice came over the speakers, echoing and digitizing where the satellite link lost the edges of the signal bandwidth. He told her that the man in the image was an MI6 intelligence officer who had gone rogue and lost himself somewhere in the city. The Brits were scouring London for him, but they were hindered by the need to do it quietly.

'*Mr. Solomon has released a considerable amount of assets in order to ensure that Special Conditions Division locate and isolate this man before the British recover him.*' Henri made a cutting gesture with the blade of his hand. '*If MI6 get any hint that we're shadowing them, Rubicon's ability to operate in the United Kingdom will be severely impacted.*'

'Copy that,' Lucy repeated. She peered at the intel file scrolling up the screen. 'Marc Dane,' she read aloud. '*Huh.* A support tech? What's so special about him?'

'*We need to know what Dane knows,*' said Solomon. '*Find him first.*'

Lucy's gaze flicked to the P99. 'And after that?'

'*We'll review the situation at that time. Be safe, Lucy.*' There was a crackle of disconnect, and the feed from the jet was cut.

She studied the data Delancort had sent, paging through it, committing Dane's face to memory.

A knock at the door brought her out of her focus, and Lucy looked up. 'Porter,' said a voice. 'I have a delivery for Miss Locke.'

She opened the door. 'That's me.'

The porter was holding a medium-sized Louis Vuitton Pullman bag. 'Hello, miss. This was just brought in to the front desk for you.'

Lucy took the handle and plucked it effortlessly from his hands. 'Hey, thanks.'

'Heavier than it looks,' said the porter, puffing out a breath. 'What's in there, sports gear?'

She pressed a five-pound note into his hand and smiled. 'Something like that.'

He camped out in the hallway as the late morning came on, propped on a cushion with the loaded Glock. When the knock came on the front door, it was like thunder, and even though he'd been expecting it, Marc still felt a jolt of shock.

He held the door open with the pistol hidden out of sight. The delivery driver offered him a pad where he could sign for the boxes piled on the stoop. Marc made a looping squiggle with the stylus that vaguely resembled a signature and the man was gone.

He made a quick survey of the empty street and recovered his purchases. It had cost a lot to get what he needed on less than twelve hours' notice, but the money wasn't his, it was fairy gold that would evaporate from the cover account in seconds the moment that his MI6 trackers learned of it.

He was rolling the dice in a big way here. If Sam's emergency accounts were flagged, what he'd done was hand Welles the location of his hiding place. Before, that sort of risk might have made him hesitate, but not now. Marc had lost something in the last few days, and he was only just starting to realize it. He'd lost some of the fear.

Opening the boxes was like Christmas morning. On the heavy wooden table in the kitchen, he unrolled lengths of bubble wrap, unpacking plastic cases and silvery static-proof bags. He couldn't suppress a small grin as he took stock. There was kit worth thousands of pounds laid out before him, and he was itching to get to grips with it.

The largest box contained a fully tricked-out laptop computer; an off-the-shelf Alienware model designed for high-maintenance videogamers with blisteringly fast internet connections. There was an IT techie's tool kit in there as well, and he used it to open the case of the laptop, getting to work on the motherboard within.

As he worked, for the first time he found himself thinking about his own place, the clean lines of the small, modern apartment he had out in Docklands. Marc's own personal kit, the computer he had spent months of his life building, was there. His bespoke machine, tuned like a Formula One racing car, sharper than anything in the arsenal of any Tiger Team hacker from Shanghai to Langley. It broke his heart to think of it in the hands of the goons from the ninth floor, who would tear it apart in search of incriminating data.

He didn't miss a lot else from the apartment, though. Maybe his Blu-ray collection, at a push. Marc had been there for almost two years, and there were still cardboard boxes unopened from the move. It had never really been a home for him, not really. It was just a storage area for his stuff, a place to park his body for sleep and food. It didn't have any history to it; it was bereft of ghosts.

Marc sighed and pushed those thoughts aside, delving into the guts of the laptop with all the care and seriousness of a cardiac surgeon performing a heart bypass.

Khadir poured dark tea into the glass and swirled it slightly, savouring the subtle aroma as a curl of vapour rose from the surface of the liquid. The tea was an ordinary thing, a common pleasure for a soldier, but he treated it as if it were a reward. Khadir had little in the manner of what other men would consider to be vices, but he was not a monk. He preferred to think of himself as a man of focus and purpose, but not one isolated from the joys of life.

Without joy there was no understanding of what was to be gained, or could be lost. The war would mean nothing without that knowledge. He smiled to himself. In the matter of something as simple as a glass of tea, that truth revealed itself.

It was quiet in the compound, save for the occasional mutter of the wind across the windows. Out in the orphanage, the youths were sleeping off the day's instruction. The cycle of training seemed endless to the young ones, but in truth they were very close to the end of it, to the start of next phase of the work. Soon the orphanage would be left behind and those considered strong enough would come with Khadir into the battle proper.

There was a knock at the door and Jadeed entered, holding a sheaf of papers. 'Commander,' he said, with the incline of his head that constituted a salute. 'We have confirmation. I thought you would want to be informed immediately.'

Khadir allowed his subordinate a nod. 'Show me.'

Jadeed handed over scans of pages from the previous day's edition of the *Washington Post*, blurred by fax transmission.

He followed the words of the article he was looking for, a grandiloquent piece discussing the subject of American educational reform, and a sneer pulled at the corner of his mouth. 'Our generous friends are proven right once again. Truly we are blessed to have such allies.'

He watched the other man sift the vague sarcasm in his tone before he answered. 'They think of themselves as more than that, sir.'

Khadir beckoned Jadeed to the table and poured more tea for both of them. 'We *are* blessed, my friend,' he told him. 'Don't question that. Like the sword, Al Sayf balances on the tip of its blade, ready to sweep up and take the head of the enemy. What we will do shall resonate in history. This will be our most devastating blow against the governments of the West.'

Jadeed baulked at the heat of the tea. 'I do not disagree,' he went on. 'But I cannot hold my silence. These foreigners, they have plans that do not walk in step with ours.' He was slowly becoming angry. 'Yes, the weapons and the equipment they have supplied to us . . . Those tools have enabled us to do great work. But they . . .' He halted, frustrated that he was unable to find the right words.

'They see us in the same way,' offered Khadir. 'As *tools*. And when the usefulness of a tool comes to an end, it is discarded.'

Jadeed gave him a sharp look. 'This is an alliance built on lies, sir.'

He smiled coldly. 'Of course it is. These men, this . . . This 'Combine' . . . What are they if not an extension of the enemy we wish to kill?' He took another sip of tea. 'They are weak men, greedy men. They desire a world where they can peddle fear to their own kind and live high from it.' He shook his head. 'Men like that, who think themselves our betters . . . Those kind of men can always be used, even as they believe it is *they* who use *us*. Our relationship with the Combine is a mutually beneficial one. But when that changes . . .'

'We will be ready,' said Jadeed.

Khadir nodded again. 'Have no doubt.'

Outside in the corridor there were raised voices, and someone gave an angry shout. A moment later, the door slammed open and two of Jadeed's men entered, dragging a third between them.

'What is this?' snarled Khadir's subordinate, rising to his feet. He glared at the third man, a husky guard with features marred by a yellow-purple bruise on his face. The man looked up imploringly.

'We found this one *assaulting* a recruit,' said one of the other guards. His words were laced with disgust, and the emphasis he placed made it immediately clear what the nature of that assault had been.

The guard's gaze flicked back and forth between Jadeed and Khadir. He started to babble, trying to explain that it was a misunderstanding.

Jadeed ignored his pleas. 'You saw this?' he asked the other guard.

'I saw it,' came the reply.

Khadir spoke to them for the first time. He touched his cheek in the same place where the man had the bruise. 'Who did that?' He asked the question in an off-hand, almost casual manner.

'It was me, commander,' said the other guard.

Khadir accepted this. 'Let him stand.'

'Sir?' Jadeed shot him a look.

'Do as I say.'

The expressions on the faces of the guards turned stony, but they did not disobey. Both men released their grip on the injured man's arms and immediately, he took a step toward Khadir, bringing his palms together in a gesture of thanks.

The commander looked the man in the eyes, measuring him for a lie.

In the next second, Khadir exploded from his chair with such velocity that his tea glass was knocked aside. His hand went to the holstered Tokarev pistol at his hip, and he drew it out, turning it to present the gun's thick, knurled grip.

The butt of the weapon came down like a hammer and shattered the guilty man's nose with the first blow. The second and third impacts cut into his face. Khadir's calm, metered manner evaporated and he was suddenly towering with anger, crossing between the two extremes in a heartbeat.

The man went down in a heap to the wooden floor, drooling blood, weeping like a widow. Khadir drew back his boot and snapped his ribs with a sharp, hard kick. 'Each one of them,' he hissed, repeating the blow. 'Each is worth a thousand of you!' He kicked him again, and the guard screamed.

'Sir . . .' Jadeed's face paled a little with shock at the sudden, brutal power of the punishment Khadir delivered.

Carefully and deliberately, the commander stepped forward and ground the heel of his boot into the outstretched fingers of the man on the floor. The bones crackled as they broke.

'Get this worthless creature out of my sight,' he said, his voice dropping back to an even tone.

Jadeed drew his own gun and worked the slide. 'Take him to the basement–'

'No.' Khadir shook his head. 'Keep him alive.' He didn't look up as he took his seat again, the matter of the chastised man dismissed immediately from his thoughts as they dragged him away.

'I despise waste.' Khadir frowned at the spilled tea, and righted the glass before filling it again.

He wasn't aware of the time until he was done. Marc opened a window to vent the smell of hot solder and called the local takeaway for Chinese food. He ate at the kitchen table, foil trays full of egg fried rice and chicken strips in thick honey lemon sauce washed down with a bottle of Tsingtao beer. Debris from his work littered the room, but he ignored it. Welles would come here eventually and it amused him a little to think of the man being forced to sift through scraps of wire and circuit board as he tried to figure out what Marc had been doing.

He took a breath and fished the IronKey from his pocket. Marc plugged it into the laptop and watched as the memory stick sniffed at the machine, looking for anything threatening. It asked for a password, and Marc stared at the prompt on the screen.

This wasn't one of those things where you got to try again if you screwed up. There was no respawn here, like in a video game. If he got it wrong, the solid state drive would lobotomize itself and Marc would have nothing. He thought about making a list of possibilities, taking some time to sift his memories of Samantha Green in hopes of finding the word or phrase that she would have used to lock up this data.

He was still thinking that when his hands were on the keys and typing, almost as if it were someone else doing it. The password panel filled up with two words and his index finger hesitated over the 'Enter' key.

Camden Market. She loved Camden Market.

He pressed the button, and like a hand of cards fanned over a table, the laptop's showed panel after panel of data, files decoding themselves from streams of unreadable gibberish into legible text.

He started reading, eating mechanically.

It was all there. Sam's off-book notes about the decision Gavin Rix had made to look into a possible breach of OpTeam security. There were things here that Marc had never even been aware of, small-scale missions handled by only one or two of the Nomad tactical officers, stuff that had never been put on the grid at MI6. Investigations that weren't sanctioned, that had originated within OpTeam Seven and contained inside the unit. He tried to read between the lines, but Sam's spare, matter-of-fact notes didn't give him much to work with.

Marc wondered where it had all began, and drilled deeper. For what seemed like the first time in forever, he felt a surge of confidence. Corridors of data, lines of intel . . . These things were *his* battleground.

He found the riches in a sub-folder full of roughly worded text files. Marc recognised the artefacts of something machine-translated, the rogue adjectives and occasional non sequitur, but it was clear enough to make his pulse race as he read on. A name repeated several times among the dense blocks of words; *Dima Novakovich.*

He knew the man, not personally, but by the ripples he left, passing through the intelligence network. Novakovich was what the Americans liked to call a 'non-state actor' – not exactly a player on the global scene in the same way as a terrorist or an agent of an aggressor power, but a moving node in the web of influence and action. The man was a criminal, that wasn't in question, but Novakovich was someone *of use*, and people like him had a way of staying beyond the reach of the world's police forces.

He was, for want of a better word, a broker. Marc had first seen his name on a list of middlemen working in Eastern Europe. Novakovich was a Lithuanian national, but stateless by his own choice, one of a breed of extra-legals born out of the rise of the *bratva*, the Russian organised crime clans. He liked the high life, expensive hotels and expensive women, and an inclination to roam from resort to resort as the mood took him. Novakovich specialised in the trade of exotic weapons systems, but nothing large enough to put him on hit-lists alongside ex-Rocket Korps generals trying to sell surplus SS-20's. No, Dima was a denizen of the dark web, the black market network buried a few layers below the internet that most of the world surfed on.

There were emails logs here, messages that had been routed through blind servers and back-channels. Marc's brow furrowed as he skimmed through them in reverse order. Rix had been talking to Novakovich for weeks, so it appeared, looking to use him for a way into the structure of the Combine. At first, Marc couldn't parse how the two of them had even got to be talking, but the unfolding narrative of the communications slowly settled into place.

The middleman had come to *them*. Novakovich wanted out. A man like him, even a minor player with his limited skill-set, he had to know about the Combine. And he did . . . More than that, he had worked for them.

Marc settled back in his chair, rubbing the fatigue from his face. He let his thoughts settle for a moment. 'They offered you a step up from the kid's table, didn't they?' He looked at the broker's picture on the laptop screen. 'But you choked. You got scared . . . By what?'

He filed that away for later consideration and read on. It was Novakovich who had confirmed what Rix and Nash and Sam already suspected, that Combine had connections, not just in foreign agencies, but also inside MI6 itself. They were talking about how to extract him, how to make sure he could never be found again, in return for spilling what he knew.

Marc had to wonder what kind of threat would motivate someone like Dima so forcefully. *Could it have been a double-game*, Marc wondered? *The Combine setting up Novakovich as the stalking horse?* It was possible, but it seemed more likely that the middleman had got in over his head, and started flailing.

Deliberate or not, whoever Novakovich was talking about had become aware of what was going on, and set up the Dunkirk ambush to deal with the problem. In keeping the investigation off the books, Nomad had unwittingly made it easier to end them.

Marc made coffee and poured the night-black liquid into a cracked mug. He set up blinds and proxy routers to mask his digital trail, then punched out into the internet, sifting the anonymous online forums and shadow chat rooms that existed in the non-space of the web. It took him hours, but from a lead he picked up from a Singaporean anti-capitalist forum, he tracked a faceless person who knew someone who knew that Novakovich had gone off the grid in the last few days.

The timing couldn't be a coincidence. The broker's business only existed on-line. His was a fully digital enterprise where buyer and seller never met, a shell game. Money went in one end, and weapons came out the other. Clean, neat, and utterly untraceable.

But Novakovich was off-line, his every virtual storefront shuttered up and silent. He was either dead already, or keeping a low profile.

The man was the next link in the chain. Marc studied his face, paging through the file on him that Sam had appended to her notes. Novakovich had a boat, a slick 170-foot super-yacht called the *Jade* that he liked to sail around the Mediterranean. If he was on board it, he could conceivably stay off the radar for months, moving from port to port and still living in the style to which he was accustomed.

That thought lodged in Marc's mind as he looked at a digital still of the broker climbing out of a limousine, a long-lensed shot of Dima with his hand on the shoulder of a woman half his age.

Her name was in the notes; Tanya Kirin, a Polish émigré with a serious jewellery habit. The file on Tanya said she was a 'dancer', a nicely vague euphemism that covered a multitude of possibilities. The couple had a history of explosive break-ups in public places and tearful reconciliations, and these incidents were usually followed by Kirin appearing with a new and bigger rock on her finger. Marc knew right away that the girl was his line to finding the broker. Novakovich wasn't a fool – he knew how to manage his digital footprint, and tracking him would be an uphill struggle . . . But pretty Tanya, with her costly tastes and shallow manner . . . Someone like her wouldn't take well to being cooped up on a boat for days on end, even if it was a luxury ride like the *Jade*.

Marc started researching the exclusive designers that Tanya Kirin liked to wear, tracking her back until he came upon a trail of ill-kept social networking data. He grinned; it was the mother lode. Within moments he was paging through Tanya's photo stream, watching as the images shifted from cell phone camera snaps of high-end restaurants and sports cars to sunlit pictures from the deck of the *Jade*.

Powder blue skies and dark water; they were out in the deeps. He checked the time-stamp. The most recent shot had been uploaded just that morning. Tanya hadn't been good enough to tag the image with her GPS location, but she had engaged in a string of messages with her friends directly afterward. One of them was an event planner who worked for the Atlantis Bay, an exclusive hotel in the town of Taormina. Marc pulled up a map search. The resort was on Sicily's Ionian Coast, and it also happened to be home to an artisan who specialised in the art deco necklaces that Tanya adored.

'Gotcha.' He leaned back in the chair, and took a sip of stale coffee. It was a chancy deduction, a shot in the dark. Marc was basing a lead on the possibility that Novakovich would want to keep his lover sweet by treating her to something new and shiny. He could just as easily be putting two and two together and making five.

But was there another choice? Novakovich was off grid because he was afraid, and with good reason. The Combine didn't like loose ends. The broker was marked, and if Dima was making for Sicily, it was a certainty that he wouldn't stay there for long. Once Novakovich had indulged his lover, the *Jade* would put to sea again and there would be no guarantee that Marc would find him.

And then there was the other consideration. If Marc could find the man, so could the Combine.

When he was done, Marc made a ghost-image copy of the contents of the flash drive, and re-coded it with an encryption to his own recipe. Marc seeded a handful of copies of the files to open access cloud servers and torrent sites out in the shadier corners of the internet, buried them deep under faked names that made the data look like out-of-date versions of office programs or ancient abandonware videogames. Anyone who downloaded the dossiers by chance would get what looked like a corrupt file. Hiding in plain sight in the margins of the net would keep Sam's intel safe. He thought about setting a time-release, a countdown clock that would automatically email the data in the clear when the timer reached zero – a digital dead-man's switch in case the Combine caught up with him. But who could he trust with this? That question, he still couldn't answer.

Marc returned to the go-bag and loaded it with the gear he had gathered, and made a place to sleep in the living room, close to the window where he could exit quickly. Lights out and in the dimness, he turned over his next move as the fatigue came on again.

He had a new mission now, one he had chosen for himself. In some strange way, that felt *freeing*. But leaving the country would present challenges of its own. Locating Novakovich meant nothing unless he could be there to look the man in the eye.

Slowly, Marc realised that he would need to call in a favour.

TEN

Stephen Parker failed to stifle a bone-deep yawn as he passed by the duty officer at the front desk of Albany Street police station. The barrel-chested man behind the high counter saw him and chuckled.

'Rough night, detective sergeant?'

'*Long* night, Mike,' he corrected.

'I thought you could run all hours.' The duty officer looked him up and down, taking in Parker's sturdy build and his round, serious face.

He shook his head. 'Get a wife and a kid and you'll see how long that lasts you.' He gave a weak grin. 'Later.'

Outside, London's morning sky was low and grey, and it threatened drizzle. He blew out a breath and marched against the flow of commuters coming up the pavement, making his way to the side street where he'd left his car. Parker was far enough down the pecking order at Albany nick to ensure that he didn't get a proper parking space to call his own, and his nondescript four-door Ford sat against the kerb, misted with condensation.

He slowed as he approached the vehicle, something in his copper's intuition ringing a warning bell. Without making it obvious, he scanned the street, but saw nothing that gave him pause. He blinked and sighed. After everything that had happened in the last few days, he was jumping at shadows. Right now, more than anything, Stephen wanted to be home with his wife and young son.

If the traffic was with him, he might be able to make it back before Kate took little Matthew to nursery . . .

Parker was reaching for the door handle when he glimpsed movement from the corner of his eye. He turned, immediately presenting himself side-on in case of an assault, but what he saw was a gangly figure garbed in rough clothes lifting up off a square of soiled cardboard. The homeless man had been concealed in the mouth of a narrow alleyway.

'Oi, mate,' said the man, raising his fingers to his lips like he was holding an invisible cigarette. 'Spare a fag?'

'Don't smoke,' Parker replied, his tone hardening. 'Jog on, fella.'

The vagrant kept his head down, dragging a heavy backpack over one shoulder. His voice shifted. 'Kate made you quit, didn't she?'

Marc Dane peeked up at him from under the bill of a threadbare baseball cap, and Parker froze. When he replied, his voice was low and hostile. 'I haven't seen you. I don't want to see you. Do yourself a favour and get lost.' He turned his back and opened the car door.

'I need some help, Steve.'

Parker stopped, and cursed himself. *This is a mistake,* said a voice in his thoughts. *Just drive on. Leave him be.*

He wanted very much to do that, to go home and never tell Kate that he had seen her brother again. But even as that thought formed in his mind, he knew he wouldn't.

'Get in the back seat and keep your head down,' he said, in a flat tone. 'Don't talk.'

He drove a few streets away until he came to a housing estate where traffic was light, and parked in a lay-by. Resting one hand on the pepper spray he kept on a belt clip, Parker turned in his seat and glared at the man sitting behind him.

'Steve, thanks–'

He silenced Marc before he could say more with a grave shake of the head. 'You've got brass balls turning up like this,' he growled. 'No bloody sign of you for over a year, and then you come to me *on the street*?'

'I'm sorry,' Marc said, looking out through the windows like he was being hunted. 'But you're the only one I could talk to.'

Parker's fists clenched with the echo of old anger. He was thinking of how he had watched his wife cry after the last time Marc had spoken to them, of the impotent fury he had felt at his brother-in-law. The two men had been civil to one another for Kate's sake, but Parker had never been able to connect with Marc, finding him hard work, distant. After the passing of Kate's mother, the rift had grown wider. Marc hadn't been there at the funeral – they said he had been on operational duty – and in the aftermath the two siblings had fallen out.

He didn't exactly know what it was that Marc Dane did for the government, but he was a copper and he knew the players in the city of London. It wasn't hard to hazard a guess.

'I told you I never wanted you to bring your spook shit to my door.' The day before, men in suits who made vague assurances of being from 'the security services' had come to question Parker and his wife, pressing them for any information about Marc's whereabouts. They had not been subtle with their threats about the consequences if things were kept from them.

'Welles,' Marc said, almost to himself. 'Victor Welles.'

'I don't know what you're mixed up with,' Parker told him. 'I don't *want* to know. The only reason I haven't already dragged you into the nick is because Kate loves you, as much as you've upset her. And I love my wife.'

Marc was silent for a long time. 'I'm sorry,' he said, at length, and Parker knew he meant it. 'I never wanted that to happen.'

He sank back in the driver's seat and felt a wave of weariness engulf him. 'You've pissed off some very important people, Marc. They told us that you're implicated in serious crimes. Murder and treason.'

'That's a bloody lie!' Marc spat. He stopped and took a moment to gather himself. 'Look, I'm going to make this right. I'm not in the wrong here.'

Parker was a good detective, and the one skill he truly prided himself on was the ability to detect a lie when he heard it. Marc was not lying to him, and for all the differences between them, he had never considered his brother-in-law to be a criminal.

On some level, he understood about the funeral. Kate hadn't wanted to hear it, so he kept it to himself, but Parker knew that the requirements of duty often failed to account for the small, human needs of people. He'd seen the flowers Marc left at the grave where his mother was buried.

Parker released a long, slow sigh. 'What do you want, Marc?'

The answer took a while coming. 'I have to get out of the country, and I have to do it in the next twenty-four hours. Otherwise, they're going to catch up to me and I'll end up buried in some Welsh peat-bog.'

'You need money, is that it?'

He shook his head. 'I need papers. Passport, driver's licence. A clean skin.'

Parker frowned. 'I can't get you that.'

'I bet you know a man who can.'

He gave Marc a sharp look. 'You understand what you're asking for, right? You're making me an accomplice to international flight. They'll put me inside for that. Kate and Matty, they won't have anything if I get pinched.'

'Help me with this and I am gone,' Marc told him. 'It won't connect back to you. I won't put my sister's family in danger . . .' He trailed off. 'She's all I have now.'

After a moment, Parker pulled out the flat black notebook he kept in his coat pocket, and scribbled down a few words. 'You'll need to be quick,' he said, as he wrote. 'Immigration is going to smash this place flat in a couple of days.'

He tore out the page and handed it to Marc, who took it like it was the ticket to his freedom.

'Thank you,' said Marc. 'And, look, Kate. Can you tell her . . .?'

Parker turned his back on him. 'I'm not going to tell her *anything*. Not that I saw you, or talked to you, or even got a sniff of you. But if your MI6 mates come back to my home and they put you on the line over my family, I will give you up without even a second's hesitation. Do you get me?'

'Yeah.' Marc said quietly. 'Yeah, I do.' He opened the door and took a last look around before climbing out.

'One more thing,' Parker glanced at him in the rear view mirror. 'If you really are a traitor, Marc . . . Never come back.'

When the door slammed, he started the car and drove away, eyes fixed on the road ahead.

The Ford sped off, leaving the unkempt man on the street watching it go. Neither the driver nor the passenger had seen the silver Nissan sedan that had shadowed them from Albany Street.

The woman in the driver's seat put the Nissan in gear, ready to pull out. 'Target's moving again. Do we stay on it?' She had a severe look about her, a tight face beneath short brown hair.

Her companion's expression was fixed in a glower, his face swollen around the bandage over his broken nose. 'No. We stay with the primary.'

'Are we sure that's him?'

The other man nodded once. 'I'm sure.' After the incident at Waterloo, he wasn't going to forget Marc Dane's face in a hurry. Without taking his eyes off his subject, he drew his smartphone and hit a speed-dial key.

'*Alpha One*,' said Victor Welles. '*Report*.'

'Echo team, on the brother-in-law,' he replied. 'We have a sighting of the primary. Request permission to isolate and extract.'

'*No*,' said Welles. The scrambler on the line made his voice sound tinny and distant. '*I know you owe him a slap, but reign it in. Your orders are to track but not to engage, is that clear?*'

The man with the broken nose shared a look with his partner, and she shrugged. 'We're not going to reel him in, sir?'

'*Now Dane is out, I want him to think he's cleverer than the rest of us. Let him get complacent. See where he leads us. He can't be in this alone.*'

'*To confirm,*' said the gruff, mechanical voice inside Lucy's helmet. '*Echo team are to track but not apprehend primary.*' She heard the burble of a reply, but it was too faint for her to decipher.

She leaned forward over the handlebars of the black Ducati 848, her face invisible behind the cowl of her visor. A wireless link between the helmet speakers and the ultraviolet laser microphone rig in her hand parsed the sounds of the voices inside the Nissan into something she could understand. The laser mike looked like a bulky flashlight, the invisible beam it generated bouncing off the passenger-side window of the Nissan and reflecting back to a sensor that registered the smallest of perturbations in the laser's wavelength. Onboard software turned the vibrations back into audio, allowing Lucy to remotely bug the MI6 team from her perch on the motorcycle a hundred metres away.

She smiled. Keyes liked the irony of conducting surveillance on a surveillance unit. Her instincts had been good, like they always were. Dane had made contact with the one person who, according to the files Solomon's connections had delivered, was the least likely choice.

'Smart boy,' she said to herself. 'Go to the guy who likes you the least.'

But Dane hadn't been smart enough. What he could think of, so could MI6, and so could Rubicon. It was a play a more seasoned field operative would never have made.

The Nissan pulled out and rolled away into traffic. Lucy gave a count of ten and then fired up the bike.

Stepping off the bus with his collar up, Marc avoided the main road where he might have been caught on a CCTV camera, and skirted the edge of Burgess Park until he found his way down the side streets to the vacant residential blocks of the Aylesbury estate.

The folded slip of paper in his pocket bore the address of a flat in one of the main structures of the complex, a crumbling series of neo-brutalist concrete blocks. Much of the site was derelict now, with a handful of die-hard residents still living among hundreds more empty apartments. The place was mired in the slow process of preparation for demolition and future gentrification, and in among the boarded-up flats there were ideal spaces for a forger to set up shop.

He followed the long, narrow terraces past lines of tin security panels bolted over windows and door frames, passing down ghost-town walkways where windblown leaves collected in the sharp-angled corners. The estate was sparse, almost beyond abandoned, empty even of squatters or the more usual low-end criminal wildlife, nothing more than hollow shells sealed tight and left to wait for the eventual march of bulldozers and wrecking balls.

The rain started, hard threads of it falling at angles that clattered against acres of grimy windows. Marc jogged across the overgrown grass verge outside the block he was looking for, and found the entry door on the ground floor propped open by a brick. Inside the air was stale. Haphazard graffiti marked the brown tile of the walls.

He climbed the stairs, catching the smell of cigarette smoke and the low mutter of conversation from upstairs. Schooling his expression, Marc walked calmly on to the landing and found two teenagers blocking his path. They eyed him, lazy and feral.

'Here to do business,' he told them. To show willing, Marc peeled off a ten-pound note and paid his toll to pass.

Another doorstop met him on the next floor up, outside the flat, but this one had a lot more threat about him. He was a heavy-set Asian man, a Sikh in a dark blue tracksuit that did nothing to conceal the obvious bulge at the waist where a fat revolver was holstered.

Marc gave the Sikh the Glock without complaint and submitted to a pat-down. Then he was in through the door, and the first thing that hit him was the smell of cooked lamb. His mouth flooded with saliva and there was an answering rumble from his stomach.

Only the living room and the kitchen of the apartment were occupied. The rest of the flat was vacant, emptied down to the wallpaper. The smell came from a young man working at a camping stove, who threw Marc a slow, disinterested look as he peered into the room in passing.

The forger was an older man with skin the colour of weathered teak and salt-and-pepper hair. He rolled toward him across the concrete floor on a chair mounted on castors, and gave Marc a level look.

'What service can I offer you?' he asked, with a politeness that seemed incongruous.

Marc took in the dining table before him, piled high with carefully ordered suitcases, each filled with blank paperwork and unused official documents. He spotted a high-definition laser printer, digital cameras and a portable computer set-up that looked more suitable for a corporate office than this decrepit domestic setting.

'The full set,' he said. 'Passport, driver's licence, identity card . . .'

'I have German, Czech, Canadian and Belgian.'

He nodded. 'German.'

'Two days,' said the old man.

Marc shook his head. 'No.' He dropped his backpack on to the bare floor and fished out the counterfeit IDs Sam Green had prepared for herself. 'I'll give you these as a sweetener.'

The forger took them and flipped through the documents. He made an appreciative noise, admiring the workmanship. 'I can offer a . . . A recycling discount for this lot. But still, forty-eight hours.'

'How much for right now?' Marc insisted.

'You're in a hurry. Everyone is in a hurry these days.'

'I don't disagree. But I still need this now.'

'Four thousand pounds.' It had to be twice the going rate, but Marc had no time to quibble. He returned to the backpack and laid a thick wedge of fifties on the table.

'Half now, half when you're done. I'll wait,' he told the old man, wandering into the kitchen.

Marc helped himself to a little of the rogan josh in the cook pot and found a corner of the flat where he could eat in silence.

The Nissan's lights flashed once as a panel van slowed to a halt and parked in front of it. The rain was a steady drumming on the roof of the sedan, a dull and monotonous sound that only served to help erode the man's patience.

He looked up as a figure jogged back across the road from the shadow of the housing estate, and opened the door.

The severe-looking woman climbed into the driver's side, and flicked rainwater off her coat. 'Took a while, but I found him. He went into one of the blocks,' she reported. 'There's a couple of louts in there, maybe some more.'

He nodded. 'No residents listed on the council tax database. More rats in a rat hole, then.'

She looked up. The rear doors of the van opened slightly and through the crack a group of men in black coveralls and tactical vests became visible. They carried shotguns and close assault weapons.

Her partner smiled coldly.

Lucy moved carefully down the length of the elevated terrace, counting off the apartments until she reached the number in her head. She had parked the Ducati near an old trash chute on one of the raised walkways, unwilling to leave the bike where it could be seen.

At the right door, she halted and used the diamond-hard edge of a military combat knife to lever open the metal security panel. She made a big enough gap to slip through and forced open the door within.

The apartment was damp and heavy with the musky stink of mildew, and a rotting grey-brown carpet gave under her boots as she threaded through to the back room.

Cold air and trickles of rain blew in through windows that had fallen open. Lucy crouched, opening her bag, looking for a good angle. Across the grassy space far below was the block that Dane had disappeared into, and from this vantage point Keyes had a view of the whole north side.

She found a broken chair and used it as a prop for the Heckler & Koch PSG-1 in the long-bag. Lucy calibrated her scope and peered down the length of the rifle, scanning across the balconies until she found the Sikh man. He was sitting on a stoop, smoking. Every once in a while, he would scowl at the clouds as if they were personally spiting him.

The sniper panned away, turning in a tight arc until the view through the scope found the road and the silver Nissan. She had chosen a good location. Lucy could see both hunter and hunted from here.

The laser microphone wouldn't work at this distance – the signal garbled by air attenuation and moisture from the rain – but she didn't need it to understand what was going on down there. The arrival of the van confirmed her suspicions.

As she watched, the rear doors opened and a well-drilled line of figures in black emerged, each of them carrying weapons. A tactical unit from MI5, she guessed, called in to do the dirty work for their sister agency.

One of the masked men in the assault unit crossed to speak to the surveillance team, who had exited the silver sedan, and very distinctly Lucy saw the man with the shotgun make a throat-cutting gesture.

A kill order. There was nothing else it could mean. They were going in to terminate Marc Dane, not to arrest him. But that didn't make sense. A few hours ago, MI6 had wanted him alive . . .

Without taking her eyes from the scope, Lucy tapped the Bluetooth headset looped over her ear and waited for the connection.

'This morning we're told to let him walk, now he's classed as shoot-on-sight?' said the woman. 'How did that happen?' She shot a look at her colleague, who continued to scowl, then back to the assault team leader.

'Countermand,' said the man with the tactical shotgun. His voice was muffled slightly by the balaclava over his face. Only his deep-set eyes were visible, and they were as grey and cold as the rainfall. 'From higher authority at Six. Target has been reclassified.'

'Welles signed off on that, did he?' said the man with the broken nose.

'Not his call,' said the team leader. He looked over his shoulder as one of his subordinates gave him a nod of confirmation.

'*This is Delancort.*'

'Put him on,' said Lucy, without preamble. 'We got a situation.'

She watched three of the men in tactical gear break off from the main group and enter one of the other residential blocks to the west. The trio all carried scoped assault rifles – short-barrel G-36s by the look of them – and with quick, precise moves they emerged on the mid-levels and took up firing posts, aiming toward the eighth floor of the other block. The guard on the stoop was totally oblivious, talking on a cell phone, making loops in the air with a lit cigarette in his hand. The rest of the tactical team disappeared out of sight, vanishing behind a line of empty garages.

'*Solomon here. Lucy, what is wrong?*'

She swung the scope back to the apartment where Dane had to be. 'You pay me for my professional opinion, right?' she said. 'Well, my opinion is that our friend Marc Dane is going to be dead inside the next ten minutes.'

'*Explain.*'

'I'm watching a strike team taking positions around an apartment where he's holed up. They're armed for bear.'

'*You're certain?*'

'I know overkill when I see it.' Lucy waited for a reply but it didn't come straight away. 'Look, if you want this Brit alive, something's gonna have to be done. He won't stand a chance.' As she spoke, the rest of the black-clad figures reappeared near the entrance to the building, and crept inside.

'*Lucy*,' said Solomon, his voice level and firm. '*Listen to me very carefully. Rubicon cannot afford to alert British Intelligence to your presence there. Your operational directives remain as they were. You are to observe but not interfere.*'

'This guy Dane is a techie. I count five roughnecks coming to his door. Those odds do *not* favour him.'

'*I am aware*,' came the reply, and she heard the frustration under his tone. '*Report in when . . . When events have reached a conclusion.*'

The signal cut and Lucy frowned. She tightened the focus on the PSG-1's scope and caught sight of something moving behind the metal security slats of the apartment. 'You better be lucky, pal,' she said to the air. 'Lucky or smart.'

The forger was good, he had to give the man that. Marc had resigned himself to waiting out the night in the grim confines of the dingy flat, but in less than three hours the work had been done.

Marc's glum, weary expression looked back up at him from the photo page of a German *reisepass*. 'Complete with holographic foil,' said the old man, placing a pencil behind his ear. He rotated on his chair. 'Impressive, yes?'

'Yes,' agreed Marc. It chilled him to think that for a bag of cash, any self-styled troublemaker with an axe to grind could do what he had.

'Marko Stahl.' He tried the new name on for size, saying it a few times to find the right inflection. '*Ja. Ich heise* Marko Stahl.'

'*Zer gut*,' said the forger with a flat smile that didn't reach his eyes. 'So, then. The balance of your fee, if you please.' He held out his hand.

Very suddenly, Marc became aware of the big Sikh standing in the corridor behind him, his tracksuit top unzipped and the thumb of his meaty brown paw resting on the elastic loop of his trousers, close to the butt of the revolver.

'Pleasure doing business with you,' Marc lied, carefully weighing out wads of notes in bundles of five hundred, from the depths of his backpack.

The old man took the money and the false warmth in his face faded. 'There's also the bill for the curry my grandson cooked.'

Marc tensed. 'And how much is that?'

The revolver emerged. 'How much you got in there?' The Sikh spoke for the first time, snarling the words. Behind him, the boy – the grandson – made his way toward the front door, a flashlight in his hand, his head bobbing as he peeked through the tin slats.

Marc frowned. 'You're gonna roll me? I thought we were doing business here.'

'You'll get what you paid for,' said the forger, unsmiling. 'I have standards. But it strikes me that someone in a hurry has little choice about making additional–'

Whatever thin justification the old man was going to give him was broken by the sound of the front door opening and a sudden, brutal crash of gunfire. The grandson came spinning back down the short hallway as if he had been kicked by a horse, and crumpled into a heap with an ugly red bloom growing large across his chest.

The front door swung open and the big Sikh was already turning, swearing under his breath, bringing up the revolver. Outside, across the way, Marc saw a flicker of yellow-white flashes in the rainy gloom and threw himself at the ground.

The air sang as rifle rounds cut across the gap between the apartment blocks and tore into the forger's bodyguard, the walls and the doorframe. The revolver gave off a sound like thunder as the Sikh jerked the trigger in his death throes. The noise reverberated, and it was a signal for the rain to come down.

Suddenly a salvo of silenced assault rifles out there were discharging, ripping through the tin casements over the windows and shattering the glass behind them, driving holes into the fibreboard walls, smashing the forger's expensive computer gear. The naked light bulb overhead fragmented, plunging the space into grey shadow.

Marc rolled over on to his back as the room hazed with plaster dust, scanning for another exit. He came face to face with the blunt barrel of his Glock semi-automatic, gripped in the old man's hand.

'You brought this upon us!' he spat. 'Son of a whore–'

For the second time, the forger's words were interrupted, but this time it was the wasp-buzz of a stray round that silenced him once and for all. The shot met his face just inside the orbit of his right eye and punched a divot of brain matter and bone out the back of his skull. The old man's legs gave out and he collapsed, falling back into his wheeled chair with a grunt of expelled air. The Glock clattered to the floor and Marc scrambled toward it, staying low, snagging it with his outstretched fingers.

The cascade of bullets halted as suddenly as it had started, and he strained to listen over the sound of his blood rumbling in his ears. Marc caught the scrape of boots against concrete out on the walkway, coming closer.

There would be a second team, he reasoned. A shooter unit dialled in to soften up the target, and an approach unit to go in and neutralise any survivors.

Marc felt sick, and suddenly the meat in his stomach wanted out again. He swallowed hard, tasting bile in his mouth. He knew this kind of operation by heart. How many times had he and Leon and Owen sat in the van and directed the same mission profile? Only this time he was experiencing it from the sharp end.

Was there someone just like him down there, out of sight in the back of a truck, watching a grainy video feed and directing a squad of killers? He shook off the thought and tried to calm his breathing.

If he knew the play they were making, then he could figure out how to avoid it.

Marc looked back toward the kitchen, where a door led out to a narrow balcony. Someone would be covering the rear of the building, that was a given, but if he could give them something else to think about, there was a chance he could create a gap he could escape through. They would expect him to go down, to head for the ground floor, and make a break for it through the front door.

He turned back and saw the forger's corpse lolling in the wheeled office chair. Drawing up his leg, Marc kicked out with a short, sharp motion and struck the frame of the chair. The blow sent it spinning and moving, describing a curving pirouette as it trundled away from him, castors rattling over the concrete floor. The chair and the slumped body sailed right past the line of the damaged windows, providing the shooters outside with a moving target.

Immediately, the heavy coughs of shotgun discharges sounded, bracketing the dead man. Each impact made the chair spin and judder, showing the gunmen on the walkway the illusion of life.

Marc was already in a crouching run, heading back toward the kitchen. He fired blindly into the ceiling of the living room as he ran, to prolong the pretence.

Metallic objects tumbled through the broken windows and clanked against the walls behind him. He didn't look back. He knew the sound, and ducked low under the kitchen table, eyes screwed shut, mouth open and the heels of his hands pressed into his ears.

A heartbeat later the flashbangs went off with a flare of brilliant white fury and Marc's nostrils stung with the hot discharge of chemical smoke. Even a room away from the stun grenade explosions, he was still dazzled and partly deafened. Blindly, Marc rose up under the table, carrying it with him, throwing it at the whitewashed windows. Glass shattered on to the balcony.

He found the dented camping stove where it had fallen and slammed the valve joint against the wall. Propane under pressure hissed back at him from the new break in the nozzle, and Marc rolled it away, back down the hallway like a bowling ball.

A figure in black, face hidden behind a scowling filter mask and ballistic helmet, appeared in the open doorway with a shotgun at the ready. The armed man saw Marc moving and fired at him without hesitating.

He was at the broken back window as the sparks from the shot ignited the propane, and a hot blast of fire channelled down the flat's narrow hallway. A plug of smoke and flame slammed Marc in the back, shoving him out on to the balcony. He heard the man with the shotgun scream.

Fighting down the trembling rush of adrenaline in his hands, he swung across the metre-wide gap to the foot of the next balcony along. They were staggered, one raised slightly higher than the next, and going to and fro Marc scrambled up past the ninth and tenth floors until he reached the lip of the roof and dragged himself up. His hands slipped on a damp lintel covered in bird shit, but he forced his way up and over, grunting in pain as he strained a muscle in his arm.

Up here the flat roof was a maze of puddles and the low blocks of ventilator units. Marc moved away down the top of the building, searching for a route to street level that would keep him out of sight of the kill team.

At the far end of the rooftop there were angled metal arms reaching over the sheer ten-storey drop, the top of a gantry built for window cleaners to use. There might be a cable drum still up there, enough for him to play out and make it down to one of the elevated crosswalks. He went for it, low and fast, limping. Glass had cut his thigh on the way through the window and it stung like a bastard.

Then a masked figure in black stepped out in front of him from behind a lift gear shed, and Marc jerked back in shock.

'Don't you fuckin' move,' growled the gunman, bringing up the SD3 sub machinegun in his hands. 'You think you actually stood a chance?' He jerked the muzzle to one side. 'Lose the gun. Put down the backpack. Hands on your head.'

'So,' Lucy said to the air, 'not lucky, then.'

Through the PSG-1's scope, she could see the Brit standing stock still, and a sliver of the assault team operator holding him up. It was impossible to get a good look at the gunman. From her angle across the park, a cluster of vents prevented the sniper from seeing all of him.

But she could fill in the blanks herself. Dane had done it again, made a risky play, and now he was paying for it. The shooter up there needed only to pitch the rogue technician off the roof and MI6's problem would just go away.

Lucy thumbed the rifle's fire selector without really being conscious of the action.

Solomon's words echoed in her thoughts. *Rubicon cannot afford to alert British Intelligence to your presence there.*

He had a very good point, but then he wasn't here, watching the last seconds of Marc Dane's life tick away. She wouldn't be on the guy now if he wasn't mission-critical – and wasn't it always Solomon who told her that her skill, her judgement, was the reason he had recruited her?

'Ah, shit,' she sighed, and pulled the trigger.

The flash and the crack of the round leaving the PSG-1's barrel was swallowed by a cylindrical suppressor, enough that someone in the room next door would only have heard the metal noise of the slide recoil.

The shot crossed the distance in a fraction of a second, windage dropping it a degree so it met meat squarely in the middle of the gunman's right calf muscle. The man was in the process of reaching up to tap his throat mike when the bullet took him down. He howled and fell to his knees. The cry shocked Marc back into motion and he came running and kicked him hard in the chest. The SD3 went flying and vanished over the edge of the roof.

'The fuck?' The gunman's voice was thick with pain and surprise. He twisted back to look up at Marc and there was real fear in the eyes behind the gas mask.

In his hand, Marc still had the Glock semi-automatic. Both of them knew what should happen next. The right choice, the expedient choice, was to put a bullet in this man's head and keep running.

Marc kept running.

ELEVEN

The thin sheeting of the ragged pergola barely served to cut the glare from the sky. Dots of sunlight marked the dust at Khadir's feet as he walked down the line of youths, each of them standing to wary attention, each of them sweating – and not from the heat.

A dry wind off the Taurus Mountains rumpled the metallic fabric, making it rattle and snap. It was makeshift cover at best, enough to hide them from thermal-optical cameras of drones or satellites.

His gaze crossed the faces of the group and he found the boy that had been discovered hiding in the compound . . . *What was his name? Halil. Yes.* The teenager didn't look away, and Khadir gave him the faintest of nods. At his side there was a thickset youth, still with a little puppy fat on him. Halil's companion had bruises on his face and stood awkwardly.

He glanced at Jadeed as he made his way back to the middle of the quad. The other men, the instructors and the guards, were all there. None of them spoke; they knew that any words today had to come first from Khadir's mouth.

'Children,' he began, looking at his young charges. 'Children are weak and full of terror.' The commander saw their disappointment and fear. They were tense, expecting some sort of rebuke.

He went on. 'For a child, the world is a place full of arbitrary rules and obstacles. It is a landscape dominated by adults, where things can be taken from you without explanation or reparation.' He walked slowly along the line once more. 'Children were brought to this place.' Khadir halted and made a point of looking each of the young ones in the eye. 'But today I do not see them. I see *men*. Warriors who have left childhood behind.'

A ripple of excitement passed through the assembled group. They were daring to hope now, just as he wanted them to.

'A child can do nothing. A man takes control. When a child is hurt, they cower and they weep. When a man is hurt, he takes the measure of his injury back from those who injured him.' Khadir stopped and placed a fatherly hand on the shoulder of a tall boy with short, scruffy hair. They shared a look that two equals would have given one another. 'Things have been taken from us. People we loved, our homes, the lives we lived.' His tone hardened. 'Our *peace*.'

Some of them nodded, others stiffened with old anger and sorrow.

'Each of you had a life crushed beneath the wheels of conflict, and you were never given a choice. But you were not broken by that experience. You were tempered, made stronger.' Khadir smiled. 'You are the best of the crop. The strongest and the most resilient. And today you are ready. Souls renewed in unity of purpose.'

They responded just as all the others had, each time he had given this speech. It was predictable. In this moment, every hardship and beating, every back-breaking hour of forced exercise and tuition was forgotten. He was giving them what the young of their age wanted; adulthood and the liberty that came with it.

He looked at them and sought the mirror of his own face as a young man, in the moment when his life had been changed. Most were the offspring of common folk, farmers and workers, the unskilled and the ordinary. They had never known the dimensions of a better life; but he had.

As a boy, Khadir had grown up in a house of wealth, the scion of a military family who had served the nation of Egypt for eight generations. And like his brothers, his father, his uncles, he was destined to be officer class. He believed the dream, dazzled by the promise of glory. He yearned for a chest of medals and the shimmering brass buttons of the elite.

But the golden patina of magnificence was a shell, a fragile skin over something rotting and decrepit. The men he respected, the mentors and elders, they had cemented their position not through prowess in battle but by cunning in the shadows. They drank tea with sworn enemies and took coin from traitors, they laid with infidels and dogs to swell their pockets. They mocked the oath they had avowed. The precious and noble uniform he had so coveted as a child was revealed as nothing but a shroud to conceal corruption and lies.

His pride, his love, all of that had crumbled into hate. He saw only greed and depravity, and a horrible stagnation of will. It shamed him to share kinship with these people.

It had been a powerful moment, the day when the young Khadir had at last fully understood. He was being groomed, not for warrior status, but to maintain the status quo of a slow, immoral decay. His family and those like them were a cancer, and they were not alone. The rot infested many cities, nations, souls.

But Khadir was not alone either. Others felt as he did, others who whispered in dark corners or dared to speak out. Those people became his new family; and on that day he was awakened. *Renewed with great purpose.*

His reverie ebbed away and Khadir's tone changed, as if he were confiding a secret truth to the youths. 'I envy you. You have been given such a great gift. The chance to take something from those who hurt us.' His voice hardened. '*Vengeance*.'

Some of them muttered approval at that suggestion.

'The nations of our enemies, our oppressors . . . The Americans and the Europeans, the Russians, even those among our own kind who would let us perish to aggrandize themselves. These are the ones who have hurt us.' He gave a solemn sigh. 'A man with courage and spirit, who can look beyond fear . . . That kind of man cannot be stopped. He may take his revenge wherever he finds it.'

He found himself in front of the boy Halil once more. '*You* are that man now,' he told him. 'Each and every one of you.'

The commander's gaze bored into Halil like lines of fire. The man's intensity seemed to radiate off him, and Halil was unable to respond with anything more than a wooden nod of agreement.

He remembered his first thoughts of Khadir – a lion among jackals, powerful as a predator. Halil's father always had a good-natured, bright charm to him . . . But Khadir's charisma was something else. He burned like dark fire, as if he were a champion out of old legends; and at that second, if Khadir had asked him to march to gates of hell itself, Halil might well have done it.

Halil could see that Tarki was enraptured by the commander. He doubted that the farmer's son had ever heard anything like it, the stirring words striking a chord with all the young men beneath the canopy.

The things Khadir said were right. It *was* an unfair world, he had been hurt, and he did want some payback for all he had lost. Some far distant part of Halil's thoughts seemed to stand outside him and watch, detached from the events. Even as he felt himself being carried away by Khadir's speech, he wondered if the man was only saying what the youths wanted to hear, manipulating them.

He was using words like a musician would play an instrument, stoking hatreds that were buried deep.

Halil could not deny it. Whenever he thought of his family, the blade of sorrow that cut into him was immediately followed by a burn of fury. He wanted to make someone pay for what had been taken from him. Khadir was promising to give Halil that, and the offer was hard to resist.

In his mind's eye, he saw his parents again, remembering the morning that they had died. Sorrow pulled him one way, impotent anger another. It would be so *easy* to succumb – but his father's face brought with it memories of his father's words. His slow, steady delivery of stories and parables, from the Qu'ran and from other books written by people in far-off lands. Halil remembered him talking of other men, men with bad souls who liked to take such books and twist their meanings so others would follow them. They took words that spoke of peace and hammered them into weapons.

Halil had not fully understood what his father had meant then, but the young man understood now. A chill ran through him as it became clear in his thoughts, as the last vestiges of anything approaching trust crumbled. *What does Khadir want from us?*

'A man takes his revenge,' the commander was saying. His second brought forward a wooden crate with a hinged lid. None of the youths spoke as Jadeed upended the container. A dozen wooden batons – enough for every one of them – tumbled out on to the sands.

Khadir picked up one of the rods and placed it in Tarki's hand.

Halil watched, not daring to move. Tarki had not spoken a word to him, or to anyone else since the previous night. The last sound he heard from his friend had been the cries of panic coming from the shower blocks. Tarki had been alone with one of the guards . . . No-one was sure what had happened in there, only that shouting brought other men running, and violence in their wake. Tarki cried himself to sleep afterward, but in the morning his eyes were dead and distant.

Jadeed shouted an order, and two of the guards disappeared into an outbuilding, returning a moment later, dragging a third man between them. He was bruised and bloody, but there was no mistaking his face. Tarki's shocked reaction was enough to be certain that it was the same man that had hurt him.

Jadeed's men threw the bloodied guard to the ground. He looked up, confusion on his face, and tried to speak, but all that escaped from his lips was a dry rattle.

The commander beckoned the youths to come closer, to form a semi-circle around the cowering figure. Tarki and Halil were pushed forward.

'This *animal* walked among us,' Khadir showed a sneer. 'He exploited his position to indulge his baser desires. He betrayed me and he betrayed his god. But worse than that, he betrayed *you*.'

It began with Tarki. A slow change on the boy's face, the fear melting away and something hateful reforming in its place. Halil saw his knuckles whiten around the baton. The seething anger in the other youth was like a taint, infecting all the others. The ones closest to the front of the group helped themselves to the pile of wooden sticks, and Halil knew then that it was not just his friend the errant guard had assaulted.

'Such things cannot be forgiven,' the commander went on. 'Such animals must be put down.'

The guard was struggling to rise to his feet, a pleading look on his face. Khadir ignored him, and his gaze found Tarki's. It was all the permission that the other youth required.

Tarki's hand blurred and there was a sharp *crack*. Then the bloodied guard was staggering backwards. He shouted a curse, muffled by the hand held to his broken nose. He called Tarki a motherless whore, bellowed that he would gut him like a fish – but his threats were buried in the rush as the rest of the youths went for him. Halil saw Adad snatch up a loose rock from the sand at their feet.

They all beat him, screaming and yelling, and Halil was pushed along with the rest of the group, another baton pressed into his grip. They followed the man down as he tried to stagger away, the rain of blows falling again and again.

Halil couldn't look away, but he could not raise the stick to strike. He heard his father's voice, the echo of his reproach warning not to do this, not to embrace the violence.

The guard's face was a pulpy, swollen mess, and his arm hung limply at his side. The voices of the other orphans crowded out everything, howling and loud. Halil felt hands shoving him forward, heard the youths spurring him on to join in.

Tarki's tormentor made one last effort to regain his footing and defy them. He came lurching toward at the edge of the ring formed by his attackers, straight at Halil. Hands raised like talons, he gurgled and spat, blinded by frenzy.

Halil struck out before he was even aware of doing it, stabbing with the length of the baton to hit the guard in the face. The blow broke the man's jawbone and he spun, shattered teeth and pink, gummy spittle drooling from his lips. Halil watched him fall once again and felt a sickly churn in his gut, suddenly aware of the speckles of warm blood spattered on his cheek.

The guard dropped and did not move again. The others made certain by kicking him until finally, with a hint of pride in his voice, Khadir told them to stop.

From the outside, the Monte Tauro seemed not so much a building, as a carved extension of the rocky hillside. Emerging from the rough stone cliffs that fell from the coastal road above, down toward the narrow shingled beach and blue shallows, the hotel was a range of terraces formed from precise slabs of reinforced concrete that mimicked the natural grey of the rocks. The suites and rooms sat behind long, flat patios, divided by circular balconies and square-cut shrubs, their wooden sundecks warming in the Sicilian afternoon. At its lowest level, the waters of a pool ringed by ranks of loungers shimmered in the breeze.

Marc leaned over the lip of his balcony and made a slow survey of the hotel exterior. Up on the road, there was only a cobbled drive leading to what resembled an elegantly appointed blockhouse of white stone and green glass. Elevators and a spiralling staircase descended through gaps cut in the cliff, tiled corridors branching off toward the rooms. Everything in the Monte Tauro had a pared-down ethic to it, like the halls of a chic gallery or a modernist office complex. Marc liked the simplicity of the building. With all its straight corridors and glassy partitions it was easy to see anyone coming. After all the rush and panic of the last few days, he actually felt a little safer here.

Still, he closed the blackout curtains until there was only a thin column of daylight showing and retreated into the room. His luggage and the gear he had bought in the airport duty free electronics store were scattered over the bed, so he took the wicker seat by the sliding doors and drank the rest of a bottle of tepid San Pellegrino. He worked hard to moderate his pulse, which hadn't slowed since he left the safe house.

The journey seemed to take forever, each little delay mounting up as if it were about to reveal the lie of his escape. He ran a hand through his hair and it came away dirty, fingers dulled by the spray-in dye that had been part of the Marko Stahl disguise. The baseball cap he had worn on the plane from England was stained dark inside, and he frowned, tossing it into the waste bin at the end of the bed. As an afterthought, he found the American Express card he had been using for the last twelve hours and snapped it into quarters, taking care to gouge out the embedded chip. As for the growth of scruffy stubble coming in around his chin, he decided to leave it unshaven, all the better to break up the silhouette of his face.

The Glock was where he had left it, concealed by the anti-detection baffles in the bottom of the go-bag. Holding it in his hand made him feel calmer, more in control, as if the cool polymer frame was leaching the dread out of him. Marc checked the rounds in the chamber even though he didn't need to, and took stock of what he was going to do next.

He was almost surprised to be here. Passing through the gauntlet of airport security, Marc had expected to be pulled from the lines of passengers. He kept looking up from the month-old copy of *Wired* he was pretending to read, expecting to see Victor Welles standing over him with that shit-eating smirk of his firmly in place. But then the blur of the trip ebbed and he was in a taxi on its way out of Catania International for Taormina, and it all seemed a little . . . surreal. Getting to where he wanted to go had slightly wrong-footed him, in point of fact. Marc allowed himself a rueful smile. *So help me, I might actually stand a chance of doing this.*

He dumped his sweaty clothes and took a shower, working out as much of the hair dye as he could, burning off the travel-lag with needles of hot water. By the time he was done, the sun was setting and out in the bay beneath the town there were a few new boats gently bobbing in the tide.

He fished out a pair of compact Pentax binoculars from one of the duty free bags and went back to the window, peeling them out of their wrapping. Marc had committed the profile of the *Jade* to memory, and it didn't take long to find her. The yacht was out in the blue waters of the Ionian Sea, moored furthest from the shore, and as he watched the anchor light flicked on. The boat was marble-white from bow to stern, accented with emerald details and lines of black glass. It shimmered in the fading sun, resembling the closed carapace of some exotic beetle resting on the water's surface.

He took a pen and made notes about what he saw. *Jade* was riding high, which made him wonder if the boat hadn't taken on fuel yet. He recognised the open solarium forward of the flying bridge where Tanya Kirin had posed to take the falsely spontaneous snapshots on her social media page. It was empty now, the windows shuttered.

The vessel was locked up tight, exactly what someone like Dima Novakovich would do if he were looking over his shoulder. Marc felt a faint pang of empathy for the man. *Yeah, pal. You and me both.*

As the evening drew in, Marc collected a room-service snack from a smiling young waiter at the door and ate on the balcony, careful to stay in the shadows cast by the open sun parasol. He watched the yacht as the air cooled, and still the *Jade* showed no sign of activity other than the soft glow of her interior lights.

Finally, he blew out a sigh. He was putting off what he knew he had to do next. Sitting here and observing, studying the target and waiting around, that was the job that he used to have. *Back then*, back in the past, in the other life before Dunkirk and the shooting and the fires.

It seemed like a million years ago.

Marc shook it off and scowled. *Old thinking*, he chided himself. *Too much note taking and data mining. Get this done.*

Back in the room, he emptied the bags and arranged all the gadgets he'd picked up on the bed, making sure everything was charged and loaded. Some of the stuff was good spec, the rest was gimmick kit Marc had gathered up for just-in-case situations. He played with a recorder pen, twirling it around his fingers, considering. In the bad old days, what he had here would have been some kind of Q Branch wet dream for any intelligence officer in the field, and now it was hardware you could buy over the counter for your kids. But tech had a way of doing that, of filtering out into the real world. It was the kind of thing that gave the security agencies of the world nightmares, the idea that some ordinary civilian could amass the gear needed to do the sort of things that once had been the sole purview of governments.

When it was past midnight, he took what he needed and packed it into a waterproof drawstring bag, before changing into something darker and less easy to read in Taormina's dimly-lit side streets.

Marc's hands slipped into the pockets of his jacket and began to drum against the lining in an aimless rhythm. He reached for the quiet spot in his thoughts and there was something else there. It wasn't fear; it was something like that, but not so poisonous.

The Glock went into a paddle holster in the small of his back, and anything that could identify him he bundled into the day-pack's hidden compartment along with his laptop. The pack would go somewhere safe; it was the one thing he couldn't afford to lose.

He looked down at his watch. 'Tick tock,' Marc said to the air. 'Rules of engagement. Approach and isolate target.' He spoke as if it were a standard OpTeam pre-brief, as if he was in the room with the rest of the Nomad agents and this was a mission for all of them. 'Get in and get . . .' He trailed off. The heavy silence of the room made it harshly clear exactly how alone he was.

Stop fucking around, Sam's voice said in his thoughts. *Green for go*.
'Green for go,' Marc repeated, and reached for the door.

It wasn't typical for such a large aircraft to wait away from the usual boarding gates, but the white and silver length of the unmarked Airbus A350 was not conventional in any sense of the word, and the Rubicon Group paid very well for their privacy.

Making her way across the tarmac, Lucy pulled her overcoat around her shoulders as the wind picked up over Heathrow's flight line. Large men in black Armani suits, big as line-backers, flanked the foot of the ramp. They scanned the apron like a pair of well-dressed gun turrets, mechanical and unsmiling.

The aircraft was plain and unremarkable – and that was exactly the impression it had been engineered to give. The uninspired livery was just similar enough to that of a handful of commercial carriers so an observer at a distance could mistake it for one of them. Lucy had heard one of Solomon's ground crew say that the jet's tail registration could be changed at a moment's notice, and its on-board IFF transponder could illegally mimic any one of a number of civilian or military aircraft codes. Looking closer, there were odd blisters along the line of the dorsal and ventral hull, home to electronic countermeasures and other gear that she had no doubt was prohibited. Lucy knew for a fact that the plane had hidden launchers for infra-red flares and chaff to throw off the seeker heads of air-to-air missiles; she tried not to let it bother her that Rubicon's CEO thought he needed that kind of protection for his private aircraft. At the rear of the Airbus, a cargo hatch was rising up to seal shut. She glimpsed the wheels of the Ducati and the silhouette of a larger vehicle back there as the compartment was locked.

A tall, waspish figure came down the mobile staircase to meet her, his hand-made shoes clacking off the metal steps.

She gave Delancort a wan smile. 'Henri. Pleasure as always.'

Solomon's assistant cut her faux compliment dead with a narrow-eyed glare. 'I think it's only fair to warn you,' he began, standing so he blocked her way, 'You've made a mess.'

She shot a look at the security guards, who both continued to behave like statues, deaf to their conversation. 'You're such a drama queen. I kept the Brit alive. Isn't that what we wanted?'

'You tipped our hand.'

All of a sudden, Keyes lost her patience with the French-Canadian and pushed past him, climbing the stairs. 'I don't answer to you.'

She entered the plane and walked down to the bar-lounge looking out over the leading edge of the wing. Lucy was aware of Delancort following close behind, but she ignored him. She was tired, tired of running all over London looking for Marc Dane, tired of the vague orders she had been given.

Ekko Solomon was there, one of the flight crew handing him a tall glass of something clear and carbonated. He gave Lucy a grave look and she tensed. At his nod, the attendant took her bags and carried them away toward her guest room in the rear of the aircraft. Delancort excused himself and disappeared into an office across the corridor.

Without waiting to be asked, Lucy stepped behind the bar and helped herself to a shot of Booker's. 'Is this the part where you dock my pay?'

'Do not be flippant,' Solomon replied, shutting her down hard. 'The choice you made has forced me to come here and recover you, do you understand that? There are operations that will need to go dark because of the notice you have brought to Rubicon.'

'Did you want Dane alive, or not?' she retorted, sipping the bourbon. 'If you wanted a corpse, I could have made that happen.'

'It is more complicated than you realize, Lucy.'

'It is?' she repeated. 'Then explain it to me. I don't work well when you decide my need-to-know out of hand. Can't give you my best if I'm cut out of the loop.'

Solomon's jaw stiffened. He didn't like it when his employees talked back to him. But Lucy couldn't care less about that. She'd always spoken her mind.

'Your actions have drawn undue attention. British Intelligence are attempting to track you as we speak. I have backstops in place to retard their investigations, but activating them has burned several key assets. And despite your unauthorised intervention today, the net result has been a loss for our efforts. Marc Dane has slipped the net.'

'Out of the country by now,' offered Lucy. 'I would be.'

'We have gained nothing. If anything, we have lost ground in Europe.' Solomon took a step toward her. 'You do understand?'

'Dane is a viable lead, right?' That got her a brief, reluctant nod of agreement. 'So better he's still breathing than not. You know what happened back there. MI6 changed gear right in the middle of a surveillance operation. They had a bullet with that unlucky son-of-a-bitch's name on it.' Lucy blew out a breath, and from the corner of her eye she saw the bodyguards boarding the plane, pulling the door closed behind them. 'While he's alive, he's still useful, right? You said we need to know what he knows. Can't interrogate a corpse.'

Solomon gave the short nod again. 'I am compelled to agree. But in the future, we will need to make sure this kind of incident does not occur again, yes?' Before she could answer, the African's eyes turned colder. 'I would not wish to be forced to terminate your employment with Rubicon over another such breach of contract.'

'No doubt,' said Lucy, covering with sip of bourbon.

The office door opened and Delancort returned, a digital pad in his hand. 'We'll be taxiing soon,' he told them. 'Departure's confirmed.'

Lucy glanced at her watch as Delancort offered the pad to Solomon. 'The file?' he asked.

The assistant nodded. 'Procurement were able to get a copy of the salient pages from Dane's jacket.'

'What's this, his personal records?' said Lucy.

Delancort shook his head. 'Not the whole thing. But we have an asset in the Ministry of Defence's medical department. We were able to get a look at Marc Dane's psychological report.' He nodded to himself. 'I think we may have enough here to start building a profile on him.' He looked at Solomon. 'I took the liberty of forwarding it to our people in Zurich.'

Lucy put down the glass. The Swiss office had a department staffed by psychologists, who did something called *extrapolative human analysis*. Rubicon used them to plan marketing strategies and stock market analysis, among other things. 'So we're going after Dane, then?'

'Everyone is,' said Delancort, with a dry smirk. 'It's just a question of who gets to him first.'

If you ignored the bright orange casing of the BladeFish, the propeller looked like a bulky desk fan. In the shallows of the bay, the sea jet's quiet electric motor dragged Marc along behind it at a steady two knots, guiding him out beneath the calm surface of the waters. He directed it with twists of his shoulders like a steering wheel, but in the dark it was easy to go off track. He halted every few minutes to rise up and get his bearings. Marc paused by a vacant mooring buoy and lined himself up on the *Jade* once more. Salt water collecting from his snorkel swilled in his mouth and he spat it out through clenched teeth. The drawstring bag on his back felt heavier and he frowned, pulling it tighter over the black t-shirt plastered to his chest. He had no wetsuit, no fins, just the shirt and dive shorts, figuring it would be better to look like an errant tourist.

Being in the water always made him feel calmer, somehow, like the waves dragged away the tension in him. He bobbed there, watching the yacht, and for the first time he saw movement.

A bulky outline passed behind a closed curtain, but it was hard to pick out any detail. He listened, hearing nothing but the slap of water against the hull of the *Jade* and the murmur of music on the wind from the island.

He pushed away from the buoy, angling the BladeFish to carry him down, and something moved at the back of the boat, out of synch with the rise and fall of the yacht, low against the waterline.

Dialling down the sea jet's speed, Marc took a deep breath and slipped under the surface, making his approach as close as he dared. When he was ten feet from the dive platform at the aft, he came up slow and steady, without a ripple.

There was another boat concealed from line of sight from the shore by the *Jade*'s hull. Featureless and matte black, it rolled gently in the slight swell. A nylon cable tethered it to a temporary suction-cup cleat attached to the yacht.

The other boat was a semi-rigid inflatable, like the Zodiacs used by the military. Big enough for five men, it was the craft of choice for anyone wanting to make a covert insertion by water.

It was the last thing he had expected to see, and Marc knew for sure that the inflatable had not been there before sunset. *Was Novakovich meeting someone out here?* he wondered. *Or is this an escape route?*

There was movement above him, the shuffle of deck shoes on wood, and Marc drifted into the shadow cast by the *Jade*, floating between the yacht and the smaller craft. He strained to listen and heard a scraping, like something being dragged.

In the next second, there was the cough of a silenced weapon, and from out of nowhere a man in short-sleeved tropical whites fell overboard and hit the water an arm's length from Marc's face.

The man turned in the swell and his head lolled, coming around to look blankly at Marc. He had a small entry wound in the soft flesh of his neck and a halo of bright blood, staining a shirt with the kind of faux-gold braid that rich men with yachts liked to make their crews wear.

The dead man slowly sank under the surface and vanished from sight.

TWELVE

For long moments, Marc willed himself to become a ghost in the water, his breath held in his chest as the seconds ticked by. He didn't dare look up for fear that he might meet the gaze of the crewman's killer.

There was a faint creak from the decking and somewhere deeper inside the boat, the muffled noise of delicate glass breaking. The shooter was gone from the rail overhead, but there was no way to know for how long. He had to move fast.

Marc pushed to the rear of the *Jade*, where dive steps extended outwards into the water. Dumping the BladeFish in a shadowed corner of the gunwale, he climbed aboard the yacht in a low, careful crouch. Seawater trickled off his shoulders in steady drops and he moved slowly, planting each foot as if he were walking through a minefield.

Tanya Kirin lay on her back on the deck before him, her head facing away, clothed in a floral-print shift dress that spread out around her immaculately tanned legs. She'd been carrying a champagne flute when she fell, and the broken stem of it was still clutched in her hand. Marc saw the black pit of the entry wound where the bottom of Tanya's jaw connected with her throat. His stomach tightened as he realized that the pool of shadows haloing the woman was a puddle of blood and brain matter.

It brought him up sharp. Poring over his laptop in Camden, he'd got used to the idea of seeing the flighty young model as nothing more than a vector of information. Now here she was, life snuffed out because she hadn't paid attention to the security settings on a messaging website.

Tanya had likely been the first to die. Marc glanced over his shoulder at the dive steps. Her assassin had come up the same way, weapon drawn, as she unwittingly wandered out to finish her glass of Tattinger.

Peering past the body, open doors led into the *Jade*'s gym and there Marc glimpsed a second figure in crewman's whites slumped against an exercise bike. Suddenly, his first impression – that Novakovich was planning to flee – seemed way off.

He pulled the Glock from his waterproof bag and snapped off the safety, holding the pistol close to his thigh, but the last thing he wanted to do was use it. A gunshot out here would not only carry clear across the bay, but more importantly it would alert the killers on board the *Jade*. And there were *killers*, plural. A lone assassin would have followed Marc's approach and swum to the yacht. The presence of the zodiac meant a team sweeping the boat, executing everyone they came across. No witnesses, no survivors.

Marc paused by Tanya's corpse and touched the skin of her neck. Still warm. Closer to her, he could smell perfume and the tang of spent cordite.

His plan of action was in tatters. He hadn't anticipated this, but now it seemed obvious. The people behind the *Palomino* were cleaning house, chasing down all the loose ends. Just as he feared, they had followed the same chains of data to Sicily, and got here before him.

He glanced back at the sea, contemplating the fallout if he abandoned his mission and fled.

Where the hell can I go?

Each second wasted was a second closer to losing everything. His fingers tightened around the grip of the Glock. Novakovich was the only lead he had.

There was a chance the accountant was still alive. Marc reasoned it through; if Dima was already a corpse, then the *Jade* would be a ghost ship.

Soft footfalls thumped on the deck above his head. They were moving forward toward the flying bridge. Starting at the top, working their way toward the keel.

Marc back-tracked through the gym and found one of the stairwells that dropped down to the lower level. He froze as a shadow passed by on the other side of the glass doors.

The figure was clad head-to-toe in the same kind of matt black tactical gear utilized by the MI6 OpTeams, his head was hidden behind a mesh balaclava and clumsy night-vision goggles that gave the shooter a bug-eyed aspect. Marc recognized the long, heavy frame of the pistol in the man's hand. A silenced Mark 23 semi-automatic, the same kind of weapon favoured by American SOCOM operatives.

He had no desire to see the gun up close, however, and when the shooter turned away to look to the stern, Marc slipped down the stairwell and moved as fast as he dared past the doors of the passenger deck. At each compartment he paused for a count of three, holding his breath to listen. *Nothing.*

Amidships, he came across an open door and used the muzzle of the Glock to nudge the gap a little wider. He swept left and right, finding no threats.

The well-appointed room was in some disarray. A tea service lay upended where it had been knocked to the floor. On the big plasma TV that dominated one wall, a movie was freeze-framed in mid-flow, the characters on screen caught shouting at one another, the 'pause' icon blinking in the corner of the display. The remote was on the carpet where it had fallen.

Marc examined it, following the trail of disruption around the room. This was Dima's cabin, the largest on the yacht. *He must have heard something*, Marc reasoned. *Paused the movie, stopped to listen.* What had come next? A shot? A cry of alarm? It had been enough to send the accountant running, tipping over the tea, heedless of the mess.

Dima was still alive because he hadn't tried to get off the yacht. He'd gone forward, deeper into the hull.

Killing time in the departure lounge at Gatwick, Marc had memorised the *Jade*'s original internal schematics from a website for boating enthusiasts, and now he ran through them in his mind's eye. Where would Novakovich go to ground?

He played a hunch.

The yacht's galley was white plastic and brushed steel, and the only light came from the soft blue glow of a giant refrigerator. There were shadows everywhere and plenty of places to hide. Panning the pistol, Marc reached out a hand to feel for a light switch and felt a sudden pain in the small of his back. He flinched reflexively, tried to turn, and for his trouble got the glinting length of a Sabatier chef's knife pressed to his throat.

A man in expensive-looking cotton slacks and an unbuttoned shirt confronted him, his pug-face filmed with sweat and set with fear. Dima Novakovich, very much alive and balancing on the edge of open panic. 'Put the gun on the table, motherfucker,' he hissed. 'I'll open you up!'

Marc felt the tip of the kitchen knife nick the side of his chin and he kept very still, raising the Glock and taking care to show he had his finger off the trigger. 'I'm not one of them.'

'Shit!' Novakovich retorted. 'Give me the gun! I slit your throat!'

'Dima, listen to me.' Using his first name actually startled the Lithuanian, and he blinked. Marc pressed on. 'I'm here to get you out. They're upstairs. They'll find us.'

The broker kneaded the grip of the blade. He wasn't a killer. According to Interpol's records, Novakovich only made money off selling weapons, never using them himself.

Marc kept eye contact with the other man. Each second that he wasn't stabbing him, Dima was losing the momentum to carry out his threat. 'Who sent you?' he demanded.

'British intelligence,' Marc lied. 'I'm a friend of Samantha Green.' Mentioning Sam's real identity was the only card he had to play. He was taking a chance that she had given Novakovich her real name in their dealings.

When the man backed off a few steps, he knew his gamble had paid off. 'Where?' Novakovich looked around. 'She is here?'

Marc blew out a breath and rubbed at the new cut on his chin. *He doesn't know about the freighter.* That made sense. It had only been days since the incident in Dunkirk, and if Novakovich was on the run from his Combine masters, he'd be out of the loop. 'We got wind of this,' Marc went on, making it up as he went, 'Sam sent me.'

For an instant, an almost child-like look of relief crossed the broker's pale Slavic features. On some level, Dima was so terrified that he wanted it to be true, he *needed* to be convinced that someone had come to rescue him; but then it passed and he became suspicious again. 'Just you?' Novakovich sized him up and frowned.

'Yeah.'

'I don't believe you.' The broker pulled a gold-plated iPhone from his pocket and pressed it into Marc's grip. 'Call her! I want to talk to her!'

'Don't be stupid,' Marc snapped, improvising on the fly with a half-truth. 'Zero profile, mate! Sam said *radio silence*!' He pressed on before the man could question his story. 'The others are ashore. Look, you want to play twenty questions or you want to get off this boat?'

'What I want is to–' Novakovich stopped short as a low gurgling rumble shuddered through the floor beneath their feet. Kitchen utensils chimed against one another as the *Jade* set slowly into motion.

Pocketing the phone in case Novakovich decided to make the call himself, Marc held up a hand to wave him back and peered out into the corridor. Through one of the portholes across the way, he saw the Capo Taormina headland slipping away as the yacht retreated from its moorings. The hit-team had raised the anchor and were taking the *Jade* out to sea, into the deeper waters of the Med. Once they were far enough out, it would be easy to scuttle the boat and let it sink without a trace. He turned back. 'Time to go. I've got a secure location on the island, we can, uh, debrief you there.' Marc had no idea how he was going to keep up the fiction that he was still an active MI6 officer, but right now he had to deal with what was in front of him. 'Is there another way off this thing?'

Novakovich emerged behind him and pointed down the corridor, no longer questioning the narrative. 'A garage. I have a launch, jet-skis . . .' He shook his head. 'But we can't go yet. I have to get something.'

Marc heard footfalls on the deck, directly above his head. 'No time!' he whispered. 'Come on!'

The broker gestured with the knife. 'Not going without it.' He set off down a narrow side passage. Marc swore under his breath and followed. Nothing about this was going as he had hoped.

The short corridor ended in what appeared to be a bulkhead panel, but Novakovich fumbled at plate in the deck and slid it back to reveal a numerical keypad. He punched in a string of digits and the bulkhead popped open on concealed hinges. The broker pushed it open and Marc caught a draft of dry, machine-chilled air and the faint ozone smell of electronics. Inside the hidden compartment was a pillar of black and silver that went from floor to ceiling. Webs of thick yellow data cables emerged from the back of it and constellations of blinking green lights flickered up and down the surface of the device.

'You've got your own server,' muttered Marc, more to himself than to Novakovich. 'Of course you have.'

It made sense. The broker's clients were, after all, people of private and dangerous natures, and the details of their business could never be entrusted to a conventional data store. By keeping his own computer server in a mobile location, isolated from the internet until it needed to be connected by satellite, Novakovich could offer security to any kind of illicit transaction. In effect, he was carrying his own little pocket of the dark net around with him.

'They punch holes in the hull,' Novakovich was saying, as he used the Sabatier to work at a set of latches in the server stack. 'Sink my

Jade. The only way to obliterate all this.' He gave a bitter smile. 'Seawater is not kind to circuits.'

He seemed a lot more upset about the loss of his yacht than the woman lying dead on the stern deck, or his executed employees. Marc said nothing. He didn't need to like the man, he only needed what Novakovich knew about the rat hiding inside MI6.

With a snap of connectors, a thick module the size of a hardcover book came free in the broker's hand and he clutched it like it was his firstborn child, discarding the knife. Marc recognized the shape of a military-grade hard drive. It looked like one of the heavy-duty models used by the Russian navy aboard their nuclear submarines, tempest-shielded to resist electromagnetic pulses, fireproof and waterproof.

'This is my passport, you understand?' Novakovich told him. 'You take me to a safe place, this will tell you what you want to know.' He pushed past Marc and made his way back up the side passage. 'We go now.'

Marc scowled. He reached for the other man's arm, trying to pull him back, and missed. 'Wait, it's not safe.'

But Novakovich wasn't listening. The broker emerged into the corridor running the length of the passenger deck and almost collided with the stealth-suited gunman moving down toward them. There was nothing Marc could do to stop what happened next.

The shooter flipped up his weapon and opened fire without a flicker of hesitation. The short-barrel MP9 submachine gun released a cluster of silenced rounds that ran up Novakovich's body, some of the bullets sparking off the case of the hard drive. Novakovich cried out and crumpled backward with a crash.

The gunman pivoted sharply at the corner of the passage and turned the muzzle of the MP9 toward Marc. His night vision goggles would easily render the space visible, and there was no cover at all.

Marc took the offensive and attacked as the weapon came toward him. With the Glock in his fist, he brought the heavy butt of the pistol across, smashing it into the lenses of the gunman's NVG rig with such violence that broken shards were driven into the shooter's cheek and eyes. The gunman jerked the MP9's trigger, but the shots went wide, chugging into the wall and the ceiling of the corridor as the magazine emptied.

Marc pushed forward with all his remaining impetus and brought up his knee into the gunman's crotch, forcing him back. Blinded and flailing, the shooter struck out with the MP9 and used it to club him in the head.

Marc's ears rang and he lost his momentum, almost stumbling over Novakovich, who lay choking on the richly carpeted floor.

With a grunt, the gunman ripped off the goggles and fumbled for the hilt of a wicked-looking combat knife, swearing under his breath. Marc remembered the moment on the tower block roof in London, but this time there would be no mystery shot, no intervention from out of the darkness.

He felt no doubt as he brought up the Glock and fired twice, putting both rounds through the other man's sternum at close range. In the close confines of the corridor, the sound of the gun's discharge was sharp and high, like firecrackers. The gunman went down and was still.

At his feet, Novakovich drooled dark arterial blood, his body shaking as it went into shock. His eyes lost focus as Marc crouched beside him. The broker's laboured breaths became wet, strangled; and then silent.

He had to wrench the hard drive from the dead man's grip, and he took off running toward the bow as footsteps clattered down the stairwell behind him. Marc pointed the Glock backward and fired blindly, sending more shots into the dark. He shouldered open the door to the *Jade*'s garage and kicked it shut behind him. Sparks flared at the gap as more silenced rounds came back in return.

Marc's heart hammered as he pushed past a small motorboat hanging from its rig and found the sloped hatch in the wall of the starboard hull. A T-shaped switch that was set in a recess, coloured bright hazard-orange, with a panel of text next to it that said *Do Not*

Open At Sea in five different languages. He wrenched it downward and the wall creased, big metal slats retreating away like folding sheets of paper. The hard drive went into the drawstring bag as he cast around, every second of delay screaming at him to *move*.

Novakovich's jet-skis sat on aluminium rails designed to act as slipways. Marc spent another bullet blowing open the locker on the wall holding the starter keys and then rushed back to the nearest wet bike, ripping off the bungee cords holding it in place.

Another spray of automatic fire rattled against the metal hatch and he knew that the shooters would be on him any moment. Marc vaulted into the saddle and shoved the jet-ski forward with his body weight. He felt it start to move as he jammed the starter key home, yanked the choke and thumbed the ignition. If the engine didn't turn over, then he was most certainly dead.

Mercifully, the Kawasaki grumbled into life as it slid down the rail, and there was a brief, stomach-turning lurch before the jet-ski hit the water and a surge of low surf slapped into Marc's chest. He landed badly and almost fell out of the saddle right there, but one hand gripped the throttle held tight and the Kawasaki bounced back up to the surface of the waves, nose pointing away from the *Jade*. Leaning low over the handlebars, Marc gunned the motor and the jet-ski shot away. For a second time, he blind-fired over his shoulder, waving the Glock in the direction of the open hatchway. The throttle vibrated under his fingers and he leaned into a series of S-turns back in the direction of the shoreline.

He heard the buzz of bullets cutting the air around him, but then the noise was lost in the hiss of the waves and the roar of the Kawasaki's engine. Marc hugged the machine, willing it to go faster.

Ellis let the MP9's muzzle drop and swore as he ejected a spent magazine and tossed it into the water, mechanically replacing it with a fresh reload from the pouches on his tactical vest.

Cruz came up behind him, an eternally blank expression visible across the Brazilian's swarthy features. 'Hayes killed the primary, but Hayes is dead.'

'Who the fuck was that?' Ellis demanded, ignoring the other man's words. 'Every bugger on this boat was accounted for, who was this *doos*?' His native Afrikaans accent always grew thick whenever he lost his temper. He slapped at the radio tab on his neck. 'Teape? Bring this thing around. We got a runner.'

There was a momentary pause before the American answered. '*Did you hit him?*' The walkie-talkie's scrambler made the channel tinny. '*This boat doesn't exactly turn on a dime. He'll be ashore before we catch up. Did you hit the runner, over?*'

'I don't reckon.' Ellis ground out the words, irritated by the admission that he had burned through a mag with nothing to show for it. 'Who was . . ?'

'*Is Novakovich dead?*' Teape cut him off before he could go on.

'Primary is dead,' repeated Cruz. 'Hayes too.'

There was a dismissive tutting noise. '*Put Hayes in the zodiac, then prep the charges below the waterline. Ellis, get his camera and bring it up here.*'

Teape locked the *Jade*'s helm on automatic and snatched up a pair of binoculars from a storage bin at the side of the flying bridge. He looked across the stern and the bulky optics brought the Bay of Taormina into sharp focus. It was difficult to pick out the jet-ski's wake among all the light pollution spilling from the town, even at this hour. If he'd had a sniper rifle and a targeting steer, it might have been possible to kill the man before he made it to the island, but none of the team had anything larger than a submachine gun.

Fortunately, Teape's employers had planned ahead. They had an option for just such a problem. He replaced the binoculars and fished a burner cell phone from a pocket, dialling a number from memory. The call connected on the second ring.

'*Si?*'

'Problem,' he explained. 'Can you find something for me?'

The voice on the other end of the line switched to English. '*Where?*'

'Coming ashore in the bay, any moment now.' Teape glanced up as Ellis came up the ramp to the flying bridge. 'Probably based somewhere local. I'll get you a picture.'

'*Okay.*' The call ended, and Teape weighed the phone in his hand.

Ellis offered a collection of cables and components to the other man. One device was a commercial digital video player. A cable ran from it to a compact brick of black impact-resistant plastic that sported a gimbal mounted digital camera at one end. No larger than a double-A battery, the low-light camera was small enough to fit in the pocket of a tactical vest and the memory pack could record hours of footage. Each member of the kill team had a similar unit on them, to keep them honest.

Ellis was also carrying something that looked like a portable fan. 'Found this lying on the sun deck,' he explained. 'That's how the bugger got out here.'

Teape said nothing, using the tablet to access the camera, spinning through the killer's-eye view until he came to the moment when Hayes had almost collided with Novakovich. He watched Hayes dispatch the broker, but it took two back-and-forth replays for him to isolate a frame of video showing the face of the man who had shot dead the other operative.

'This him?' He showed a grey-green low light image of a washed-out face framed by light-coloured hair, caught in the middle of grim exertion.

'Could be.' Ellis was sullen. He didn't like being party to mistakes. '*Ja.*'

Teape captured the image, then slipped the cable into a port on the phone. Within moments, the picture was sent to two distinct destinations. The first was Faso, the watcher he had left on the island. The second was the first link in a chain of blind digital relays that would eventually channel the still to someone who could put a name to the face.

Marc ditched the jet-ski on the pebbled beach and threw the key into the surf. The faint notes of soft piano music filtering down from the terraces of the San Domenico Palace hotel up above were a stark counterpoint to the drumming of his heart in his ears. He ran toward the steep path leading up the cliffside and into the town.

A short way up, beneath the thin trees clinging to the rocks, he dragged the dark tracksuit out of his waterproof bag and pulled it on over his wet swim gear. Swallowed up by the warm night, Marc looked back over the bay and out to sea. There was nothing to indicate that the *Jade* had ever been there.

The hard drive was bulky and awkward on his back, and he felt hyper-conscious of its weight and the potential of the data it contained. As an afterthought, he opened the neck of the drawstring back and fished out the dead man's cell phone, crackling open the casing with his thumbnail. Marc pulled the device's battery so it couldn't be used to track him, and tossed it back in.

He couldn't make out anyone following him, so Marc made the ascent up the long and winding path, moderating his pace so he wouldn't be winded by the time he reached the narrow road at the top of the cliff. Deliberately, he took a long, roundabout route, going away from the Monte Tauro hotel, up towards the Corso Umberto, the main thoroughfare through the town. The medieval streets came in close and offered plenty of shady alcoves. Marc picked his way along them, diverting down cobbled alleyways as he cut back in a loop, in the direction of the parkland at the Villa Comunale.

Finally, he followed a group of boisterous German tourists making their way back to the hotel and slipped in behind them, crossing the Tauro's foyer while they dithered and chatted.

Marc was reaching for the door to his room when some unnamed instinct stilled him in his tracks. Outwardly, nothing was amiss, but after a night of seeing every part of his plans come apart, he was suddenly seized by the certainty that something wasn't right. Holding his breath, Marc pressed against the wall and leaned as close to the door as he dared, straining to hear.

For long minutes, *nothing*. He started to wonder what he would do if one of the hotel staff appeared.

Then, very distinctly, he heard the sound of movement on the other side of the door. The creak of the wicker chair out by the balcony, shifting under someone's weight.

The blood drained from his face. All the while he had been burning off time taking the long way back to the hotel, thinking he was being clever, but these people had found him anyway. Was there someone like the German assassin waiting in there for him, a silenced gun aimed at the door? The chair creaked again and he knew for certain.

Silently, Marc drew back from the door, retreating away. Strangely, he felt partly vindicated for his own paranoia. Before setting off to the *Jade*, his last act had been to secret his daypack in a hide outside his hotel room. Instead of stowing it in the room safe – which was hardly secure in itself – he'd opted for a more basic option.

There was a maintenance closet off the corridor, with a hung ceiling. Marc stood on tiptoe to dislodge a tile with his fingers, and found the daypack's strap hanging behind it, exactly where he had left. He grabbed it and fled.

Instead of going up the rise toward the town, he retreated back down the small slip road that served the hotel, following the curve around the hillside toward the beaches. With his hood up and a shemagh taken from Sam's go-bag around his face, Marc avoided the gaze of the Monte Tauro's security cameras and scrambled over a wall a few meters further on, climbing around a dusty fibreboard sign on scaffold poles, dragging the backpack behind him.

The sign sported a sun-bleached picture of idyllic three-storey beachside apartments and text promising the completion of construction the previous year. On the other side of the wall was the debris of a forsaken construction site, overgrown by the march of the local greenery. The plot sported the frames of the promised apartment but little else. The unfinished holiday homes resembled something a patient but unimaginative child might have made out of building bricks, breeze-block cubes open to the air in many places where walls had not been added. The air was musty with the smell of animal urine and neglect, the ground littered with windblown trash and dead leaves. Marc slipped into the nearest of the skeletal buildings and worked his way to the uppermost floor, through the gaps where staircases would have eventually been installed. The boom and bust in the European construction industry over the last decade had left dozens of sites like this scattered around the holiday resorts of the Mediterranean, snapped up by speculators unable to complete contracts, or sell on in a hostile marketplace. The apartments were out of the way here, out of sight from Taormina, forgotten and isolated. A good bolthole, and well placed to watch the hotel.

It was what Marc needed, a place where he could rest and think on his next move. Too much of what was happening to him was reactive, forced on to him by the actions of people who wanted him dead. If he was going to get ahead of the curve, that had to change.

He found a corner of the unfinished building, a space that probably would have been a well-appointed bathroom had the Euro crash never happened. He put on his last change of clean clothes and, making certain that there was no way any light would be seen from the streets above, he booted up his laptop.

The hard drive sat on the floor. It was an ugly object, all sharp edges and steel plates. Numerous ports and jack sockets dotted the flanks of it, many of them non-standard sizes deliberately chosen by the Soviet military to make it difficult for anyone without the correct gear to access the contents.

Difficult, Marc reflected, *but not impossible*. He set a suite of high-level intrusion programs to work on the device, letting them probe its firewalls for weaknesses. It would take hours for the software to map the whole scope of the drive's memory, like a scout circling an ancient fortress in search of loose stones in the walls. Marc could only sit back and watch the slow, inexorable motion of a progress bar across the screen.

One at a time, feeling the tightness in his muscles, he marched bullets into the magazine of the Glock and waited for the dawn.

THIRTEEN

The port of Mersin appeared to Khadir as little more than a drab collection of grey boxes, stacked alongside quays extending into the gunmetal sea. The Turkish docks were alive with activity and the noises of commerce, as containers were loaded and unloaded on to the slow hulks of cargo ships resting at anchor.

The driver threaded his car between the forklifts and trucks until they emerged in the shadow of a black-hulled freighter flying a Bolivian flag. Khadir gathered up his bag and walked away without looking back. The *Santa Cruz* rose high over his head, the ship's curved stern like the battlement of an iron castle. He immediately spotted a man in a heavy weather coat at the rail, the distinctive silhouette of an AK-47 resting low over his belly, not quite concealed from sight.

Others were waiting at the foot of the gangway, and as Khadir approached, a parked van was disgorging his soldiers on to the quayside. The youths saw him and they kept their manner circumspect, even though he knew that many of them had never glimpsed the sea before. Jadeed descended from the ship, barking out an order, and they fell into a loose rank and marched up the walkway.

Khadir's subordinate had travelled ahead of the group, arriving a day earlier to meet the arrival of the *Santa Cruz*. The rest of them had made the trip from the orphanage by various means, moving separately. Khadir favoured the train; it gave him time to reflect and take a rare moment of respite.

Jadeed intercepted him before he reached the foot of the gangway and the expression on the other man's face spoke volumes.

'What is wrong?' said Khadir, meeting the issue directly.

As usual, Jadeed wasted no time with preamble. 'The equipment is in place, the doctor is here as well, but the material is not on board.'

Khadir covered his annoyance with a slow nod. 'Reason?'

Jadeed shook his head. 'He refused to account for it.'

'*He*?'

'The Britisher is on the ship.' Jadeed inclined his head toward the vessel. 'His paymasters sent him. He will only speak with you.' There was something else left unsaid and Khadir gave his man a level look, waiting for him to reveal it. At length, Jadeed scowled. 'He insults me. My temper is tested.'

Khadir snorted quietly. 'I would expect no less.' He advanced up the walkway, striding on to the ship as if he owned the vessel and everything aboard it.

The one with the rifle was waiting for him, along with a second man. The rifleman was of Eastern European stock, Khadir guessed, perhaps a Serb, but the other could only have been the Britisher. He didn't need to confirm that it had been this man's voice on the other end of the satellite phone, days earlier. The cold twist of his lip confirmed it.

'Well now. The famous Omar Khadir. Here you are,' he began, the rough edges of his words broken and crude. The man had dark hair cut close to the scalp and the unkempt new growth of a beard. His eyes were of note, though. They were the only thing that gave Khadir pause. He knew immediately that this was not a man to underestimate. 'You brought a school outing with you.' The Britisher surveyed the group of the youths as they milled in the middle of the deck, eyes darting around as they took in the scope of the ship. 'This a joke, is it?' Khadir said nothing as the man came close to him. 'You bring a couple of men and what, a pack of *kids*?' He grunted. 'Be lucky if you could find one of 'em whose balls have dropped.'

The youths were all watching now, and even if they didn't understand the words, they could guess what was being said. 'They are soldiers,' Khadir replied. 'They are loyal. That is all that matters.'

The Serb made a negative noise and spat on the deck in open contempt, and the Britisher walked toward the group, glaring at the youths. 'Can they even hold a rifle?' He shot a look back at Khadir. 'You really think this shower of little shits is up to it?' He didn't wait for a reply. 'What kind of amateurs are you people?'

'They understand this war,' Khadir told him. At his side, he could sense Jadeed seething at the Britisher's tone. 'They are old enough to fight. You should understand that.'

'You what?'

'Your nation practically invented the idea of child soldiers, after all.' Khadir went on. 'The young ones who signed away their lives to fight in your First World War? Britain's boys, old enough to carry a gun, old enough to die for King and Country.' He allowed a shade of mockery to enter his tone. 'What is it they called those infantrymen? *Tommy Atkins*.' Khadir sounded out the name. 'Like you. You were once a soldier of the crown, yes? It's a good name.'

The twist in the Britisher's expression showed that Khadir had touched a raw nerve. His guess had been accurate. He knew this kind of man well, the thuggish and cunning sort that swelled the ranks of armies the world over. Men who fought for the sake of it, not for ideals.

'You wanna call me Tommy . . .' said the Britisher. 'I don't give a toss if you call me Mary bloody Queen of Scots . . .' Without taking his eyes off Khadir, his hand came up and pointed toward Jadeed. 'I'll tell you this, *Saladin*. Your dog there keeps on eyeballing me and I'll fucking gut him. We clear?'

'We are.' Khadir glanced at his second-in-command and Jadeed scowled and walked away. Behind him, the gangway was retracting and the *Santa Cruz*'s horn sounded as the ship's crew began to cast off.

Tommy – that was now the name Khadir had fixed the man with – came back toward him, dismissing the Serb with a jut of his chin. 'You keep your little boy band off the deck and out of trouble, right?'

'Explain something to me,' he replied, ignoring the demand. 'What makes you think you are in charge here?'

That earned him a rough burst of laughter. 'Did you miss a memo, pal? Did you forget who's bankrolling your little junior jihad?'

Khadir felt his tolerance waning. 'Al Sayf does not answer to you, mercenary, or your Combine. We have paid our way in blood.'

'Whatever you say.' The other man shrugged. 'But the fact is, the gents I work for can cut you out of it and you'll be shit out of luck. So you'd best not piss me off.'

'They sent you to watch us. Who is the dog now?' Before Tommy could reply, Khadir advanced on him. 'That was not part of the agreement. Where is the hardware we were promised?'

'Down below.' The Britisher looked away as the dock began to slip back from the ship, the engines giving off a low, muttering growl. 'Set up just like you wanted.'

'You know what I mean!' Khadir snapped. 'We were promised the Thunderbolts in return for the strike in Barcelona. Where are they?'

Tommy folded his arms. 'Not here. Not yet.'

'That was not–'

'The deal, yeah, heard you the first time. But things change. Circumstances beyond our control and all that. There are some loose ends that need to be cleared up.'

Khadir was silent for a moment, recalling the sudden and unexplained removal of his previous contact with the Combine. The Britisher must have guessed his line of thinking.

'No room for mistakes, you know that as well as I do. So we've got people cutting off any chances for blowback. Thing is, one particular little fucker is taking more effort than expected.' He said the last with some venom.

'That is the Combine's problem, not ours.'

Tommy shook his head. 'Wrong answer, Saladin. It's *everyone's* problem. And my new bosses? They don't like that. So we're dialling it back until things are sorted.'

An icy rage manifested itself in the slow tightening of Khadir's fists. 'Al Sayf have burned many bridges to reach this point. I will not allow the fears of old men to stop our call to vengeance.' His eyes glittered with cold fire. 'You are like them, a man without conscience and faith, so I do not expect you to appreciate such ideals. But understand *this*.' He leaned closer, his voice falling into a leopard snarl. 'Tell the ones who hold the leash around your neck that if they betray us, there is nowhere under heaven where they can hide.'

When Marc awoke the first thing he did was tap the laptop's keyboard, ignoring the aches across his back from having slept sitting up. He scowled at the progress bar on the monitor, still incomplete, the endless train of data calls on an inset panel showing the unrelenting, inexorable advance of his scan programs as they mapped the stolen hard drive. He ate a crumbling energy bar as a makeshift breakfast, and hazarded a look out of the empty window frame, down toward the hotel.

A patrol car was parked outside the lobby entrance, and he could see a Polizia Municipale officer talking animatedly with the one of the desk staff.

Marc shrank back, scanning in every direction for any signs that he had been discovered. He drew the pistol, checked the safety was off, and then slipped back to his hiding place.

His eyes fell to Novakovitch's iPhone, still lying where he had left it, half-stripped on the dusty floor. He wondered if it might hold some clue that could help him with the hard drive. Carefully, Marc reassembled the device, but not before using the thin blade of a screwdriver to tease out and disconnect the handset's GPS chip.

The phone came on and emitted a soft, melodic chime. The tiny tape-spool icon indicating a waiting voice-mail blinked in the corner of the screen. The message was just over three hours old, and the phone displayed Tanya Kirin's picture as the sender's ID.

Unless the dead girl was calling from her watery grave, someone else was reaching out to him. Marc tapped the playback key and gingerly raised the phone to his ear.

'*I assume you have Dima's phone, Mister Dane,*' began a smooth, metered voice, in an accent that could have been Swiss or Austrian. '*My name is Grunewald. We should have a conversation.*'

Marc's heart thudded in his ears and a wash of fear rose and fell in him. He held the phone away, as if it had suddenly become poisonous. A hundred questions churned in his thoughts, but he swallowed and took a deep, long breath. It took an effort to step back from the moment, to look at this new development from outside himself.

They know my name. But that wasn't a surprise, the leak inside MI6 could have made sure of that. *They know I'm here on the island.* Had someone on the yacht got a look at his face? That had to be it.

Abruptly, another thought occurred to him. *But they don't know where I am.* If this Grunewald guy had that information, Marc would already be dead.

Looking again, he saw that the voice mail message had an attached link with it, a web address for an on-line map site. Marc opened the laptop's browser and copied the code in by hand, revealing a street-level view of a sleepy residential district. An avenue in the Hammersmith district of London.

Marc's gut filled with ice. He knew the street and the house with the yellow door framed in the middle of the screen, knew it well even though he hadn't been there for years.

Katie's house. *His sister's house.* He had a flash of memory – a dinner party, feeling awkward and out of place, a few months after Katie and Stephen had married. Back when Mum was still alive.

He put down the phone and for long moments, Marc lingered on the thought of smashing the handset into pieces under his heel and making a run for it. But that was never going to be an option, not for him. Maybe Sam could have done it, just walked away and not looked back, but Marc was not that person. He had made a promise.

He drank the last of the water he had in his pack and gathered his thoughts. He tapped the key to return the call and on the third ring the line connected.

'*I see I was right.*' The same voice, calm and unhurried. '*Do I have your attention?*'

Marc resolved to give them nothing more than they already had. 'Say your piece.'

'*Straight to business. Good. I'm glad we didn't have to go through any needless chest-beating.*' There was a brief pause, and Marc strained to listen for any background noise, anything to give him a clue as to who he was talking to or where they were. '*Mister Dane, you've made yourself an irritant. You're getting in our way. Now you've taken something that my employers would very much like to have in their possession, yes?*'

Marc glanced at Novakovich's hard drive, but said nothing.

'*I think you can see where this conversation is leading,*' Grunewald continued. '*Give me the storage device, or there will be consequences.*'

'Come and get it.' His throat was dry and his reply came out gruff and terse.

'*You're quite clever for a technician, Mister Dane, but you're out of your depth. Let us be clear about this, so you understand.*' The man on the other end of the line read off the street address of the Parker household. '*It only requires me to make one call and my men will enter that house and kill everyone they find there.*' The bloodless, matter-of-fact delivery of the threat made it all the more chilling. '*Don't do anything so foolish as to try to warn them. That would be a grave mistake.*'

Having seen the work of the hit team on Novakovich's yacht, Marc had no doubt that he was dealing with people who were more than capable of such an act. 'You kill them and I'll upload the contents of that hard drive to every news agency on the planet.'

He heard the brief sneer in the reply. '*That's a poor bluff. The device is encrypted.*'

'Maybe so,' he retorted, 'but I am *quite clever*, remember?' Marc shot a look down at the laptop. In truth, he doubted his software was going to be able to harvest much of use from Novakovich's files, but if he could make Grunewald think otherwise . . .

'*Let us deal with this matter like two professionals, then,*' said the other man. '*A trade.*'

'You get the hard drive, you call off your men.'

'*It is that simple. Now, you will come to–*'

'No.' Marc spoke over him before he could begin to set out his demands. 'No, you listen to me. I make the rules. I say where and when we meet.'

There was a moment of silence as Grunewald muted the call at his end, and when he came back he sounded almost amused. '*As you wish. Go on.*'

'Midday,' said Marc, his thoughts racing. 'Come alone. It'll be a public place. I'll send you a location.' Before Grunewald could say more, he cut short the call and sank back, breathing hard.

'*Shit.* Shit shit *shit.*' Marc buried his face in his hands. The last thing he had ever wanted was to drag his family into this mess, but now it was happening, and he was losing control of the situation.

He desperately needed another option, but there was none. Katie was his weakness, his vulnerability, and her life was not a price he was willing to pay, not for anything.

Marc went to the empty window, walking off the nervous tingle in his limbs, and glanced out, off to the west over the hills towards the volcanic mountain rising up in the distance.

If there was even a chance he could keep a handle on this, get through it alive, then he had to think fast. He looked away from the dark slopes and began to punch in a text message.

Victor Welles sat on the far side of the conference table, idly stirring a cup of coffee with a slender spoon, and he graced Royce with a dismissive glance as the mission director entered the room.

Royce's lips thinned as he took a place directly opposite the other man. Talia Patel sat next to him, laying her digital pad flat on the polished mahogany.

Royce took a breath and opened his mouth to say something, but whatever it was became lost in the thud of another door opening, this one at the head of the room. Sir Oliver, his expression every inch that of a scowling hound, came striding in. The deputy director trailed a thin, bespectacled man in his wake, who clutched a legal pad and a fat fountain pen in his long fingers.

Welles and the others made a cursory effort to rise in his presence, but Sir Oliver angrily waved them back to their seats. He didn't wait for his assistant to finish assembling a cup of Earl Grey for him from the server tray by the wall; instead he launched into a savage glare that took in all of them.

'The Americans have a word for this sort of thing,' he began. 'They call it a *clusterfuck*.'

Talia flinched at the deputy director's choice of language. Sir Oliver rarely swore, and when he did it was the precursor to heads rolling.

'What the blazes are we doing?' he went on, eyes flashing. 'One cock-up after another? This will not stand.'

'We can take something from this,' Welles ventured. 'At least now we know for sure that Marc Dane is our double. We can start damage control–'

'Don't talk to me like I'm a fool, Victor,' Sir Oliver snapped back. 'You're on the bloody hook for this as much as K Section. You can start by explaining why Dane's capture order was inexplicably replaced with a termination warrant at the last moment.'

'Yes, do tell,' said Royce. 'Since when are we authorising Five to murder our officers?'

Welles laid his hands on the table, and at the very least he had the good grace to look contrite. 'There was a communications error. A kill order was issued without my knowledge.'

'That doesn't just *happen*,' Royce went on. 'There are safeguards in place. It's not like accidentally ordering too many boxes of paperclips.'

Sir Oliver snapped his fingers and the man in glasses put a piece of paper on the table, a print-out of the order in question. 'Someone will be for the high jump when this is sorted out, be sure of that.' He leaned forward and took a proffered cup of tea. 'For now, move on. Let's review, shall we?'

Talia swallowed and took her cue, reading from her notes. 'The subject escaped custody en route to an off-site secure location and a full security alert was sent out. Surveillance teams on Dane's family made contact and tracked him to a housing estate in South London.' She glanced at Welles, then away again. 'Tactical entry was made in order to secure him, but Dane slipped the net and tracking was lost.'

'He's out of the country by now,' added Royce. 'He was gathering false identity papers when the team moved in.'

'What's being done about that?' demanded Sir Oliver.

'We have all the materials from the flat where the forger was working. He's dead, but we're backtracking through what he left behind.'

Talia nodded. 'Our spotters are currently running facial recognition sweeps on CCTV footage from airports, ferry terminals and railway stations. Interpol have been notified, flagging Dane on the terrorist watch list. We've cut off all possible lines of support, but for now he's in the wind.'

'The fellow had help,' said the deputy director, measuring the words. 'If not from inside this organization, then from very close at hand. This is what I find the most troubling.' Sir Oliver took a purse-lipped sip from his tea, his anger turning frosty. 'Tell me about the sniper.'

Welles stiffened. 'We don't have any read on him. All we know is that a marksman in a neighbouring building fired a single shot at one of the pursuing officers. The recovered round was from a 7.62 NATO bullet.'

'How far away?'

'Around four hundred meters,' he continued. 'Whoever was covering Dane's escape wasn't much of an expert. The shot missed the tactical operative, only clipped his leg.'

'I don't agree,' Royce replied. 'There was no usable evidence left behind in the shooter's hide. That shows a professional's attention to detail.' He turned to Sir Oliver. 'I don't think that was a miss, sir. I think Dane's guardian angel shot that officer exactly where they meant to.'

'And Marc . . .' Talia paused. 'Dane had the opportunity to terminate the injured man to cover his escape and he didn't take it. Hardly the actions of a cold-blooded killer.'

Welles shook his head. 'Miss Patel, is it? With all due respect, I'm wondering if you had best remove yourself from this meeting. I have grave doubts you're capable of proceeding in an objective manner.'

Her eyes narrowed. 'How dare you. I could say the same. It's abundantly clear you're seeking to use these events to harm the reputation of K Section–'

'You're doing a good enough job of that on your own–'

Sir Oliver put down his tea cup with a hard *clack* of china, silencing them both. 'I want to make this very clear,' he began, ice forming on the words. 'This agency is not an arena for games of one-upmanship. I won't have it. You will work together to locate this rogue officer. You will recover him, he will be put to the question, and responsibility will be fully apportioned to whomever must bear it. Then this sorry episode will be buried deeper than Tartarus and that'll be the end to it.' He looked at each of them in turn, waiting for a nod of acceptance. 'If there is any other outcome, I will personally ensure that each of you spend the rest of your careers at some godforsaken listening post in the Falklands.' He stood up abruptly, brushing a fleck of lint from the lapel of his jacket as he turned back toward the door. 'Now get out of my bloody sight, and do your damned jobs.'

The cable car rose into the white haze wreathing the volcanic peak, and Marc looked back, turning to watch the barren slopes below as they receded. A wide field of craggy, dark rock extended away from him in a massive fan, dotted by sparse patches of hardy lichen and the brick-red streaks of oxide dust deposits.

The basalt cone of Mount Etna was broken by the grey ribbon of the highway, curling like a snake up the southern face of the sleepy volcano, the greenery of the foothills beneath a diminishing tide. Down at the far end of the cable line, the hotels, restaurants and gift shops of Nicolosi Nord ski station lay in a curve overlooking the views toward the coastline. The wood-framed buildings and parked cars were toy-like and artificial against the alien landscape. If not for the signs of human activity, it could have been the surface of an asteroid captured by the cameras of a space probe.

Marc blended in with a Canadian tour group up from the cruise liners in the bay and rode with them in their coach all the way up to the nearby hotel Rifugio Sapenza, before slipping out and away. He was as certain as he could be that he wasn't followed, and after judging the ebb and flow of each bus-load of arrivals, he waited until he could board a cable car on his own. The trip afforded him the time to recheck the Glock's ammunition magazine and the contents of his backpack. He peered at the cell phone, re-reading the terse message he had sent to Grunewald.

Bocca Nuova. Four Hours.

The mountain seemed like a good spot to meet, and despite his concerns that the day's foul weather might turn away the tourists, there were still crowds of them all around. The volcano was always a draw, with people eager to climb the three thousand plus meters of the cinder cone towering high over the island. A public place, with only one way in or out. It was the best Marc could come up with on short notice.

Etna's crown was all but invisible, shrouded in clouds, but every now and then a glimpse of the stark black summit showed though, the edges of the great crater silhouetted by shards of sky. The cable car lurched as it rode over the last support tower and creaked to a walking pace, the doors sliding back. Marc didn't wait for the operator to wave him out and bounced down on to the platform.

Outside in the damp, chilly afternoon, ragged patches of snow peppered the black moonscape around the cable car terminus, and a dirt track led away into the mists. Bulky Unimog trucks in white and red liveries waited for each new clump of tourists, and Marc joined the back of another group, watching their faces for anyone who seemed less interested in the sights and more in him. Engine grumbling, the high-sided 4x4 set off, swaying as an indifferent driver threaded them back and forth along the last few hundred meters of the lava fields before the peak proper.

From there, it was a footpath where an equally disinterested tour guide led the sightseers on a walking circuit around the edge of Bocca Nuova, the so-called 'new crater' formed in the last set of eruptions over a decade ago.

The mists cut visibility down to less than a hundred meters. As they approached the roped-off cordon around the fissures in the rock, the haze closed in even further, thickening for a few moments before the wind drew it away again. Ahead Marc glimpsed the steaming pits of fumarole vents, the steep sides stained dull yellow with tracks of sulphur deposits. To the eastern edge, a sheer drop fell into the Valle del Bove, revealing more flashes of blue sky between the shifting walls of fog.

He halted by a rocky outcrop near the beginning of the rough path, one hand slipping into the cavernous pouch of the hoodie where his pistol was resting.

Three figures emerged out of the mist, and one of them gave a languid nod as he caught sight of Marc's face. 'Here we go,' he said, in a flat, characterless American accent.

The man who spoke had a long, gaunt face and the kind of economy of movement that Marc associated with soldiers. The second, a muscular Latino guy who stood off to the side with a glower from under a ski hat, said nothing. But something about him triggered a flash of recall. Marc was sure he had been one of those shooting at him on board the *Jade*. The third man had a Germanic cast to his features and a shock of stark blond hair. Like his compatriots, he wore a black ski jacket of military cut, bulky enough to cover the bulge of any concealed firearm. He gave a bleak smile.

'Mister Dane. You actually came.' He drew a ten euro note from a pocket and handed it to the blank-faced American. 'I had my doubts, even as my colleague Mister Teape thought otherwise.'

Marc felt hot and cold all at once, the chill of the altitude and the icy sweat on his brow warring with the warmth of the fleece hoodie. 'I told you to come alone.'

'I chose not to.' Grunewald opened his gloved hands. 'Cruz?' He glanced at the Latino man. 'Show him.'

The man reached into a pocket and pulled out a smartphone. He dithered over it a moment, tapping at icons, then held it so Marc could see the images it was displaying.

The picture was remarkably crisp. It was a video feed, captured by someone holding a camera and panning it around the interior of a panel van. The viewpoint showed three men, all in dark clothes, with their faces concealed behind ski masks. They ignored the camera watching them, busy with the loading of the silenced pistols in their hands. One of the men had a crowbar lying across his lap.

'Thirty seconds,' said Grunewald. 'From the moment I say go to the moment they're inside your sister's house. A minute after that, maybe two, for the kills.' He took the smartphone from Cruz and pretended to use it to take a snapshot of Marc as another gaggle of tourists walked past them. 'I make one call, and . . .'

Marc licked his lips. 'You can't do that.'

'You know how to stop it,' said the mercenary. He held out his hand.

'No,' Marc shook his head, and smiled tightly. 'I mean you *can't*. You can't call your men on that.' He pointed at the air. 'No cell phone coverage up here, no signals. Nice video there, shame it's not live.'

Grunewald's insouciant manner slipped, just a little. 'Of course. Quite correct. And you would know that, wouldn't you? Being a *techno-geek*.' He sounded out the words, scornful of him. 'So that means you know what *this* is, too.' He snapped his fingers and Teape produced a block of grey and yellow moulded plastic, handing it to him. It resembled the old brick-sized mobile telephones of the 1980's, with a stubby tube for an antenna.

Marc's heart sank. 'A sat-com.'

That earned him a look that was indulgent, almost pitying. Grunewald weighed it in his hand. 'This *does* get a signal, Mister Dane,' he said. 'Your clever little tactic to cut off our communications failed to account for that.'

'This ain't our first rodeo,' said Cruz, offering the comment with a sneer. 'Not so smart now, *ese*?'

'No,' Marc admitted, his gut tightening.

Grunewald gestured with the satellite phone, pointing with the antenna. 'So. The threat still remains. If my operators don't hear from me, they'll go in anyway.'

Marc sniffed in the cold air. 'If I give you what you want, I have no guarantee that you're not just going to kill them anyway.'

The other man's expression shifted. He actually seemed *offended*. 'What do you think I am, Mister Dane? A common thug?' He came closer, his tone hardening. 'I am a professional. I don't condone needless collateral damage. Terminating civilians out of spite is for criminals.' Grunewald folded his arms. 'We both want the same thing. We both want my men in London to turn around and go home.' He shook his head. 'The murder of a police officer and his wife and child, in such a heavily populated area? Do you have any idea of the risk factor of such a sanction? The gentlemen I work for don't want such attention. But you've driven them to these ends. You've forced me to risk my team.' The man paused. 'I will give the order if I must. But wouldn't it be better for everyone to sleep soundly tonight?'

Marc felt numb inside as he reached into the folds of his hoodie and withdrew Novakovich's hard drive.

Teape was on him in a moment, snatching the device from his hands and peering owlishly at its surface. 'Looks secure,' he reported. 'I don't think he opened the casing.'

'Tried,' Marc admitted. 'Couldn't get in. Old school heavyweight encryption, thick as boiler plate.'

Teape took the smartphone from Cruz and used a thin cable to connect the two devices. After a long moment, the phone trilled. 'It's the genuine article.'

'How difficult was that?' Grunewald raised the sat-phone to his ear and pressed a speed-dial button.

The square grip of the Glock pistol was clenched in Marc's hand, and his finger rested on the trigger guard. Marc resolved that the mercenary would be the first to take a bullet if he did anything other than keep his word.

It was almost a shock when that was exactly what he did. 'It's me,' he said. 'Condition abort. I repeat, condition abort. Fall back to extraction.' He cut the call and studied the look on Marc's face. 'What did you expect? I told you they would live. Your family don't need to pay for your mistakes.' He gave the other man a quick look. 'Cruz, take his weapon.'

Marc reacted, but he was too slow to stop the swarthy man from shoving him back into the rocky outcrop. Cruz had a curved karambit blade protruding from his fist, which had come from nowhere. He pressed it into Marc's side, hard against his belly but out of sight from any passing gazes. 'Don't be stupid,' muttered the man, palming the Glock quickly and cleanly. None of the civilians milling around had noticed anything.

'You got what you want,' Marc said. 'We're done here.'

The pitying look returned. 'Not so,' Grunewald replied. 'This is the end of the line for you, I'm afraid.'

'We had a deal–'

Grunewald raised a hand to silence him. 'Which I honoured. But nothing we spoke about pertained to *you* getting off this mountain alive.' He shook his head, as if he was a parent disappointed by an errant child, and turned away, walking back down the slope.

Cruz's knife jabbed Marc through his clothing. 'Walk,' said the man, nodding toward the pathway leading up to the steaming crater. 'You wanna see the top, don't you?'

FOURTEEN

The mist rolled up over the lip of the fissure in a ghostly wave, bringing with it the acrid tang of sulphur. Marc could make out the cold weather coats of the tourists filing along the edge of the crater. He could hear them talking, snapping photographs. None of them were remotely aware that a murder was about to take place.

Cruz shoved him in the small of the back with his balled fist, the wicked arc of the mercenary's karambit concealed there, ready to slash open Dane's back at a moment's notice. 'Keep walking,' he growled, white exhales of breath wreathing his face. 'To the edge.'

Marc saw the crater fall away before him, past a line of iron rods and the red rope cordon strung between them. The hard chemical smell in the air made his nostrils ache. Down in the pit, gurgling fumaroles frothed, coughing out volcanic gas and superheated water.

The cleft in the dirty black rock was sheer-sided, rough walls of compacted basalt sand wet with snowmelt and condensed steam. Anyone who slipped over the edge would have nothing to grab on to, and the steep fall would take them all the way down into the mouths of the fumaroles, into the ragged plumes of searing vapour.

Cruz would make it look like an accident. Leave Marc to die in agony while his killer faded away, back down the slopes.

'No,' Marc muttered, the thought becoming a word, cementing his next action.

'The fuck you say–' Cruz began, but Marc was already moving, as another breath of cold wind brought fog down around them.

He deliberately tripped and fell, toppling like a cut tree away from the mercenary's grasp. Marc landed hard on the crumbly stone path and rolled as he hit, ignoring the bolts of pain through his shoulders. He heard the hiss of the knife slashing through air.

His hands clawed at the dirt and filled with clumps of damp black sand. Blindly, Marc threw the muddy mess back at Cruz and instinctively the other man put up his hands to shield his face.

He didn't waste the moment the crude distraction provided. Marc pivoted and scrambled forward toward the mercenary's indistinct shape, colliding with him at a low angle. He knocked his legs out from under him in a clumsy rugby tackle, and Cruz went down.

Punching blindly, Marc hammed blows into the other man's midriff and sternum, desperate to keep up the momentum. Cruz's talon-like blade cut the mist again and Marc swallowed a cry of pain as a line of heat drew across his shoulder, the tip of the karambit making brief contact as it moved in a wild, defensive arc.

Marc got a good look at Cruz's face as the mercenary's perpetually angry scowl briefly became an almost childlike expression of terror. The killer's footing was stolen by Marc's artless attack and Cruz's right leg went out from under him as the fragile lip of the crater crumbled under his weight. He went into the red rope and fell over it, dragging one of the iron stakes out of its hole as he tumbled.

Shouting in vain, Cruz dropped a good ten metres before he was silenced by slamming face-first into the sheer wall of the fissure. He whipped into a spinning, flailing tumble to fall the rest of the way into the crater.

Marc scrambled to his feet and broke into a run back down the path, the first screams of shock from the sightseers echoing behind him. Clutching his wounded arm, he tried to block out the burn of the pain and focus on escape.

He had to warn Katie and Stephen. He had to reach a landline, call them and beg his brother-in-law to get his family away. It didn't matter if he never spoke a word to them again after today – but Marc could not let them pay the price for his mistakes. They were all he had left.

The material of the dark hoodie masked the knife cut's spill of blood from the other people on the path and he was back at the end of the rough-hewn road even as word of the terrible 'accident' at Bocca Nuova was spreading.

Shrinking into the depths of the hood, he walked quickly toward a parked Unimog, threading around a group of tourists ready to be ferried back to the cable car station. He was just a few steps from the vehicle. Once he was on board, the misted windows and the hoodie would hide his face–

Marc's breath caught in his throat as his gaze crossed the snow-dusted tables in front of the *baita delle guide* hut and hung on two figures standing together, one busy lighting a cigarette. Grunewald and Teape were less than twenty metres from where he was, conversing in low tones. Marc turned sharply away as a woman behind him said something in polite Italian.

He was hesitating, holding up the queue and she was urging him to board the vehicle. Before he realized what she was doing, the woman reached up to shake him on the shoulder, and he flinched as she touched him where Cruz's blade had cut.

The woman's hand came back wet with blood, and the scream she gave hung in the wet air.

Grunewald and Teape both saw him. The American rocked off his heels and came marching forward, his dull gaze unblinking.

Marc shoved the woman out of his way and barged through the rest of the queue. A hut raised off the rock on wooden stands was directly in front of him, and without looking back he moved around it, putting it between himself and Teape.

He was counting on the reluctance of the mercenaries to start shooting or otherwise draw attention, but that would not last forever. Rounding the hut, Marc heard the rattle of a motorcycle engine and saw a shape moving through the mist along the rough highway – a four-wheeler Kawasaki ATV, ridden by a tall youth wearing a fluorescent orange crash helmet.

Marc ran into his path and the rider skidded to a halt, flipping up his visor. '*Cosa c'è?*' he asked, frowning. Marc pointed in a random direction and the young man looked, peering into the haze.

'*Scusa.*' With his other hand Marc threw a brutal left cross that slammed the rider hard enough to unseat him. He fell back over the rear axle, dazed and reeling as Marc leapt into the saddle.

Teape turned the corner of the hut. There was the angular shape of a silenced pistol in his hand.

Marc twisted the ATV's throttle and it leapt forward, spraying a fan of loose grit as he wrenched it around in a tight turn. He caught a glimpse of the gun in Teape's hand jolting but the cough of the shot was swallowed by the snarl of the Kawasaki's engine. Leaning low over the handlebars, Marc pointed the ATV into the fogbank and roared away, on to the path that snaked around Etna's lower cones toward the cable car terminal.

A long, foggy straightaway let him build up a good clip of speed, before suddenly fading into a hairpin bend that almost put him into the rocks. Marc leaned up and away like a yachtsman pulling against a sail and the ATV howled as it went into a rasping sideways drift. The ugly little bike chopped off the tip of the corner and bounced back down on to the ice-rimed path, violently weaving left and then right.

He had barely recovered any equilibrium before a set of white headlights appeared over a low rise directly in front of him, lancing out of the wall of mist. Swerving over the track, he cut across the path of another Unimog on its way up to the summit, earning a thunderous chorus of disapproval from the truck's air-horn.

Then he was into a series of descending switchbacks, passing the Cisternazza crater. *Almost there.* The cold wind whipped at his exposed face, numbing his cheeks and making his eyes run. In the middle distance he could see the glow of the lights from the restaurant atop the cable car station. Marc leaned into another tight turn and he glimpsed a shape – white and red, big and fast – looming large in his peripheral vision.

More from instinct than conscious thought, Marc put the ATV into a slalom path as another Unimog vaulted the tip of the last bend and thumped onto the road behind. Roaring with acceleration, the truck came surging after him, flooding the grey landscape with engine noise and dirty exhaust.

The Unimog's front bumper crunched against the back of the ATV, shattering one of the tail-lights. The impact almost sent Marc into a skid, but he kept the four-wheeler stable, rocking it back as it threatened to tip. If he lost control now, his body would meet the road and a heartbeat after that, the truck would grind him beneath its tyres.

Marc dared to take a swift glance over his shoulder, wind whipping the hoodie off his head. He saw Teape glaring at down at him from behind the Unimog's steering wheel, the high 4x4 coming on like a charging rhino.

They went into the next bend and the bigger, heavier truck lost momentum as it cornered wide. Marc concentrated on the apex of the turn, threading a good racing line as the road became a chicane, but, distracted by the pursuit, he saw the turn-off toward the terminus too late and was past it before he could react. The walls of sharp black rock around him receded and suddenly the path was taking the ATV out over a wide delta of old, solidified lava flow. The incline grew steeper, and gravity pulled on the lighter Kawasaki's frame.

He felt rather than heard the advance of the Unimog as the big truck shortened his lead, the drumming rumble of the engine vibrating through his chest. He concentrated on steering a zigzag course across the rough-hewn trail.

They passed a towering pillar of green-painted steel rising out of the earth toward the sky, thick wires leading down toward Nicolosi Nord. Cable cars cranked past over Marc's head as he emerged from their slow-moving shadows and into an area lit by bright sunshine.

He took a risk and veered off the cracked roadway, on to the undulating plains of the lava field. The Kawasaki was catching air every few seconds as every little rise threatened to buck him out of the saddle.

Teape was still on him, the heavy truck bulling its way over the uneven going. The stolen Unimog was going to follow him all the way down unless he could do something about it.

Leaning hard into the handlebars, Marc swerved the more agile ATV into a turn that carried him around a patch of black sand that had collapsed in on itself, forming a wide pothole. High up in the Unimog's cab, Teape wasn't aware of the hazard until he was right on it.

The 4x4's rear right wheel fell sharply into the pit. The tall-sided vehicle over-balanced and rolled, crashing hard against the rocky slope, finally coming to a clattering halt back on its wheels.

There was little time to celebrate any kind of victory, though. Marc had well and truly lost any sign of the proper pathway and it was all he could do to cling to the yowling Kawasaki bike as the steep incline and the basalt shingle collaborated to unseat him.

He was a hundred metres from the highway when one of the ATV's front tyres finally burst and showered Marc with shreds of rubber. The wheel hub sank into the loosely packed dirt and with a grinding hiss, the four-wheeler bike juddering to a halt.

Marc stumbled away from the bike, his heart hammering in his chest and his breathing laboured. The thinner air up here on the mountain was draining the energy from him. He staggered down the last length of the slope to the parking lot.

A pair of payphones under plastic hoods stood close to a nearby vendor, who was hawking colourful postcards and odd little souvenir statues made of black volcanic glass. Marc lurched into the closest one, snatching up the orange handset and jamming a phone card into the pay slot. He blindly dialled the only telephone number he never had to think to remember, and fought down the trembling in his numbed fingers.

Stephen Parker's gruff voice answered. '*Yeah*?'

'Don't talk, just listen.' The words spilled out of him in a rush. 'Get Katie and Matt and get out of the house right now, go to the station, stay there, there's men with guns in a van outside, you have to go now–'

'*Marc*?' He felt the anger and disappointment in the growled reply. '*What the hell have you done?*'

'Just *fucking do it*!' Marc bellowed, drawing apprehensive looks from day-trippers examining the tourist mementos. 'Go, Steve! Do it right *now*!'

His brother-in-law never graced him with a reply, but in the seconds before he hung up, Marc heard Stephen calling out urgently to his wife.

The next sound he heard was the roaring snarl of the Unimog as it smashed through a chain link fence behind him and came hurtling across the footpath. Smoke snorted from the truck's engine as the mercenary aimed it like a missile, mashing the accelerator to the firewall.

Marc ignored the screaming tourists behind him and at the last possible second he threw himself aside, diving toward a heap of dirty slush gathered by the side of the road. The out-of-control Unimog missed him by an arm's length, colliding with the payphone where Marc had been standing and beheading it, ripping the stand from the ground with a shriek of torn metal. Bleeding off speed, the truck went into the side of the vendor's hut, caving in a wall and collapsing the sloped roof as it ground to a stop.

The tang of a gasoline fire reached his nostrils and Marc slipped away as flames caught and spread, chewing down jolts of pain with every limping step.

Lucy feigned dozing, but it was a poor act. Despite the comfort of Solomon's private jet, she still couldn't surrender to sleep. The best she could manage was some kind of vague nap-state, hovering at the edge of real rest but never really getting there. It wasn't that she was a nervous flyer, far from it. If anything, conventional air travel bored the hell out of her. No, Lucy Keyes guessed that on some level, she just couldn't release herself from a baseline level of alertness while thousands of feet in the air, inside a pressurized steel tube. Instead she cat-napped, letting her mind drift.

She heard the thud of the office door down the corridor, and blinked as Delancort appeared in the lounge area. Shifting planes of light moved slowly around the cabin as the jet began a slow turn and he was illuminated by the glow.

'What is it?' she asked, spotting the smartphone in his hand.

'Caught a fish,' he replied, with a faint smirk. 'A priority message just came through from the London office. It appears that our good friend Marc Dane has broken cover.'

Lucy frowned at the thought of that and got up, holding out her hand to demand the phone. 'Gimme.'

'I don't–' Delancort began, but he made only a vague attempt to prevent Lucy snatching it from his grip.

The message on the handset was from the Rubicon Group's UK headquarters, and it had an audio file attached. She pressed the 'play' button and two voices emerged from the device's tiny speaker, layered by the distortion effect typical of a digital phone tap.

'*Yeah?*'

'*Don't talk, just listen.*'

'Second one is Dane,' Delancort explained. 'First is his brother-in-law, an officer in the London police.'

'I know.' Lucy let the brief, terse conversation play through. 'Brother sounds pissed,' she offered. 'What the hell is this all about? Dane talking about men with guns outside a house?'

'Blowback from his escape, perhaps?' Delancort shrugged. 'It's likely the cop helped him get out of the country somehow.'

'This doesn't sound like two guys happy to help each other.' Lucy handed back the phone. 'So we got this how? Tapped the line?'

'It would be more accurate to say that we tapped the tap. British Intelligence put a wire on Dane's sister's phone the moment he went off grid.'

'I'd like to know exactly how we seem to be reading MI6's mail.'

Delancort gave that thin, unctuous smile that always made Lucy want to smack him upside the head. 'Rubicon has a lot of assets in Europe.'

He wasn't going to give her more, so she let the question go for the moment. 'Where'd the call come from?'

'A public payphone in Sicily, in the Etna National Park. And obviously, if we have that information, then so do Dane's former employers.'

Lucy was already marching past him, heading toward the cockpit. What was Dane doing in Sicily? It was a short hop from the UK and as good a place as any to lay low – but then he'd blown that in a hot second by phoning home.

Men with guns, he had said. Was that MI6 again, threatening his family to pressure Dane into surrendering, or someone else?

'What are you doing, Lucy?' Delancort trailed after her as she approached the flight deck.

The door was open, and as she came up, a broad-shouldered man with dark hair in close-cut curls emerged, rolling up the sleeves of his white uniform shirt. Captain's epaulets on his shoulders made him resemble any one of countless civil aviators, but it was his eyes that betrayed a youth spent in the cockpits of warplanes. Ari Silber had that kind of rugged early-forties look that handsome Jewish doctors and Hollywood actors struggled to cultivate. He had an easy smile but a killer's gaze. Lucy liked that about him; she knew another shooter when she saw one.

From what she had gathered, Silber had come to work for Ekko Solomon after a distinguished career flying an F-15I *Ra'am* strike fighter for the Israeli Air Force. She wondered if it bothered him to have gone from top gun to a rich man's chauffeur. *Or does he owe the African something too?*

'Looking for me?' he asked.

'Where are we at right now?'

'Over the Med,' he replied. 'I'm guessing you have forgotten a bag in London and you want us to go back for it?'

'If we divert, how soon to get us on the ground in Sicily?'

Silber paused, doing the calculations in his head. 'Three hours at the inside, touching down at Catania airport.' He glanced at Delancort, nodding toward the flight deck. 'You want I should make that happen?'

'No,' said another voice, and the conversation stilled.

As ever, Ekko Solomon was dressed as if he was about to step out to a business meeting. He held a digital tablet in one hand and Lucy guessed that he had seen the same message from the London office.

'We know where Dane is,' Lucy noted.

Solomon shook his head. 'We know where he *was*.' He gestured with the data pad. 'This man is running and he will not stay in one place. He knows he has burned his hiding place in Sicily. He will flee.'

'We're playing catch-up with his people,' said Lucy. 'Unless we can get out in front of Dane, we're not going to be able to grab him before the Brits. If there's a lead we can find–'

'Marc Dane is desperate,' Solomon went on. 'He needs help. So he will go to someone that he trusts.'

Delancort nodded. 'That's what the behavioural model suggests, based on the data from Zurich. Everyone Dane is close to is back in England.'

'Not so,' replied Solomon. 'Captain Silber, we *are* going to divert this aircraft, but not to Sicily. Contact Cairo, have them adjust our flight plan. This is our new destination.' He handed the pilot the digital pad.

'Yes sir.' Silber nodded and vanished back into the A350's cock-pit, leaving Lucy to frown at the new orders.

'I want this man in our care,' Solomon said firmly. 'This is an imperative.'

Marc was alone in the train compartment for the first time since he had boarded, the other passengers – a pair of animated Austrians – having disembarked the moment the carriage had halted, eager to get some holiday snapshots.

Outside the window, an identical coach blocked any other view. The train from Palermo had been stacked, one line of wagons arranged next to another, inside the belly of the ferryboat that was now crossing the Straights of Messina toward Naples.

Within the hour, Marc would be on the main line to Rome. The border crossing, such as it was, had been twenty minutes of queues and fretting that he would be made but the Marcus Dale passport, a spotless Canadian snap cover that had never been used before, got him through.

The German identity Marc had used in Sicily was gone, ashes in a corner of the unfinished apartment complex. Destroying it had been the last thing he did after coming to rest there. His escape from Etna had been touch and go, but an empty seat on a tourist coach had been enough to get him away in the confusion. Cleaned up as best he could, Marc recovered the daypack with his laptop and the rest of the gear, and bolted. And now he was on the move again, he had no clear picture of what to do next.

This wasn't how it was supposed to have gone. Marc's plan was in tatters. He'd seen it playing out a whole different way. Finding Novakovich, getting the information he needed on the turncoat at MI6. Sneaking back into the UK, coming in from the cold with all he needed to clear his name and put the loss of Nomad to rest. He felt like an idiot, like he was cursed. With every day he was away, the chances of him ever coming home were receding into the distance.

This is how they're going to get me, he thought. *They'll keep the pressure on and keep coming, cut off every escape route until I have nowhere left to run.*

His options were narrowing, and if he knew that, then the people who wanted him dead knew it too. The moment was coming – and it would be very soon – where Marc would have to risk his liberty on one last gamble, or run for his life and never stop.

He scowled at the thought and looked down at the screen. The computer seemed to take forever to boot up, and he drummed his fingertips on the edge of the keyboard. It was running slow, and he wondered if the cause was the volume of data his counter-crypto software had gathered from Novakovich's hard drive.

His attempts to make a 'ghost' copy of the drive – to essentially clone the whole thing – had been doomed to failure. Perhaps, if time hadn't been against him, if he'd had access to the kit back at the OpTeam data lab at Vauxhall Cross, there might have been something he could have retrieved.

But whatever secrets the broker had been protecting were lost, traded away for the lives of Katie and her family. Instead, all he had were layers of redundant data, the remnants of buffer files and digital tags left behind by the movements of the *actual* encoded information. Less sensitive than Novakovich's precious files, this data was the equivalent of the wake left behind by the passing of a ship, or the footprints of a long-gone animal. Just vague indicators as to where the electronic communications had gone, devoid of any useful content.

He recognized some of the code fragments. They corresponded with encryption patterns used by the secure email servers at MI6. On their own, these were nothing but circumstantial evidence, phantoms of proof that wouldn't hold up in any court of law. But they were enough for him, confirmation of what he now believed was true.

Information had been delivered from an unknown source inside British Intelligence to Combine assets elsewhere in the world, and Dima Novakovich had been paid handsomely to be the middleman. At least, up until the point when it was cheaper to buy his silence with lead instead of gold. But without evidence of what intelligence had been sold and more importantly, who had leaked it, Marc was nowhere. At best, he had enough to throw suspicion on the deaths of the Nomad team and force MI6 into a mole hunt. It was not enough to absolve him of any guilt, and turning it in now would only give the Combine's source the opportunity to cut and run. By the time anyone managed to reconstruct the origins of the communications and track down which user had sent them, the person responsible for Sam's death would be gone.

Marc watched the columns of abstract numbers and letters drift down the screen in a digital waterfall. This would only work if he could do it himself. If it was possible to gain access to a secure MI6 server and drill down into the communications records . . . Then even if the Combine source had used blinds or shell processes, it was possible Marc could reconstruct at least part of the emails to see what Novakovich had so carefully protected.

But it was a pointless exercise to even consider it. Wary of the regular covert cyber-attacks from Chinese and North Korean hacker-ops units, the network for the British intelligence ministries was entirely stand-alone, isolated from the global internet to prevent intrusion. Short of finding a way to reprogram one of the deep net's impossibly complex orbital satellite relays from the ground, the only other method to connect would require Marc to physically be *in the same room* with a secure MI6 terminal. And to do that, he would have to gain entry to a building filled with people who would all be on the lookout for him, some of whom might want him dead.

His gut tightened as an audacious and utterly insane thought came together. Marc actually let out a nervous laugh at the idea of it. The train would be in Rome by late afternoon. He would have to work quickly.

One last gamble, he thought. *All or nothing.*

FIFTEEN

Callum Torrance crossed the lobby of the St. Regis, his jaw set and his pace quick. One of the hotel's porters stepped out of his way with a curt *scusi* but Torrance ignored him. He didn't really *see* staff in the way that he saw other people; they were movable appliances that brought him what he needed when he needed it, and that tended to be the start and finish of his interactions with them. Unless they had done something to piss him off; then, they became very visible, if only so he understood where to direct his sense of entitlement.

He looked around to orient himself and found the reception, scanning the atrium as he walked. Like anyone who had come up through the ranks in Hollywood, he had developed the ability to sift a room for faces and dismiss anyone who wasn't in the business, or at least in the orbit of what he considered important. He registered that there was no one he knew sitting in the lobby, and more importantly, there was no one who looked like paparazzi. The last thing the shoot needed right now was more negative publicity.

Callum's gaze dwelled briefly on a light-haired guy, dressed in an unimpressive suit. He was absorbed in a laptop, but he didn't have a camera, so Callum had forgotten his face in the time it took to walk to the front desk.

He picked a receptionist and talked at her. 'What the hell is so important that I have to come down here?' He demanded. 'Can't you people send a messenger?' He pulled at the collar of his shirt and grimaced. Rome's sultry evening heat made him sweaty and irritable.

'Mister Torrance,' the receptionist said smoothly, 'please accept our apologies.' She knew exactly who he was. Callum's studio paid a sizeable stipend to the St. Regis to hold rooms for their top people during the European shooting schedule. 'Sir, the message was from a Mister Black? He expressed a desire for discretion.' She offered him a note.

Callum's face drained of colour. It would not be an exaggeration to say that Harlan Black was one of the more turbulent film directors Torrance's studio had ever worked with. His last film had brought home a truckload of Award gold, but he was a perfectionist and the erotic period drama they were filming out at Cinecittà was already falling into serious budget overruns.

Black's message was exactly what he had been dreading. *Filming suspended*, it said. *Creative differences. Car coming for you.* Callum could hear the sound of his plans for the evening disintegrating around him like peals of breaking glass, and he shot a look at the Patek Philippe on his wrist. Tonight was when they were supposed to get the last night shots in the can.

'Where's the car?' he said, in a dead voice.

The receptionist gestured with a perfectly manicured hand. 'Your driver is waiting outside, Mister Torrance.' He stalked away. 'Have a nice day,' she said to his back, never once showing any sign of registering his rudeness.

Blinking at the low sun, Callum climbed into the town car, cursing under his breath.

Looking across the top of his screen, Marc waited until he saw the car move off. The clock was running.

He stood, tucking the laptop under one arm, and extended the carry handle on the new Pullman case he had purchased at the railway station. In a moment, he was across the hall and approaching the elevators, mentally ticking off the time.

The density of Rome's evening traffic and the distance to the Cinecittà studios outside town meant that Callum Torrance's journey would last somewhere between twenty-five and thirty minutes. Add another ten or twenty to that for the producer to get out to the back lot . . . Marc estimated that it would be forty minutes before Torrance would discover that he'd been sent on a fool's errand. It was Marc who had called the front desk pretending to be Harlan

Black's assistant, dictating the false message, Marc who had called Cinecittà's usual car service and told them that Torrance wanted a pickup at his hotel.

He waited until he had one of the elegant wrought-iron elevators to himself, and tapped the button for the executive suites. As he rose, Marc flipped open the laptop, quickly connecting the computer to a cable which ended in a blank smartcard. A progress bar filled as the laptop transferred data to a programmable radio-frequency ID chip in the card. The chip was the same as those embedded in the smartcards used by the St. Regis as room keys. It had been easy for Marc to use a wi-fi reader to pinpoint the key card in Torrance's pocket. In a fraction of a second, MI6-issue ripping software sent a radio 'ping' to the key, spoofing it into thinking it was talking to the door mechanism. The key responded with the lock code, the laptop copied it, and now Marc had unfettered access to Torrance's hotel room.

He exited smartly, passing down the corridor to the Ambassador Suite. The ersatz key worked perfectly and he entered, closing the door quietly. Inside, Marc sagged back against the door and took several deep breaths. The linen shirt beneath the sandy-coloured jacket he wore was suddenly sticking to his chest.

Leaving the case so it blocked the door, he stalked into the suite, drawing the Glock but keeping it out of sight. Marc had gambled on Torrance being here by himself, and it looked like he was right. The one other variable that could derail Marc's plans was Torrance himself. If he changed his mind and came back to the hotel, if he used his cell phone to call the studio during the car journey . . .

Marc caught sight of a black rectangle of glass – Torrance's iPhone – lying forgotten on the bedside table and smiled in relief. *One less thing to worry about*, he thought.

Satisfied the room was secure, Marc locked himself in and set to work. Recovering the Pullman case, he dumped it on the sofa in the living room and tore it open, checking his daypack and the rest of the contents before going through Torrance's wardrobe. The producer was a little broader across the chest than Marc, but they were a close enough match that he could fit into one of the Armani suits hanging there.

He looked at his watch as he changed clothes. *Fifteen minutes elapsed.*

The suite was easily six times the size of the dingy little room where Marc had spent his first two days in Rome. The shabby hostel in a backstreet off the Satzione Termini was cheap, commonplace and the grim-faced old woman who ran it spoke no English and asked no questions. Living off supermarket pasta cooked on a tiny hot plate and biding his time, Marc's plan had slowly come together.

To get access to an MI6 terminal meant getting into a building in Rome belonging to the British government, and that was a short list. OpTeam safe houses were out of the question, which left him with just one single – and highly secure – location; the British Embassy on the Via XX Settembre.

To find a way in, he back-tracked. Torrance's studio was a patron of European art, including the exhibition that was opening later this evening in the grounds of the Embassy, before an exclusive guest list of the city's best and brightest. It didn't take long for Marc to discover that Torrance's latest film was in choppy waters, and a trawl of entertainment gossip websites provided the names of the players in the producer's current drama. From there, it was just a question of building a convincing series of reasons for the man to be out of his hotel room.

If Marc Dane could hijack Callum Torrance's life for the next hour or so, he could get to what he wanted.

It was his final roll of the dice. The last of the cash he had left had gone to pay for a passable suit and haircut that had allowed him to walk unchallenged into the lobby of the St. Regis, along with some NATO Meal-Ready-to-Eat packs from an army surplus store and a mix of materials from a gardening supplier.

He'd ditched the hostel that morning, skipping out to avoid the concierge, leaving a mess of paper cups, plastic spoons and a chemical odour lingering in the tiny, unventilated room. At the bottom of the Pullman case were a dozen polythene carrier bags, each wrapped into a clump the size of his fist.

Marc hacked the electronic lock of the suite's digital safe with the same method he'd used on the door, helping himself to a wad of cash in dollars and euros, but most importantly locating Torrance's all-important invitation.

Thirty minutes now. That was the zero line, the maximum Marc was willing to allow his carefully engineered break-in to last. He checked the contents of the Pullman one more time, stuffing his clothes inside, then left. Marc had left traces of himself all over the suite, and it went against the grain to leave without cleaning up. But if this went to plan, it wouldn't matter.

The elevator deposited him in the hotel's basement car park and Marc handed a valet a couple of notes and a ticket stub he'd found in the producer's jacket.

The hefty tip was enough for the valet not to question the identity of the man claiming Torrance's car. A moment later the concrete walls of the parking garage echoed to the snarl of a highly tuned engine, and a canary-yellow Ferrari 458 Spider rolled to a halt in front of Marc.

Despite the tension of the moment, and the very real danger he was in, it was all Marc could do not to cast his eyes over the sleek sports car and break into a grin. He slid in behind the wheel, throwing the Pullman into the passenger foot well. Taking a breath, he put the Spider into gear and eased it away from the kerb. The car responded smoothly, propelling him on to the street with a mutter of revs.

In the hostel, Marc had memorised the route as he alternated between mixing small batches of chemicals and watching the door. Now, pressed against the leather upholstery of the Ferrari in a suit that was worth a year's rent on his London flat, that moment seemed like it had happened in a different world.

I could take this and just go, Marc thought. *Find my way to the motorway and put my foot down . . .* The sudden presence of that temptation alarmed him. He was so tired, and he badly wanted to be free of all this.

He scowled, shaking those thoughts away. 'Too late for that now,' he said aloud, catching sight of his own eyes in the rear-view mirror. 'You had that chance, mate.'

The British Embassy had the kind of late Sixties modernist design that would have made it look at home in some dystopian science fiction movie. Poured grey concrete formed a rectangular outline that stood off the ground on thick pillars. Beneath it, shimmering pools fed by fountains glittered in the fading light and the grassy lawns surrounding them were populated by a temporary installation of lights and statues. In ranks that went back and forth across the embassy plaza, stages had been set up to display paintings and other works to the milling attendees.

Torrance's invite got Marc through the gate and allowed him to take the Spider into the embassy's small parking lot, shrouded by a line of trees from the main building.

At the last moment, just before he had turned up the drive, a black sports utility vehicle had filled the rear-view, emerging from the tailing traffic like a tank cresting a hilltop. Had the vehicle been following him all the way from the hotel? He didn't think so. The SUV passed in a grumble of engine noise and he exhaled. There were enough real threats to watch for without inviting more.

Leaving the Spider parked nose-out and unlocked, Marc slipped out, moving low and quick between the other parked cars, making preparations for the next phase of his solo mission. Again, he peered at the Cabot dive watch on his wrist. 'Twenty minutes?' he asked the air. 'Hope that's enough.'

A metal detector at the entrance let him enter without complaint. The Glock was in the car where he had left it, and Marc felt vulnerable without the pistol on him. He hadn't been without a weapon to hand since fleeing London.

The cream of Rome's rich list were already at the gathering, indulging themselves. Marc moved through knots of chatting, laughing people, most speaking in animated Italian and a few in more sedate English. A server with a tray of elegantly prepared fish canapés passed him, and with a start, Marc realised that he was hungry. Taking a flute of wine to blend in, he trailed after the waiter and helped himself to a few bites.

He paused before a complex piece of modern art and used it to cover his examination of the plaza. Security was everywhere. He recognised the regulation cut of jacket and trousers that characterised the diplomatic protection detail. Were they on alert because of him? It was likely. It would only be a matter of time before one of them got a good look at his face, and then his thin cover would be blown. But no one would want to create a scene here, of course. Not tonight, with civilians everywhere and the British reputation on the line. They would come discreetly, with threats that were quiet but no less serious.

Embassy staff weren't the only muscle here, either. Marc spotted groups of personal bodyguards orbiting close to their principals.

One of the security officers, a severe woman in a black pantsuit, turned in his direction and studied him for a little longer than he was comfortable with. Marc moved away, quicker than he should, without watching where he was going. He bumped into one of the bodyguards he had seen earlier, gaining a cold-eyed glare in return. The man had the build of a wrestler, and he seemed as if the expensive jacket he wore was only barely keeping him confined. The inky blue nubs of tattoos poked up over the collar of his shirt. Marc knew the icons of the *bratva* when he saw them.

'What do you think of this?' The voice came from behind him, educated and unhurried, with a Russian accent. 'What does it *mean*?'

Marc turned and saw a face that hitherto he had only encountered on the front pages of newspapers or in MI6 briefing documents.

Pytor Glovkonin was a very rich man. Tall and imposing, he had features that were all hard angles, with a light and perfectly trimmed beard that did nothing to soften him. A billionaire energy tsar with massive holdings across the Russian Federated States, he was the very model of the ex-Soviet oligarch, politician and mafiya, a captain of the New Russia's industry with a shady past that British Intelligence could only guess at. Glovkonin's name and that of his pet conglomerate G-Kor had risen to the attention of both MI6 and MI5. The billionaire had many investments in the UK, and rumours of his connection to organized crime did not sit well with the British government. But there had never been anything other than hearsay, nothing actionable, leaving the man free to spend his wealth buying up choice parts of Knightsbridge and the occasional premier league football team.

'Well?' he prompted, gesturing at the sculpture before them. 'I would think a man paying this much attention to such a piece would have an opinion.'

'It's complicated,' Marc offered, actually *looking* at the sculpture for the first time. Art had never really been his strong point.

Glovkonin gave a grunt of laughter. '*Life* is complicated. Art is supposed to be simple.'

'You think so? The roof of Sistine Chapel is pretty busy.'

That got him a nod. 'Of course. But the ideal behind the work is uncomplicated. *God meets man*. That's all there is to it.'

'Well, then maybe what this piece means is *art isn't simple*.'

The other man shrugged. He had the easy, magnetic charm of someone used to being the master of his world. 'The intent of the creator is meaningless. Only what we, the audience, believe is of importance. What I say this means, it means.'

'That must be a nice position to be in.' He glanced away. Three of the security staff had gathered near one of the fountains, talking quietly. Marc knew that any moment now they would turn in his direction. He resisted the urge to steal a peek at his watch.

Glovkonin gave him a considering look. 'You're English. From London, yes? Are you part of the embassy staff?'

Marc shook his head. 'I'm here to see a friend.' He didn't like Glovkonin's scrutiny. The man had eyes like a wolf, constantly searching for weakness.

'Is it a woman? This friend of yours?'

'No . . .' For a moment, Marc caught sight of a girl with long dark hair, and her face blurred, becoming Sam Green's. 'No,' he repeated more firmly, banishing the thought.

'You have the air of a worried man,' said Glovkonin, as if he were reading Marc's thoughts. 'In my experience a man with that look only has it for two reasons. The first is always because of a woman.' He shared a smile with his bodyguard. 'The second comes from having a knife at the throat.' He placed his thumb to his neck to underline his point. 'So if it isn't a woman, then what concerns you, Mister . . . ?'

'Pardon me, Sir?' The woman in the black pantsuit had appeared beside him before he could answer. 'There's a telephone call for you.' Close up, he could see the grey comma of a wireless radio earpiece hidden under the cut of her hair.

Glovkonin met Marc's gaze and it was clear that the other man knew there was no telephone, no call, nothing but trouble waiting for him. 'Here she is,' he noted, with deceptive lightness.

'If you'll come with me, please?' The woman gestured for Marc to step away. Her other hand drifted toward the small of her back. *What did she have holstered there? A pistol? Too noisy. More likely a stun gun.*

Marc very deliberately looked back to Glovkonin. 'What time do you have?'

The other man raised an eyebrow, then drew out an antique watch from a fob pocket and snapped it open. 'Thirty minutes past seven.'

'Now, sir.' All pretence at politeness was now gone.

'Nice meeting you,' Marc said, with a wan smile. He walked away, and the security officer fell into step with him.

'Mister Torrance is very upset about losing his invite,' she said quietly, looking him up and down 'Also his suit. And his car.' She was leading him to the rest of the waiting security team.

He halted a few feet away and they all flinched. 'My name is Marc Dane,' he began.

'We know who you are,' said the woman. 'Don't make us do something you'll regret.'

'You're not going to make a fuss,' he snapped, and jerked a thumb in Glovkonin's direction. The billionaire was still watching with interest. 'Not in front of him and the rest of these people.' Before she could threaten him again, Marc went on. 'I'm here to turn myself in. I'm going to surrender, but only to someone I know.'

'You don't get to give orders, Dane.'

His lips thinned. 'You bring me John Farrier.'

'There's no-one here by that name.' She was going to say more, but then Marc caught the faint buzz of a voice from the woman's earpiece and she hesitated. 'Stand there. Don't talk and don't move,' she said, at length.

Marc did as he was told, and within a few moments he recognized a familiar figure threading his way through the party-goers. John Farrier's expression was a mix of relief and disappointment.

Farrier gave the woman a nod. 'Lane, stand down.'

'Not bloody likely,' she retorted. 'This man is a rogue agent.'

Marc drained his wineglass and set it down on a nearby table, acutely aware that by now there was probably a sniper on the roof with crosshairs on his skull. He offered Farrier a weak grin. 'Hey man. Glad to see me?'

'Fuck, no.' Farrier shook his head. 'What the hell are you doing here?'

'Take me in, and I'll tell you all about it.'

'Sir,' began the woman, 'I don't think you–'

Farrier raised his hand to silence her. 'Tracey, I've got this, all right?' He glared at Marc. 'Come with me.'

He followed his friend toward the main building, chancing a last look over his shoulder.

Pytor Glovkonin had watched the whole interchange from afar, and he raised his glass to Marc in what could have been an expression of good luck, or a farewell to a defeated man.

They took him to a holding room on the first floor and took everything he had on him. Lane put a hand on Marc's shoulder, digging into nerve points under his flesh, uncomfortably close to where he had been injured a few days ago.

'Sit down.' She shoved him into a chair and stalked around the table in the middle of the room, glaring at him. Farrier took the seat next to him, and outside the door, through a glass partition, Marc watched another man take up a guard position. The man in the corridor was armed with a pistol, holding it out and to the ready.

'You've got some nerve,' said Lane, circling him. 'Did you really think you could walk in here using another man's identity without us noticing?'

'No,' Marc admitted. 'But it took you a while, didn't it?'

She ignored the comment and addressed Farrier. 'He was talking to Glovkonin. What was that about?'

'He likes art,' Marc explained. 'You've got a problem with me sneaking in, but apparently its okay for Six to let shady Russians come to the party, as long as they're billionaires, yeah?'

Farrier sniffed. 'He's never been charged with anything.'

'Unlike *you*,' Lane insisted.

The door opened and another man brought in Marc's case before exiting again without a word, leaving the luggage open for Lane to paw through. In short order she pulled out the daypack bundled up inside, the scuffed laptop and the pistol. Lane laid them out on the table next to the contents of Marc's pockets, his wallet and wrist-watch, all arranged neatly like items of evidence at a trial.

'I travel light.' Marc feigned indifference. 'What time you got?'

'Seven forty,' offered Farrier, leaning forward. 'I wouldn't worry about the clock if I were you. There's a lot of people back home who have a lot of questions for you.'

Marc said nothing, measuring his old friend's expression. John's manner betrayed little. With Lane in the room with them, he couldn't speak openly about what had happened at Vauxhall Cross.

What little he could read of Farrier spoke to frustration, maybe even sadness. Marc saw the slightest edge of it in the other man's eyes. *What is he thinking? Is he angry with me because I didn't run when I had the chance?*

'Who was the sniper in Walworth?' Farrier's question came out of nowhere. 'The one who covered you when the strike team went in?'

He remembered the subsonic hum of the gunshot coming out of nowhere on the damp rooftop, the man sent to kill him falling away wounded. 'I have no idea,' he replied, and it was the truth. 'All I know is that tactical team was there to shoot me dead, not take me in.'

Farrier blew out a breath, his expression softening. 'Someone buggered up the paperwork. Big stink about it at HQ.'

'Oh.' Marc sat back. 'So it was a clerical error, then? That makes me feel a lot better, cheers.' He looked up at the neon strip light over their heads, then away.

'Should you even be telling him any of that?' Lane demanded.

Farrier didn't answer her. 'I've got to say, I'm amazed you made it this far, Marc. You know Welles was on you the moment they picked up that call from Sicily? Bad tradecraft, mate. You sent up a flare. He warned me you might try to make contact, but I told him you wouldn't be that stupid.'

'I'm not as smart as I look.' Marc's retort was dry. He knew that as they spoke, someone in the security detail was trying to contact

Welles back in London, perhaps dragging him away from some pricey dinner date. As soon as he and Royce knew Marc had been captured, the hammer would fall hard and his window of opportunity would be closed permanently.

He glanced at Lane. 'Tracey, right? What time do you have, Tracey?'

Her irritation deepened. 'Why do you keep asking that?' she snapped.

Outside, there were muffled thuds of concussion, and then a hooting chorus of car alarms.

Acrid clumps of white smoke churned from the wheel wells of a dozen vehicles, the sudden stink of burnt sugar and rotten eggs hanging in the air. Predictably, the result was an immediate surge of panic as the embassy's guests discarded their vols-au-vent and sought to put as much distance as they could between the outbreak of 'fire' and themselves. Private security details clustered around their principals, and the embassy guards – already on high alert, thanks to Dane's gate crashing – went out in full force.

The smokers were not really IEDs in the real sense of the term. Barely-dangerous nuisance devices at best, Marc had cobbled them together in the dingy little hostel from innocuous, store-bought ingredients. A thick paste of potassium nitrate and sucrose in the right formulation yielded 'wet' smoke bombs that were less risky to homebrew than more volatile pyrotechnics. Marc had discarded or eaten the sachets of food in the surplus NATO-issue MRE packs, but kept the flameless chemical heater pads that soldiers used to warm them in the field. Wrapped around the bricks of putty, the activated heaters took around twenty minutes to bring their contents up to flashpoint. The distraction was good, but it would only last until the non-lethal nature of it was revealed.

Marc didn't waste a second. He threw himself across the table and snatched up the Glock. To her credit, Tracey Lane didn't waste time trying to beat him to it, and she reeled back, tearing a short-framed Sig Sauer semi-automatic from a paddle holster in the small of her back. He registered the firearm with a distant, passing thought, realizing his earlier surmise about Lane carrying a tazer had been very wrong.

She was shouting something, but Marc wasn't listening. He was back on his feet, yanking Farrier up out of his chair, shoving him forward as a human shield. His blood thundering in his ears, Marc jammed the Glock's muzzle into the soft tissues of Farrier's throat.

'*Back the fuck off!*' he bellowed, his voice rebounding off the walls of the office.

Farrier went limp in his grip and Marc pulled him close, blocking the path of any shot Lane might be thinking of putting his way. The door behind her slammed open and the guard outside came in, his weapon drawn.

Marc pulled his hostage back to the wall and edged around the table. Lane was still shouting at him and he glared at her over Farrier's shoulder, choking out a threat. 'I will shoot him. Don't test me.'

In her eyes there was raw hatred. Marc had validated the woman's initial reading of him, and she must have felt a brief flash of conceit as she told herself how right she'd been.

'Mate,' Farrier was saying. 'Stop this now. You're only making things worse.'

'Don't talk,' he snapped. 'You!' He jerked his chin at the armed guard. 'Put the laptop in the backpack and slide it over. The wallet and watch too.'

Lane gave the guard a wary nod and he did as he was told. 'You won't escape,' she said. 'You know that.'

A harsh, broken chuckle threatened to push its way out of Marc's mouth. Escape wasn't his priority. As if to underline his point, the embassy's fire alarms belatedly started to sound. He prodded Farrier with the pistol. 'Pick up the bag.'

'Where are you going to go?' Lane demanded.

He answered her with gunfire. Shoving Farrier toward the open door, Marc fired two rounds up into the humming neon strip hanging over the table. The shots struck home, and the lighting tube exploded in a shower of sparks, plastic and glass. With nothing but evening twilight coming in through the window blinds, the interview room was plunged into shadows. It was the impetus Dane needed to shove Farrier out into the corridor, shouldering him through the doorway like a rugby full back bulling a flanker into the mud. He kicked the door closed and tipped a nearby rack of shelves across it, blocking the room enough to hinder Lane and the other guard for a few moments.

He turned in time for Farrier to come at him with the daypack, swinging it like an ungainly club. Marc deflected the blow before it could connect with his gun hand and swore violently. 'Move!' he shouted, pointing down the corridor with his free hand, waving the pistol with the other. 'Just bloody move!'

'You've lost it,' Farrier managed, as they threaded through the first floor corridors. 'Oh shit, I can't believe I helped you.' He stumbled to a halt and rounded on Marc. 'Did you do it? Fuck me, did you *actually* do it, you bastard? I know you never liked Nash, but Sam and Rix–'

The icy calm came back from where it had been hiding all this time and Marc shook his head. 'I'm innocent of that, if nothing else.' He nodded toward a door leading to one of the embassy's communications rooms. 'In here. Before they see us.'

'That's not a way out,' Farrier told him. 'No windows, no other doors.'

'I know. Go on, get in.'

Inside, the whine of the fire alarms was lessened by the thick sound-deadening door. The communication room was colder than the rest of the building, chilled by the action of air conditioning fans working to keep a small computer server and mainframe system operating, even in the most dazzling of Roman summers.

The moment they were alone, Marc spun the Glock around in his hand and offered it to Farrier. 'I'm sorry, John. But this is the only play I had.'

Farrier gingerly took the gun and made it safe. He rubbed at the reddening patch on his throat. 'I direct you to my earlier statement,' he managed. '*You've lost it.*'

'Likely,' Marc agreed, taking a seat before a monitor and keyboard. Faster and more secure than the old Aramis networks of the previous decade, MI6's intelligence messaging network booted up in short order. With a couple of quick commands, he bypassed the first layer of the emergency lockout triggered automatically by the fire alarm, and brought up a screen demanding a password and login. 'If you would do the honours?'

'You . . . want my network access? What good is that going to do? My clearance can't get you anything useful.'

Marc shook his head and snatched the backpack from him. 'You'd be surprised.' He opened the laptop and set it next to the monitor, snaking a thin cable between the two. Marc had programmed a quick-and-dirty search macro to match the pattern data taken from Novakovich's hard drive with the signal records in MI6's communication's database. He explained the high points of this to Farrier as he double-clicked a string of icons on the screen. 'I've got scraps of information, nothing more,' said Marc. 'But if I can compare it with Six's email logs, I can see who was talking and maybe even what they were talking about.' He shot Farrier a look that had more pleading in it than he liked. 'Proof, John. It'll be proof that someone gutted my OpTeam and hung it on me.'

Farrier put it together. 'That's why you did something as ball-achingly idiotic as coming to Rome. Because you knew I would be here?'

'Because *I trust you*,' Marc retorted. He lifted his hands up from the keyboard. 'Was that a mistake?'

The other man sighed heavily. 'You think someone's dirty back at the Cross, then?' He didn't wait for Marc to give him an answer.

'Ah, I'd be lying if I didn't say that I was suspicious about everything that happened at Dunkirk. And frankly, I never liked how that nasty little turd Welles has it in for you. He wants to fix the blame and call it done, take the win like a trophy or something.' Farrier shook his head.

'Welles says he's a team player, but I reckon he would set fire to K Section if you gave him matches and petrol,' Marc replied. 'I don't know the ins and outs of it, but he and Royce hate each other's guts.'

Farrier considered this, glancing back to the door to check it was secured. 'You reckon he's on the wrong side of . . . all that?' He gestured at the laptop.

'Not sure,' Marc admitted. 'But this'll help me find out who is.'

The other man put the Glock aside and came to the keyboard, typing in his codes with deliberate, two-finger precision. 'The moment I log on, it's going to raise a flag with security. They'll figure out what terminal I'm using and send a team.' He hesitated over the 'enter' key.

'Yeah,' said Marc, tapping it for him. 'They will. So step back and let me work.'

Farrier's codes were still valid. With a few short-cut commands, Marc drilled down through the layers of the secure communications framework and set a search running. He had already drawn up a file of parameters for the program to look for, a list of time and date tags, keywords from message headers, even commonalities in encryption methods. 'Think of it like a freight train timetable,' he said, speaking in a low voice, almost to himself. 'I know where the trains were. I know how many carriages they had. But what I don't know is where they went, or what was on them . . .'

'Suppose you find what you're looking for,' said Farrier. 'Then what?'

'Then I surrender. For *real.* And you get to be my character witness when I stand up in front of the Old Dog and tell him exactly who has been taking the fucking silver . . .'

Marc trailed off, and just as fast as it had come to him, the cold-eyed focus he had felt in the corridor bled away. His cheeks were suddenly hot and he felt light-headed. Farrier was saying something, but Marc didn't hear it. His world collapsed to the monitor in front of him and the dialog window across the middle of the screen.

Each sliver of data Marc had been able to glean from Novakovich's hard drive had a header string of letters and numbers. One by one they scrolled by as the search program sent a virtual shout out into the network, listening for the call back, for the echo of data that would signify a hit.

Every one of them was returning the same result; a single word in bold, repeated over and over until it filled the search column.

Failed. Failed. Failed.

'Oh hell.' The room swam around him, and Marc gripped the arms of the chair. 'No . . . That's not right. It should be there.' His voice rose. '*Why the fuck isn't it there*?'

Farrier saw the endless string of negative hits. 'Okay, I don't know this computer stuff like you, but I'm going to go out on a limb and say that looks bad.'

'It's bad,' Marc's reply was brittle.

It confirmed beyond the shadow of a doubt that someone was working against Marc at MI6, that with very deliberate and exacting care, all traces of covert electronic communications between Vauxhall Cross and Dima Novakovich had been excised.

'No loose ends,' he breathed.

SIXTEEN

Marc was propelled up from the chair by a burst of directionless fury. Frustration crowded in on him, and he snatched up the wireless keyboard from in front of the monitor, every last impulse in him wanting to smash it against the desk. In that second, all he wanted to do was *break something.*

It had been a waste, everything he had done. His elaborate ruse to gain access to the embassy, getting himself in a room with John Farrier so he could use his old friend's pass codes . . . All for *nothing.* His prize was gone, his targets one step ahead of him, just as they had been in Dunkirk and every day since.

'*Fuck*!' He let the keyboard drop and stood there, every muscle in his body tense with rage. He could almost hear the sound of his luck running out, like some far-off crash of thunder rolling down the hills toward him.

And then, as if fate was playing a joke at his expense, a single string of text in green appeared among the endless stream of dull red *Failed* fields.

Two words. *File Found.*

Like a drowning man grabbing at a rope, Marc snatched back the keyboard and his fingers scrambled across the buttons in a clattering rush.

'What is it?' said Farrier, frowning at the lines of impenetrable code.

'A temp file . . .' The words spilled out of Marc's mouth. He was almost giddy, snapped back from the bitter edge of failure in a heartbeat, desperate to see what single piece of data his search had recovered. 'It's something stored on the MI6 comm server while being moved from one stack to another . . .' He had to stop typing and physically force himself to take a calming breath. What lay before him was the ghost of file, a fragment of digital chaff caught in the cogs of the electronic communications system.

Whoever had gone through the server at Vauxhall Cross had been very thorough, but they had missed this one record because it was in the wrong place. 'It's like you scrunch up a bit of paper and toss it in the rubbish, only you miss and it falls between the bin and the wall, you don't find it for weeks . . .' Marc swallowed, aware that he was talking without thinking. 'It's an image.'

'Can we see it?'

Very carefully, Marc sent a copy to the laptop, then to make doubly certain he added a macro to send another out via email to the dozen anonymous file sharing data banks he used. Inside the shielded walls of the embassy building, the laptop's wi-fi wouldn't be able to accomplish that, but the moment Marc was outside it would zap off into the cloud, replicating itself in blind servers all over the globe.

The picture unfolded on the bigger monitor, a complex swirl of dull earthy colours, whorled like a fractal and dappled by shadows.

'Satellite imagery,' offered Farrier. 'Russian sourced, judging by that.' He pointed at a Cyrillic digital watermark at the bottom of the shot. 'Desert, mountain foothills . . .' He scanned the screen with a practiced eye.

'What have we got here?' Appended to the picture were notations in a language Marc didn't immediately recognize.

'That's Turkish,' Farrier went on. He leaned in to read. 'And this is Turkey. There's map coordinates here. Somewhere near the north-western border of Kahramanmaraş Province.' Off Marc's questioning look, he gave a shrug. 'I had some work there a while back.'

Marc knew better than to ask for more details. He pointed at a cluster of buildings at the foot of a hillside. 'This looks like a compound of some kind.' He wondered why the MI6 mole thought this image was important enough to email it to Novakovich.

'Not a military site, though . . .' said Farrier. He tapped the screen, indicating two words. *Yeni Gün*. '*New Day*,' he translated. 'I know the name. It's a charity group for kids in that region. Waifs and strays, war orphans, all that.'

They're just kids . . .

Farrier's words sparked a flash of recall in Marc's mind. For a second, he could smell burnt metal and hear Gavin Rix's voice in his ear as it crackled over the secure radio link. The memory made his skin crawl and he frowned.

Was there a connection, or was he just forcing two disparate pieces of data together to create a correlation that didn't exist? It wasn't something Marc had time to dwell on. Lane and the rest of the embassy security team were on their way by now, and every second he spent considering the fractional sliver of intelligence he had recovered was a second less he could spend making his next move.

Whatever the hell that is going to be, he said to himself.

Marc pulled the cables on the laptop, erasing the search program but leaving the secure terminal open. 'I've gotta go,' he said. 'Thanks again.'

'I can't cover for you this time,' Farrier told him, his eyes solemn. 'You can't come to me again, Marc. It's too risky, for both of us–'

'I know,' Marc said, cutting him off. 'And I'm sorry too, mate.' Without warning, he brought up the Glock and used the butt of the gun to club his friend across the temple. Farrier went down in a heap, dazed and bleeding.

He flinched at the violence of the act, but it was necessary if he was to keep Farrier blameless. The twist in his gut still felt like betrayal, though. Marc ignored it and slipped out of the office, sprinting away down the narrow corridor.

The embassy's first floor windows were designed to trap the shade of the day and keep the offices cool. Security concerns meant that from the outside, they were almost impossible to open, but from within it was a different story.

Marc would have liked the opportunity for a subtle approach, but that wasn't to be. His mind kept spooling back to a single toxic dread; *he had no plan for this*. The way he wanted it to play out, the way it *should* have, he would find the files he wanted, then offer a surrender – secure in the knowledge that he had the proof he needed to clear his name. He cursed himself now for being naïve, foolish enough to think that things might actually go his way this time.

Off the administration wing there was a room with a window that peered out over the ornamental pond at ground level. Marc loaded a trolley with cartons of copy paper, turning it into a makeshift battering ram. He shouldered it into the window with a crack that popped the seams around the toughened safety glass. On the second attempt, the window yawned open wide enough for him to scramble out with the daypack secure on his back.

From a distance, it hadn't seemed so high, but now as he contemplated the fall, Marc realized that there was enough of a drop from the first floor to the shallow pond to break his bones. He took it anyway, lowering himself as much as he could before letting go.

He cut the water with a hissing splash and hit the concrete bed beneath, hard enough that lines of fire shot up his legs and shocked his spine. Soaking the stolen Armani suit, he ran across the width of the pond, dodging around the spray from the fountains.

The white glare of torch beams bobbed among the embassy's pillars, crisscrossing as they searched for him. He glimpsed figures carrying the spindly shapes of Heckler & Koch MP5 SD3 sub machineguns. Marc had fired those during training, the snapping sound of the discharge reminding him of the pop of Christmas crackers. The weapons were discreet enough that the sound would be swallowed by the steady hum of the traffic out on the Viale del Muro Torto.

He moved into the wooded area of the embassy gardens, staying low. There was little doubt that any capture orders on him would now be shoot-on-sight as a matter of course.

Escape and evade, he told himself. *Easier said than done.*

The daypack bounced as he moved, staying in the shadows. He threw a glance back toward the main entrance where he had driven in with Torrance's Ferrari. Blue strobe lights shimmered on the other side of the big gates, an Alfa Romeo from the Polizia parked nose-to-nose with a fire tender from the Vigili Del Fuoco. Even if he could cross the open ground between here and there, the guards on duty would catch him well before he had a chance to step off British territory and back into Italian jurisdiction.

He did what was least expected of him – and the most risky. Marc turned back toward the main building and headed toward the far side of the compound. There was a service entrance over there for delivery vans and maintenance vehicles. As he moved, under the noise of the traffic and the steady bleating of the fire alarms, a low-pitched buzz caught the edge of Marc's hearing and he reflexively looked up – but then it was gone and he shook off the distraction. He moved around a skinny cypress tree, behind a leafy bush on a rise overlooking the service gate. The secondary entrance opened out on to the Via Palestro, and while the big metal gates had been partially drawn open, the retractable bollards blocking access to the road were still up.

Marc's hopes withered as he counted six armed figures forming a cordon around the gate. He caught sight of Lane, her pistol still drawn, in conversation with one of the guards. He couldn't make out what she was saying, but Lane's body language was more than enough to convey her ferocity.

'Not that way, then,' he whispered, drawing back into the shadows. Marc was about to turn away when he glimpsed a slow, black shape through the open gate as it passed by. A Toyota RAV4, identical to the vehicle that Marc had seen in his rear-view mirror on the way from the St Regis, crawled by at a steady, deliberate pace before disappearing behind the wall.

He wanted to tell himself that there was no way it could be the same vehicle, but the shape of the SUV and the tinted windows were identical. Marc moved back through the trees, paralleling the path of the side road. *If the SUV was* something, *if it wasn't MI6 . . .*

The buzzing noise interrupted his train of thought, and this time he was certain he had heard it. Marc aimed his pistol in the direction of the sound and saw a blur of motion; a spindly shape like two joined figure eights, clustered around a spherical pod.

The little drone flyer hovered a few meters over his head, bobbing in the light breeze, and he drew a bead on it. Wherever the thing had come from, it sure as hell wasn't Foreign Office issue, and if it was feeding images of him back to embassy security, he would never have heard the bullets that would have taken him down. Marc hesitated to fire at it, knowing that a gunshot would announce his location to everyone in the compound.

Slowly, the drone dropped down to head height. Then, with little flicks of motion, it buzzed toward the wall, stopping to wait for Marc to follow it.

'What's that, boy?' he asked it, as if he was talking to a dog. 'What have you got for me, huh?' The entire thing seemed surreal, and it was almost enough to make him burst out laughing.

He was close to the sheer grey expanse of the embassy wall when the drone suddenly zipped up into the air and over the coils of razor wire at the top. A second later, Marc heard a hollow cough of compressed air and a black nylon cord came streaming back over the wall, trailing from a grapnel head. It landed at his feet, an open invitation.

Marc threw a last look over his shoulder in the direction of the embassy, and holstered the Glock before snatching up the cord. He tugged it twice and got an answering pull in return. He barely had time to brace himself before the line went taut and he was yanked up off his feet. For one worrying moment, Marc feared he would be dragged through the sharp tines of the razor wire, but his ascent halted just short of the top of the wall, allowing him to gingerly negotiate the coils. From the far side, he could hear angry voices and see the flicker of torchlight reflected off the tree canopy.

Discarding the cord, he gathered himself as a door opened on the side of the SUV idling at the kerb. An athletic black woman with short hair and a wry curl to her mouth looked out at him. 'Hey,' she said, by way of a greeting. Over her shoulder, Marc saw what looked like a mil-spec equipment case packed with low-light video screens and control boards.

'Hey,' he replied, because he didn't have a better response.

'So I guess you need a lift.' Her accent was East Coast American, confident with it. She beckoned him with her index finger. 'C'mon.'

Marc made the snap decision and vaulted into the vehicle, hearing the wheels hiss against the asphalt as the Toyota bolted away and into a slewing turn that threw it down a narrow side street. He rolled with the motion and bounced on to a seat, struggling to keep his balance. Behind the woman, he caught a glimpse of sandy hair and a sallow face, but little more of the vehicle's silent driver.

The woman showed Marc a smile. 'So this makes it twice I saved your ass,' she told him.

'Twice?' he echoed, even as one of Farrier's questions came flashing back to him. *Who was the sniper in Walworth?*

'You don't have to thank me,' she added, pulling something from the folds of her jacket.

More police strobes flashed past as they turned on to the main boulevard, and Marc shot a worried glance out of the window. 'Where are we going?'

When he looked back, she had one of those dart guns in her hand, the kind that zookeepers in wildlife documentaries used to drug tigers. 'Out,' she told him, and the pistol chugged.

Marc saw a fast blur, as if a giant bee had thrown itself at his neck and stung him. He slapped at the pain as a wash of cold went through his veins, and his hand came away with a little blood on it, a feathered dart falling from his numbing fingers. He tried to talk, but his lips and tongue had suddenly turned into lifeless meat.

The inside of the SUV spun around him and warm darkness rose up to smother him.

The wind off the ocean rolled up over the decks of the *Santa Cruz*, plucking at the places where tarps had not been firmly tied down. Emerging from out of the threatening cloud, the helicopter seemed to approach in total silence, all sound of its rotors stolen away by the stiff breeze.

It passed up the length of the freighter and turned around. The loud clatter of the aircraft came from nowhere and the wedge-shaped fuselage of the German-made MBB BK117 dropped toward the deck of the ship. The loading hatch over the *Santa Cruz*'s main cargo bay had been reinforced to act as a helipad, and the pilot lined up the skids for a careful touchdown.

Two men watched the helicopter's arrival, the Serb with the eternally disdainful expression and the grimacing Englishman, who glared into the fading light of the day.

The BK117 landed with a heavy thud and the rotors were barely spooling down as the Serb barked out orders to a pair of crewmen, sending them up to secure the helicopter against the deck. Three figures climbed out of the aircraft, one less than there was supposed to be.

The Englishman wasted no time, shooting a look at the man who had piloted them to the ship. 'You Grunewald?'

The man shook his head. 'Ellis,' he said in a dry growl, jerking a thumb at his chest. He indicated the two others with him, one with a blank, hollow-eyed countenance and another with a sardonic measuring gaze. 'That's Teape. And the posh one, he's Grunewald.'

'You're the new man,' said the Swiss mercenary. 'Pleased to–'

He was cut off before he could continue. 'They said there were four of you coming. Where's the other one? What's his name, Cruz?'

'Ah,' said Grunewald. 'Let's just say his contract came to an unexpected conclusion.'

'Silly bastard fell into a volcano,' offered Ellis.

'You what?' The Englishman's face soured. 'Are you taking the piss?'

'It's not as dramatic as it sounds,' Grunewald replied, stepping down on to the weather deck. 'Your boy Dane has quite the survival instinct.'

'He ain't my boy,' came the reply.

'As you wish,' Gruenwald shrugged. 'But I'll say this for him, he's tenacious.'

'What the fuck?' The other man shook his head in disbelief. 'Shit, I've got here just in time, because obviously you lads don't even know how to deal with one slippery little prick!' He advanced on Grunewald. 'Listen. I don't know what the SOP was before, but now I'm on side, there will be zero screw ups, you read me?'

'You got a lot of mouth on you,' Ellis said, his eyes narrowing. 'Who the hell are you again?'

'Who am I?' The Englishman's fist came up in a blur and struck Ellis in the throat. Not enough to do any real damage, but enough to make him choke and stagger back against the lip of the cargo hatch. 'I'm *Tommy* fuckin' *Atkins*, pal. I'm the one running you now, so less of the lip.' Ellis reeled, and stopped himself on the verge of trying something in return. The other man looked back at Grunewald. 'So. What's that, two dead now? He's doing better than you.'

'It's not all bad,' insisted the mercenary. 'We leveraged the family to recover the hard drive from the yacht.'

'It's intact,' said Teape. 'I checked.'

'So push that, then.'

Grunewald shook his head. 'Dane's sister is under police protection. We can't get near them.'

The Englishman spat on the deck. 'Bollocks.'

The mercenary had the good grace to look contrite. 'Faso delivered the drive to the courier, as ordered . . . But I think we need to go up the line.'

That earned him a challenging glare. 'Oh yeah? You want to talk to the men in charge?' He shook his head. 'That's not your call to make.'

'I know they are not pleased,' insisted Grunewald. 'We have a lot of loose ends here, and I know there's been talk about going dark until the Dane issue is dealt with.'

'Yeah, well that ain't going to wash with Saladin and his fucking children's crusade.' He stopped as two figures approached from the stern, hunched forward against the wind. 'Speak of the devil.'

Khadir advanced, his face as stormy as the clouds. Jadeed hovered close to his side, his gaze in constant motion – back and forth between the mercenaries. 'Why was I not told a helicopter was meeting us?' demanded Khadir. 'Who are these men?'

'Consultants,' said the Englishman.

'This is *our* operation,' Khadir insisted, bristling at his tone. 'The Combine involved you in order to assist *us*.'

'And that's what we're doing,' replied Tommy. He looked back at Grunewald. 'Tell me you got one thing right, at least. Did you bring him his toys?'

The mercenary gave Teape a nod, and the dour American went to the rear of the helicopter. He opened the curved cowling around the BK117's cargo compartment, and removed a pair of long slab-like containers. Khadir jerked his chin and Jadeed stepped up to assist him.

'Open them,' he commanded.

Teape gave Grunewald a questioning look, but the other man waved him away. 'He bought them. Let him see them.'

'*Al Sayf* bought these weapons,' Khadir corrected.

Jadeed produced a lock-knife and used it to slice open lines of bright red security tape around the latches. Cracking the seal, Jadeed gave a grunt of approval as the contents were revealed.

Each container held a trio of narrow white tubes just under three meters in length, terminating in bright red caps and festooned with safety pins and warning tapes. Fins sprouted from the rear and the front of the tubes, and down the length of their bodies were lines of component numbers.

'From Hangzong Nanfeng, via Pyongyang, to you,' said Grunewald, with a smirk. 'The PiLi-5 short-range air-to-air missile. Accept no substitutes.'

'Happy now?' Tommy demanded.

Khadir met his gaze. 'And what of the other issues you spoke of?'

'That's a work in progress,' offered Grunewald. 'He got away from us in Sicily and resurfaced in Rome, but British Intelligence lost track of him there.'

'Fucking morons,' snapped the Englishman, and his use of foul language made both Khadir and Jadeed glare at him with open disdain. He didn't appear to notice, gesturing at Grunewald. 'They're worse than you are. Can't find their arses with a torch and a road map . . .' He shook his head. 'Doesn't matter. The Combine have a contingency is in place. Dane thinks he's clever, so we let him be clever. We're gonna kill two birds with one stone. We set out a box, we just have to put him in it.'

At first Marc thought he was drowning, and it was that hot flash of naked panic that kicked him back up above the surface of the chemical sleep dragging on him. He struggled against the pull of waves that wrapped themselves around him, catching him in a net he could not escape from.

Marc remembered the impact as the Lynx collided with the white-caps off Truro Shoal, the cold waters of the South China Sea filling the helicopter's cockpit and battering him back against his seat. He remembered it as if it were happening now, only this time he wasn't getting out, this time he was going to follow the crashed aircraft down into the deeps along with the rest of his crew–

And then he was kicking weakly at a snarl of fine cotton bed sheets, sliding against his own clammy skin. Marc rolled back and saw a curved arc of ceiling lit by soft lamps. His head felt thick and heavy, and it made it hard for him to think straight. Everything seemed to have an unreal, dreamlike quality.

'What was in that dart?' he said aloud, croaking the question through an arid mouth. Marc's hand went to his throat where the needle had gone in, and there was the raised dot of a fresh scab there.

As he climbed from the embrace of the bed, Marc was rewarded by a thudding headache that emerged from the depths of his skull and set up residence right between his eyes. Blinking owlishly, he surveyed his surroundings. He appeared to be in a small, oddly-shaped but very well-appointed hotel room with no windows. The air tasted dry and even draining the water glass he found on the bedside table didn't lessen that.

There was a vibration underlying everything that put him off-balance, but Marc couldn't tell if that was real or just some strange artefact of the drugs working themselves out of his system. A set of clothes – an expensive Nike tracksuit and matching trainers – had been left out for him, and he dressed as quickly as he could. Of the suit he had stolen from Callum Torrance, the daypack, the Glock pistol and his laptop, there was no sign.

Marc tried the door handle, expecting it to be locked. The fact that it wasn't caught him off-guard.

Stepping out of the room, he found himself in a thin corridor, and suddenly the reason for the unusual dimensions of the 'hotel room' became clear. The curve of the ceiling over his head, the steady vibration, the narrow confines; he was on board a wide-body airliner, one that was clearly designed around the needs of some very well-heeled passengers.

Marc crossed to a window and peered out. He saw the arc of a wing and an engine in the spill of illumination from the cabin, the pulse of a running light flashing steadily. He guessed that the jet was at cruising altitude, but in the darkness it was hard to be certain. After a moment, he gave up looking for landmarks and used the visible stars to figure a rough directional fix. They were flying east. He wondered about what that could mean, and turned away.

Across the cabin there was a man of average build and pale skin, his hair hidden under a watch cap. He gave Marc an even look, showing no sign of alarm at finding him up and around. Then, almost carelessly, he jerked a thumb at a door leading toward the aircraft's forward compartments. Without a word, he walked away, down the corridor Marc had emerged into and disappeared through a door to another cabin.

In its own way, Marc reflected, that was almost insulting. The pale man – Marc was pretty sure it was the same one who had been driving the RAV4 in Rome – considered him so little a threat that he didn't call for help or otherwise raise the alarm.

Scowling at the thought, he went through the next door, revealing a large conference room that filled the width of the aircraft. On one wall was an oil painting of the African veldt, and Marc's eyes were drawn to glassy plates in the surface of the table that dominated the room. He guessed that there were projectors, screens and other digital tech embedded in the rich wood. Like everything else on the plane, it was a bespoke setup.

The next compartment was a lounge area with a curved bar made of glass, dark red leather and brushed steel. Seated by a window, the woman who had drugged him looked up from the pages of a glossy French fashion magazine.

'Enjoy your nap?'

Marc held up his hands. 'I really don't want you to shoot me again.'

She cocked her head. 'I really don't want you to give me a reason to.'

His frown deepened, and he went to the bar, helping himself to a bottle of mineral water, draining it halfway in a single pull. 'What am I doing here? Maybe I should start with that.' His eyes flicked around the small sink behind the bar. There was a sharp cocktail knife for cutting limes within arm's reach. He thought about palming it.

'You're being kept alive,' she replied. 'All part of the service.'

He didn't like the way that came out, but before Marc could question her further, two men approached from the corridor leading to the jetliner's nose. Both well-dressed, one of them slender with a Gallic face, the other tall, dark and imposing, a serious cast to his expression.

He surveyed Marc with a measuring look, taking him in with a nod. 'Mister Dane,' he said. 'I am Ekko Solomon. Please accept my apologies for the manner in which you were brought here. I hope you understand it was the most expedient choice under the circumstances.'

'Right. Of course.' Marc met the man's gaze and found what seemed like honesty looking back at him.

'You've already met my driver Malte and Miss Keyes.' He nodded toward the woman.

'Call me Lucy,' she smiled.

Solomon indicated the man at his side. 'This is Henri Delancort, my executive assistant.'

Delancort inclined his head. '*Bonjour*.' He showed a brief, practiced smile that didn't reach his eyes. 'I apologize about the clothes. Your . . . suit . . . was quite soiled by your escape.'

'It was on loan, anyway,' Marc replied. 'Where's my gear?'

'Your computer is safe,' Solomon explained. 'I hope you'll understand that I had Henri examine it.'

'Custom encryption, very good,' said the other man. 'Not standard MI6 issue.'

'I don't work for Six,' Marc corrected. 'Not anymore.' He carefully put down the bottle. 'Look, if you're after Novakovich's drive, I don't have it. The Swiss guy took it.'

Solomon sighed and took a seat. 'Mister Dane . . . I think you may be operating under a mistaken assumption.' Marc listened as he spoke, trying to place the man's accent. East Africa, at a guess, perhaps Kenyan. It was hard to be certain. 'My people have been tracking you since you walked into Vauxhall Cross. I have been very eager to have a conversation with you. What I want . . . is to hear your side of the story.'

Marc said nothing for several moments, turning the man's words over in his thoughts. 'I know your name,' he said, at length. 'You're the founder of the Rubicon Group. A bit of a mystery man, someone likes to who keeps himself off the stage.'

'That is so,' Solomon allowed. 'I prefer my anonymity.'

'I also know that your company has a small division that's active in the field of private military contracting.' Rubicon, like any number of other PMCs working in the global theatre, were monitored as best they could be by British Intelligence. K Section back in London were peripherally aware of Rubicon's involvement in kidnap and recovery operations in Chad and Bolivia, work on close-protection details in Iraq and China, but that was their above-board stuff.

There were rumours that Rubicon had a hand in a number of less than legal incidents as well, but as with most ghost stories in the spec ops community, actual details were sketchy. Marc said as much to Solomon, watching the man for any reaction.

'There's a good reason for that,' said Lucy, answering for him. 'We work very hard at staying off the radar. And my boss here is pretty wealthy.'

'We don't fight wars for people, Mister Dane,' said Solomon. 'The majority of the operations my employees take on are subsidized by Rubicon itself, not those whom we assist. I have a different take on what soldiers without flags can accomplish for the world. Do you follow me?'

'Not really. And to be honest, corporate mercenaries don't have the best reputation these days.' Marc saw a glitter of silver as Solomon leaned forward, a thin chain showing against his throat through the open collar of a sea-blue silk shirt. There was something hanging at the end of the chain, but he couldn't quite make it out, some abstract piece of curved metal.

'That is so,' Solomon went on. 'But let me offer you a simple truth as a counter. It is a regrettable fact that no government can ever be fully trusted to make the truly right choice when confronted by an impossible situation. People elect their leaders in the hope that they are moral souls, but no-one is perfect. Inevitably, men are loyal in one of only two ways. They are loyal to their nation, even if that nation is misguided or wrong. Or they are loyal to avarice and greed, interested only in power and wealth. They do what they will to serve one of those masters.' He brought his hands together. 'When the time comes to make a moral choice between right and wrong, few can faithfully follow that path to the end. Men will do what is right *for them*, not what is *right*.'

Marc shifted uncomfortably. He didn't know where this conversation was heading, but he didn't like the tone of it. He couldn't be certain if Solomon was trying to convince him or threaten him.

'I built Rubicon from ashes,' said the other man. 'Ashes of war. I have worked hard to raise myself up from the poverty I was born into. Believe me when I tell you I have seen every kind of injustice, all across the heartland of my mother Africa. And now I have made billions of dollars from land and mining and technology. Now I can do something about it. As Lucy says, I am a very rich man.' He reached up to his neck and pulled out the silver chain between his fingers. 'I see you looking at this. Do you recognize it?'

Marc gave a slow nod. Now it was clear to him, he could see that the odd bit of discoloured metal was actually part of a weapon. It was the trigger from an AK-47 assault rifle.

'This is a reminder of the reasons I built Rubicon,' Solomon told him. 'I did it with one thought in mind. To serve no nation but justice.'

The other man's words didn't sit well with him, and Marc couldn't stop himself from showing doubt on his face. 'So . . . You're telling me that you founded a PMC force to act as, what? Vigilantes on a global scale?'

'That's one way of looking at it, I suppose . . .' said Delancort. 'But Mister Solomon prefers to consider the group's work as a force for good.'

'And what gives you the right to do that?' Marc studied Solomon, his own circumstances forgotten for the moment. 'What makes it okay for you to take the law into your own hands?'

'Many nation states have done that in the past. Your own Great Britain once did so. But it is not about power, Mister Dane. It is about *responsibility*. In a lawful, moral society, it is the responsibility of the rich man to see that the poor man does not starve. It is the responsibility of the strong man to see that the weak man is not preyed upon.' Solomon stood up again. 'Once a man has power, as I do, he has a moral imperative to use it for the betterment of the world.'

'That's a very laudable goal,' Marc replied, after a moment. 'How exactly do I figure into it?'

'You put your foot in something nasty, and some of it has stuck to you,' said Lucy. 'The Combine.' She said the name and Marc couldn't help but grimace. 'Rubicon have been tracking their network for a while now. We think your people at MI6 got caught up in something they are planning, and . . .' She trailed off. 'It hasn't gone well.'

Marc felt an irrational flash of annoyance at the woman's words, but he pushed the emotion away. 'I may be on the run from my own countrymen, but if you think I'm going to compromise MI6, you're way off base.'

'That's not it at all,' insisted Delancort. 'After we learned that you fled, we deduced that you would most likely come to Rome looking for John Farrier. You trained with him, *oui*? You trust him?'

'We are trying to do the same thing you are,' said Solomon. 'I want to find the members of this group and expose them. They are anathema to Rubicon and its ideals. The Combine exists solely to supply weapons and support to terrorist groups around the world. To maintain a state of global instability and gain wealth by abusing that imbalance.' He hesitated, glancing at Lucy. A silent communication passed between them, as if he were giving her permission to reveal a truth.

'We believe that the radical terror group Al Sayf are working with the Combine to prepare another major strike against the West. You're familiar with the bombing in Barcelona . . . That was just the curtain-raiser. All indicators point to an imminent attack on a major American city, but we don't know which. Rubicon was tracking a consignment of six Chinese-made missiles bought illegally from North Korea, and we believe that the Combine is going to supply them to Al Sayf.'

'We have lost our lead on the missiles,' Delancort admitted. 'The North Korean general brokering the deal died in what appeared to be a road accident.'

'Emphasis on *appeared*?' suggested Marc.

Delancort gave a grim nod. 'That is representative of a major alteration in Combine tactics. It is what the Americans would call a 'game-changer'. They are moving from dealing in weapons to being pro-active in organizing a terror strike. Al Sayf are the partners they have chosen for this unpleasant endeavour.'

'So why don't you alert the CIA or Homeland Security?' Marc replied.

'The Combine has penetrated several intelligence agencies,' said Delancort. 'A fact I think you are well aware of.'

Marc's jaw stiffened, but he let the comment pass.

'Will you work with us?' asked Solomon. 'We want the same thing, Mister Dane. To expose these men and stop them before another atrocity happens.' He hesitated. 'I know you have your doubts. But consider that if I simply wanted your knowledge, there are more . . . direct methods that could have been employed to get it. Lucy's intervention in London allowed you to escape death on that rooftop. And again, we assisted you in Rome. These are not the acts of those who wish you harm.'

There were reasons why this was a bad idea, Marc knew that. But he also knew that his luck had run dry in Italy, and the fact was he had no more cards to play. Without Keyes riding to the rescue, Marc would have most likely ended his life in a hail of bullets, or at best spent it buried in some ghost prison until he was old and grey.

He turned it around in his thoughts. There was an opportunity here. All that stuff about the Chinese rockets was news to Marc, but it fit the profile. If Solomon was on the level, if Rubicon really did have their own leads on the Combine, then having the backup of a multi-billion dollar corporation could come in very useful tracking down the people who had ordered the deaths of Nomad team.

Solomon's speech about responsibility had struck a chord with Marc, as much as it might have been idealistic, but he wasn't going to let that blind him to what was important to *him*. Marc saw Sam's face in his mind's eye, and once again a horrible second sense-memory came back with the smell of blood and fire. He drew a breath and let the moment fade.

'I'm certain the Combine have someone inside MI6,' he told them. 'I want to know who that is.'

Delancort and Solomon exchanged a look. 'We don't have that information.'

'Will you help me get it?'

Solomon nodded. 'If we can, we will.'

'Okay.' A strange sense of relief washed over Marc. 'I found something called *Yeni Gün*. It's a charity for war orphans in Eastern Europe.' He said nothing else. Marc wasn't about to trust these people with everything he knew, not yet.

'Henri?' Solomon gestured to Delancort, and the other man produced a data tablet from inside his jacket.

'*Une moment* . . .' He tapped at the device's screen, typing with his thumbs. 'I have it. The New Day . . . They have a number of 'rescue centres' for displaced and orphaned youths in Anatolia and the surrounding regions. The main office is in Ankara.'

'I found the location of what is supposed to be a New Day orphanage out in the foothills of the Taurus Mountains. I'm not sure what's there, but if the Combine's mole in MI6 thought it was important, it must mean something.'

Solomon went to an intercom panel on the wall and tapped a button. 'Flight deck.'

'*Silber here, sir,*' said a male voice. '*Are we dropping off our new passenger?*'

'No. Mister Dane has agreed to work with us,' Solomon replied. Marc didn't want to consider what exactly *dropping off* might have been a euphemism for, had he chosen to reject the billionaire's proposal. 'I need you to change course. Take us to Central Turkey.'

'*Will do*,' said the pilot.

Almost immediately, Marc felt the floor beneath his feet tilting gently as the jetliner eased into a slow turn.

Solomon came closer and offered Marc his hand. 'Thank you, Mister Dane, for your trust. I promise you it will be worthwhile.'

Marc took the other man's hand and found Solomon's grip was firm and steady. 'It's not like I had a lot of choice, yeah?'

He got a rueful nod in return. 'When someone's heart is honestly governed by what they believe,' noted Solomon, 'that is all too often the case.'

SEVENTEEN

Dawn was moving in as Solomon's A350 rolled to a halt at a private hangar on the far side of Erkilet International Airport. It was going to be another hot, arid day in the Turkish heartland.

Delancort produced another fresh set of clothes for Marc, comprised of German-made tactical boots, rip-stop cargo trousers and a lightweight jacket, and at length returned his daypack with the contents intact.

Marc didn't hesitate to activate the laptop and check the portable computer's security. His firewalls and lockout protocols had been tested but not penetrated, just as he had hoped. Still, he resolved to crack the laptop's case at the first opportunity to check for the presence of any bugs, key loggers or other unwanted additions. The daypack had also gained some extra content in the form of an emergency survival kit and a box of 9mm ammunition for the Glock. The pistol was in there too, and he was surprised to note that someone had cleaned it for him. *Five star service*, he thought.

'You may need that,' Delancort noted, nodding at the weapon. 'But let us hope not, eh?'

Marc walked down the jet way, blinking into the rising sun. He dug in the bag for the USAF-issue sunglasses that he habitually carried and wiped them clean. Lucy was waiting at the foot of the ramp, dressed in the same kind of almost-neutral clothing as he was. She was peering at a sheaf of paper maps, and among the sheets Marc saw a blow-up of the satellite image he had provided to Rubicon, the errant picture salvaged from the comm files.

'We can make this by late afternoon if we hustle,' she told him. 'A helo would draw too much attention. We'll take the highway.' She jerked her thumb at a battered Land Rover parked in the shadow of the jet. Malte, the taciturn driver, was in the process of loading the 4x4 with two equipment cases, one labelled with a red stripe, another with blue.

'Is he coming with us?'

Lucy shook her head. 'Just you and me, pal.'

'Oh, good.' Marc shrugged. 'I mean, he's such a talker. Wouldn't be able to get a word in edge-wise.'

'That's funny,' she said, in a way that suggested she thought the exact opposite.

She walked away toward the car and he trailed after her. 'Hey,' he said to her back. 'I, uh, suppose I should thank you. For Walworth.'

'Where?' Lucy didn't turn, giving Malte a smile as she passed him going the other way. The driver didn't even glance in Marc's direction, climbing back up the jet way without looking back.

'London,' Marc clarified. 'The roof.'

'Oh.' She paused to give the Land Rover's tires a desultory kick. 'Yeah. That guy was gonna smoke you, all right.'

'You didn't kill him, though,' Marc noted. 'I mean, you must have had the shot, right?'

She glanced at him. 'Wasn't my choice. It was yours.'

'He was just some tactical bod, he wasn't . . .' Marc halted, frowning. 'He wasn't Combine.'

'Whatever you say, slick.' Lucy climbed behind the Land Rover's steering wheel, pausing to fix a dun-coloured headscarf in place over her hair.

Marc took the passenger seat and found a threadbare cap he could pull down low to shade his eyes.

She glanced at him and smiled thinly. 'Relax, Dane. I'm not going to drive you into the desert to put a bullet in your head and dump you in a ditch. That's not Solomon's style.'

He tugged self-consciously on the bill of the cap. 'In the last few days, almost everyone I thought I could count on has tried to arrest me or shoot me. So I may have some trust issues at this point.'

Lucy chuckled and put the car in gear. 'Buckle up,' she told him. 'We'll work on that as we go.'

The early hour meant that traffic on the local roads was thin, and as they joined the D300 highway heading southeast out of the city of Kayseri, there were few cars but regular lines of trucks moving down the dual lanes. If there was a speed limit, Lucy Keyes didn't seem to have any desire to obey it, and she kept the Land Rover at a swift pace, weaving the vehicle around the larger, slower-moving cargo carriers. Beyond the edges of the dusty road, the landscape was an expanse of brown and grey, patched by slivers of greenery that flashed past in ill-defined blurs. The hills and the mountains dominated the view ahead, growing larger as they closed in.

At first, Marc's conflicted mood threatened to drag him away into a morose silence as his thoughts turned inward, but the last thing he wanted to do was dwell on the chain of events that had forced him into this situation. Second-guessing himself would only undermine his confidence, and right now he needed to keep his doubts at arm's length, until he could be sure that Solomon's people were really what they said they were.

'So.' He took a breath and looked across at Lucy. 'You're from New York City, right? But not Brooklyn, I'm guessing. I'd say Queens, yeah?'

She nodded, pursing her lips. 'Not bad. That's a pretty good call for a Brit, most of you guys can't tell the difference.'

'I'm good with accents,' said Marc, making a circular motion with his finger. 'Like some people have an ear for music, you know? Also I watch a lot of American telly.'

'Let me guess, cop shows?'

He shook his head. 'Nah, sit-coms. Cop shows are too close to the job. Plus they never get the little stuff right, and it pisses me off.'

'I heard that,' she agreed. 'People in Hollywood think if they park a yellow cab at the end of a street in LA, it's a dead ringer for Manhattan . . .'

>

'Or if there's a double-decker bus and some rain, it's London.'

'What, you guys have sunny days?' She smirked. 'Huh. Who knew?'

Out of nowhere, Marc felt an unexpected pang of regret. He'd grown up in London and lived there for most of his adult life. The sudden possibility that he might never get to return carried more weight than he was ready for. 'You . . . miss it? New York, I mean?'

'I miss the food,' said Lucy, with feeling. He sensed a moment of shared regret between them, as if they were both some kind of exile.

'How did you end up in all this? Working for Rubicon, I mean?'

She shot him a look, and he wondered if he had touched on a sore point. Lucy guided the Land Rover past a sluggish tanker truck and set her gaze on the view through the grimy windshield. 'It's no big deal,' she said, at length. 'I was Army green for a good while. No job for a lady, so my mom used to say. But I got a good eye, and I like guns. Delta was recruiting for Foxtrot Troop, so I opted in. Stayed for a tour.'

'I thought that was a myth,' said Marc. 'About Delta Force having an all-female squad . . .'

'Sure it is,' Lucy replied evenly. 'Just like it's not true that British Intelligence has its own covert strike teams.'

'Fair point,' he allowed.

'Uncle Sam may be old-fashioned, but he ain't stupid. Sometimes girls can get where boys can't.'

Marc nodded. 'You'll get no argument from me.'

'So you're ex-Royal Navy, right?'

He tensed. 'How do you know that?'

Lucy pointed at his arm. 'Cabot wristwatch. It's a dead giveaway.' Marc frowned. The military-issue dive watch was the only connection he still had to that part of his past. 'And also my boss is a billionaire, remember?' The woman went on. 'Information gets bought real easy, if you know how to deal.' She smiled again. 'So you're all about Queen and Country. From navy puke to covert spook, all for the union jack.'

'Something like that,' he muttered. 'And just so you know, we only call the flag the 'union jack' if it's flying on a ship.'

'Oh yeah?' Lucy cocked her had. 'How about that? Every day's a school day.'

They passed another car and the other driver leaned on the horn to show his displeasure at Lucy's cavalier attitude to the rules of the road. Marc cinched his seatbelt a little tighter.

'So why did you pack it in with the army?' He was aware that she'd tried to steer the conversation away from that subject, but Marc wasn't ready to let that drop without pushing a little more.

'Solomon made me a better offer,' she said. Lucy seemed as if she was going to say something else, but then the impulse faded. That was all he was going to get. Marc guessed there was more to the story, but he wouldn't hear it today.

She pointed at a road sign as they approached the outskirts of a town at the base of a low mountain. 'Pinarbaşi. We turn south here, to the provincial border. Roads will get rougher once we start into the foothills.'

Marc threw a glance over his shoulder, back down the highway. 'I can take the wheel for a spell, if you want.'

'No need.' Lucy didn't look away from the road.

Without an operation in progress, the Hub White command room seemed hollow to Talia Patel, still haunted by the ghosts of the events of OpTeam Nomad's fatal mission. For now, the room's large main screens were the only active system, each paired with the discreet bulb of a digital camera looking down on the table and the rank of chairs that faced them.

Welles and one of his ninth floor men were already there when she entered behind Royce, and he spared them both an arch look. 'Here we are again,' he began. 'We should stop meeting like this, Donald. People are going to talk.'

'Oh, Victor,' Royce said quietly as he sat down. 'Do sod off.'

Talia blinked at her superior's off-hand insult. It wasn't like him to so easily rise to the bait, but then the stress of recent days was starting to tell. Royce had repeatedly ignored suggestions to take some time away from operations, and Talia was aware that he hadn't been home for the last few nights.

Welles thought better of digging up any kind of comeback and covered the moment with a sniff and a glance at the clock on the far wall. The minute hand snapped around to the top of the hour, and the three screens lit up, along with red LEDs beneath the cameras. The displays showed an almost identical conference room set-up. Only the quality of the daylight and the time-stamp in the corner of the images broke the illusion. The other end of the teleconference was a room in the British Embassy in Rome.

Two people looked back out at them, a woman Talia didn't know, helpfully identified by the screen's image recognition software as LANE, T; and John Farrier, who seemed to have aged ten years since she last saw him in the flesh.

'*Secure*,' reported Farrier, his lips thinning. '*Let's get to this*.'

Ignoring any pretence at protocol, Welles leaned forward and launched into a cold-eyed snarl. 'I won't waste time by going through a laundry list of your security detachment's shortcomings. I don't care how Marc Dane got into the compound, but I do want to know how he got out of it again.' He glared at Lane and Farrier. 'Any takers?'

'*He had outside help*,' said the woman.

'Of course he bloody did!' snapped Welles. 'I wonder if he had some inside as well.'

Farrier's gaze sharpened. '*If you've got something you want to say, spit it out*.'

Welles produced a data pad and laid it on the table. 'I have information on a piece of OpTeam hardware Dane used to cause a road accident in the middle of Central London, tech that as far as my investigators can determine, he wasn't issued with.'

'*I don't know anything about that*,' Farrier replied, and Talia saw a stony cast come over the other man's face. Had Farrier actually intervened in order to get Marc free? She didn't want to think about the implications if that were true.

'I find it interesting that when Dane was on the run, when he had a million different places to hide, it was you he came looking for.' Welles cocked his head. 'According to the details from Lane's report, you were out of contact for almost fifteen minutes while Dane had you as his so-called hostage.'

'*He trusted me*,' Farrier snapped. '*Because you didn't give him any other option. That's why he came to my door*.'

'What did he say to you?' Royce spoke up.

'*I told him to surrender*,' Farrier went on. '*He wouldn't listen. He said he was innocent, that he had nothing to do with the loss of Nomad*.' The other man paused. '*And for the record? I believe him*.'

'What you believe is of little interest to me,' said Welles. 'Dane's a fugitive. He had the chance to come quietly and now he's racking up criminal charges like they're going out of style.'

Royce sighed. 'He wanted access to the secure messaging network. Your report says that he coerced you into giving him your passwords.'

Farrier nodded. '*That's right*.'

'Why?' said Royce. 'What was he looking for?'

'*Marc believes there's been a penetration at the Cross*.' Farrier let that statement hang for a moment, and Talia found herself stiffening at the possibility. '*He thinks the ambush that took out Nomad was expedited with the help of someone inside the circle*.'

'Which is exactly the kind of explanation he would give if *he* were that insider,' Welles insisted. 'An innocent man doesn't run.'

'He might if he thinks he's going to vanish down a deep, dark hole and never see the light of day again,' noted Royce.

Welles dismissed the comment with a snort. 'How long were you alone with him in the embassy comms room? What did he do while he was there?'

'*A few minutes. He got nothing,*' said Farrier. '*Check the logs yourself. He tried to break through the firewalls, and botched it. In the end, he gave up.*'

Talia glanced at her own pad, which contained the same reports Welles was referring to. A records dump from the embassy mainframe showed that someone had attempted to access the MI6 network through a secure terminal, but all the activity log contained were dozens of rebuffed calls as the system denied entry over and over again. The log made it seem like Dane had spent several frustrating minutes repeatedly trying and failing to get in.

But then Marc Dane was one of the best OpTeam field technicians they had, and Talia imagined that he was more than capable of erasing an *actual* activity log and replacing it with something like this, to blind them to what he had really been doing.

'For the moment, let's move on to a different concern.' Welles threw a glance at his pad. 'His escape route. The vehicle, the woman. Let's talk about them.'

Talia had given image captures from the embassy's exterior security cameras a priority run through every available database, and now she manipulated one of the screens to bring up a ladder of images. 'We're working on getting traffic camera footage from the police in Rome, but the Italian secret service are dragging their heels. They said, and I quote: 'The Servizio per le Informazioni e la Sicurezza Democratica expect complete disclosure of the situation in order to facilitate full co-operation'. They're making a lot of noise about what they see as a terrorist incident in their capital.'

'*We're telling them it was a hoax,*' said Lane. '*They're not buying it.*'

Talia went on. 'Without street footage, we can't lock down where the vehicle went after leaving the area, but our teams in image analysis have some facts about the car itself.' She showed them a computer model of the dark-coloured Toyota RAV4. 'Based on the weight distribution and axle height, the car was fitted with bulletproofing and other modifications. There's also evidence that they launched some kind of surveillance drone.'

'Show us the woman,' said Welles.

Off a nod from Royce, Talia brought up a different image, this one a blurry still of a dark face peering out of an open car door.

'Facial mapping gave us a good hit,' she explained. 'We found a seventy-one percent probability match.'

'Who is Dane's new friend?' Welles studied the still, taken just as Marc had vaulted toward the waiting SUV.

'When I ran her through the NATO force records database, we came across this.' The picture of the woman was replaced by a different image; the same face but younger, somehow harder. In the second photograph she was dressed in the sand-and-brown shades of a United States Army desert camo uniform.

'Lucille Roshanne Keyes,' said Welles, reading out the name appended to the file. 'Says there she was in the logistics corps.'

'*That's American shorthand for special forces*,' noted Farrier.

'Why would the cousins want to grab Dane?' said Royce.

'We don't think they did.' Talia shook her head. 'Keyes isn't with the Americans any more, at least as far as we can tell.' She put up a different file, and this one was an arrest warrant. 'Full details are classified, but there was an incident that resulted in Keyes being dishonourably discharged and convicted of criminal conduct. She was sentenced by a closed military court and remanded to the Naval Consolidated Brig in Miramar, Florida. Information on what she did and the terms of her punishment are redacted.'

Welles pointed at the screen. 'She can't be in a military prison and a Rome backstreet at the same time.'

'We have fragmentary reports about an escape four years ago from Miramar,' Talia went on. 'Keyes's details appear on a fugitive watch list very shortly afterwards. I'll need to reach out to the US Department of Defence or the CIA if we want hard data.'

Royce shook his head. 'Don't do that unless we have absolutely no other option. The last thing we want is the Langley boys getting involved in this. Sir Oliver would hang the lot of us.'

'Still time for that,' Welles retorted. 'So we have a former US spec ops shooter, possibly still being run by the Americans but more likely selling herself to the highest bidder, acting as taxi driver for a rogue British intelligence officer. Who wants to be the one to break news of this delightful development to the director and the JIC?' No-one spoke, and so he turned his glare on Farrier. 'You listen to me. I want you on the next RAF transport back to Brize Norton, is that clear?'

Farrier looked to Royce for support, but the other man just shook his head. 'There will need to be a more thorough debriefing,' Royce said.

Talia saw Farrier's stony expression slip for a moment, before it hardened once again. '*All right*.'

'Lane, you handle things there. Lean on the locals, get that camera footage,' Welles told her. 'We need to know where Keyes took him, if they're still in Italy or not . . . Get it done.'

'*Yes, sir*.' Lane gave a nod and the screens went dark.

Welles rounded on Royce. 'A redacted file. You know what that suggests, Donald? This Keyes woman did something so unpleasant that her commanders wanted her buried alive.' He drew in a sharp breath through his teeth. 'That's our phantom sniper. And I wouldn't be surprised if she was there in Dunkirk to kill Dane's team mates as well.'

'You don't know that–' Royce began, but there was no strength behind the denial.

'Open your eyes!' Welles barked, startling Talia. 'You think I'm trying to shaft you because of the chequered history between us? Well, let me make this crystal clear.' He leaned in. 'As much as I dislike you, I will bring Marc Dane to book because I believe he's responsible for killing British servicemen and betraying his oath to the crown, not because I want to knock off K Section. Now, you either get on side with me and fix the holes in your leaky ship, or you'll go down with him.'

He pushed past Talia and out of Hub White, his assistant trailing silently behind him.

She turned to Royce, but he wouldn't meet her gaze. 'Sir, I . . .'

'Just find him, Talia,' he said bleakly. 'Before he can cause any more problems.'

The road degraded with every mile they travelled, losing the asphalt and then the dust and gravel until it was only the most basic suggestion of an actual track.

A sun-faded *Yeni Gün* sign, the colours bleached away into nothing, rattled gently in the dry winds by the entrance to the orphanage compound.

There was no movement around the discoloured walls, and Lucy turned the Land Rover about in a slow crawl, the tires crunching on the desiccated earth. She scanned the windows, black squares punched through the sides of the silent blockhouses, looking for threats.

As the grumble of the engine died, Marc heard the moan of the steady breeze, and the desolate cluster of buildings seemed like the loneliest place on Earth.

'Stay alert,' said Lucy, reaching down into the wheel well to grab her backpack. 'We don't know what we're gonna find here.' She reached inside and her hand came back with the compact shape of an MP7 sub machinegun. She cocked it with a snap of the receiver, and handed Marc a walkie-talkie. 'Just in case,' she added.

Marc followed her out of the Land Rover, slipping out of the door with his bag over one shoulder. He had the Glock ready, close to his chest and his finger resting on the trigger guard. He felt acutely aware of every tiny detail around them, the crumbling rocks beneath his boots, the heavy heat of the late afternoon sun, the weight of the loaded gun.

Lucy called out something in a language that sounded like Arabic and then again in English. 'Anyone here? Show your face.' No answer came back to them, and she moved off.

Marc kept with her, glancing at the razor wire fences. All that was needed to hammer home the ghost town nature of the compound were some rolling tumbleweeds. They approached a covered quad near two long, low huts. Thick tent cloth kept the whole area in shade, and it snapped as the wind passed over it. Marc paused in the shadow and peered up at the underside of the material, noticing the strange metallic weave. 'That's thermal baffling up there. Designed to reflect heat. Russians used it during the Cold War to fake out spy satellites with infra-red cameras.'

'Whoever ran this place was taking precautions,' Lucy noted. Her manner had shifted from the attitude she displayed on the ride up here. Her dash of the brash was replaced by something cooler, more professional. She pointed at one of the dusty pre-fabricated huts. 'Let's take a look.'

The outbuildings were repurposed Quonset huts, Second World War vintage, curves of rusting galvanized steel vibrating with the heat of the day. A musty odour hit him as he entered, sparking unpleasant recall of sweaty changing rooms in the comprehensive school where he had spent his early teens. Ranks of bed frames stood in lines all the way to the far wall.

'This is where the kids slept, I guess . . .' said Lucy. 'Beds are too short for adults.'

Marc fell into a crouch and used his phone to snap a couple of pictures. 'Scrape marks on the floor.' He pointed them out. 'No dust on the frames, so they must have been used recently.'

'The hallmarks of an evacuation,' she said, looking around. 'Move on. The main building next, I reckon.'

They crossed the covered quad and headed toward the only two-storey building in the compound. Marc thought he saw something more than just shadows in the lee of one of the support poles, a dark, rust-brown patch on the sandy ground, but he didn't draw attention to it. He followed Lucy's silent hand gestures to stack up either side of the front door and slowly ease it open.

The door was already hanging loose, and it gave a sullen creak as it came the rest of the way. Marc braced himself, imagining that there could be some angry thug with an assault rifle waiting within, but there was no hail of bullets, no sudden report of fire.

The building was as dead as the rest of the orphanage, dark where the shadows feel deep, lit only by shafts of sunshine that caught motes of dust as they advanced down the main corridor. The first room they came to had towers of wooden cubby-holes either side of the door, and Lucy used her booted foot to kick it open. Over her shoulder, Marc glimpsed an almost empty space with a few scattered cushions in one corner and a thick red carpet on the floor, the colour worn pink by years of feet and hands upon it.

'Classroom,' he suggested.

Lucy scowled, seemingly reluctant to enter, and she peeled back the headscarf she was wearing to set it around her neck and shoulders. 'Prayer room,' she corrected.

Marc drifted across the corridor to the next door, which opened on to a windowless space with reinforced walls. Empty rows of shelving filled every available corner, and the scent of machine oil was soaked into the brickwork. The shine of brass caught his eye and he plucked a lone bullet from where it had fallen to the floor. It was a live 7.62 round, the ammunition of choice for the venerable Kalashnikov assault rifle. 'They missed one,' he said, placing it on the shelf, standing alone like a tiny, tall-hatted sentry. 'What kind of orphanage has an armoury?'

She didn't answer him, instead pointing with the MP7. 'Anything we can use will probably be on the upper floor. We need actionable intel.'

Marc followed her back out and then up the creaking stairs, wondering if this expedition would bear fruit.

He thought again about Rix's words on the *Palomino*, in those moments before the ship had been consumed in fire. Rix had said there were children on the ship, and Marc couldn't help trying to connect that with the lead that had brought them here, thousands of miles away, to a place that was supposed to care for lost youths and war orphans. If the *New Day* charity was cover for a partnership between the Combine and Al Sayf, then it was singularly callous one.

On the upper floor, there was the heavy trace of burnt paper in the air. Low on one wall, Marc saw a scrawl of writing in hasty calligraphic script, scratched into the peeling paint across the brickwork. 'Kilroy Was Here,' he said aloud, guessing at the significance of the tiny act of defiance.

'It's a name,' Lucy told him. '*Halil.* It means 'good friend'.'

'You read Arabic as well, then?'

'I got a lot of talents,' she replied. 'Trigger-puller is just my best one.' Lucy pointed across the hall. 'Check this out.'

Marc followed her into another room, and inside the stench of dead fires was thick, the roughness of the soot collecting at the back of his throat. Along one side of the room, a desk had been piled high with papers and set alight, left to burn until all that remained were ashen piles that retained some ghost of their original shape. Battered filing cabinets sat with their drawers hanging open, emptied of anything that might have been useful.

Lucy stopped suddenly and dropped to her haunches, shouldering her MP7 on a bungee sling so she could have both hands free.

'Problem?' said Marc.

'Look-see,' she replied, pointing.

Marc peered at the floor and made out a thin line of fishing wire suspended at ankle-height. 'Oh bollocks,' he breathed, as he followed it to its end. Hidden in the debris was a roughly egg-shaped object Marc recognized as a Soviet RGD-5 anti-personnel fragmentation grenade. The part of his memory that belonged to his techie soul – the bit of him that was the legacy of a bookish child who could name a hundred kinds of dinosaur or recognize all the variants of a Spitfire – dutifully reeled off the specs of the device in a way that wasn't at all comforting. Most notably, he remembered that the Russian grenade had a timer that could easily be set to anything from twelve to *zero* seconds.

'Yeah,' agreed Lucy. 'Stay back . . .'

'No, I got this,' he said, pulling a folding multi-tool from his belt. Without waiting, Marc moved in and severed the line. In a few moments, he had made the booby-trap safe.

'Huh,' she said, and there was something new in her eyes, something that could have been respect. 'You're good for something.'

Grunewald looked up as the hatch banged open and the Englishman that the jihadis called Tommy strode in. His thuggish glower swept the compartment and found the mercenary. 'Well?' he demanded. 'What have we got?'

'See for yourself,' said Grunewald. What had once been one of the *Santa Cruz*'s smaller cargo bays had been converted into a makeshift operations room with video monitors and a military communications rig. A blurry ten-second loop of footage, black-and-white imagery shot from great altitude, showed a sparse landscape and a cluster of buildings.

Teape, who sat before the workstation, pointed a long finger at the bottom of the screen. 'There.' The video loop ended and started again, and where the American indicated, a light-coloured rectangle moved into the frame and performed a slow circle. 'Mid-size vehicle,' he noted. 'Two people get out.' Ellis stood watching off to one side.

'Where's this come from?' demanded the Englishman.

'Camera time leased off one of the Indian government's 'weather' satellites,' Grunewald sniffed.

'That could be anyone down there,' Ellis spoke up.

'It's him,' said Tommy, nodding to himself. 'Yeah. No other fucker is going to grind up miles of dirt road to that shit-hole without good reason. He took the bait.'

'What bait?' said Ellis.

Tommy answered without looking at him. 'The problem with clever bastards is, they like being clever. So you give them something that makes them feel smarter than you, they're at it like a rat up a drainpipe.' He leaned in and tap-tapped one of the moving dots on the screen, as if he could speak to the person it represented through the gesture. 'You hear that, mate? We led you there, you little prick.'

'We lost direct video a couple of minutes ago,' said Grunewald.

The Englishman ran a hand over his chin, rasping at the stubble there. 'Khadir's boys left booby-traps, might have done the job for us . . . But best to make sure. Belt and braces.' He pointed at another monitor, which showed a tactical map of the area off the Turkish coastline. 'The Yanks are still out there, right?'

Grunewald nodded. 'But we won't have access for much longer. If we are going to use them as an asset, we have to do it soon.'

Tommy grinned wolfishly. 'Well, then. Better let them have some.'

'Proceed,' said Grunewald, placing a hand on Teape's shoulder. The American nodded, and typed in a pre-designated communications code into the keyboard in front of him.

Hundreds of kilometres to the east, a task force from the United States Navy's Sixth Fleet out of Naples lay on station. The flotilla sat in a staggered row across a small corner of the Mediterranean, almost following the sword-tip line of Cyprus's Cape Apostolos Andreas, toward the edges of Syrian territorial waters. The US Navy's mission brief in the area was defined to the rest of the world as 'tactical presence', a very visible deterrent to the belligerent forces of ISIL in the local theatre and a way of rattling America's sabres at nearby Russian military assets. There were also other facets to the operation that were less perceptible to global observers.

One of them was designated as Tasking Element Argonaut, a rapid-reaction mission that could be deployed within minutes from the task force's main aircraft carrier. Argonaut's objective was simple and direct – to use fast, stealthy UCAV drones to take out sites designated as terrorist training camps or other 'targets of opportunity'. Battle planners in the US Navy, kept out of the evolving drone war by the dominance of the USAF, had been only too happy to secure their future budgets by taking on the mission, showing that sea-based unmanned combat aircraft could do the job just as well.

It was no coincidence that assets managed by the Combine were also embedded in the command and control pipeline of Argonaut. Under the guise of orders direct from Washington, signed off on by military chiefs sympathetic to Combine interests, it only took a few short moments for Teape to contact the flotilla and impersonate a naval officer halfway across the world.

'Stormline. Action order,' announced Teape, speaking into a headset microphone, using the carrier's radio ID code. 'Tasking Element Argonaut, expedite immediate. Deployment confirmation is–' He paused to peer at a slip of paper on the folding table before him. 'Romeo Nine Seven Kilo Two Zebra Lima. How copy?' The value of that string of letters and numbers was measured in the ghostly coin of the Combine's power and influence.

There was a crackle of static, and then a voice responded. '*Good copy, code matches, Stormline confirms. Deployment under way. Stand by.*'

Grunewald smiled thinly. Somewhere out in the Med, a robot aircraft was being hustled to a deck elevator, and within ten minutes it would be airborne. He glanced at another screen, where the details of a 'strike package' were displayed. This was the pre-programmed mission for the UCAV, a series of waypoints and direction markers now being uploaded to the Navy drone. The strike had been planned months ago, as just one more constituent of a larger plan, as another method of erasing a loose end left behind by the collaboration with Al Sayf. The mercenary glanced at Tommy. It had been the Englishman's idea to delay the use of the drone after the problem with the technician Dane had blown up, to use it now and, as he put it, *kill two birds with one stone.*

After the launch, the drone jet would vanish below radar detection height and cross the Turkish coastline, powering northward. Such an action would be a violation of the borders of a NATO member nation, so all the more reason to ensure that no human pilot would be part of the mission loop, and that no direct control by the mothership would be in place by the time the UCAV reached its target.

In an hour the drone would be back over the Med, circling the carrier it had launched from, its weapons load a little lighter and its mission record scrubbed clean. And they would have one less problem to concern them.

'*Argonaut Two is away*,' reported the radio voice. '*Good launch*.'

'Confirmed,' Teape responded.

An unpleasant sneer tugged at the corner of Tommy's lips. 'If this don't do it,' he said, almost to himself, 'I'll walk out there and strangle the bastard myself.'

EIGHTEEN

Marc had assumed that after the whole trip-wire situation, Lucy's rather confident attitude might have toned down a little, but that didn't appear to be the case. He winced as she used a swift kick from an army boot to smash open the lock on a door, the mechanism coming away with a crunch of fresh splinters. The upper floor's corridors converged on this one doorway, and Marc guessed that the building had been deliberately constructed to have two distinct 'sectors' that could only be accessed via chokepoints. His theory was confirmed when they found poorly-built walls extended out into the passage, making it into a chicane.

Lucy threw him a look. 'See those?'

He nodded. 'To slow down anyone coming through. Blockades to break up lines of fire.'

'Which means the people here were paranoid about getting a SEAL Team wake-up one dark night.'

'Yeah, something like that.' With the Glock held close, he eased open a door off the main corridor and peeked through. It was another dormitory, but unlike the ones in the outbuildings, this was better appointed. Of course, 'better' was subjective, in terms of having actual glass in the windows, and a ceiling that wasn't pock-marked with holes. The denuded bedsteads were clearly adult-size bunks, with cloth privacy curtains hanging between them like limp flags. A widescreen television set up in one corner of the room was the only thing that seemed out of place, and Marc noticed a DVD player and a pile of discs at the foot of it.

'I'm guessing those aren't rom-coms,' Lucy offered.

'They bunked the adults here,' Marc moved away, back down the corridor. 'Like tutors and pupils in a boarding school.'

She followed him, frowning. 'Safe bet they weren't teaching them about peace and harmony.'

The corridor ended at a lightless stairwell that went straight down to the basement, vanishing into the hot shadows. Lucy held out a hand to him, her expression turning stony. She said nothing, instead making a silent gesture that told Marc to keep behind her. He nodded and let her take point.

Lucy brought the MP7 up, the muzzle hunting for targets. Marc held his pistol out and down, ready to snap it up to firing position if he saw a threat.

They descended into the darkness, and the air closed in on them, thick and unmoving. A cloying smell seeped into Marc's throat and nostrils. Lucy eased open a rusty door and the odour came at him full force.

Charred meat. The same awful, charnel house stench from the docks in Dunkirk. He swallowed hard, tasting the acidic burn of bile in the back of his throat, and gripped the gun tighter.

The room was a large space, floor and walls tiled in washed-out sea green. Illumination blazed from a buzzing neon tube that threw stark light across everything.

In the middle of the room was a discoloured drain grille set at the hub of a dozen shallow gutters, and gathered around it were patches of what could only be blood. Flies spun around the freshest of the brown puddles. Marc turned slowly in place, not wanting to but unable to stop himself from picturing what had taken place here. A metal autopsy table had been shoved off to one side.

'Gunshot kills,' Lucy announced, her voice flat and empty.

'What?' Marc's mouth was dry.

She pointed at the patches. 'If a knife had been used, there would be spray. Someone . . . More than one . . . Was brought down here and shot dead.'

Marc forced himself to study the scene dispassionately, and he saw holes in the tile where some eager executioner had missed with their first shot, or else put a bullet right through the body of their subject. 'What the hell is this all for?'

She didn't answer him. Instead, Lucy made for another steel door on the far side of the room. Poorly-oiled hinges gave a low moan as it opened and dry, dusty air wafted out.

The other section of the basement took up the rest of the building's lower level, dominated by a large furnace. It was barely alight, but still a weak glow shone through the gaping maw of the fire pit, and Marc glimpsed spindly shapes among the ashes that he didn't want to study more closely.

Lucy didn't share his reticence. She peered inside, before turning her head to spit. 'Fuck,' she breathed.

Marc's gaze dropped to the floor and he found himself looking at pieces of torn paper, probably dropped from piles of documents as they had been taken to be burned. He crouched, grateful for something else to focus on. The paper was yellow, tissue-thin, the kind of tear sheet that you would be handed by a deliveryman. He used a pen to tease the fragment open and saw strings of symbols he couldn't read. 'Hey,' said, without looking up, 'what does this say?'

Lucy loomed over him, scowling. 'A date? Not sure. You think that could be something?'

He nodded. There was part of a letterhead visible, and a logo that showed outlines of a truck, a plane and a boat. 'Might be a bill of lading.' Marc cast around and found more bits of paper with the same colour and form. 'Maybe several.'

She drew a black rectangle out of her pocket and offered it to him. 'Take pictures. Use this.' Lucy paused to look at the device – it was a smartphone of some kind, but Marc couldn't see any manufacturer's mark or identifying symbols. The phone beeped and came alive. *A facial recognition lock,* he realized. Rubicon were clearly serious about operational security for their field agents.

He smoothed out the pieces of paper on the dusty floor and took a string of shots, the smartphone's bright flash lighting up the room like a strobe. 'I've got some image processing software on my laptop we could use on this . . .'

Lucy shook her head. 'Solomon's got a whole lab full of geeks for that.'

'Oh. Right.' Marc nodded to himself. He'd become used to working alone in the past few days, and it seemed strange to think about being part of a 'team' again, even if it might only be a temporary state of affairs.

She snatched the phone from him and tapped out a string of text on the screen. 'No signal down here.' Lucy handed it back again. 'Go outside, see if you can get a couple of bars. It'll send the email automatically.' She looked away. 'I'll see what else I can find.'

Marc took the opportunity without hesitating, grateful for it. The sickly air of the basement was oppressive, and all he wanted at that moment was to be out of there.

Marc came to a halt and shielded his eyes with the flat of his hand, blinking owlishly into the sunlight. He took a deep breath of fresh air and tried to convince himself that the death-stink from the basement hadn't followed him out here. As much as he wanted to think about something, *anything* else, his thoughts kept returning to Dunkirk, to the weight of Sam Green's body in his arms and the ashen stench that was that all that remained of her hours later, clinging to him as if it had soaked into his pores.

'Piss off!' He spat the curse at nothing, angry at himself, dispelling the horrible moment of recollection with a snarl.

The Land Rover was nearby, and he trudged over to it, opening the passenger door to find a bottle of mineral water lodged in the footwell. The water was warm and tasted of plastic, but it helped wash away the scent-memory. Marc drained most of it and then on impulse, he tore off his cap and splashed the remainder over his face and neck. It seemed to help.

Pulling Lucy's ghost-phone from his pocket, he held it up and moved around in a circle, squinting at the line of signal bars as he wandered across the quad. He must have looked like an idiot, arm out above his head, waving at nothing. Out here a decent cellular link was more rare than a rainy day, but Marc was willing to bet that Mister Solomon would equip his people with something a little better than the latest device from Apple. The device gave off a sonar-like ping as it found the thinnest margin of a carrier signal, and presently a little icon flashed into life, showing a letter zipping away into the ether.

'Done . . .' Marc began, dropping his arm. He was turning back toward the main building when he saw sunshine flicker off something moving fast against the distant hillside.

He was still processing what he saw when the wind brought him the rolling whine of an aero engine. The sound immediately seemed *off*. The pitch was all wrong, too high for a fighter jet, not enough bass and chop for a helicopter.

Then he saw it again, and Marc's mind caught up with him at shocking speed. Still distant, but clear as it crested a scrub-covered hill, he saw a torpedo-like fuselage sporting twin tail planes and sharp-edged wings, with the dark void of a jet intake across its dorsal hull.

Marc snatched the walkie-talkie from his belt and mashed the transmit tab. 'We have a problem!' he shouted. 'We got incoming aircraft!'

The American woman's voice crackled back at him. '*Turkish Air Force?*'

He shook his head, not that she could see the gesture. 'Only if the US Navy has started selling them Sea Avenger UCAVs.' The drone passed behind another hill, banking toward the compound. 'It's definitely coming this way–'

Marc's words cut off as the unmanned aircraft made a fast pass over the orphanage, and the whining engine echoed off the landscape. The sunlight flash came again, and now the drone was close enough that he could see it reflecting off a pod along the centreline of the aircraft, a cluster of lenses feeding images back in real-time to whomever was directing the machine.

When Lucy's voice came over the radio again, he heard the grim resolve in her voice. '*That thing is here to kill us.*'

'I'm pretty damn sure I haven't done anything to annoy the American government!' As he spoke, Marc was keeping low, watching to see where the drone would pop up.

'*The Navy didn't send it*,' she said flatly. '*It's a loaner. Listen to me, small-arms won't be enough to deal with it. I need you to get to the car, get the gun case.*'

Rather than answer, Marc broke into a sprint across the quad, back toward the Land Rover. As he moved, he heard the echo of the drone's engine. It was turning, gaining height. That first low-level pass had been to scope out the target. The next approach would be rolling in with weapons hot. Marc knew the Avenger UCAV could carry a reconnaissance package, a load of 250-pounder bombs or – as this model did – clusters of lethal AGM-114 Hellfire air-to-ground missiles. Even a near-hit from one of them would be enough to bring an explosive end to Marc Dane's fugitive odyssey.

He slammed into the side of the Land Rover and scrambled to the rear door, wrenching it open. The two cases he had seen Malte loading that morning at the airport were still there, one with a red stripe across it, another with a blue stripe resting on top.

As Marc's fingers closed around the handle of the blue case, from behind him he heard a distinct shift in engine pitch as the drone came around. Marc hauled the long case out with a grunt of effort – it was heavier than he had expected – and he couldn't stop himself from casting a look over his shoulder.

It was a decision he immediately regretted. He saw the drone in the near distance, nose-low and framed against the afternoon sky. There was a flash of ignition beneath the Avenger's belly as one of the missiles dropped from its internal munitions bay. The Hellfire came curving in, a trail of white smoke describing its approach.

He vaulted away from the Land Rover, the case held in a death-grip, running as fast as he could across the quad. Marc heard the shrill, falling shriek of the missile as it dove at the parked 4x4, the warhead meeting the metal of the sun-warmed hood with a massive thud.

He left the ground and tumbled as a wave of burnt air hit him from behind and blasted him off his feet. He lost the gun case and landed hard on his shoulder, rolling across the ground. Hot, petrol-stinking fumes washed over him and he choked on dust.

Marc scrambled to his feet. The Land Rover was gone, what pieces of it remained reduced to blackened twists of steel. A flaming pit marked the strike point, a pennant of dark smoke curling up into the air. The wind pulled at it, dragging the haze across the compound. His ear felt wet and he touched it, his finger coming away bloody. Some tiny fragment of the exploding car had nicked him as he fled.

Up above, the drone was already turning inbound for another attack run.

'Good kill,' said Teape, watching the feed from Argonaut Two. The screen in front of him resembled some abstract war game simulation, the buildings of the orphanage compound rendered as blank boxes and the contours of the local landscape a series of nested green lines. The feed was coming in with a near-zero delay, beamed right to the *Santa Cruz* by a clandestine link off Stormline's network.

'If he's still breathing, then it's no kind of kill at all,' sneered Ellis. He was watching a different monitor, this one a side-looking view from a video camera in the Avenger drone's recon pod. He pointed to a flicker moving below as the UCAV banked. 'Still got a live target down there.'

Grunewald said nothing, turning to glance at the Englishman. The soldier's face was set in a hawkish glare, watching every return on the main screen in front of Teape. Tommy leaned forward and pointed. 'Cover,' he noted. 'Target that and hit him again.'

Teape nodded and moved a mouse pointer over the tactical display, click-dragging a targeting box over the tent-like structure the Englishman indicated. He wasn't strictly piloting the drone – the Avenger's on-board computer was smart enough to manage something as simple as a standard flight path – but it was still necessary for an element of human input to be required for the firing of an actual weapon. The drone obeyed Teape's new orders and shifted position, bringing its nose to bear so the next Hellfire could acquire the designated target.

At the other screen, Ellis was running the video feed back a few moments. A hard drive stored a digital recording of everything the drone observed, and now he set the playback running in slow reverse, the moment of the first missile hit unfolding backwards. Grunewald watched the orange fireball shrink and fade, the Hellfire rebuild itself and retreat from the parked Land Rover. At length, Ellis found what he was looking for and drew the other mercenary's attention. 'There he is.'

Grunewald looked, and saw that Ellis had captured a single frozen image. A man, running at full tilt to escape the destruction of the vehicle. It was undoubtedly Marc Dane, the same ragged hair and the unshaven face he had seen atop Mount Etna. 'He should be dead five times over,' Grunewald said sourly.

'Luck,' offered Ellis, the word like a curse. The dour Afrikaans would never be willing to accept that someone like Dane had slipped their grasp though any other means. 'But we're gonna run that clock out, *ja*?'

Marc found the gun case where it had fallen and grabbed it, lurching away from the remains of the Land Rover. The heat from the explosion made his skin feel sunburnt and his ears were still ringing from the detonation. He was only aware of Lucy when she grabbed his arm, yanking him toward the thermal-cloth tent with a hard tug on one of the daypack's straps.

'This way!' she shouted, but her voice was woolly, like it was coming to him from underwater. 'Back to the building!'

Marc nodded and let her lead him back the way she had come. As they made it to the entrance hall, he felt, rather than heard, the second missile hit. The blast put them both down, and they stumbled as a wave of displaced dust churned in though the open doors.

'Six Hellfires,' Marc said, his own voice sounding oddly muffled. 'Enough to blast this hill into rubble.'

Lucy wasn't listening to him. She pulled at the gun case and her expression turned thunderous. 'You . . . got the *wrong goddamn box*!'

'What?'

'These are the non-lethals!' She wrenched the lid open and grimaced at what lay inside. 'Red for dead, blue for *screwed*!'

Mark threw a glance over his shoulder, out through the doorway toward the burning pit. Whatever had been in the back of the Land Rover was splinters and wreckage, same as the vehicle. 'How was I supposed to know?' he spat back at her. Inside the case there were a few flash grenades, along with other kit he didn't recognize.

Lucy grabbed at a tazer pistol, and then angrily threw it down. 'Great. We can't even dent that thing with this *Star Trek* shit.'

Mark ignored her, and reached for the largest device in the case. It unfolded as he removed it, a skeleton stock snapping open to reveal a trigger and pistol grip beneath. The weapon was the size of a short-frame assault rifle, but where a conventional firearm would have had its mechanism, there was a solid block of electronics resembling a fuse box. The device terminated in a curved dish antenna, giving the whole thing the look of a sci-fi ray gun built from electrical spares. Fluorescent warning stickers covered the weapon, forbidding users to operate the gun without protective gear, for more than ten seconds at a time, not to look directly into the emitter head . . .

He saw a tell-tale hazard symbol, a yellow triangle showing a stylised radio mast beaming out ripples of radiation, and understanding clicked into place. 'This is a HERF gun.'

'It's useless, that's what it is.' Lucy looked up at the ceiling, listening for the drone's return. 'Unless you wanna microwave a burrito before we buy the farm. That thing's a crowd control prototype, not for anti-aircraft fire!'

It was also all they had. 'We need to get to the roof,' He thumbed the on-off switch. 'High Energy Radio Frequencies, yeah? Enough of that shot at anything will cook it from the inside out. Even a drone.'

'You are going to get killed.'

He shook his head. 'No, *we* are going to get killed when that drone spears us with a missile, so we may as well go out swinging.' He broke into a run and heard Lucy swear again as she came after him.

Marc emerged on to the roof of the building, blinking furiously in the bright sunshine. The HERF gun was large and cumbersome, banging against his chest as he dashed across the flat roof. He was aware of Lucy a few steps behind, panning around with her MP7.

Marc slipped and dropped to a clumsy halt at the eastern end of the building, on his knees behind the raised parapet. From here, he would have had a view of the entire New Day orphanage, had parts of it not been on fire or blown apart by missile impacts.

He raised the HERF gun to sight along the top of it, and became aware that the thing was humming gently to itself. Directly in his eye line was a warning panel reminding Marc that what he held in his hands was essentially the guts of a powerful magnetron, and that prolonged use of it was likely to blind him. Lucy's earlier comment about heating food wasn't entirely facetious; the same technology behind an ordinary microwave oven was also present in the HERF, but reconfigured and focused along very different lines. As a less-than-lethal combat option, the HERF worked best as a deterrent device, temporarily subjecting its targets to a painful 'heat ray' effect that even body armour couldn't attenuate. But against anything non-organic, the weapon's track record was unpredictable at best.

'There!' Lucy shouted and pointed out to the south. The UCAV was starting in on its third pass, and from the angle of attack, it was clearly targeting the building they were standing on.

'One.' Marc began to count, bracing himself to draw a bead on the prow of the drone as it turned inbound. 'Two.' He put his finger on the trigger switch and took a deep breath. 'And three.'

There was no howl of tortured air, no showy bolt of energy that leapt from the dish-muzzle of the gun. Instead, Marc became aware of a hazy lensing effect that blurred his vision, and a deep, unpleasant oscillation inside the gun's casing.

'What are you waiting for? *Shoot*!' Lucy shouted.

'I have. I am!' he snapped back, holding the weapon steady, his aim never shifting from the Avenger's nose cone. It was still coming, swift and deadly. Marc kept the firing switch depressed, and past the count of five seconds a yellow light blinked on, warning him to release the button. He ignored it, continuing to ten seconds, twelve, fifteen.

The yellow light turned red, and the HERF gun's humming grew loud and insistent.

'What are you waiting for?' demanded the Englishman. He prodded Teape in the shoulder. 'Blow the building.'

But Teape was shaking his head. 'This isn't right.' He moved he mouse pointer, but the display on the main repeater screen had crashed, the tactical display frozen with the UCAV in a banking turn toward the point of missile release.

Grunewald and Ellis crowded around the secondary video monitor, which showed the grey-on-grey blur of the hillside flashing past beneath the Avenger's fuselage. 'No Hellfire launch,' said the mercenary.

'Looks like jamming,' said Teape. 'Signal is breaking up. The drone isn't answering commands.'

'Stormline are cutting us out,' said Grunewald. 'The Americans must have severed the link.'

'No,' Teape shook his head. 'This is on-site, we're losing–' He fell silent as all the screens linking the *Santa Cruz* directly to Argonaut Two abruptly went dark.

Tommy grabbed him by the shoulder. 'Get it back!' he snarled.

At twenty seconds, the HERF gun was uncomfortably hot and the plastic casing was in danger of burning the skin off Marc's face. The UCAV seemed unaffected, its high-speed approach vector unchanged – but then it suddenly struck him how close the Avenger was to the walls of the compound. By now it was well inside the optimal release envelope for the AGMs, but still it hadn't fired.

A whiff of acrid, burnt-plastic stink filtered out of the HERF gun as he exceeded the experimental weapon's safety margin and the device abruptly went dead. He almost threw it down, the palms of his hands red raw from surface searing.

'Look!' Lucy pointed. 'Holy shit! That actually worked!'

Marc saw the drone's nose dip as it passed over the outer wall, and the robot aircraft seemed to sag in mid-air, as if all the fight had gone out of it. Streamers of smoke issued out of vents in the Avenger's fuselage where the drone had been coming straight at him, right into the apex of the HERF gun's invisible beam.

The port wing rising in a too-late course correction, the drone went in toward the rubble-strewn road that led to the main building and the starboard wingtip clipped the edge of a water tower. With a screech of twisting metal, the drone was flipped around. It dived at the ground and dashed itself against the dirt with a thunderous roar. An explosion flared orange-red, throwing the burning fuselage back up into the air, turning it into a tumbling mass of fire.

A fleeting moment of elation at defeating the UCAV faded in Marc as he realized the wrecked machine was going to come crashing into the building.

'*Run!*'

He sprinted away from the edge of the roof just as the burning drone struck and a pair of Hellfires went off in the collision. One of the missiles was thrown free of the fireball and shot away into the sky on a wild trajectory, spiralling away into the mountainside miles distant. The other blew out the front quarter of the building and forced blazing drafts through the lower floor, turning everything into an inferno.

Marc felt the sickening lurch as supports crumbled and the building shook, slumping in on itself. The entire roof structure dropped two metres beneath his feet and great cracked sections of it tilted away behind him at sharp angles. Marc stumbled to his knees and twisted in time to see Lucy lose her footing and drop. Her boots couldn't find purchase and she skidded down the slope of the broken roof, toward the fires below. He launched himself forward, snatching at her.

Lucy's hand caught his sleeve and pulled hard, almost enough to drag him down with her. He fell flat, clinging to a section of air vent that showed something approaching stability, and for long, precarious seconds they both hung there. 'Any . . . Anytime you're ready . . .' he wheezed.

She used him like a climbing frame and pulled herself back from the edge, before the two of them rolled back on to the creaking roof and lay there, gasping for breath.

'Okay,' said Lucy, her throat raw with effort. 'Let's not do that again.'

'Stormline reports loss of signal from Argonaut Two.' Teape spoke in his usual monotone, his voice so bereft of affect it was almost robotic. 'No confirmation on third weapon release.'

'They shot it down . . .' Ellis said, looking around the compartment at the blank screens. 'How could that happen?' He looked at the Englishman. 'This is the same punk from Etna, how is he capable of–'

Tommy wasn't listening to him. He prodded Teape with a finger. 'What did you do?'

'Not me,' Teape replied. 'I just did what you said.' He pointed at the mouse. 'Moved the clicker where you wanted it.'

The Englishman swore and for a moment it looked like he was going to punch Teape out of anger. But then he turned away and his glare found Grunewald, who stood watching the interchange. 'Why didn't you just put a bullet in that prick when you had him?'

Ellis answered for him. 'Because we were told to deal with this problem discreetly.' He nodded at the blank screens. 'Although that directive seems to have gone out the window since you turned up.'

'The compound suffered a sustained missile bombardment,' said the Swiss mercenary. 'There's no reason to assume the targets didn't perish.'

'No reason to assume they *did*, either,' Tommy snarled back. He threw up his hands. 'Bollocks. All right, we've done enough, wasted too much time on this already.' He shook his head. 'Yanks'll be pissed off about losing their toy, so we can't let this connect back to the Combine.' He shot a look at Teape. 'Close off the link to Stormline, wipe all this and put it in a fucking box. Khadir's operation is where we're supposed to be at. We concentrate on him from now on, stop wasting time and effort on distractions.'

'My thoughts exactly,' insisted Grunewald. At last, the Englishman was starting to see things his way.

Tommy closed the distance between them. 'Find a local, get them out to the orphanage to check the site. That'll put the lid on it.'

Ellis sniffed. 'Someone is still going to have to talk to the higher-ups,' he said, fixing the Englishman with a sideways look. 'Don't envy you telling them you got no bodies.'

The other man glanced at Grunewald, indicating Ellis. 'How do you stand the sound of this twat's voice in your ear all the time?' Tommy snorted. 'Listen, Dane is dead, or he's not. And if he's not, he's still an international fugitive on about fifty different terrorist watch lists. So either way . . . He's *fucked*.'

Marc found a crate full of empty soda bottles and dragged it into the shade before using it as a makeshift stool. He glanced around the sparse village, the first sign of civilization he and Lucy had found after striking out from the burning compound. He thought to begin with that the building shading him from the setting sun was some kind of garage, and it clearly did perform that function, with an oily old Skoda up on blocks inside. But it also seemed to serve as a sort of general store and cafe for the settlement as well. Across the way from him, a group of older Turkish men sat around a card table in plastic lawn chairs, alternating between sipping from cups of coffee and giving him unfriendly stares. He managed a weak smile and saluted them with the ice-lolly that Lucy had taken from the garage-store's grumbling refrigerator. She handed a fold of hundred-dollar bills to the man in the mechanic's overalls who met them on their arrival, and in return he offered bottles of water and the cooling popsicles. Marc sucked on the orange-flavoured ice and stared morosely into the distance.

The two of them had barely made it off the crumbling roof, scrambling down a corroded fire escape before the building gave a final, howling moan and collapsed. Coated in dust and soot, they had little choice left but to abandon the compound and start walking. Lucy's smartphone had been lost in the drone attack, and Marc's was broken. He tried and failed to get a response from his laptop, wincing at the rattling that came from the device when he shook it.

So they walked in tired silence, with the sun falling toward the horizon behind them. The roads returned – such as they were – and Lucy spotted the nameless village as the hillside began to flatten out around them. Walking into the town proper set Marc thinking about a scene from a spaghetti western, as the two strangers were greeted with suspicion.

Marc glanced at the men again, and watched them talking about him. They had to have heard the drone, he thought, or at least the sounds of the explosions. And if this was the closest town to the *New Day* orphanage, these people had to know the men who worked there. Marc wondered how that would figure with him and Lucy. Was someone nearby already making a phone call, reporting back to an Al Sayf cell member or a Combine contact?

He was tired, and some part of him was telling him to pack up and run. Fatigue seemed to be winning the argument, though. He sat on the crate, feeling every ache in his body, crunching the ice between his teeth until only the stick was left.

Marc pulled the sliver of wood from his lips and studied it as Lucy emerged from the garage. 'No joke,' he said, without thinking.

'Say what?'

He showed her. 'No joke, see? When I was a kid, they used to print gags on lolly sticks. *Why did the chicken cross the road?* That kinda thing.'

'I know that one,' she said. '*Because the poor feathered asshole was being chased by a drone.*'

Marc gave a shrug. 'I suppose comedy is less funny when it's happening to you.' He tossed the stick into the gutter. 'You find a working telephone?'

Lucy nodded. 'They got a landline. Put a message in the Rubicon dead drop. Now we wait.' She jerked a thumb at the floor above the garage. 'I rented us somewhere to crash. Cost us more than a night in the Ankara Hilton, but then I'm buying his silence.' She nodded at the coffee-drinking men, who had now been joined by the mechanic. 'Theirs too.'

'I would really like a shower,' Marc noted.

'You really need one,' she replied, with a nod. 'But sadly, they can only spare enough water for one of us, so you're out of luck.' Marc hesitated, and before he could say more, Lucy went on. 'And don't ask if we can share. I know we both got shot at and all, but that doesn't mean I'm going to sleep with you.'

'I wasn't going to say that,' he retorted. 'Bloody hell.'

Lucy sniggered, and he realized too late she had been making fun of him. 'God, you Brits. You're so easy to troll.'

'Hey,' Marc sighed. 'You don't get to do sarcasm. You're an American, you people aren't supposed to understand irony.'

'You'd be surprised.' She blew out a breath and fell silent for a long moment. When she spoke again, Lucy was staring off over the hillside. 'So that was a trap back there. Not just the grenade, I mean. The whole place. Your lead from MI6.'

'Yeah.' Admitting it felt like a weight settling on him. 'The Combine cleaned house, but they left the New Day info behind as a snare. I mean, I knew that was a possibility, but I never thought . . . I mean, a US Navy UCAV? I did not see that coming. In both the literal and figurative senses.'

'Look on the bright side,' she said. 'We just torched a few million dollars' worth of taxpayer's money back there. Someone will have to carry the can for that. That's blowback the Combine won't like.'

Marc scowled. 'I'm going to flinch every time a plane passes over from now on.'

'Them's the breaks.' She yawned and worked a muscle in her shoulder. 'It's not a total bust, though. We're alive, we got new intel. That's a win, of sorts.'

'So we know that Al Sayf and the Combine were working some kind of angle out here,' Marc said, thinking aloud. 'Not a pleasant set-up. Using a camp for war orphans as, what? A weapons dump? Training facility?'

'Both?' she offered.

Marc nodded at the grim possibility. He still had no idea how the orphanage connected to the *Palomino* or the Barcelona bombing, but he couldn't escape the chilling certainty that those acts of terror had just been the opening shots. He thought about the horrors in the bloodstained basement and his lip twisted in disgust.

'I get one thing now,' said Lucy. 'Solomon has been chasing this hard, and that place is the reason why.'

'The orphanage?'

She nodded. 'I think . . . It's personal for him.'

'What do you mean?' Marc lowered his voice. Lucy was bringing him into a confidence.

'You know what Rubicon is, but most people don't know where it grew from. Solomon was a war orphan himself. Family wiped out during the civil war in Mozambique. You've seen those pictures of kids in knock-off Nikes and soccer shorts carrying assault rifles? You go back thirty years . . .' She let the statement hang.

Marc's eyes narrowed. 'He was a child soldier?'

'Think on that,' said Lucy. 'And then maybe you get what he's about.'

He nodded, taking it in. 'Is that why you fell in with Rubicon?'

Lucy's body language shifted immediately, and she leaned away from him, the brief moment of openness melting away. 'I told you, he offered me a deal. And working for someone who wants to do the right thing is good for my karma.' She looked out over the hillside. 'What about you?'

'What *about* me?'

She turned back to study him. 'How'd you end up a techie? I mean, you got skills, that's clear enough. You're kind of random, but I've seen worse in the field. How come you're not an agent?'

'*Officer*,' he corrected. 'In Britain we call them field officers, not agents.' He knew Lucy was deliberately steering the conversation away from herself, but even as he saw that he was already falling into old patterns of explanation and denial. 'I didn't make the cut.' He sighed, and the next words came from nowhere. 'I didn't want the risk.'

'The safer bet, huh? I get that.'

Her tone touched a raw nerve. 'You really don't,' he shot back. 'People don't *get it*.' Marc shook his head. 'It's not about courage or weakness or anything like that. It's about understanding yourself. I know my limitations.' Suddenly he was on his feet, scowling at her, the memories of dark sea and thunderous sky at the edges of his thoughts. 'I never asked for this. I never wanted any of it to happen. I went right to the ragged edge once and that was enough for me. I don't want to be here.'

'And yet, you are,' she said mildly, his anger rolling off her. Lucy stood up and turned to walk away. 'Not dead yet, when by all rights you damn well should be. What does that tell you, Dane? Where's your limit now?'

NINETEEN

With each step Marc took, the dust streamed off him in waves. He was walking into the teeth of the windstorm, the pressure of it pushing back as he advanced. He raised a hand in front of his face and his mouth opened in shock. The dust wasn't sand, but particles of his flesh, tiny pieces of him being ablated away by the howling wind. His fingers were becoming translucent and glassy.

Distantly, he heard the sound of a thudding, urgent heartbeat. Each pulse of noise was loud like a hammer-blow, coming closer with each second. Marc tried to shield his eyes, but the sand was everywhere, ripping at him like a million tiny razor blades.

Someone was standing there, up atop the rocks, looking down upon him. Dark hair caught like a pennant snapping in the breeze. *Sam.*

He tried to call her name, but his throat filled with dust. She was sad, and her face was streaked with blood. The pulsing sound grew louder, shifting pitch and changing–

Marc was suddenly *awake*, blinking away cold sweat. He rolled off the mattress and peered around the room. The grubby space resembled some post-apocalyptic bedsit, pieces of dismantled machinery among a threadbare couch, a table and a trio of mismatched chairs. He dressed quickly, his clothes feeling stiff and scratchy against his skin.

There was no sign of Lucy, only a neat bed-roll atop the couch where she had slept the night before. Marc's daypack was where he had left it, and he grabbed at the bag, fishing inside for his pistol. The gun was still there, next to the battered laptop.

It was then he realized that the thudding sound he remembered from the vivid dream had not faded with the phantom image of

Sam Green. It wasn't in his head; it was coming from outside, a low beat changing into a mechanical crackle even as he listened. *Rotor blades.*

He went to the door and opened it a crack, looking out on to a metal fire escape. Behind the garage there was a field populated by a couple of shacks and a dozen dead Trabants that had been stripped of parts. Above, a grimy white helicopter was circling as the pilot looked for somewhere to put down. It was an aging Russian Mil Mi-8, a civilian model of the workhorse 'Hip' that had been in service since the Sixties. As it turned, Marc could clearly see the crew through the windows of the cockpit. They didn't look like military types.

'Hey!' A voice called out and he looked down to see that Lucy had appeared at the foot of the stairs. She held her bag in front of her, one hand inside. From above, he could see she was gripping the MP7, keeping it out of sight. She jerked her chin at him. 'C'mon,' she continued. 'I think our ride is here.'

People were gathering to see what was going on, so Marc wasted no time in swinging his daypack over his shoulder and climbing down to her. Safety on, the Glock went into the back of his waistband. 'Are you sure?' he asked, as he got close.

Lucy gave him a cool-eyed look that reminded him more of Sam than he would have liked to admit. 'If it's not,' she replied, raising her voice to be heard over the noise of the helicopter touching down, 'then we neutralize the crew and take it ourselves.'

Not for the first time, he couldn't be certain if she was joking. But then the point became moot as the Mi-8's passenger compartment hatch slid back and Henri Delancort stepped lightly down to the ground. He ducked low, holding his hand to his face to shield himself from the dust being kicked up, and somehow still managed to do it with an air of arch poise. In his brown suit and handmade shoes, Delancort looked as if he had been dropped in from a fashion shoot.

He flashed a tight smile. 'You visit the most delightful places,' he told Lucy. 'I take it we will not be getting our deposit for the car back?'

'Send the bill to Uncle Sam,' Lucy shot back.

He beckoned them to follow. 'Mister Solomon has gone on to Cairo for his meeting. He wants us to proceed with the investigation.'

'You found something?' said Marc.

'We found something,' agreed the other man.

Lucy bounded up into the helicopter, while Delancort took his time, frowning at the dust collecting on his trousers. Marc was the last aboard, hesitating for a moment before he scrambled in and pulled the hatch shut.

Delancort gave him a measuring glance. 'Problem?'

Marc shook his head. 'It's a backseat driver thing. Don't like riding in choppers when I'm not in the cockpit.' The aircraft trembled, and he felt the lurch in the pit of his stomach as they left the ground. Marc found a seat and strapped in.

The other man sat opposite him, with Lucy at his side. 'Let me tell you what our imaging team at the Palo Alto office made of those pictures.' He leaned forward. 'The document fragments appear to be from shipping manifests.'

'For aircraft?'

Delancort shook his head. 'Seagoing, not air freight. Sadly, you did not catch anything that gave clues to the registration of the ship involved, or any information on the cargo. But what we *did* get was a destination.' He glanced at Lucy. 'The Port of New Jersey in the United States.'

Marc considered this new detail. 'We have to be looking at something pretty recent. How many ships have sailed out of Turkish ports for the US in the last week or so?'

'More than you would expect,' Delancort replied. 'But confidence is high that the manifests are connected. They correlate with data we have been tracking from some of Rubicon's other intelligence assets.'

Lucy nodded grimly. 'The chatter about Al Sayf launching an attack on American soil. If the Combine have sourced transport to get them to the East Coast . . . That's as good as a confirmation.' She fell silent for a moment. 'Can we assume they're gonna hit New York?'

Marc thought he heard a catch in her voice as she mentioned her hometown. Delancort was shaking his head. 'We cannot presuppose anything at this stage.'

Marc watched the landscape roll past beneath them as the helicopter turned back toward Kayseri. 'Okay. We need to get this in front of someone at US Homeland Security, right? It's a good bet that whatever ship they're using, they won't have docked in New Jersey yet. The Americans can seal the port up tight and catch these sods before they get off the boat.'

Lucy and Delancort exchanged a loaded look that rang a warning note in Marc's mind. 'Combine penetration has not just reached into European intelligence organs,' said the other man. 'They have people everywhere.'

"That was an American military drone that attacked us, remember?' Lucy added. 'If they can co-opt the US Navy, they can get their claws into CIA, FBI, Homeland . . .'

'But you don't know for sure?' Marc insisted.

'If we take the risk of revealing this information, we could lose any lead on Al Sayf's operation.' Delancort cocked his head as he spoke. 'All it takes is one informant to warn the Combine and they will go dark. They will shift targets. The next attack could be over and done before we are aware of it.'

'So, we just sit on this?' Marc reeled back in his seat. 'For all we know, the people responsible for the Barcelona bombing and killing my team could already be on the streets of New York!' He glared at Lucy. '*Your* streets.'

She reacted with an angry snarl. 'You think I like the idea any more than you do? But just think for a goddamn second, Dane! We have the drop on these sons-of-bitches, we know where they are gonna be.'

'Our data-mining group are already working on analysing sea traffic going in and out of the port,' said Delancort. 'We can narrow down the possibilities and isolate the suspect ship before the Combine can proceed.'

'And if you're wrong? Or a little *late*? What then?' Marc aimed a finger at Delancort. 'They blew up a police station in Spain and a ship in France. What if next time it's a school? A hospital? A shopping mall?'

Lucy reached across the gap between them and placed a hand on his forearm. 'Marc. Listen to me. *We* need to get these people. Not Homeland Security, not some other agency that leaks like a damn sieve. This is our shot, and, yeah, it's a risk. But that's how Rubicon works, and if you want to be part of that, you can be. Because we could use your help.'

'And you are quite uniquely motivated,' said Delancort, with a sniff.

Marc shot him an acid look, but said nothing.

The *Santa Cruz* was steaming at a steady rate of knots as it approached the coast of Newfoundland. A low sky of clouds as grey as oily wool had descended on them and visibility was no more than a mile, but soon enough America would reveal itself, and for the first time in his life Omar Khadir would look upon the land of this enemy with his own eyes.

It was necessary to wound these people to make them understand, Khadir decided. Unlike others of his kinsmen, Jadeed or the angry men whom he had recruited to teach the youths in Turkey, Khadir did not see the United States of America as the wellspring of all the world's degeneracy. They were no 'Great Satan' – there was no such thing. The potential for corruption, for dishonour of soul and self was something that no single nation had primacy over. To lay the blame for such things at the feet of just one people was naïve, a choice made by men of narrow mind. Any society, even those who declared themselves the most pious, could be rotting within. Khadir knew that from first-hand experience.

The colour of a man's skin, the flag he revered, and the god he prayed to . . . *None of that mattered.* They were all convenient hooks upon which one could hang an ideology that would fit the needs of the war.

He did not blame the Americans for all the decay he had witnessed. They were victims of it as much as he, but that did not mean he would spare them. So bold and so arrogant, they had painted a target upon themselves and dared those who hated them to take a shot. A strike against the United States was simply the most expedient option for Al Sayf, for their media liked nothing more than to show the shedding of blood for all the world to see.

When it was done, the work would be broadcast around the globe, burned into history alongside every other act of terror that had changed the face of human civilization. And it would just be the *start*. The British would be next. Al Sayf would make good on their promises to that nation.

'Commander.' Khadir turned as he heard Jadeed approaching, and he took a deep breath of briny air. Further down the hull, the helicopter was being made ready for departure, the ship's crewmen removing the weather tarps over the cockpit and checking the fuel tank.

'Report,' he told Jadeed, looking away from the aircraft.

The other man bobbed his head, removing the wool cap he had been wearing. 'We are ready, sir. The recruits are prepared.' Ever-present in a tight coil around his wrist, his *misbaha* beads clattered against one another as he gestured toward the ship's island across the weather deck.

'Where are they now?'

'They have been returned to the quarters to recover. I have stationed men to watch them.'

'Good . . .' Khadir saw a man in a green smock loitering in a shadowed corner beneath the island, sucking greedily on a cigarette. He was one of the doctors the Combine had found for them, a Brazilian thoracic surgeon who had lost his licence after developing a taste for his own medications. Patches of dark arterial fluid patterned the front of the smock, making him look more like a butcher than a healer. 'How many did we lose?'

Jadeed swallowed hard. 'A few,' he admitted. 'No more than expected. We always knew there would be wastage.'

Khadir gave a nod. 'Just so.' As he said the words, some of the Serbs emerged from the hatch near where the doctor stood. They carried a stack of black body bags between them. With a waddling gait, the men shuffled the bags toward the rail of the weather deck.

'I gave the order to dispose of the remains,' Jadeed explained. 'I thought it best to do so immediately . . . If we wait–'

Khadir raised a hand to silence him. 'You did the right thing. We close the distance to America with every hour. Disposing of them now ensures these brave soldiers will not wash up on the shores of our enemies.' He frowned. He wanted to say something. He felt as if there should be words spoken to mark the passing of the young men, but now the moment was here, he had nothing to offer up.

Jadeed's attention kept straying to the helicopter. The Britisher was there, talking animatedly with the other mercenaries. The tone of Tommy's harsh, jarring voice reminded Khadir of the sound of a barking dog, and the fitting nature of the image provided him a moment of cold amusement.

'I know you resent the Britisher,' Khadir told his second. 'And you are right to. But you must go with them. It is required, for the success of the work.'

Jadeed's eyes narrowed and he ran a finger over the line of beads. 'I will say this to you, sir. He is the son of a whore and I would very much like to beat the pride out of him.' There was genuine longing in the other man's eyes, the need for violence strong beneath the surface of Jadeed's self-control.

'Rise above him,' Khadir replied, the words both order and warning. 'But be watchful.' He did not need to say more. Both of them knew that the Combine's alliance with Al Sayf was temporary, and that once the act was done, the relationship between them might change very sharply.

There was a crash and a string of curses behind them. Khadir's head snapped around to see the Serbs beginning an argument over which one of them had slipped up and allowed the body bags to fall across the deck. One of the bags had split open and a pasty length of arm, a sliver of torso and a face emerged from within.

Khadir grimaced. The dead youth's eyes looked up at him, the corpse's chubby face now sallow, flesh sagging on the skull beneath. He searched his memory for the name of the teenager and did not find it – but he did remember him, the boy who had been assaulted by the degenerate guard at the orphanage. *A pity to lose that one,* he thought.

The youth had shown promise, ever since he taken up a weapon and led the beating of the man who had hurt him. The kind of raw hate that lurked inside the boy was exactly what Khadir was best at moulding. It was the same fury that he had tempered in himself many years earlier.

Jadeed shouted at the Serbs with such force that the two men stopped their argument and meekly gathered up the dead once more. Khadir sensed someone approaching but did not turn as the Britisher came closer.

'What's all this shit, then?' he demanded. 'You topping your own now?'

'Are you shocked?' Khadir replied coldly.

'I don't fucking care,' Tommy snarled, with such thuggish disdain that it made Jadeed's hands draw into fists. 'Clean up your mess if you have to, but we're on the clock.' He jerked his thumb at the helicopter. 'On the hurry-up, Saladin.' Without looking back, the Britisher stalked back down the deck, and the aircraft's rotors began to turn lazily in the damp air.

Jadeed met Khadir's eyes and his annoyance softened under his commander's hard gaze. 'Go,' he ordered. 'Make sure the mercenaries complete their tasks ahead of our arrival. Without you, we will never be able to reach our objective.'

The other man bowed slightly. 'I won't fail.'

Khadir gave him a smile and placed a hand on his shoulder. 'I know.'

Jadeed sprinted across the deck to the helicopter, scrambling into the back with one of the other loyal men. The Britisher took the co-pilot's seat next to the thickset, sour-faced one called Ellis; the other mercenary worked the controls and Khadir watched the aircraft lift off and slide into the breeze. Low and fast, it powered away across the waves and vanished into the rain.

Beneath radar coverage on a course that would thread through the gaps in Coast Guard patrols, the 'advance team' would smooth the way for the final execution of the work.

'Soon, brothers,' Khadir said aloud, closing his eyes and listening to the ocean. '*Soon*.'

Within a couple of hours the Rubicon jet was back in the air and heading directly toward Newark Liberty International. Marc showered off the trail dirt and the lingering smells of cordite and fire-smoke, too wired to appreciate the rare novelty of enjoying such luxuries at twenty thousand feet. His hair still wet against his scalp, he wandered shoeless down the length of the aircraft until he found the bar, and there he helped himself to a cup of bitter brown coffee. The light in the open common area was good, so he took a bar towel and set out the laptop and his micro-tools on it. The computer looked as if it had been thrown down a flight of stairs, and Marc cracked open the damaged case, checking and cleaning the interior, sifting little piles of sand from the cooling fans and around the central processor unit.

The task gave him focus, let his mind sieve through recent events while his hands moved with the rote motions of muscle memory.

He was almost done when Lucy arrived. Unlike him, the woman seemed fiercely awake. Marc peered into the dregs of his coffee and thought about the not inconsiderable fluid weight of caffeine currently coursing through his system. She watched him carefully rebuild the laptop's battered case.

'I've seen guys with that same face,' she said, pointing at him. 'Same look, working on something like their life depends on it. Difference is, they were Delta boys prepping their guns.'

Marc laid his hand on the flat of the keyboard. 'I could kill a man with this,' he said, and the words were out of his mouth before he knew where they had come from.

Lucy gave him an odd look. 'Like . . . with hacking?'

'Yeah.' Marc nodded once, then showed her the thick rod of the power pack that slotted into the laptop's battery compartment. 'Or maybe with this. Cracked a man's skull one time.'

She took the battery and weighed it in her hand like a club. 'Improvise and adapt.' Lucy returned the unit and folded her arms across her chest.

'Something like that.' The power pack slid home with a hard click and the laptop came to life. Patched and dented, with an ugly glitch in one corner where the screen had been damaged, it still worked – and that gave Marc a kind of satisfaction that brought a brief smile to his lips. It struck him that at this moment, the machine might well be the closest thing he had to a lifeline. He thought about the Glock, lying forgotten in his cabin. The gun would keep him alive . . . but the data he had might actually save him.

If I can just live long enough to figure it out.

Delancort emerged from Solomon's office across the way and caught sight of them. 'Ah, *c'est bon.* I have something you both should take a look at.' He used a wireless link to relay images to a television monitor that unfolded out of a hidden panel.

Marc craned his neck to see a series of stills fan out across the display. 'What are we looking at?'

'The first pass from our data forensics people on the New Day orphanage,' said Delancort. 'No prizes for guessing that it has as many shells as a *matryoshka* . . .'

'A what now?' said Lucy, leaning against the wall.

'Nesting doll.' Marc made the shape with his hands. 'One inside another.'

Delancort gave a curt smile. 'Pardon the metaphor, but I thought it particularly apt when this gentleman's name floated to the surface.' A patrician face snapped into view, a man with a severe beard and close-clipped moustache, the hard hunter's eyes of a wolf glaring back at them.

'Pytor Glovkonin,' breathed Marc. 'Well now . . .'

'He's a patron of many charitable groups, of course,' Delancort went on. 'Most of them seem legitimate. It could be a coincidence that one of the richest oligarchs in the Russian Federated States has a connection to the New Day orphanage . . .' He let the sentence trail off. 'I do not believe any of us would lean toward that version of things, *oui*?'

'A day ago, I was as close to him as I am to you,' Marc noted. 'Ships that pass, and all that.'

Lucy took this in with a nod. 'I get that this guy is big money and dirty with it. But we're saying he's Combine too?'

'It's a good fit,' said Marc. 'MI6 have nothing actionable on this bloke. He's got assets all over Europe and Russia. He operates up high, where the air is rare and the cash is thick.'

Delancort tapped a finger on his lips. 'Rubicon is well aware of Mister Glovkonin's more questionable business enterprises.

G-Kor and Rubicon have crossed swords in the past, financially speaking.'

Marc shot him a look. 'How so?'

'G-Kor are connected to a holding group in Irkutsk, which host an array of secure internet servers from the safety of a decommissioned nuclear missile silo.'

'Dark net,' Marc said, with a grimace. Off Lucy's questioning look, he went on. 'It's like a shadow internet, yeah? A web *below* the world wide web. Servers in countries with an elastic view of data law. They operate information banks, hosting sensitive material for rogue states, drug cartels, arms dealers, you name it. They bounce digital files from place to place, sometimes in deep storage like the silo thing . . .'

'That's what Novakovich, the broker guy, was into?'

He nodded. 'He had his own little piece of the ghost web, right on his yacht.' Dark net servers were what allowed criminals like the Combine to continue to function on a global basis. Marc didn't add that the reason why many such data havens *stayed* in operation was that dozens of larger nations also secretly used them as remote hosts for material they didn't want on their own servers.

Delancort was watching Marc carefully. 'Will you tell us what else you have?' The question seemed to come out of the blue, and Marc knew immediately that he hadn't schooled his expression quickly enough to hide his reaction.

'I told you about New Day. I told you what I want.'

The other man nodded. 'Yes, the identity of the person or persons responsible for the loss of your team in Dunkirk. But I think you're holding something back.'

Lucy came and took a seat across from him. 'He's right, Dane, isn't he?' Her eyes narrowed. 'Look, after the drone and all, if you still don't think you can trust us, then–'

Marc cut her off with a wave of his hand. 'It's not that. It's just . . .' He sighed. 'What I have isn't anything at all. It's worthless.' He explained about the email data he had recovered from the MI6 network. 'It's all circumstantial stuff, traces of traces, nothing solid or even remotely provable.'

'Digital information never dies,' Delancort countered. 'You may not have access to it, but it is out there in the web. Everything leaves an impression.'

'Maybe so,' Marc admitted. 'Maybe there are some fragments caught in a buffer somewhere, but I can't track it down. There are only two places in the world that could reconstruct the data, and neither are open to me.' He shot a look at Delancort. 'Or your boss's money, for that matter.'

'Are you sure?'

'I'm sure. You may have been able to get into my MOD files, but Rubicon can't break the encryption at GCHQ, can you?'

Delancort paled slightly. 'No. No, we cannot.'

Marc nodded to himself. British Intelligence's electronic surveillance centre monitored a huge volume of emails, data, radio and cellular traffic, but its security was airtight. 'As we know, I'm on MI6's shit-list right now, so they'd never turn over their data to me.'

'You said *two* places,' noted Lucy.

'The second one is an even tougher nut. The National Security Agency.'

'Oh, yeah,' she said. 'That whole PRISM thing.'

His lip curled. 'That's just the program you know about.' MI6 had been aware for years that the NSA's data trackers watched all the British intelligence agencies. But while the security services publically appeared to be turning a blind eye to it, GCHQ were doing exactly the same thing to American assets in Europe with their Tempora initiative.

Delancort sniffed. 'The NSA would never admit to having the data you need to trace the emails.'

Marc nodded. 'So I'm back to square one.'

Lucy shot Delancort a glance and he sighed. 'Mister Dane, I understand that you are wary of incurring any obligation to Rubicon, but

Mister Solomon has told me to offer you, within reason, any and all help the group can provide for your objective.'

The offer was a genuine surprise to him. 'Why would you say that?'

Delancort seemed confused by the question, as if it had never occurred to him. 'Because it is the right thing to do,' he replied.

At first, Halil thought he was drowning.

His throat was clogged and his arms and legs were numb. They felt like distant things, vaguely connected to his body. He tried to open his eyes, but the pain of the bright lights above him forced them shut.

It took effort, but he turned over, feeling the sagging mattress give as he shifted his weight. Sharp, jabbing pains prickled all across his belly and sternum, making him gasp. He rolled back, and forced one hand to his face to cover his eyes. Minutes passed, minutes that seemed like hours, and finally Halil managed to lift himself to a sitting position. The pain across his torso was constant, and he found it hard to breathe.

He sorted the sounds around him. The creak of rusted metal, the distant lap of waves. Other youths, some talking in low voices, others crying softly. Halil slowly dropped his hand and placed his bare feet on the cold floor. He was dizzy, even sitting still, and his flesh felt strange. It was hot to the touch.

Halil's laboured breathing sounded loudly in his ears. He had no recollection of walking back to the long, chilly room where the teachers had billeted the youths after boarding the ship. He remembered them marching out to the mess hall in a loose group. They were all hungry, stomachs empty and growling. The teachers had forbidden them to eat for over a day, and there was talk among the group that someone had done something wrong that the lot of them were being punished for.

But when they trooped into the mess, the men there were eating. The food had been a meat stew, and remembering the smell of the greasy soup now made Halil gag in reflex, the acid boil of bile tickling the back of his throat. He desperately wanted water.

He fixed on the memory again, trying to replay it in his mind's eye. The mess hall. The food. Jadeed had been there, and he smiled at them. At first Halil was wary of any pretence of warmth from the commander's bullying second, but he had brought a reward – gassy American sodas that fizzed and popped in sculpted bottles with garish labels.

Tarki had guzzled his like it was nectar, belching loud and long. Everyone had laughed, and for a moment they forgot they were young men, all of them acting like children. The teachers didn't censure them, so they all drank and they laughed, and it was only when Halil drained the bottle that he saw the powdery dregs in the bottom. White crystals, like refined sugar.

Then a heavy sleep came in a wave, swallowing him whole. Through blurry vision he saw Tarki slump against his bench. Colour bled out of Halil's vision and then there was nothing . . .

Except that there *was*. A collection of sensory details that meant nothing in isolation. There was the hard metal smell of rust, the burning chemical odour of powerful cleaning agents. Metal, bright and mirrored and full of pain. Blood, cold and wet. *And the screaming.*

He shuddered as that came back to him, a door in his memory opening wide, bringing a torrent with it. At the time, he had not processed the sound correctly, but now he knew that it had been Tarki. Tarki, screaming in absolute agony, weeping and bawling.

And perhaps some of the screams had also come from Halil's lips.

He touched his face, feeling the tracks of dried tears. The prickling pain in his stomach was so fierce, he could only breathe in quick increments, panting like a dog.

Where did they take us? With mounting horror, he found that the cotton *thawb* he wore was marked with dots of fresh blood. His hands shaking, Halil rolled back the garment to bare his torso to the air. He shivered and fought to keep himself from bringing up vomit.

A wadding of cotton wool was across his belly, held there by strips of yellow medical tape. Blood was soaking through the pad.

Tears gathering in his eyes, Halil picked at the tape, fingers trembling as he did so. It came away and allowed him to peer under the pad.

The prickling pain seemed to double, and he felt a wash of cold across his face as the colour drained from his cheeks. Vertical lines lay across his belly, from his crotch to his sternum. Each one a livid, fresh suture, held closed by rows of tiny plastic staples beneath a thin mesh bandage. Halil let the garment drop back, suddenly too terrified to look at what had been done to him. He saw others among the group with expressions that mirrored his own, brimming with fear and uncertainty.

It was then he realized that the bunk where Tarki had slept was empty. At last, he found his voice and managed a few words. 'Wh-where . . . is he?'

The gangly youth called Adad was sitting nearby, and he fixed Halil with a sleepy gaze. 'A teacher said he was sent back.'

Halil shook his head sharply, making himself giddy. That wasn't possible. They were on a ship, miles from their homeland. It was a lie, and he said so.

Adad didn't seem to hear him. He was gingerly probing at the bloody stitches in his distended stomach with a finger, their patterns mirroring those on Halil's belly. 'I know a story,' he said. 'A man put drugs in people's food and then cut them open. Took their kidneys to sell to the Saudis. They've done that to us.'

Halil forced himself to take shaky steps across the cabin, becoming lucid as he felt the chilly metal beneath his bare feet.

There was a teacher blocking the doorway, and he glared at the youth. 'Go back to bed. You are unwell.'

'Why did you do this?' Halil managed. 'What did we do wrong?'

'Nothing,' snapped the teacher. 'Idiot. It was for your own good. You were ill. Now you will be better. *Rest.*' The man gave Halil a shove, and the teenager staggered back.

Returning to his bunk, he saw that Adad was at a porthole, his pasty face pressed to the glass. 'Do you see this?' he asked.

Halil peered out of the window and saw pale skies over a wide bay, framing a concrete shoreline and a forest of towering blue cranes. Beyond were lines of cargo containers as far as he could see.

'Is that Africa?' said Adad, his pain momentarily forgotten.

Halil caught sight of a design painted on one of the mammoth cranes. Horizontal lines of white and red, a field of stars on a dark rectangle. 'Not Africa,' he said, shaking his head.

TWENTY

The teachers turned the youths out of their beds, making them stand in a line against the bulkhead. Anyone who had even the slightest wisps of facial hair was made to shave them off, and so attended, they seemed years younger than they actually were, men reduced to boys once again.

Halil could see the edge of a porthole from the corner of his eye, and the movement of light and shadow through it told him that the freighter had docked at the American port.

America. It seemed impossible to believe that he was there. As much as he had been fed propaganda tales of the unholy United States, he also knew the country from the snatches of stories he had seen from television and books. In his mind it was a riotous collision of all these things, stitched together from hearsay, the lyrics of overheard pop songs and the fiery rantings of angry imams.

A teacher told them to take off their clothes, and when they hesitated, the closest youth got a backhanded slap across the face. Halil and the others did not need a second lesson, and he rolled the *thawb* off his body. The others did the same, forming piles of dirty clothing at their feet. Soon they were shivering and naked, hunched forward to protect themselves from the cold air.

All of them had the same scars that Halil had on his belly, some so pale they were fish-belly white. He tried to understand what that meant, once more taking a hand and pressing it lightly on his stomach. The prickling pain flared and he hissed to himself, blinking furiously.

One of the ship's crew rolled a laundry trolley into the cabin and upended it on the deck. A pile of new clothes spilled out, their colours impossibly bright, along with dozens of blue cardboard boxes.

Inside each were brand new running shoes that smelled of plastic and processed leather.

'Dress,' the teacher told them, pointing at the pile.

Halil joined the others as they warily came forward and dug through the heap of trousers, t-shirts and sweatshirts. They fished out socks and underwear and garbed themselves in silence. Halil found a pair of jeans that were a size too large, a blue t-shirt bearing some incomprehensible logo and a dark, voluminous top to wear over it. Fiddling with the zipper, he went to the shoes and recovered a pair that matched the size of his feet.

'These are the clothes of infidels,' Adad whispered, pulling moodily at the front of a hooded sweatshirt. 'I don't like them.'

Halil said nothing as he knotted the complex laces of the shoes, just happy to be warm again. He looked up as the teacher accepted a box from another of the instructors. The teacher threw away the lid and began pawing through the contents. He removed laminated cards, and wandered back and forth between the youths, handing them out. Each of the youths also got a small paper bag.

When it was Halil's turn, the teacher peered at his face and then pressed a card into his hand. He looked down and saw that it was an identity pass, the same thing he had seen on the chests of police officers or government officials. Halil's face was there, a photograph of him he remembered being taken on his arrival at the orphanage.

In the paper bag there was an odd collection of things; a cheap digital watch, some boiled sweets, a packet of disposable tissues and at the bottom, foreign money. It didn't seem like much, a dozen copper and silver coins of varying sizes, and a fold of green paper notes that felt strange to the touch. The items seemed alien to Halil, but he followed the example of the others and found pockets to stuff them in. He ate one of the sweets, crunching it nervously between his teeth.

When each had dressed and been issued with a card and bag, they were marched along the snaking corridors of the ship. The teacher led them down below the waterline, and despite the pain and the anxiety of their new scars, there was a growing air of excitement among the young men. A hatch creaked open and they emerged into a tall, cavernous hold.

Halil glanced up and saw that the roof of the hold was open and one of the blue cranes he had glimpsed from the window was hanging over the wide cargo bay. Drops of fine rain were finding their way down, and he felt them touch his cheek. A jolt of panic shivered through his body.

Where are they taking us? What has become of Tarki?

The teacher took them to a container made of corrugated steel and cranked open the door at one end, then gestured sharply. 'Get in. Remain silent once this door closes, or you will be beaten. When the container moves, do not cry out, do not try to open the door.' He glared at them, and they returned solemn, cautious nods.

Halil was the last to climb in, chancing a look upward in time to see the crane's hoist descending. The teacher shoved him in the small of the back and the door slammed shut, trapping the dozen or so of them in the dank, metallic box.

He found a place to sit, his back to the wall, and Halil lowered his head, drawing up his knees. None of them dared to speak as metal clattered on metal around them, and then came the sickening lurch as the container rose off the deck. In the darkness, Halil heard some of the others praying but he did not join in with them. He had the chilling sense that if there was a god out there, it had abandoned him long before now.

The container creaked as it swung about, before settling hard on another platform. Halil heard the hoist wind back, and they moved again, this time atop some chugging hauler that grumbled like the trucks that had visited the orphanage.

Then there was silence, for perhaps an hour. It ended with an abrupt rattle of chains at the door, and the container was opened by a towering figure.

'Come,' said Khadir. 'Take your first steps across the battleground.' He backed away and let the youths scramble out.

Halil looked around, trying to take it all in. The container and the truck it sat upon were inside a warehouse. The roof over their heads was rattling with the steady patter of rainfall, and there were men here and there. Some had guns, some were teachers and some not. The commander was dressed similarly to Halil and the other teenagers, his features disguised beneath the bill of a black baseball cap. He said something Halil didn't hear to a man with a flat, dead expression, and got a nod in return.

At the back of the warehouse was a narrow, orange-yellow bus. On the side of the vehicle were the words *Wayne County School District*; again, they meant nothing to the young man. But he had seen vehicles like this one before, when the television had shown footage of American towns. He had the idea that they were commonplace here.

Khadir was speaking. 'This is the beginning of your most important mission,' he told them. 'And it requires a serious mind.' The commander held up one of the laminated cards. 'This will protect you as we travel into the heart of the enemy's territory.' The cards were a lie, telling others that the bus was from a school that taught only the deaf and the mute. If they did not speak, they could not accidentally reveal anything to their foes. 'It is imperative you maintain this fiction. If you fail, you will be abandoned here to die.'

Khadir's eyes fell on Halil and the youth's blood ran cold. *Tarki is dead.* Meeting Khadir's icy gaze was the catalyst for the sudden understanding of that truth, and Halil realised that he had known it from the moment he had seen his friend's empty bed. *Khadir, Jadeed, the teachers, they used him. Killed him. They're going to do the same with the rest of us.*

The commander walked away to talk to one of the mercenaries from the boat, and a teacher snapped at the young men, telling them to board the bus. The ragged group marched to the vehicle, but Halil's panting breaths came in shorter and shorter bursts. He could feel a rising tide of panic welling up in him. Sweat beaded his forehead and his eyes darted around. His thoughts were slippery and hard to hold on to; Halil wanted to flee, to escape from these strangers who pretended they were his mentors. Khadir was coming back now, marching toward him.

Halil looked away, afraid the commander would read the doubt on his face, and caught sight of a door leading to the docks. *But what is beyond it?* He couldn't answer his own question, visions of the strange America that existed in Halil's thoughts like a patchwork thing. It terrified and enticed him at the same time. *Didn't they say that America was supposed to be a land of freedom? Was that a lie too?*

In that moment, Halil understood that he would never be allowed to know the answers if he climbed aboard the bus. He was almost at the step, following the other youths inside.

The animal fear in him made Halil's choice before his rational mind could process it. The burning pain jabbing at his chest, he suddenly burst into motion, shoving Adad out of his way, pushing the other teenager on to the bus. He broke into a run and scrambled toward the warehouse door, colliding with it in his haste. It juddered open, exposing Halil to the rainy air outside. Behind him, Khadir was shouting.

He ran; but each as each footfall slapped hard against the concrete dock, it was like the echo of a bell striking, the pain cutting into him with every jarring motion. He slowed and staggered, eyes prickling with tears. Halil coughed and brought up a stream of thin, watery puke. He stumbled to a halt and retched, no more than a few hundred metres from the warehouse.

Blinking against the rain, Halil wheezed and looked up, seeing canyons of metal boxes ranging away in every direction. Towering light poles marked off the distance, making it seem vast and impossible to gauge. He felt terrified and utterly lost.

Then Khadir was suddenly at his side, dragging him up from his knees, shouting at him. The commander's dark eyes were aflame, and he cocked back his hand to strike at the youth. Halil flailed, trying to deflect the blow he knew was coming, and missed. His hands snatched and caught the bill of Khadir's cap, blindly pulling it away.

The punch hit the youth in the side of the head and it tore his footing out from under him. The world turned around Halil, and wet tarmac slapped him in the face. New pain bloomed, hot and red.

Khadir hauled Halil back up once again, grabbing back the cap and pulling it down low over his brow. 'You disappoint me, boy,' he snarled, shoving Halil toward the warehouse. 'I thought you had steel in you.'

Halil wanted to curse the man, to demand he tell the truth about Tarki and all the others who went missing, 'sent back' into oblivion. But he was too weak, too afraid to do anything else than fight the tight agony contracting his chest. He waited for a death blow to come, for the whisper of a drawn knife. There was no such release.

Back inside the warehouse, Khadir forced him to climb into the bus, under the sullen gazes of the other youths. *I am the lesson for today*, Halil realised.

The commander drew the shape of a pistol from under his jacket and rested it on Halil's forehead. 'If every life were not vital to the work, I would end this one now and toss him into the ocean,' Khadir snarled. 'Any more foolishness, and death will come early and without honour to the weak of spirit. Do I make myself clear?'

The youths all nodded meekly, and Halil was allowed to find a seat toward the rear of the bus. He collapsed into it, his head falling forward.

'You are stupid,' hissed Adad from the seat in front. 'Where did you think you were going?'

'Don't know,' he managed. 'Out there. *Not here*.'

Adad said something about doing as you were told and showing respect, but Halil wasn't listening. For the first time since they had left Turkey, he heard voices speaking in English – he recognized Khadir's clipped, educated diction and the monotone drawl of the dead-eyed American in the driver's seat.

'You know the details?' Khadir was asking.

The American snorted. 'Yeah, don't sweat it. Willard and Pershing is the fall back, I got it.' The words registered with Halil. The seemed like names, but they meant nothing to him.

'Then drive,' said the commander. 'I want us there by morning.'

The engine grunted to life, and the bus rolled away into the drizzle.

'We're here,' said Malte, and Marc came out of a light doze with a start. They were the first words he had heard the driver say.

He looked up, blinking away the edges of the sleep he had fallen into, rocked into it by the swaying motion of the SUV as it rode down the New Jersey Turnpike. Marc rubbed his face and peered out of the window.

Thin rain streaked the glass, disrupting the radiance of passing streetlamps and the headlights of other cars on the road. The weather was turning, the drizzle just the leading edge of a glowering storm front that was already hitting Manhattan Island and would soon be here across the bay.

He stifled a yawn. Despite the amenities aboard Solomon's private Airbus, Marc had found it difficult to snatch any rest on the flight. He skipped off the surface of sleep like a thrown stone skimming a lake, in the end having to make do with a vague simulacrum of it that now left him feeling strangely hollow. Delancort handed him a bottle of water and he drank from it, watching the Canadian set up a collapsible console that snapped into place against the back of the seat in front of him.

He recognized some of the systems – radio frequency and wi-fi sniffers, an encrypted cellular communications hub. It was a cut-down portable version of the kind of gear he had operated along with Leon and Owen in the back of Nomad's forward operations vehicle. But this time, it was Delancort who would be running comms and digital, and it was Marc who would be *getting out of the van*. The thought made him shudder unexpectedly, and he tensed. In the opposite seat, Lucy caught the moment and gave him a curious look. 'You okay?'

'Fine,' he lied. 'Green for go.'

She didn't say anything else, zipping up the black tactical vest over the rip-stop jumpsuit she wore beneath. Marc was dressed in identical fashion, although his vest differed from Lucy's by the number and distribution of ammo pouches and gear packs.

'Are you sure you are ready to proceed?' Delancort cocked his head, watching Marc carefully. 'Perhaps it would be better if Malte accompanied Lucy instead.'

Marc shot the other man an angry look. 'It's a bit bloody late to ask me now, don't you think?' He turned away irritably, angry at Delancort's question and the doubts it brought up, angry at himself for letting it get under his skin.

Lucy carefully lifted a spindly grey battle rifle from a case at her feet and checked the weapon's action before loading a twenty-round magazine of 7.62mm bullets. Marc recognized the gun as a Mark 14 EBR, a combination assault rifle and marksman's long arm. Lucy seemed completely at home with it, adjusting the extendable shoulder stock by feel as she glanced out of the window. The SUV was turning as it manoeuvred through an open gate.

For Marc's part, he had a slab-like Vector K10 sub machinegun lying across his lap, the weapon's rhomboid shape broken up by a slim noise suppressor and a holographic peep sight.

In the driver's seat, the blond-haired Scandinavian killed the lights and pulled the SUV in behind a cargo container. Black shadow swallowed the vehicle, and now Marc could only see by the soft glow cast by the displays on Delancort's console.

'You know how to use these, right?' asked Lucy, pressing a set of Ortek night vision goggles into his hand. Marc nodded and pulled the NVGs down to hang around his throat, next to the tab of an inductor microphone.

Delancort reached for handle of the double doors at the rear of the vehicle. 'Malte is going to stay close, keep the entry point safe. You two . . .' He trailed off. 'Well. You know what to do.'

'Usual rules,' said Lucy, her tone turning business-like. 'We're caught, we're burned. Rubicon will deny having anything to do with us.'

'I don't even work for Solomon,' Marc muttered.

'Then you're halfway there already,' Delancort smiled, a little unkindly. '*Bon chance*.' He twisted the handle and Marc followed Lucy out into the rain, their boots clattering against the wet concrete of the dockside.

Lucy stayed near the metal wall of the cargo container and Marc walked where she walked, feeling the familiar adrenaline tingle in the tips of his fingers. He held the Vector tighter, trying to stop himself from drumming out a mindless rhythm on the grip of the gun.

It was all moving fast now. It seemed like just a moment ago they had been coming in to land at Newark, then discreetly ushered off to a private hangar where equipment and a vehicle were already waiting. The set up might have been very different, but the vibe was exactly the same; the moment Marc had stepped off the plane, he had felt it – that identical tension in the air, the same razor's edge sense of a mission about to launch.

And I'm in it, he told himself. *All the way*.

He heard Delancort's voice buzz over the bone-induction radio and saw Lucy nod. 'Copy. Berth nineteen. The *Santa Cruz*.' She looked over her shoulder at Marc. 'We're moving. Stay out of the floods.'

Rounding a line of containers, there, rising like the wall of some ancient fortress, was the hull of the freighter. Rubicon's intelligence team had narrowed down the probabilities and made the informed guess that the *Santa Cruz* was the vessel Al Sayf were using. Marc wanted to see the data himself, but Delancort had dismissed the idea. It came hard to Marc, accepting the fact that not every element of what was going on around him was his to manage. Back when he had been a part of Nomad, he would never have balked at the notion of taking a risk based on someone else's tradecraft – but his days on the run had burned that away. He dug deep and tried to find trust, but it was running thin. Once again, he told himself that he would only work with Rubicon until he had what he needed, until he could find a way to get to the Combine.

The *Santa Cruz* was lit by a halo of orange work lamps, giving it a hellish cast. Looking up at the ship, he slipped into cover behind the support leg of a massive crane and took a long breath. His mind couldn't help but slip back to a different night on a Dunkirk dockside.

'We need to get aboard,' Lucy whispered. 'Can't go up the gangway.' She pointed out men on the ship where the walkway met the weather deck, all of them trying to hide the fact they were armed with rifles. 'I got an idea.'

'Right,' said Marc.

'Hey.' She came closer and tapped him on the shoulder. 'Focus, Dane. You wanted to come with, I need you in the moment.'

'I'm here,' he insisted, mentally shaking off images of a burning ship. 'What's the plan?'

Lucy pointed up at the great angular frame of the cargo crane rising above their heads. 'Up and over.'

Breaking the lock that kept the crane's upper tiers secure, Marc pulled open a safety gate and let Lucy take the lead. They climbed the steel staircase that zigzagged up the leg of the massive crane, and to Marc the ascent seemed to go on forever, his boots ringing on the metal as the rain spattered his face. Then abruptly the stairs ran out and they had reached the very top of the gantry, twin booms extending out from the dock and over the black waters of the bay. Up here, the wind wasn't cut by the bulk of the ships or the walls of cargo containers, and steady gusts buffeted the two of them as they advanced along a narrow service catwalk.

Marc chanced a look down and saw the distance back to the concrete far below. A strong burst of wind could easily make one of them lose their footing and go over, into a fall just long enough to let you realize exactly how dead you would be on impact. He hung the Vector on its sling and made his way forward using both hands to slide along the guide rails.

A red beacon blazed bloody red light across the end of the gantry, pulsing to warn off any low-flying aircraft that might venture too close to the harbour. The beacon gave Lucy's dark skin a strangely dead look. She shouldered the Mark 14 and fished two rectangular pods out of a pack on her belt. She peered at the drop, gauging distance, then used a thumb-wheel on each of the boxes to make an adjustment. 'Here, take one.'

Marc examined the object. About the size of a house brick and just as heavy, it was made of matte black plastic with bone-white wheel at one end. A karabiner spring hook dangled from it, at the end of a length of fine wire. 'What am I looking at here?'

Lucy dropped and looked over the edge of the crane gantry, out into empty space. Hundreds of metres below her lay the weather deck of the *Santa Cruz*, the big hatches open to reveal the first and third cargo bays to the air. Bay three, directly below them, was already empty, while unloading was still taking place at bay one. Floodlights lit the working bay, revealing the cavernous space inside the freighter, but Marc caught sight of the bay two hatch still firmly shut, and wondered why it wasn't also in operation.

'The box is something from Rubicon's engineering division,' she told him, drawing back to press hers against part of the crane's superstructure. It clanked into place, powerful magnets holding it firmly. Lucy pulled on the D-ring and secured it to a load-bearing hook on the back of her gear vest, just below the shoulders. Marc suddenly had a very clear idea of what the device was for. 'Don't touch the bare wire,' she told him. 'Some kinda graphene super-cable, or something. Take your fingers clean off.'

Marc nodded and copied her actions, securing his own unit far enough away that their wires wouldn't get snarled together. 'Maybe climbing up the anchor chain is a better idea?'

'Where's the fun in that?' Lucy asked, and rolled over the edge of the gantry like a swimmer dropping off the back of a boat. The box emitted a waspish buzz as it played out the wire, and Marc watched her fall toward the open cargo bay, the motion almost graceful.

'Ah, bollocks,' he said to the rain, and leapt, slipping back into the attitude he had learned during parachute training.

The ride was faster than he expected, and it happened in an odd kind of stillness. The open maw of bay three yawned beneath him as the *Santa Cruz* rose. As he descended, he glimpsed what seemed to be a figure, a guard on patrol walking around the ship's flying bridge – but he went unseen. The armed man was looking out toward the sea, watching for boats. Dropping from the sky on silent spider-wires, Lucy and Marc were almost invisible.

They fell past the level of the deck and into the rusty cavern of the cargo bay. Marc saw the bottom of the compartment coming up fast and swung his legs out, bending his knees to take the shock of the landing. Somewhere far above, the inertia reel mechanism in the box was tightening as the cable reached its limit, slowing his fall. Marc bobbed to a halt a meter over the deck and reached up to disconnect. He fell the rest of the distance, and caught a flicker of silver as the karabiner, now without his weight upon it, shot away as the box retracted it back.

Lucy crossed to him, her NVGs already set across her face. 'Enjoy the ride?'

'Yeah . . .' He managed. 'I did, kinda. Just give me a second, though. I have to wait for my balls to drop back out.'

She chuckled and tapped the goggles around his neck. 'Eyes on, Dane.'

He nodded and activated his NVGs. The full expanse of the cargo bay was suddenly revealed to him in lunar hues of grey and green.

'Entry complete,' Lucy was saying, pressing a finger to her throat mike. 'Where to first, over?'

Delancort's voice sounded in Marc's earpiece. '*The number two cargo bay. According to the port authority's logs, the ship's manifest says the loader hatches can't open because of a mechanical issue, but the captain has turned down the offer of a maintenance crew to help fix it.*'

'If anything is being hidden on this tub, that's where it'll be,' Marc concluded. He raised the Vector and checked the safety.

Lucy's head bobbed and she unlimbered her rifle. 'Okay. You're the ex-sailor. Which way?'

'Over there,' he said, indicating a hatchway on a raised gantry. 'That should take us through the companionway between the hull frames.'

'I got point,' she told him, and set off, climbing the stairs to the gantry two at a time. Marc came after, panning the Vector. She put her shoulder to the hatch and it creaked as it came open. Marc winced at the sound, convinced that the noise would be heard throughout the ship, but no alarms brayed.

His lips thinned. The monochrome world seen through the NVGs was unpleasantly close to the similar view he had watched via a remote feed from the members of OpTeam Nomad, only here and now, Marc was experiencing it first-hand, embedded in the danger instead of removed from it. He pushed away those thoughts and moved on.

Beyond was a corridor that branched off into other walkways, or stairwells that went back toward the upper decks. Marc silently directed Lucy, and she inched forward until they found the door they were looking for.

Another grunting snarl of rusted hinges brought them into bay two, and immediately Marc saw why the overhead hatches had not – and probably never would – be opened.

The bay had been refitted, sections of decking welded into place in order to turn the cargo compartment into some kind of workshop. There were a few lights in there, so Marc slipped the NVGs up to his forehead and scanned the chamber for any indication of what it was being used for. The work lamps revealed benches scattered with cutting gear, mechanical tools and electrical components.

'Hey,' called Lucy, from another bench. She held up a circuit board to show him. 'You know what this is?'

He let the SMG drop on its sling and came over. The circuit board was just one of dozens, long and thin, connected by flat bunches of wire. He held one up to the light and saw Chinese characters etched among the copper tracks and embedded CPU chips. 'This is military,' he announced. 'At a guess, part of an avionics package?'

Lucy accepted this without comment. Her attention was on something else, a support frame covered with a dust cloth. She grabbed a corner and pulled it away.

Ice formed in the pit of Marc's stomach as the objects under the cloth caught the light. The unmistakable shapes of two air-to-air missiles lay on the frame, their casings cracked open, more wires trailing from within like the tendrils of an uprooted plant.

He looked back at the circuit boards. 'Those are from these.'

'The PL-5's we were tracking,' announced Lucy, peering closer. 'Serial numbers match. Missiles built for the Chinese air force, traded to the North Koreans and sold on to the Combine by a general with an eye for dollars. But it doesn't make sense . . .'

As Marc looked around, he saw other cylindrical parts, other components that revealed themselves as pieces of the dismantled rockets. 'They took them apart. Why would they do that?'

Lucy shook her head, tapping her mike. 'Thunderbolts have been located, state is inert. I say again, *inert*. But something isn't right.'

'*I'm monitoring*,' said Delancort. '*Proceed. Report as you go.*'

She turned to Marc. 'When these were taken, we thought we were going to find Al Sayf converting them for use in an aerial attack. Maybe mounting them on a civilian light aircraft . . .'

'I get that. They could use them to shoot down airliners, fire at buildings . . .' He scowled at the idea, moving to examine one of the missiles more closely. He visualized the shape of the weapon and the parts that comprised it, as if it were an exploded engineering blueprint. 'But instead, they gutted them, and–' Marc's words died in his throat as a sudden realization made itself apparent. He turned about, looking in all directions. 'It's . . . gone.'

'Something wrong?' said Lucy.

'Look at this.' He held up a section from the front end of the missile and showed it to her. 'Tell me what is missing.'

And now she saw it too. 'Oh shit.'

'Yeah.' A single PL-5 missile had a warhead packed with one of the most powerful explosive compounds on earth, a substance known as HMX – but each rocket's load had been removed. 'Six missiles, you said. That means around thirty, thirty-five kilos of military grade explosives if they harvested the lot?' Even a small amount of that material, correctly placed, would have been enough to cause the sinking of the *Palomino* and the carnage in Barcelona.

He tapped his throat mike. 'These . . . thunderbolts . . . They weren't the first ones to fall into the hands of our friends, were they?'

Delancort's reply came back after a moment. '*It is possible. We are not certain. But we think they may have had more.*'

'They never wanted the missiles,' said Marc. 'They just wanted the warheads. Military-grade HMX makes the bathtub plastic explosive most terrorists use look like a joke. They're building bombs, Lucy. Bigger and nastier than anything we've seen them use yet.'

The woman didn't respond immediately. She was standing in front of another hatch on the far side of the workshop, studying the decking at her feet. 'Check this?'

Even from across the compartment, he could see the distinct mark of a boot print in front of the hatchway, left as if deposited by someone walking into the chamber. The print glistened, dark and oily in the half-light.

'Blood,' Lucy announced, matter-of-factly. 'No more than a couple of hours old. Tracked in here from the next compartment.'

Marc looked up as Lucy reached for the handle to release the latch and open the door.

But before her fingers could brush the metal, the hatch suddenly yawned wide and a figure filled the doorway; a thickset man with Slavic features set in angry surprise. In his hands he had an AK-47, the muzzle pointing directly at Lucy Keyes.

TWENTY-ONE

The guard caught Lucy by surprise, and she reacted a heartbeat too slow. Her hands were snatching at her rifle as the big Slav spun up the wooden stock of his AK-47 and cracked her hard across the face. She staggered back, her night vision goggles broken by the force of the impact.

He hit her again, this time a hard blow in the centre of her sternum, and she cried out in pain. Lucy fell against the raised gantry and lost her grip on her rifle. The guard swore at her. Catching sight of Marc, he rotated the Kalashnikov, ready to rip a burst of gunfire across the woman and then toward him.

Marc snapped the Vector to his shoulder as the door banged open, but he wavered as the guard stormed in, hesitating to shoot in case he caught Lucy in the fire zone. Now she had fallen clear, that moment of vacillation melted away, and he squeezed the trigger.

The silenced Vector gave a chattering snarl, the muzzle rising as a stream of .45 ACP bullets blasted out and caught the Slav straight on. The shots hit him in the stomach and chest, slamming him back into a guide rail near the open hatch. His legs gave out beneath him, and the guard toppled forward, falling over the edge of the gantry and down past the makeshift deck, into the murk along the keel-line. Brass shell casings clicked off the gridded platform at Marc's feet, rolling this way and that.

The entire encounter lasted less than twenty seconds.

Breathing hard, Marc ejected the magazine and reloaded before moving to help Lucy to her feet.

She growled through gritted teeth as she stood. 'Motherfucker,' she said, with feeling. Lucy probed the skin over her cheekbone and winced, turning her head to spit out blood.

Marc peered over the guard rail and saw the dead man splayed in a peculiar position a few metres below. His legs were at an unnatural angle, his chest a red ruin. 'That's a problem,' he muttered.

'Only if he's missed,' Lucy said thickly. 'Which he will be, probably sooner than we would like.' She gathered up the Mark 14 from where it had fallen. 'C'mon, we have to keep moving. If he was in there, he was protecting something.'

'Okay. Yeah.' Marc pushed past Lucy, not waiting for her to complain about him taking the lead, and crossed the companionway into another refitted compartment.

The metallic stench hit him as he opened the next hatch, and he wanted to tell himself it was just seawater and rust; but the odour had the tang of death about it. The light inside the chamber gathered in streaks of reflection across the black tarps that lay scattered across the decking. It was like the execution room back in the basement of the orphanage, but worse. Much worse.

Blood, on everything, as if someone had uprooted an abattoir and placed it here in the middle of the cargo ship. Lucy said nothing, but he heard her sharp intake of breath, the faint sound at the back of her throat that might have been a stifled gasp.

The compartment resembled a battlefield operating theatre, the kind of thing one might have expected to see in some Vietnam War-era firebase where soldiers were chewed up by withering enemy fire. An operating table, racks of equipment and gas cylinders were ranked to one side, visible behind olive-drab sheets that had been hung from wires to create some kind of partitioning. Large plastic cubes inside steel cages were filled with water, taps draining into grates below, perhaps to allow whomever had worked in here to sluice the blood from their hands.

Marc nudged open cases to find packets of sterile syringes, scalpels, bandages and more, still sealed and ready to be used. There were cool-boxes too, the kind you might take on a picnic to fill with ice and chill your beer. Inside Marc saw antibiotics, morphine and fentanyl ampoules.

'God, not again.' Lucy's voice was rough and scratchy. 'What the fuck were they doing in here?'

The machine shop and the dismantled missiles had been ominous enough, but this . . . Marc's thoughts fell toward the darkest, the most horrible of possibilities as he circled the compartment, taking it all in. On one gurney he found a plastic tray laid out with little spiders of electronic components. He recognized coin-sized lithium batteries connected to the stripped-down guts of Bluetooth earpieces, hand-assembled things constructed from repurposed off-the-shelf hardware. Each unit ended in a tiny metallic tab, an electric igniter of the kind used to set off fireworks. 'These are remote detonators,' he said tonelessly. Each one was sheathed in a furry covering that resembled cotton down.

'What you got?' asked the woman.

'*Shit.*' Marc felt bile rising in his throat and sat heavily on a stool. 'Oh shit, I think I know.' He looked up at her, swallowing hard, breathing through his mouth. 'Those things are wrapped in Gore-Tex. The stuff they line waterproof coats with.'

'I don't follow you–'

He waved her to silence. 'These are *implants*, Lucy. That material is what they use to coat medical implants, like replacement bones or organs . . . It fools the body into ignoring the immune response, stops it getting rejected . . . ' He trailed off. It was all coming back to him, clear as day. The long and complex explanation the doctors had given him and Kate when they talked about Mum's kidney replacement surgery, a lifetime ago. 'Do you get it? You can cut someone open, put those inside them, stitch them back up.'

Lucy's eyes widened in shock. 'Along with, what? A pound of HMX?'

He nodded bleakly. 'More than that.' Marc was finding it difficult to swallow. He couldn't get the acid taste out of his mouth. 'Get into the space around the gut . . .' He pressed a hand to his belly. 'Surgeons call it the peritoneal cavity. You could put, hell, I don't know . . . Wads of the fucking stuff in there, chunks the size of cricket balls.'

'And then you got yourself a walking weapon.' She spat on the deck. 'That's how the orphanage figures into this. It wasn't for training soldiers. It was for finding *mules*.'

'There is problem,' said the bullish Serbian, cradling an Uzi in his hands, his thickly-accented words hard and percussive.

Grunewald looked up and took a moment to flick a speck of lint off the lapel of his leather jacket. He wanted to be off the *Santa Cruz* and away from here, but closing up the back end of this stage of the operation was taking longer than he wanted.

The Eastern Europeans the Combine had supplied as low-level muscle were competent but they were not efficient, and they dragged their heels with any work that didn't include intimidating people or shooting at things. Grunewald had ordered them to clear out any materials that might immediately link back to the group and pack them into a cargo container to go overboard.

'What now?' he asked. 'This needs to be done by dawn, you understand that?'

The Serb shrugged and held up his radio. 'Man is silent. No call.'

Grunewald frowned. 'A guard missed his check-in? Where is he supposed to be?' It was a problem with using these criminal types, not professionals. They were easily distracted.

'No call,' the Serb repeated. 'Man was in hold. Hospital. Sergey up on deck heard noise.'

'What kind of noise?'

The other man held up his weapon. 'Gun,' he explained.

The mercenary's face twisted in irritation and he stood, pulling a pistol from an inner pocket. 'Get Sergey and some other men. Then show me where.'

Marc and Lucy were silent, both of them struggling to process what they had discovered in the makeshift operating room.

At length, she took a look around. 'This is what you'd need,' she said to the air. 'A surgical theatre, somewhere more or less sterile, enough antibiotics to stave off any infection. Anaesthetic, oxygen, couple of pairs of hands who know their way around the ER. All that would be a piece of cake for the Combine to source.'

Marc was only half-listening to her. He was thinking back to the intelligence reports that had come out of the Barcelona bombing. The Spanish had been stymied by the data they had recovered from the building's metal detectors; according to the scanners, nothing had gone through the doors that could possibly have concealed an explosive device powerful enough to level the police station.

But clearly, it had. *Some poor bastard with a bomb sewn inside him*, Marc thought, horrified by the grisly prospect.

It was a hideously ingenious strategy. With security systems like advanced chemical sensors or millimetre-wave body scanners capable of peering through outer layers of clothing and even false limbs, the conventional suicide bomber was no longer the most expedient option for militant extremists. Terrorists couldn't just strap a bomb vest under a big coat and walk on to an airliner or into a protected location without being identified . . . but someone carrying a device actually *inside* their bodies would be virtually undetectable.

Lucy's thoughts were taking a similar path. 'This is the next evolution of suicide bombing, right here,' she said, eyes flashing. 'You know about the al-Asiri bomb in Jeddah, back in '09? One guy, promising to give up his pals working for Bin Laden, just as long as he gets some face time with the head of the Saudi counter-terror force. He gets the meet, makes a call on his cell and the fucker just *explodes*. He had a hundred grams of plastic explosive stuffed in his gut, and that only has a fraction of the potential of HMX . . .' She caught herself and tapped her throat mike. 'Hey. You getting this horror show out there?'

'*Yes*,' said Delancort, and his tone was muted and sober through the buzzing distortion of the radio link. '*Every word. Unfortunately.*'

'Did you know this was what they were doing?' Marc demanded.

'Hell no!' Lucy snapped back, and he believed her.

Marc got to his feet and straightened. The revulsion of what they had discovered here would have overwhelmed any rational person, but he couldn't allow that feeling to rise up in him now. He had to be cold and clinical about this, remain focused on the situation at hand and figure out how they were going to deal with it.

He stared at the operating table. 'We've missed what they were doing in here,' he said. 'They must have been implanting the devices during the voyage . . . So either the bomb carriers are still on board–'

'Or they've already been deployed against their targets,' Lucy concluded. Then all the work lights in the compartment died and plunged them into pitch darkness.

Marc snatched at the NVGs and pulled them down over his eyes as the shooting started.

With the strike to her head still echoing through her bones, Lucy felt as if she had been plunged to the bottom of a well as the cargo bay went black. For dizzying seconds, she could see nothing at all as her eyes adjusted, and she silently cursed the guard Marc had dispatched for smashing her goggles beyond repair. She was starting to pick out shapes inside the compartment when muzzle flashes flared yellow-white on the gantry above, and through the shadows she heard the humming of heavy calibre rounds cutting the air about her head.

She fired blindly with the Mark 14, shots kicking off as fast as she could squeeze the trigger. She dodged away, scrambling for cover behind one of the big cube-shaped water barrels. Lucy thought she saw the glitter of glassy eyes up there, mechanical insect faces staring down at her. The mercs had low-light goggles too, the more complex four-scoped versions that gave better coverage with the trade-off of making the wearer look like a mechanical cockroach. She saw Marc shooting back, but the attackers had the numbers, and they were getting their range.

Shots punched holes into the far side of the plastic barrel, causing water to jet across the bloodstained deck. Lucy pivoted and fired a couple of bursts at the point where she estimated the incoming rounds were originating. She was rewarded by the keening shriek of ricochets as her shots sparked off the walls of the freighter.

They were rats in a trap here, and she could only guess at how many men the mercs had to pour in after them. *The guard*, she thought, *they found us because we smoked that unlucky son-of-a-bitch.*

'We gotta move,' Marc called out. 'I'm coming to you!'

He burst out of cover, a shadow against shadows, spurts of exhaust gas from the Vector's muzzle dancing in the air. Lucy did what she could to give him covering fire, shooting wildly until the mag was empty.

Marc didn't pause, just grabbed at the strap of her tac vest and pulled her with him. With Lucy virtually sightless in the depths of the ship, only he could see well enough through the Ortek goggles to guide her to some kind of safety. She ran with him, gripped by a horrible, naked sense of vulnerability.

Marc's gun ran dry, and he shouted 'Hatch!' as they both collided with the closed doorway on the far side of the compartment.

Her hands scrambling over the old metal, she found the lever and threw her weight behind it to shove it open. Shots clipping at their heels, they fell through into the dark corridor beyond – and for a second Lucy was afraid the fall would go on forever.

Marc helped her up, and she could make out his silhouette, hear him gasping with effort.

'Where are we?' she asked, becoming aware of pain across the backside of her right thigh. Lucy reached down, found a rent in material and her hand came away wet. *Damn.*

'Another space between the hull frames,' Marc was saying. 'Walkways and gantries in here going all the way up to the weather deck . . .'

They ran down the corridor, each footfall making her wince. She chanced a look up and saw glimmers of light like faraway stars. Lucy could just about make out the lines of the metal struts holding the *Santa Cruz*'s superstructure together.

Marc was looking at her, catching up to her situation. 'You're bleeding.'

'Grazed,' she corrected, being generous about the bullet wound. 'Hurts like hell, though.' Lucy heard movement back down toward the doorway, and shoved him in the chest. 'Get up higher.' The empty ammunition magazine fell out of the rifle as she flipped the ejector tab and slammed home a fresh twenty-round box in its place. 'I need a shot-caller.'

She dropped into a crouch, hissing at the pain, and pressed herself into the cover of a thick iron stanchion. The Mark 14 pointed back toward the doorway they had come through and she fired off a couple of rounds, watching them spark off the lip of the hatch.

'They're gonna come in there,' Marc told her.

She nodded. 'And I can't see them. But you can. So get up. Spot for me. We need to thin them out, else they'll run us down before we can get topside.'

He didn't say any more, and Lucy heard his footsteps retreat, the grunt as he climbed the closest maintenance ladder.

'*Copy*?' Marc whispered into the radio, sounding in her ear.

'Copy,' she repeated, working to moderate her breathing and reduce the motion of her rifle's barrel. 'Anything?'

'*Wait one.*'

Marc's world was a hazy landscape of fuzzy emerald shadows and white shapes that loomed out of the murk, like some lo-rez vision of an underwater scene. Twice he bumped into supports, or reached out to grab something that turned out to be far beyond his reach. Doubling back, he skidded to a halt on an iron platform suspended between two ladders. A narrow walkway extended off in both directions toward the stern and the bow, another access channel running the length of the ship. The decking swayed unpleasantly as he put his weight on it, and he snapped back to the guard he had shot, the man going over a similar rail. It would be a longer drop from here, he noted, and after the high-speed descent from the crane, he decided he had done enough falling off of things for one night.

Settling to his haunches, Marc fumbled with the unfamiliar Vector, making a meal of reloading it by feel alone. But he didn't want to take his eyes off the open hatches – there were more than one, he realized – and put Lucy at risk.

'Watch your fire,' said an angry voice, carrying out of the other compartment. It echoed off the walls, making it hard to be sure exactly where it had come from. Marc tensed as he recognised the clipped accent. 'We need them breathing, one of them at least.'

'I know that voice,' Marc said into the radio. 'Grunewald. He's a hired gun working for the Combine.'

The professional, he thought. The man who had threatened the lives of Marc's only living family, who had left him to be brutally murdered on the peak of Mount Etna.

Through the dull eyes of the NVGs, Marc saw white shapes moving at the open hatches as men tried to inch their way forward. 'Multiple targets,' he said, pressing the throat mike. 'Twelve and one o'clock.'

Lucy's reply was a snarl of three quick shots, so close together the sound of them ran into one long report. Someone screamed as she struck meat and bone, another fell back without a cry.

'A little low,' he corrected. 'Come up a couple of degrees. More on the way now.'

Beneath his feet, Lucy was effectively shooting blindfold, guided only by her own senses and by his vantage. Still, she was brutally effective when her shots struck home, and as the guards boiled out into the corridor in an attempt to rush her, the sniper killed enough of them to make the rest dodge in and out of their sparse cover.

Marc was calling out clock numbers again when he felt the suspended walkway under his feet vibrate as someone put their weight on it. He looked up and saw more white blurs, these ones coming for him, angular shapes in their hands.

But Marc saw the jerk of shock as they laid eyes on him, surprised to see him up on the higher gantry. Marc turned and brought up the SMG one handed, pushing himself back with the other as he fired. The Vector brayed and shots sprayed out in a corkscrew pattern, killing one man and wounding a second. The third had more time to react and fired back at him, the thunderous boom of a pump-action shotgun roaring. Marc flinched away and more by luck than judgement the blast was wide of him. He caught a couple of hot specks of thirty-ought buck as they raked his shoulder. Marc fired again, his free hand coming up to slap the Vector's fore grip and hold it steady. This time, a burst of rounds took off the top of the shotgunner's head and he collapsed on the walkway with such dead-weight force that the entire thing creaked and swayed alarmingly. Choking on fresh cordite fumes, Marc scrambled back to his feet and looked straight down.

Lucy was still shooting, pacing shots to keep the advance pressed back, and that was why she hadn't noticed the hatch *behind* her swinging open. Marc cursed himself for missing the other doorway where it lay buried in shadows, and shouted out her name.

She heard him and rolled over, coming around with the gun. The men behind her were a large, bull-necked guy aiming an Uzi and the Swiss merc from the mountain. Before Lucy could get off a shot, before Marc to do anything to intervene, Grunewald fired a taser into the woman's side and discharged a surge of crackling electricity through her. Her scream resonated, bouncing off the iron walls of the compartment. Shots from the other man's Uzi followed, sparking as they clipped the walkway at Marc's feet.

He bolted forward, slamming into the next hatch along, and tumbled through into the next length of the walkway, swearing violently.

Her body on fire, her nerves as tense as steel rods, Lucy's teeth ground together as powerful hands dragged her back along the metal deck and into the reeking space of the improvised operating room. She had been hit by stun gun discharges before, and she knew that all she could do was ride it out. Although only a fraction of the weapon's charge got into her body through the protective material of her tactical vest, it was still enough to temporarily rob her of control of her limbs. Finally, the shuddering tremble that ran through her began to ease away, and in its place she felt a deep ache in every joint and muscle. Lucy rolled on to her hands and knees, gulping in air. She tasted blood in her mouth and retched.

She looked up in to the eyes of a man in a black leather jacket, artful designer stubble on his face and a disappointed air about him.

'Who are you?' he asked, toying with a Sig Sauer semi-automatic. His accent was middle-European – this was Grunewald, the voice Marc had identified earlier. His gun wasn't exactly pointed at her head, but it was close enough that she wasn't willing to make any sudden moves. 'Who are you with? How many of you are there? Pick one, any one. Take your time.' He cocked the weapon to show that last part wasn't true.

'You need . . .' She tried to speak, and it was hard, her tongue lolling in her mouth, thick and heavy in the wake of the taser shock. 'You need *to get the fuck out of here*!' She shouted the last part, slapping at the throat mike in hopes that her words were transmitted to Dane and Delancort.

Grunewald's face soured and he leaned in and pulled at her collar. He saw the microphone rig and ripped it away. 'Stupid. We're going to find your playmate.' He turned to the balding thug at his side and prodded him in the chest. 'Tell them to get the other one. Use the tazers, that's why you have them. Bring him back alive.' He looked back to Lucy and blew out a breath. 'This really is inconvenient. You're disrupting my timetable.'

'My heart bleeds,' Lucy retorted. She moved her head and saw the other guards dragging in the bodies of the men killed in the firefight. 'Theirs too.'

He glared at her. 'I'm going to have to find out who you are, and because I don't have time to waste, it will be very painful.' He paused to consider his own words, and looked down at the Sig. 'Then again, I may just shoot you dead.'

'We know all about the bombs,' Lucy told him, probing to see what kind of response she got.

'I doubt that,' Grunewald replied, turning to one of the other men. 'There's a blowtorch in the workshop. Bring it to me.' The mercenary held the throat mike pickup to his neck and pressed it there. 'Do you hear me? I'm going to burn her to death unless she talks.' He threw the comm rig away and stamped on it. 'Last chance,' he told her. 'I know you're an operator, I can tell. So, one soldier to another, let's find a solution that works for us both, yes?'

She thought for a second, and tried a different tack. 'I work for an organization with very deep pockets. They'll buy you out.'

He clicked his tongue against his teeth. 'I'm not greedy enough to double-cross the men who currently employ me. You understand. But tell me what I want to know and we might be able to negotiate something.'

'Can't do that. See, my boss wants all your bosses in shallow graves.'

'Ah.' Grunewald tapped the barrel of the Sig against his lips, almost as if he were blessing it. 'We seem to be at an impasse, then.' The other guard came in with the blowtorch and the merc opened his hand to accept it. 'Tie her to a chair,' he said, putting the gun down on a nearby bench.

'*You need to get the fuck out of here!*'

Lucy's words robbed Marc's legs of any forward momentum and he came to a halt, reeling back against a hull spar. There was something in the woman's voice he hadn't heard before. It wasn't fear. Desperation, perhaps, laced with cold dread at what they had seen in the operating room.

You should run. That icy little voice again, the one that sounded like Sam. *She's right. Leave her and get away.* Because people needed to know what they had discovered on board the *Santa Cruz*, they had to be warned. And maybe Lucy Keyes could buy Marc enough time to get off the boat and raise the alarm.

Marc gripped the guard rail hard, as if he was afraid he would fall. And perhaps he would, fall away into some deep, black nothing inside himself if he just let it all happen *again*. Everyone in Nomad had perished and it had been on *his watch*. Sam and Rix and all the others, they should still have been alive. Marc was their support, he was supposed to have seen the contingencies, known what to look for. But they were dead, and everyone else was telling him he was to blame, *and what if they were right?*

Why was he out here doing this, running headlong into something that he could only just about grasp? It would be safer to flee. It had *always* been safer, he knew that. The path without risk, that was what Marc Dane had settled for. Why did he think that this time would be any different?

He made a low, angry noise in the back of his throat, growling at the self-doubts. He forced himself to remember the moment at a ratty little café in Camden Town, of how he had felt and what he had decided.

Not here, Marc told himself. *Not today. Not again.* Lucy Keyes was not going to die because of him.

Below, Marc heard the clank of a hatch opening and pulled his goggles back down. A man emerged carrying a shotgun, his face lost behind the bug-head mask of the big NVGs. He was looking in every corner, leading with the gun's pistol grip in one hand, the hazard-striped bulk of a tazer in the other. He was coming closer, and Marc saw an opportunity. *Improvise and adapt,* he thought.

Acting quickly, Marc grabbed the edges of a metal ladder and slid down it, feet off the rungs. He made enough noise to get the shotgunner's attention, dropping squarely into the middle of the walkway a few metres from the other man.

'Looking for me?' He let the Vector fall to the deck and raised his hands. 'It's okay, mate,' Marc said conversationally. 'I surrender.'

The shotgun's muzzle drooped, and the steel tines of the tazer emitter aimed toward him.

Lucy's head had gone as far back as the metal chair would let her, the zip-ties around her wrists and ankles cutting into the flesh as she wriggled against her bonds. The burbling flame from the blowtorch threw jumping patterns of orange light off the walls of the makeshift operating room as Grunewald brought it closer. The mercenary twisted a dial on the back of the nozzle and the jet of fire became a blade of blue-white heat that seared her face, even a hand's length away.

'Talk to me,' he told her. 'Be reasonable. You're fairly attractive, and I imagine you would like to remain that way.'

'You're gonna ugly me up?' she said, eyeing the flame. 'I've heard that threat a few times. I gotta ask . . . If I was a guy, what would you say then?'

He paused, genuinely considering the question. 'The same,' he said, moving the blowtorch to his other hand. 'I mean, no-one wants third degree burns on their face, no matter what gender they are.'

'You're an equal-opportunity bastard.'

Grunewald nodded. 'Pain doesn't discriminate.' He leaned in. 'And so . . .'

The hatchway on the far side of the compartment clanked open and the mercenary swore under his breath at the interruption.

Lucy looked across the room as a guard in one of those four-eyed low-light rigs pushed a slack, barely conscious figure before him, hands bound behind his back. She recognized the Ortek NVGs covering the face of the prisoner, and the same matte black tac vest that she was wearing. 'Dane . . . ?' Her heart sank. 'Why didn't you run, dumb-ass?'

He had clearly been electro-shocked to within an inch of his life, trousers stained wet where his bladder had given out. The guard was struggling to hold him up, and finally let go, allowing him to collapse in a heap. The other guards in the room fingered their weapons, uncertain how to proceed.

'Dane?' Grunewald's eyebrows rose. '*Marc Dane*?' He flashed a grin. 'You came here with him? That *is* interesting. But sadly, I have neither the time nor the inclination to interrogate *two* people.'

He snatched up his Sig Sauer and put a bullet through the right eyepiece of the NVGs, the shot blowing a bloody divot out the back of the crouching figure's head. The dead man spun away, falling into the shadows beneath the operating table.

TWENTY-TWO

Shock gripped Lucy's chest like a vice closing on her ribcage, before the sensation was ripped away by a tidal wave of anger. '*You son of a bitch*!'

'Was he important to you?' Grunewald asked her, without concern. 'You should thank him. The fact that you are connected to that fool has just made your value to me increase considerably.' He put the pistol back down on the bench. 'We suspected he had some outside help, especially after intercepting the report from the British Embassy in Rome, but . . . Coming here? Coming *after* us? I have to admit, that was a dangerous choice to make.' He gestured toward the corpse. 'As you can see.' He hesitated, torn between taking a closer look at his handiwork and attending to Lucy. Unluckily for her, he turned away and picked up the blowtorch again, moving it from hand to hand. 'So. I have decided not to kill you. But that still means I will need to inflict a lot of pain.'

'Fuck you and the horse you rode in on,' Lucy spat back. Her training told her that what she *should* be doing right now was acting as if she were weak, maybe crying or begging for mercy. Anything to make Grunewald and his thugs underestimate her, to make them lower their guard. But she couldn't go to that place, not with Dane's body lying there in front of her. She had been starting to like him.

The mercenary sniffed. 'You think I did that out of some sense of enjoyment?' He chuckled and looked around at the other guards, the man who had brought the prisoner in, as if seeking agreement from them. 'Perhaps you're not aware of the previous attempts to end Mister Dane's life and the annoying ability he demonstrated in avoiding them. That bullet? That was just the clock re-setting. That was death catching up to him. An end he should have had back in France, along with the rest of his team.'

He nodded to the nearest man, a stocky figure with lank hair. 'Put the body with the others.'

The guard nodded and came forward, crouching over the corpse. He reached down.

Grunewald kept talking, gesturing with the blowtorch, the flame dancing. 'Dane couldn't live,' he said, as if the idea was ridiculous. 'Every second he was still drawing breath, he was making us look bad. My employers disliked being led on a merry chase by a man who couldn't even make the grade as an MI6 field officer.'

Lucy saw the guard stiffen as he pulled the NVGs off the dead man's face. Even from where she was sitting, she knew immediately it was not Marc Dane that Grunewald had executed.

The mercenary saw her expression change and he spun as the guard muttered another name under his breath. 'Sergey . . . ?'

What happened next was so fast it blurred into one frantic burst of motion. The guard that had brought 'Dane' into the room flipped up the bug-like visor over his eyes and nose, revealing Marc's pale, sweating face beneath. In the same instant, he pulled the trigger of the Remington M870 shotgun in his hands. The muzzle was low, aimed in an angle toward the deck that caught the thighs and torso of the crouching guard, buckshot ripping into him with a deafening report.

Lucy had been waiting, preparing for the moment when Grunewald would come into her range – and she instinctively knew that there would be no second chances. Her feet were back and slightly below the seat of the chair as far as the zip-ties around her ankles would allow, her coiled muscles now propelled her forward in an explosive movement. She came up and on to the balls of her feet, strength and momentum rolling her headfirst toward the mercenary. Lucy's forehead and right shoulder collided hard with Grunewald's ribs and she heard the satisfying snap of bone breaking. He lost the blowtorch with a grunt of expelled air, the tool clattering to the deck, and he went down under the weight of the woman and the seat she was attached to.

Grunewald cried out in pain, but Lucy was already rolling herself off him, spinning violently around so that the right arm of the metal chair and the zip-tie securing her wrist to it cracked against the deck plates. She rocked back and did it again. The second time, the tiny block of plastic that acted as the zip-tie's lock fractured and the binding loosened.

She caught the oiled *snap-clack* of the shotgun's slide being worked and a second boom of fire, followed by a third and a fourth. Ragged holes appeared in the cloth partitions hanging across the operating theatre, and trays of bandages were shredded into downy confetti by the wild blasts as Marc fired at the other guard.

She was aware of a hot fuel-oil odour in her nostrils, and saw the blowtorch searing a partition, fire jumping up its length. Grunewald was back on his feet and she tried to swing out and block him, but the mercenary kicked her and dove for the bench where he had left his pistol.

The second guard fell hard, another shot from Marc ripping into him, and he collapsed against one of the cases of drug ampoules. Lucy snapped off the tie holding her right ankle and turned awkwardly, still half-bound to the metal chair.

Grunewald snatched up his weapon and spun around, shooting wildly. Bullets cut the air and Lucy ducked, catching sight of Marc as he pumped the shotgun's slide once more. A dead cartridge tumbled out of the ejector port and he pulled the trigger. The hammer fell with a hollow click.

'Idiot,' growled the mercenary, and he sprinted for the far hatch, leaving them both to the hissing, spitting flames that swarmed across the discarded medical equipment and the flimsy cloth dividers.

Marc dropped the empty shotgun and came towards Lucy, throwing off his stolen goggles. 'Hold still!' he shouted, and from a pocket he pulled a small silver multi-tool. A keen knife flicked out and made short work of the remaining zip-ties.

Lucy booted the chair away from her with a grimace and coughed. The compartment was rapidly filling with smoke. 'We have to go after him.'

Marc was nodding, pulling at the bodies of the guards, searching their pockets. He found a short-frame Ruger revolver and claimed it. 'He's going to know where the bomb carriers are.'

'We can hope.' Lucy's eyes lit up as she came across her Mark 14 EBR, lying on a bench where Grunewald's men had discarded it.

Fighting back another racking cough, she slipped through the hatch, aiming with the rifle. Fast footfalls echoed above her, and she saw a shadow moving up the zigzag tiers of the support gantries. Grunewald hesitated for a second in the middle of his ascent to fire back down toward them, the shots ringing as they rebounded off the hull. A thin sliver of light, bright like a strobe, briefly blazed somewhere up there, cutting a purple after-image on her retina.

'If he gets off the boat, if he gets reinforcements, we're buggered,' Marc was saying.

Lucy didn't feel the need to voice her agreement and grabbed the rungs of the ascent ladder. She started upward in pursuit, lungs scratchy with the smoke. Marc was right behind her, the wheelgun in his hand clanking against the rungs with each step.

'Trick with the goggles . . .' She managed, as she climbed. 'That was clever.'

'Yeah,' he panted. 'Got his tazer turned round on him. Swapped my gear and vest with the poor bastard.' Marc gave a weak chuckle. 'Not much of a disguise, but down here in the shadows . . .' He trailed off. 'Thanks.'

'For what?' Lucy said, out the side of her mouth. They reached a companionway and a set of steel stairs leading the last few metres up to the deck.

'For being pissed off that I was dead. Most people don't seem to give a toss about me these days.'

'*De nada*,' she shot back, but her words were lost in a slow rumble of noise that came from the hatch ahead of them. All at once Lucy's brain caught up to the constant rattling noise, and she kicked open the hatch, ducking out of sight as she did so.

A blast of torrential rain gusted in through the open doorway, propelled across the deck by the winds that had brought a storm from New York City. A deluge of water lashed down, sheets of it moving across the weather deck and ringing off the empty cargo containers.

'Advancing!' Marc shouted, and he bolted out of the doorway, still clutching the revolver. Lucy came up with her rifle and saw movement further down the deck. Grunewald's attention was on the Brit, and he fired twice, trying to bracket Marc as he ran.

The Mark 14 bucked against her shoulder and the round was a near-hit. Yellow sparks flashed off a container wall near the mercenary's head, making him flinch away. He put a shot in her direction and ran as quickly as he dared along the suspended walkway over the weather deck's mid-line.

'He's going for the stern,' Marc called out. 'There'll be more of them in the island.' He was pointing at the towering section at the rear of the ship, atop which stood the freighter's bridge and crew decks.

Between Grunewald and the island was the open maw of the number three cargo bay, now sheathed with flexing sheets of tarpaulin while the unloading was temporarily halted. The cranes on the dock couldn't operate in conditions above a certain wind speed, and the storm was moving fast. Under the cover of the rain, Marc and Lucy ran quickly, weaving back and forth so as not to present easy targets.

At least, that was the idea. In reality, the mercenary was fixating on Dane, shooting at him every time he got a clear line of fire. Lucy was soaked through, drenched by travelling the distance across the deck in the teeth of the storm, and she fought off shivers. Dropping to one knee, she let Marc press forward and brought up the rifle again. In the cold and the pouring rain it was difficult to keep her hands steady, but as Grunewald surfaced from cover to make one more attempt to put a bullet into Marc's skull, lightning lit up the sky and she had him in her sights. Clear as daybreak.

Her shot hit him in the outside of the left thigh, ripping out a chunk of flesh, and through the rain she heard the man's scream.

Grunewald vanished behind a support stanchion, and she saw Marc hurdle it, before he too was lost from sight.

At the edge of the open cargo bay where the catwalk connected to the suspended companionway, the rain was already sluicing away the blood Lucy's shot had released. Marc came carefully to the lip of the bay, the Ruger leading him, and there he found the Swiss mercenary.

A few feet below the frame of the massive cargo hatch was a maintenance ledge, and it was immediately clear that Grunewald had slipped down on to it. The rain made it treacherous, and the wind had given him an unexpected push. He was bleeding badly, colour draining from his cheeks. The mercenary's nickel-plated Sig Sauer lay out of reach, lost on the weather deck along with his footing.

In desperation, Grunewald was trying to climb back up on to the lip of the hatch, but his left leg was nothing but dead weight, unable to push him that last metre to safety. Marc could see he was hanging on by his fingers, clutching at the iron hull braces as if he could dig into them by sheer force of will.

Grunewald gasped and spat rainwater. 'Don't,' he snapped, seeing the revolver. 'Help me.'

It was a long drop from the gantry to the bottom of the cavernous cargo bay. Marc moved closer, trying to find a place where he could brace himself and take the mercenary's weight, if it came to that. 'Make it worth my while.' He was oddly surprised at the tone of his own voice. It seemed flat, the words coming out of his mouth disconnected from him. 'You told me up on the mountain that you were a professional, yeah? So act like it. I'll trade you this . . .' He held out his hand a length shy of the man's grip. 'For Al Sayf. Targets. Routes. Names.'

Grunewald nodded, a defeated look in his eyes. 'I only know what vehicle they took. Pull me up and I'll tell you. I *will* tell you. I didn't lie about your sister, I won't lie about this!'

'Tell me first.' Some decent human fraction of Marc's soul wanted to reach out and grab Grunewald before he could fall. Being party to the death of a person in the act of trying to kill you was one thing, that was survival. But looking on as someone inched toward their end was very different.

He resisted the urge to take Grunewald's hand. It would make him seem weak in the other man's eyes. This had to go to the edge. He shot a look over his shoulder. Lucy was coming. He had to do this before she got here. 'Deal?' he asked.

'*Schysse*!' The curse burst from the mercenary's lips. 'All right! A school bus, Michigan state plates, southbound on I-95. *Now help me*!'

'Cheers.' Marc nodded his thanks. Then, very deliberately, he drew back his hand and folded his arms across his chest.

Grunewald's eyes widened, and the last of the cool, superior aspect he wore finally crumbled away. It revealed fear and fury beneath, as the mercenary bellowed at him. Grunewald scrambled at the metal in a last, frantic attempt to haul himself up from the fatal drop below.

Marc sat watching him, unmoving. That moment of brief empathy had been remarkably easy to silence. It wasn't a surprise, after all the things the Combine and this man had done to try to end him and the people he loved. 'I know we made an agreement,' he said, watching Grunewald's grip ebbing away. 'But I can't be as *professional* about this as you are.'

The gantry gave a shuddering clank and Grunewald was gone, spinning silently into the floodlit depths of the cargo bay. The sound of his body striking the keel was swallowed up by another grumble of thunder.

Halil leaned forward until his head was resting on his knees, but the throbbing sensation in his temples did not lessen, and the sickly pressure in his stomach grew worse. He gulped in air, feeling dizzy.

Adad and the others on the bus were avoiding him, not meeting his gaze, not daring to speak to him. Halil's disobedience in the warehouse had marked him as toxic and they did not want to share in the commander's displeasure.

He looked away, sliding closer to the windows, trying to catch some fresh air through the open slat near the top. Outside, he saw a brightly-lit veranda and rows of fuel pumps. The bus was parked at the furthest pump from a nearby garage, and Halil couldn't make out much inside the building. The American with the dead eyes was nearby, a cap pulled low over his head. He was feeding the bus's tank and never once looked up.

Halil could only guess at where they were. They had been driving along this highway for hours, hemmed in by walls of tall trees, back-lit by the slow crawl of a grey dawn. Once or twice he had seen a road sign for somewhere called Pennsylvania.

Some distance away from the gas station he saw another building, low and close to the road. It was faced in shiny chrome and glass, with lines of red and blue neon that danced in the windows. A café of some kind, he guessed, but bigger than any he knew from his home.

Thinking of food made him blanch, and Halil turned away, becoming aware of Khadir looking in his direction. Standing at the front of the bus, his arms were folded across his chest.

New pain prickled Halil's gut and he let out a low gasp, rubbing his face to hide the watering of his eyes.

Then he thought of Tarki, poor gullible Tarki and all the others who had been 'sent back'. Had they been sick like he was now? It was too much for him and his shoulders began to shiver, involuntary jerks of his throat making Halil heave and choke. He felt acid bile rising up in his throat and slapped a hand to his mouth, trying to keep it down.

Suddenly Khadir was pulling him out of the chair, shoving him down toward the open door at the front of the bus. 'You will not foul this vehicle,' he snapped.

Halil held it until he stumbled down the steps and then threw up the meagre breakfast they had been given after departing the docks. He had been punished with only a half-ration, and now it was all on the tarmac, a mess of thin drool and undigested bread.

'Shit,' said the American, as he returned, his nose wrinkling. 'What's wrong with him?'

Khadir ignored the question and gave Halil a shove, addressing him in Arabic. 'Get back on. Do not add to your shame.'

Halil nodded weakly and stumbled aboard. His joints ached and he dropped into the first seat that was free, near to the open door. He ducked his head to try and breathe in the outside air, and heard the two men speaking in English.

'What did you do to them?' said the American. 'That kid's got a face like curdled milk. Like he's gonna die.'

'All soldiers die,' Khadir replied coldly.

'Uh-huh.' The other man shrugged. 'Well, that one ain't going to make it.'

'He will serve the work.'

'Right.' The American zipped up his jacket and climbed into the bus. 'How much did you put in all of them, anyhow? Stuffed them like turkeys, huh?'

Halil's jaw dropped open. *How much did you put in?* The question hit him like a splash of freezing water, and his hand dropped to his stomach again, the pricking pain gnawing at him in response.

He pressed harder than he had dared before, gritting his teeth, and he felt something foreign *inside him*.

The teachers had not cut them open to help them. They had not taken something *out* of them, they had put something *in*.

Halil retched again, but he had nothing to bring up. He felt a great fear settle upon him, stronger even than the day when he had learned his parents were dead.

'We did what was required to make them warriors,' Khadir was saying, dismissive of the American's questions. He turned and met Halil's gaze – and the lion's feral instinct flashed in the commander's hooded gaze. 'You . . .' He advanced toward Halil, who stumbled back out of the seat and into the walkway down the length of the bus. 'You are listening . . .' Khadir searched his face, and Halil was shaking his head in terror. In that moment, he felt like glass, as if the commander could see right into him. '*You were listening*!' Khadir bellowed the last words at him and swatted Halil with a powerful backhand blow.

It was only then that Halil realised Khadir had still been speaking in English. He babbled out a fawning apology in Arabic, but it was too late. In his fear, Halil had revealed the truth and doomed himself.

'In the orphanage,' Khadir spat, towering over him, 'You were hiding in that room. A whore's son spy, listening to our secrets. Who did you tell, boy?' He hit him again, drawing blood. '*Who did you tell*?'

'No-one!' he cried out. 'I never spoke of it!'

There seemed to be no limit to the commander's fury, and when he met his gaze Halil knew that the man was going to murder him, wring his neck and abandon him in some roadside ditch in this alien country. He begged, but Khadir didn't hear him, and all around the other youths were a silent audience to this brutal moment.

'This is a liar and an animal,' the commander told the rest of them. 'I offered greatness, a purpose . . . In return there is only lies!' He raised his hand for a blow that would shatter bone.

'Watch it!' The American called out from the front. 'Company!'

Outside, a car was pulling into the gas station, rolling to a halt outside the garage. The vehicle was white, with a dark stripe along its length, a cluster of lights on the roof and a heavy black bumper at the prow. Everyone inside the bus froze, and Khadir's hand dropped to his side.

Policemen looked towards the bus as they climbed out, looked away and went inside the garage workshop. Halil seized on the moment of distraction and threw himself at the emergency exit door at the back of the bus, out of Khadir's grasp. The door gave under his weight and he tumbled out and on to the tarmac, landing badly on his hands and knees.

Desperately, he pulled himself up and into a stumbling run. *This time*, he told himself, *I won't stop. No pain will stop me.*

Khadir came to the yawning door and stopped on the threshold, throwing a wary glance towards the police car, and with each second that he hesitated, Halil was staggering further down the highway, making for the truck stop a few hundred meters distant. The garage door opened again and the two police officers – State Troopers, judging by their uniforms – paused to discuss something. Neither of them were looking in the right direction, neither of the men saw the youth skirting the pathway and making his bid for freedom. But they did look toward the school bus, and for longer than Khadir wished.

He snagged the handle of the emergency door and slammed it shut, then turned and glared at Teape. 'Start the engine. Pull out to the road.'

'But, the kid . . .' The American worked the lever that closed the front door and put the vehicle in gear. 'You're gonna let him go?'

'Of course not.' Khadir stalked to the front of the bus, ignoring the questioning looks of the other youths and his men. The latter, he gave a burning glare, turning his anger on them for failing to stop Halil from making a second escape bid. 'He betrayed us,' he told them all in Arabic. 'For that he will die.'

The bus lurched on to the highway, but Khadir tapped Teape on the arm. 'Drive past the truck stop, keep going for a short distance. Then pull in.'

'What do you want to do?' Teape asked flatly, as the truck stop flashed past. 'We don't have time for complications.'

'I am aware,' Khadir shot back. He pointed at a section of shoulder by the side of the road. 'Stop here.'

Teape studied the rear view mirror. 'Cops are still back there. Not following.'

'Yet,' he added. Khadir made a decision and went to the backpack he had brought with him. 'One of us will stand out,' he told the American. 'It has to be you.'

'You want me to go bring him back?'

Khadir paused, then shook his head with grim finality. 'That opportunity has passed. The boy is a liability now, that is apparent. But he can still be of use.' From the pack, he removed a bulky smartphone and a black zip-case the size of a book. He offered the case to Teape, who opened it and studied the contents blankly.

It took only a moment to explain what was required. As the American stepped off the bus, Khadir switched on the phone and navigated the screens with swipes of his finger, finding a custom program and activating it. The phone gave a soft ping as its wireless connections initialized.

Gina's Place had stood by the side of the highway since the 1950's, and although it had changed hands a dozen times since it was built, none of the owners had been able to bring themselves to strip away the old airstream shell around the truck stop's frontage. A generous critic might have suggested that added to the place's charm, but it was an understatement to say it had seen better days. The diner was too faded, too beat-up to be considered *kitsch* or *retro*. Booths lined the walls, patterned in pale wood, and stools with red vinyl heads marked out the distance along a bar in front of the serving area.

Gina's was just hitting the dawn rush, populated by overnight truckers who kept themselves to themselves, sipping bottomless coffee or working their way through fry plates with their noses in the sports pages. Halil came in, almost colliding with a gumball machine and a rack of tourist leaflets. A bell over the door rattled, drawing the attention of the waitress on duty. She flashed a plastic smile, not really registering the young man, and continued to top off the drinks of two weekender bikers from Upstate New York who looked to be heavy tippers. It was busy enough for him to become lost in the noise of the place.

In another time, Halil might have just stopped and stared at the inside of the truck stop, at this slice of Americana that seemed pulled through time from the country he knew from faded old books and the heavily-dubbed sitcoms that made his father laugh. But now the place seemed threatening and scary. It was so *different* from the world he knew. Fear had taken away the bold and adventurous child Halil had once been. Now, all that was left was a young man lost in his own desperation.

His eyes fell on the doors at the back of the diner, spotting the stick-figure sign for a men's room, and he moved quickly in that direction. Halil passed a rank of payphones and his hand reached for one of them. He pulled it back and frowned. *Who would he call? The police?* They would arrest him for entering the country illegally. They would be deaf to his pleas. American policemen were no different from those at home, bellicose men with guns and corrupt souls. *A doctor, then?* But doctors in this country were like shopkeepers. They would not even consider looking at a dying man unless he had a fistful of money.

Before anyone could question him, Halil went into the restroom. He almost fell into the closest toilet stall, locking the door shut behind him. Inside, it reeked of pine disinfectant.

He removed the bandages, unwinding them from about his body. Halil wadded them into a ball and stuffed it down the back of the cistern. His swollen, livid belly hung uncomfortably against his belt. Now he was aware of what had been done to him, he seemed to weigh twice as much as before. Halil fingered his lips and wondered if it might be possible to induce vomiting, to bring up whatever was inside him; but then he pushed the thought away. Throwing up outside had done nothing.

He thought about the school bus passing him on the highway as he sought cover under one of the big tractor-trailers. Khadir had threatened to leave behind anyone who did not obey orders, so was that to be Halil's fate?

Was he safe here, surrounded by these foreigners? Would Khadir come looking for him? Had he doomed all these people just by walking into the diner?

Halil rose shakily to his feet. *I have to warn them*, he told himself, and for the first time in too long, he felt his mother and his father at his shoulders. They were telling him it was the right thing to do. He could not allow his fear to put others in danger. He had to tell them. *He had to ask for help*. Halil slipped the latch on the inside of the stall and pulled it open.

The dead-eyed man filled the doorway, a ghost of curiosity in his expression.

His other hand came swinging around and Halil took a punch in the chest that threw him back. He collapsed on the toilet seat, gasping in pain.

Without betraying any flicker of emotion, the American forced his way into the cramped stall with the youth and locked the door. He held his hand around Halil's throat in a vice-like grip to stop him crying out.

The man pulled a plastic case from his pocket with his other hand, and opened the clasp with his thumb. With quick, dextrous motions, he plucked a narrow syringe from inside, and used his teeth to remove a safety cap covering its needle.

Halil's eyes widened and he put all the effort he could muster into a call for help, but then sharp pain flared in his neck where the dead-eyed man stabbed him with the hypodermic.

A creeping chemical chill washed through him, spreading out from his throat. His thoughts became slow, each sensory input growing sluggish and detached. The cold filled his body, and Halil fell unconscious, dreaming that he was being covered in frost.

'Cops are gone,' offered Teape as he approached the parked bus. He paused for a long draw on his take-out strawberry milkshake. 'Saw the cruiser go north.'

Khadir stood on the steps of the bus, glowering back at him. 'I told you to be quick.'

Teape shrugged and stirred the dregs of his drink with the straw. 'Had to make it look normal.'

'Where is the boy?'

'Men's room, back of the truck stop,' he replied. 'Gave him enough to put him down for at least an hour.'

The other man considered that. 'How far away will we be in that time?'

Teape shrugged again. 'Depends on the traffic.' He lost interest in the milkshake and threw away the remains. 'Outskirts of Baltimore.'

Khadir nodded and drew out his cell phone. The application displayed there had many settings, multiple functions that could allow him to activate any number of the weapons at any time, provided they were within communications range. From the phone, it was a simple matter of selecting a length of timer, a start point, and then pressing *SEND*.

He selected a single weapon, designated on the display as Number Seven, then dialled in a countdown of one hour and thirty minutes. He tapped the key and the phone gave an answering beep. A clock display began to spool down, and Khadir watched the seconds as they began their slow march toward zero.

To simply murder the traitorous youth would have been a waste of effort and material. Now, although it deviated from the agreed plan, he would serve a useful purpose by sowing confusion among the enemy, by misdirecting them. When the moment came, it would at first seem like a tragic accident – a gas explosion perhaps – and by the time the authorities got a scent of the true nature of the weapon, the endgame would already be in motion.

'So, we should probably get going,' Teape offered. 'Unless you wanna stick around to watch.'

Khadir slipped the cell phone into his pocket. 'Drive,' he said.

TWENTY-THREE

The rain drummed on the raised tailgate of the Toyota SUV, and Lucy leaned in to stay out of the wet. It was moot, really; their sortie across the deck of the *Santa Cruz* had soaked her to the skin, and even after dropping her sodden vest in the trunk, she still felt heavy and cold.

A pair of police cruisers rushed past as fast as they dared on the slick turnpike, making for the Port of New Jersey. From where the SUV was parked near a disused warehouse, she could see a tinge of orange glow in the belly of the storm passing overhead, most likely the spill of light from the fire aboard the freighter.

'Why are we sticking around?' she said to herself.

Delancort looked up from the back seat, his face lit by a laptop screen. 'This day is just getting started,' he told her. Lines of cables connected the computer to a pair of metal boxes as big as house bricks, and on the screen there was a flickering jumble of video images. The angle of the display meant that she couldn't get a clear look at it, but Lucy could just about make out that the footage was a grainy surveillance camera feed from the docks.

'How'd you get those, anyway?'

He nodded at the silent man in the driver's seat. 'Malte recovered them from the port authority security office. I sent him in while you were boarding the freighter. It seemed like a good idea.' Delancort indicated a wireless antenna module clipped to the roof. 'The New York office are in the loop. They are running real-time analysis of the imagery.'

'Right.' Lucy had guessed as much. Solomon leased several floors at the top of an expensive glass tower off Park Avenue, and as well as dealing with the minutiae of the Rubicon group's more mundane corporate interests, there was also a 'crisis centre' there – a vague name for a department staffed with technicians, hackers and other specialists with skill sets that skirted legality. Those people had been called in at oh-dark-thirty to provide back-up for the operation on the *Santa Cruz*.

Delancort glanced at a text feed in the corner of the screen. 'That confirms it. The local authorities have been alerted, fire and police only so far. Which is good. If luck is on our side, it will take hours for them to get to the heart of what happened on the ship.'

'By then this will all be over, one way or another,' Lucy said grimly. She glanced away and found Marc, standing off to one side under a corrugated steel awning. The Brit was staring out into the rain, his expression unreadable.

'*D'accord*,' said Delancort. 'But still. We cannot afford to waste time. The police arriving on the scene reported men fleeing from the ship, some of them possibly armed. Those are likely mercenaries in the employ of the Combine.'

Lucy thought about Grunewald, and she couldn't keep a sneer from her lips. He had fallen to his death by the time she reached the edge of the cargo bay, and as she stood there next to Marc, peering over the side, she asked the question. *What happened?*

I got what we need, he told her, and that was all he had offered, aside from parroting the dead man's description of the school bus to Delancort.

The French-Canadian was still talking. 'If one of those runners reports in to their masters, this could end before we can find the bus. They may pull the plug.'

'That's the smart call,' Lucy agreed. 'But I don't know if these guys are into being smart over making their statements.'

Delancort agreed. 'All the more reason to act swiftly.'

She nodded and fought off a shiver. 'Which brings me back to my first question.'

Delancort looked up at her. 'This is not waiting, this is regrouping. I am certain you would be the first to agree that what you found inside that ship was not what any of us expected to discover.'

'Yeah,' replied Lucy, thinking of the smell of blood and machine oil. 'You pass that on to the office too?'

'Mister Solomon has been informed.' Delancort's expression grew bleak. 'This is quite the horror our English friend has led us too.'

'How long d'you think someone could live with . . .' She fumbled at the words. 'With those *implants* inside them?'

'Not long.' The answer came from Malte, who looked back at her in the rear-view mirror. 'Two days?'

'Which means the attack will happen in the next twenty-four hours, if not sooner.' Lucy pushed away the sickened sensation inside her gut and tried to think like the men behind this vile matter. 'You got your weapons primed, you want to deploy them as soon as you can.'

A bell-chime drew Delancort's attention back to the computer and he clicked open a window on the screen. A stream of still images shuffled themselves across the display. He scrutinized a text attachment and muttered under his breath.

'What is it?' Lucy leaned in to get a better look.

He showed her. 'It seems our friends from the ship have planned this very carefully. There is some partial video of a vehicle matching the description Dane gave us exiting the docks. The image analysis team extrapolated possible locations inside the port complex where it could have been waiting. The driver clearly knew the sweep patterns of all the security cameras down to the second.'

She saw shots that seemed empty, until one looked closer and noticed that each contained a fleeting glimpse of a moving vehicle – a flash of tail-lights in one, the blur of movement in another, but nothing distinct.

'Our people are very good, though,' added Delancort. 'Look here.' He brought up a still of a length of dockside, and just visible in the edge of the shot was part of a warehouse. 'That's where the school bus was waiting. Out of sight.'

'How do you know?'

Delancort tapped a key and the still image came to life. 'Watch.'

For a moment, the black-and-white footage showed nothing of note, just the jerky motion of strung cables between light poles shifting in the breeze. Then there was a sudden tug of movement at the extreme edge of the picture. A figure came into shot, moving with difficulty. A gangly kid, Lucy guessed, judging by the motion of his arms and the too-big sweatshirt he was wearing. He walked like he had been hurt. For a second, the youth looked up into the air and the camera got a good look at his face.

'The New York office are running recognition protocols on him as we speak,' noted Delancort. 'But he's likely a clean skin.'

'He's scared out of his mind, is what he is.'

'He has good cause.' Delancort pointed at the screen, back to where the youth had first appeared. 'Keep watching.'

A second figure appeared, a bigger man in a baseball cap, and in less than two frames he was on the youth, grabbing him firmly. There was a ham-fisted scuffle and the cap came off. Lucy's lips thinned as she watched the youth get beaten down and dragged away, out of camera. The man snatched up his hat and put it back on, but not quickly enough to stop the video from capturing a shot of the side of his face. 'Who's the tough guy?' she asked.

'Someone we know.' Delancort dragged up another window and showed her the facial match. 'There is an eighty-one percent chance that is Omar Khadir. Extremist militant, known terrorist and the most active combatant in the Al Sayf organization.'

Lucy's mouth went dry. She knew Khadir by name, had been briefed on him when Rubicon had begun to suspect that Al Sayf were involved with the Combine. This was the first concrete evidence of his presence. The man had a reputation for pitiless action and unerring focus. If he had dared to enter the United States, it was only because he had an atrocity planned.

She thought about the HMX, the operating room and the nauseating possibility of the 'body-bombs' Marc had described. 'Maybe Dane was right. This is getting out of hand. We should talk to Rubicon's contacts at Langley. Get them on this. Khadir is on the Central Intelligence Agency's most-wanted list. They should be told.'

Delancort eyed her. 'Do you want to make that call? Do you want to read out the long list of laws we have broken to get to this point?'

She shot him a hard look. 'There comes a time when saving lives becomes more important than protecting your own ass.'

Another police car sped past and Delancort cocked his head. 'Then by all means, flag down the next officer you see. If you're right about the timeline . . . And from my experience of working with you, you usually are . . . You will still be in a holding cell when Al Sayf's latest act of violence happens.' He cocked his head. 'Tell me I'm wrong.'

Lucy sucked her teeth in irritation. 'You're not wrong.' She sighed. 'Okay. I'll need copies of all that.'

'Already in motion.'

'Car is here,' said Malte.

She turned to see a sleek Ford Mustang slowing as it approached. Black and shiny, the muscle car sported some silver trim and a feral-looking grille. Lucy raised an eyebrow; the car looked like some rich man's plaything – and she realized it was precisely that, one of Solomon's large stable of high-end vehicles.

The sound of the Mustang drew Marc from where he had been brooding, and he gave the vehicle a measuring look. 'What's all this?'

'Our ride, I guess.'

The Mustang's driver climbed out. She was a slight Chinese girl wearing a Bluetooth headset, a glossy red jacket and matching skirt. 'Delivery,' she said, with the hint of a local accent, rattling the keys in her hand. 'This okay? They said you wanted something quick.'

Delancort peered out from inside the SUV, not wanting to get out into the ongoing downpour. 'Lucy. Take the car, follow the school bus. They cannot have more than a couple of hours headstart. Interstate 95 tracks along with the coast for hundreds of miles, so you have a good chance of catching up to them. Just try not to get caught breaking any speed limits.'

'What about you?' asked Marc.

'We are going to the office in the city. We have to co-ordinate with Mister Solomon. In the meantime, if you make contact, call me *immediately*.'

'Hey. I'm Kara.' The girl in the red jacket nodded at the car. 'There's clean clothes in the back, weapons and some ammo.' She pulled a thin wallet from an inner pocket and handed it to Lucy. 'This is for you.'

The wallet turned out to contain very good imitations of a Federal Agent's badge and identity card in the name of Tracy Reese, one of Lucy's snap covers. She pocketed it before Marc could ask any questions.

Kara produced two thick smartphones and passed one to Lucy and the other to Marc. 'Compliments of Mister Solomon, so you don't need to fret about running out of minutes. Intel data has already been uploaded.'

Marc turned the phone over in his hands, studying the featureless black slab. 'No manufacturer's marks . . .' He paused to reach into the Toyota's trunk to grab his weather-beaten backpack.

'That's right,' Kara was opening the door of the SUV. 'More *Spy-Phone* than *iPhone*. Both got face-pattern keys so they won't unlock for anyone but the designated user, just look at the screen and you're golden.' She flashed a grin. 'You're MI6, right? It's virtually identical to the ones you guys give your field officers.'

'How do you know that?' asked Marc.

'Because we copied the design from a stolen one found on the body of an FSB agent.' Kara tossed a set of keys toward Lucy.

With a speed she didn't expect, Marc's free hand shot out and snatched the key fob from the air before it could reach her. 'This time, I'll drive,' he said firmly.

Kara's grin faded. 'Does he know how to handle an American car?'

Marc placed his hand on the Mustang's rain-slick hood. 'Shelby Cobra GT-500. Solomon's got good taste in motors.'

'Girl makes a point,' said Lucy, as she slipped into the passenger seat.

He didn't look at her as he put the car smoothly in gear. 'Belt up,' he said, fastening his seatbelt.

She barely had the connector snapped in place before the Mustang snarled, shooting away from the kerb and into the sheeting downpour.

Exactly at the instant the clock's hour hand snapped to ten, the door of the briefing room opened and the men holding John Farrier's future in their hands entered. It was the first time he could recall seeing Royce and Welles side by side, under any circumstances. An example, he supposed, of exactly how serious this whole situation was. Shaking off his travel lag, he swallowed a yawn and Farrier looked up as they took their seats. He had decided on the flight from Rome that he wouldn't get up for either of them, not until they gave him something that approached a degree of respect. Welles had one of his thick-necked security people with him, but Royce was alone. If anything, the head of K Section looked more strung out and weary than Farrier was.

'You look like I feel, Donald,' he told him.

Royce gave him a sideways look that was empty of anything. 'We're all making allowances,' he said vaguely.

'Some more than others.' Farrier drew himself up and turned to Welles. The bumpy ride in one of 99 Squadron's C-17 transport planes had burned a steady bad mood into him, and given Farrier more than enough time to stack up plenty of stinging rebukes for the man who had dragged him home. 'Let's get this colossal waste of effort dealt with.'

Welles looked at him for the first time, as if he had just noticed Farrier was in the room. 'In a hurry?'

Farrier leaned forward. 'I don't know what favours you called in, Victor, but you pulled me out of an operational cover in the middle of a major security incident without so much as a by-your-leave. I hope you think it was worth flying me back to London, because I'm going to make sure the director and the whole bloody operational committee know how you're throwing your weight around.'

'You arrogant prick.' Welles delivered the insult calmly. 'I mean, really. You have the temerity to bark at me when it is you that deserves the dressing down.' He shook his head. 'Where do you think my authorization came from? Are you really so monumentally self-assured that you believe everyone at the Cross would just *accept* you had nothing to do with Dane's appearance at the embassy?'

'It's not like I gave him an invitation,' Farrier shot back. *But then again, maybe I did, just without realizing it.*

'Oh,' Welles tapped his fingers on the table. 'That's the line you're going to follow? Because that's as tissue-thin a denial as I've ever heard. You aided and abetted a fugitive, John. And the more I think about it, the more I'm certain that Rome wasn't the first time.' He waved his hand at the walls. 'Remember this room? Where we held Dane when he walked in off the street? You were with him.'

'I don't recall that,' Farrier lied. 'Try again.'

'I think you helped him get away,' Welles insisted. 'And then you let him wander around a secure MI6 station like he owned the place. Which makes you culpable, in my book.'

'He was armed. I was being held hostage–'

Welles snorted with derision. '*Please*. I've read your file. If you wanted, you could have disarmed Dane and shot him dead before he got ten feet away.'

Farrier's lips thinned and he looked toward Royce. 'That would have worked out for you?'

Royce pinched the bridge of his nose. 'Marc Dane was ... *Is* keeping secrets from this agency. If he had nothing to hide, he had no reason to run.'

'I'm looking at one right now,' Farrier retorted, shooting a glance at Welles.

Royce shook his head. 'Point taken. But even so, when he came to you . . . To somebody who trusted him, he still used you.' The other man sighed, and he seemed to age ten years with the next statement. 'Marc is off the chain, John. He is associating with non-state actors, criminals and mercenaries. He's working to an agenda out of step with ours. That is not the behaviour of a loyal MI6 officer.' Royce looked at Welles. 'As much as I despise saying it, Victor is correct. Dane has gone rogue and we have to treat him as such.'

Welles sat back in his chair. 'You recruited him from the Navy, helped train his team. You thought you could bring him back into the fold. You were protecting him. But that was the wrong call.'

Farrier hated the small part of himself that was agreeing with the internal affairs investigator, and he tried to silence it. 'Marc is not a traitor,' he insisted. 'But someone wants us to think that he is.'

There was a knock at the door that forestalled any reply, and it opened to admit Talia Patel. She gestured with the ever-present digital tablet in her hand. 'There's been a development,' she began.

Welles beckoned Talia into the room. 'Let's have it.'

She frowned. 'The woman from Rome, Lucille Keyes. We found a few appearances between the time she dropped off the radar and the present day. Analysis points to a very strong likelihood that Keyes is currently in the employ of the Rubicon Special Conditions Division.'

Royce seemed surprised. 'This is the first I've heard of any connection to a private military contractor . . .'

Talia seemed contrite. 'It was a weak lead, or so we thought. I wanted high confidence intel before I brought it to you.' Her boss didn't seem happy with that answer, but he didn't press the point.

Welles turned back to Farrier. 'Did Dane mention this to you?'

He shook his head, uncertain what to make of the new revelation.

'What does this get us?' Royce demanded, his apparent fatigue fading. 'Do we have a current location on Keyes?'

Talia's lips thinned. 'We have something, but not a confirmed sighting. After this came to light, I had GCHQ watch Rubicon's data traffic for any unusual increases in activity, and there has been a lot going on at their New York office over the last five hours.'

'Up with the larks over there?' offered Welles. 'But then I suppose it is the city that never sleeps.'

She went on. 'Newark Airport traffic control logged the arrival of a jet registered to the company late last night. I took the liberty of having our station in Manhattan put surveillance on the Rubicon building. One of their cars left in a hurry, and we tracked it across the bay to New Jersey.'

'How does that connect to Marc or Keyes?' said Farrier.

Welles took this in, ignoring the other man's comment. 'Where did the jet fly in from?'

'Kayseri, Turkey. But before that it made a brief stop-over in Rome.'

'He's there.' Welles stiffened. 'But we need to know that for sure.'

'There's something else,' Talia added reluctantly, looking to Royce for support. He gave her a nod and she continued. 'Our people on the ground are hearing reports of an incident aboard a ship at the Port of New Jersey. It's not that far from the airport. Details are sketchy, but there were gunshots. A fire. Bodies have been found.'

Welles leaned forward. 'We need to get on top of this right now. If Dane is on American soil, his potential to embarrass this country and this agency grows exponentially. If the cousins get a whiff of this, Six will take the blame for whatever happens next.'

Royce pushed back his chair and stood up, gathering himself. 'Talia, contact our team in New York and tell them to mobilize whatever assets they need. Their orders are to search for Marc Dane and whomever he is now associating with, as quickly as possible. Make every attempt to secure a live capture . . .' He paused. 'But lethal force is authorised.'

Talia said nothing, gripping the data pad in her hand. Farrier shook his head. 'This is a mistake.'

'Your opinion is duly noted,' Welles retorted, and fixed Royce with a hard look. 'Donald. You're going to keep me in the loop on this, no arguments. And I'm sure I don't have to remind you that we need to make sure that the Americans remain completely ignorant of any operations on their turf. All it would take to put the damn cap on this mess would be blowback from the CIA.'

Royce gave a nod. 'Agreed.'

'Bring me in,' Farrier insisted. 'If Marc's out there . . . I know him. I can help you reel him back.' John considered the possibilities, weighing betrayals against secrets, truth against potential lies. It worried him that he didn't have a clear sense of what was right and what was not.

The withering look Victor Welles gave him told Farrier that nothing he could say would change the man's mind about Marc Dane's guilt. 'You just sit there, John,' he said. 'You just sit there, and wait. If you're a good lad, I might be able to get you the cell next to Dane's.'

The voices were thick and strange, and they came to Halil through a haze of noise like rushing water.

'Are you okay, son?' A man, an older man, with confusion in his manner.

'He looks real sick to me,' said a woman, and Halil thought he smelled something sweet on her. 'I reckon he's some kinda junkie. A Mexican.'

'You don't know shit, Sally.' Someone poked him, a brisk shove in his chest, a gruff voice close by. 'He ain't a Mexican. He's one of them Ay-rabs. I seen enough of them when I was in Desert Storm.'

Halil tried to open his eyes, but the effort was great. His limbs were slow and heavy.

The woman snorted. 'We all heard your war stories one time too many, Jake.'

'Hey, I *know* what I'm talkin' about . . .'

The jumble of accented words was difficult to follow, and Halil gave up. His senses slowly returned, the world stitching itself back in about him, layer by layer.

Through blurred vision, shapes took form and crowded in. He reacted with fear, trying to retreat back, but there was nowhere he could go.

Faces loomed large over him. The old man, clad in a stained apron that smelled of stale fried food. The woman in a server's uniform, peering at him like he was some kind of unusual creature. A heavy man with a scraggly ginger beard and deep-set eyes beneath the peak of a greasy trucker cap. They were all too close, all talking at once.

The whole world had a peculiar, dreamlike quality to it, and with sudden realization he knew it was horribly familiar. His hand slapped limply at his neck, where the American with the dead face had stuck the needle in him. *Drugged*, Halil thought, the concept large and ponderous like a glacier cutting through a turgid sea. *Like before, on the ship. Drugged to sleep.*

Another figure joined the three surrounding him, and Halil's heart leapt into his throat. A man with skin as dark as ebony, his gaze hard and pitiless. He wore a uniform with a large metal badge, and the heavy shape of a handgun at his hip. 'What the hell is this?' He seemed angry at Halil's mere presence.

The dark man brought a tide of memory rising up from Halil's thoughts, of other men in other uniforms, other policemen who had come to him on the day his mother and father had perished. They brought death with them. Panic surged through his veins, an electric shock of fear that made him flinch.

'Hey!' The dark man's expression grew stern. 'Are you high, son?'

'He's on somethin',' offered the woman. 'Been shooting up in the restroom!'

'You don't know that,' said the old man, but no-one was listening to him.

'Maybe he doesn't understand.' The trucker waved a hand in front of Halil's face. 'Could be he's like, one of them re-tardeds.'

'*Habla espanol*?' said the policeman. He was so close Halil could see the jumble of foreign words on his badge.

Halil tried to reply, but it was hard to form speech

'They don't teach Ay-rab kids nothing,' added the trucker, with a sage nod.

The dark man suddenly pulled back, and his hand dropped to the butt of the pistol in his belt. 'Goddamn it. The kid is high,' he told the others. 'I'm sick of these tweakers. See his pupils? Gonna have to get him out of here, take him somewhere safe.'

Somewhere safe. The words cut through the fog of Halil's thoughts like a searchlight. He remembered the officers who had come to the door of his family's home, in their uniforms and wearing their bright badges. They too told him they would take him somewhere safe. Because he was just a boy with two dead parents and no-one to care for him, and an orphan could not live all on his own.

And no matter how much he had cried, they had refused to let him stay. The policemen struck him with a baton just like the one the dark-skinned man carried at his waist, dragged him weeping into the street. His life shattered in that moment, the broken pieces of it falling until they came to rest in the dust and the pain of Khadir's orphanage.

Halil would not let that happen again.

They were all talking about him, talking about what they would do with him as if he were not even there. As if he were a child, without the will to speak for himself. Now the policeman was drawing a pair of handcuffs from his belt.

Then it was happening, and Halil could not stop himself. He did not *want* to stop himself.

Halil's hand slipped across the table and clutched a glassy cylinder full of sugar. He put all his strength into a sudden jerk of movement and slammed it into the side of the man's head.

Glass exploded in a crunch of sound and the police officer's face was doused in a torrent of powdery granules. The woman let out a cry as the man lost his balance under the force of the surprise attack. Halil saw him fall away and crack his temple against the countertop, eyes rolling back to show whites as he continued his drop to the floor. There was blood.

He stumbled forward off the seat and went to the semi-conscious policeman. Halil tore the big pistol from its holster, and the woman's cry became a full-throated screech.

The sound made Halil wince and he involuntarily tightened his grip on the weapon. Thunder sounded inside the diner as the gun discharged a single round into the floor, cracking the aged tiles.

Now Halil's panic washed out of him and infected everyone else in the room, as the figures seated at other booths all bolted into motion, running for the door. There was chaos all around, and he winced in pain as the prickling agony in his gut returned.

Halil stumbled, the gun in his hand heavy and dangerous, the muzzle swinging back and forth past the faces of the man with the cap, the woman, and the old man in the apron. None of them dared to move, not with the threat of death in his grip, and not with the injured policeman lying on the floor.

Marc kept the Mustang at a steady pace down the arrow-straight highway, holding the car just under the speed limit. He lost himself in the action of the drive, his world narrowing to the sparse traffic sharing the road and the feel of the vehicle over the wet asphalt.

Lucy was nimble enough that she could slip back over the gap between the front seats to the small space in the rear. In the mirror he caught glimpses of tawny skin, a flash of white underwear as she shucked off the damp tactical gear for something less military-looking.

'Enjoy the show?' she asked, as she climbed back into the passenger seat and snapped her seatbelt into place.

'I'm driving,' he replied, by way of denial.

'That you are.' Lucy loaded one of the fresh Glock semi-automatics Kara had brought from the Rubicon office. Satisfied, she seated the gun in a paddle holster under a loose black flight jacket. 'Where'd you learn to handle a muscle car?'

'I play a lot of *Forza* when I'm on downtime.'

'Uh huh.' He could see her studying him out of the corner of his eye. 'So, you gonna tell me what happened back on the boat?'

'You were there.'

'Not for all of it.'

He shot her a look, eyes flicking briefly from the ribbon of black before them. 'We got the intel. That's all that matters, yeah?'

'You killed that merc. Grunewald.'

'No-one's going to weep for one less assassin in the world.' Marc's lip pulled into a sneer. 'And for the record? It was gravity that killed him, not me.'

'Did you do that for Sam?'

His hands tensed reflexively on the steering wheel. 'What do you mean?'

Marc heard her sigh. 'Back in Turkey, that night . . . I heard you say a name in your sleep. I'm guessing it's someone important to you.'

'She died.' He told her before he could stop himself. 'They made it happen.' Marc didn't need to explain who *they* were.

'You don't have to justify it to me,' Lucy said gently.

'I'm not,' he snapped. 'Grunewald threatened the lives of my family. The Combine murdered my team. I've got all the bloody reasons I need.'

She was silent for a long moment. 'It's not an easy thing to end someone in cold blood. Takes more out of you than you'd think.'

A hard retort was forming in Marc's thoughts, but then he caught up to the woman's tone of voice and remembered exactly *what* Lucy Keyes was, what it was that she did best. He said nothing, just nodded.

Bright colour blinked behind them, and he glanced at the wing mirror, seeing the flicker of red and blue strobes. The skirl of a siren reached his ears and Marc eased off the gas, pulling the car over into the slow lane as the boxy shape of an ambulance screamed by in a flash of lights and spray, hooting at everything else on the road.

Lucy leaned forward. 'What is that? Up ahead?'

They crested a low rise, following in the ambulance's wake, and there in the middle distance were more flashing strobes from a cluster of emergency vehicles. Cars and trucks formed a tailback behind a line of smoking road flares that cordoned off the highway around a gas station and roadside diner. Marc slowed. He could see policemen gesturing to the drivers, trying to turn them around.

'Ah, hell.' Lucy rocked back in her seat. 'Must be an accident or something.'

Marc tapped the sat-nav set into the Mustang's dashboard. 'If we have to double back, we're going to lose the bus for sure.' He rolled to a halt, and one of the cops started toward them.

'Then we'll need to bluff our way through.' She reached into her pocket for the fake ID. 'Let me do the talking.'

Marc gave her a sideways look. 'Hey, I can fake the accent,' he said, in something fairly mid-Atlantic.

'What is that supposed to be, Canadian?' He didn't get to reply as the deputy was at the window.

'Hey, folks,' said the policeman. He made a stirring motion with his finger. 'Gonna have to ask you to go around and head back to the off-ramp. We got ourselves a situation here, nothing to worry about, but we're gonna need you to move out of the immediate area.'

Lucy's whole body language changed as if a switch had been flipped. She was suddenly stiff and purposeful, and the FBI badge came out on the end of her raised arm. 'Deputy, I'm Special Agent Reese with the Bureau. This is Sergeant Major . . . Day . . . He's with the RCMP.'

The police officer's eyes widened. 'The Feds are into this already? Holy Smokes, you guys are fast.'

Lucy gave a nod, doing nothing to correct the assumptions the deputy had made. 'Has anyone been hurt?'

He returned her nod. 'One of our guys, Deke, a patrolman. Some drugged-up gang kid got Deke's weapon and now he's holed up in the diner with hostages. A shot was fired. SWAT's on the way, but the roads are washed out . . . No idea when they're gonna arrive.'

'Okay.' Lucy put the badge away, and Marc could guess what she was thinking. They couldn't afford to get caught up in some local trouble. With every minute that passed, Omar Khadir was a mile further away.

But the next words out of the cop's mouth changed all that. 'Saw the perp myself when we tried to roll up in there. Arab-looking kid waving that gun around like anything. We backed off . . .' He swallowed. 'I mean, folks around here remember what happened in Boston and all–'

'Arab?' Marc said, remembering to feign the accent again. 'Was there a school bus that came through here?'

'Michigan plates,' added Lucy.

The cop gave a slow nod. 'Yeah. One of the Staties mentioned it. Stopped for gas, then drove off, I think. What's that gotta do with anything?'

Marc pulled out the smartphone Kara had given him and paged to one of the still images from the dockside security cameras, holding it up.

The cop peered at the screen. 'Hey, that's him. That's the kid!'

'You're sure?'

He nodded again. 'Oh yeah.'

'I need to speak to the senior officer on the scene, *right now*,' Lucy insisted. The deputy's head bobbed and he jogged away into the drizzle. She glared at Marc. 'Didn't I just tell you *not* to talk?' she snapped, and gestured for him to guide the car over to the shoulder. 'Ah, shit . . .'

'You told him I was a Mountie.'

She shrugged. 'First thing I could think of.'

'I don't have any ID for Sergeant Major Day . . .'

'I'll get Henri to make something up for you. But in the meantime, less talk is better.'

He swung about, parking the Mustang, and turned to face her. 'So you're thinking what I'm thinking, right?'

She peered out at the diner. 'That maybe Khadir has left a little something-something behind at Gina's Place? Yeah.' Lucy hands tightened into fists. 'This complicates things . . .'

'You reckon?' His thoughts raced. 'We've got to get in there. I mean, if this lad is . . . I dunno, *live*, we got no idea how long he's going to stay that way.' Marc remembered pictures of the rubble that was all that remained of the Nou de la Rambla police station, and wondered what kind of devastation a similar bomb blast would wreak out here on Interstate 95.

Lucy laid her hands on the dash. 'Let's you and me be clear on this. We're talking about the difference between blowing through this roadblock and following a lead on the bus, a lead we *know* is rock solid, or getting tangled up in something that just dropped into our lap on the *chance* it's one of Khadir's soldiers in there.'

'And if it is?' Marc insisted. 'If there's some mule with a belly full of military-grade explosives just waiting to be martyred?' He pointed toward the local cops gathered around one of the newly-arrived paramedics. 'Those blokes have no idea what they're dealing with.' He shook his head, opening the car door. Part of him knew she had a point, but he couldn't be cold-blooded about it. 'You want to drive on? Go ahead, keys are in the ignition. But I know what *I'm* doing.' Marc climbed out of the Mustang and walked away toward the ambulance.

TWENTY-FOUR

The soporific effect of the injection was wearing off. Everything in the diner was becoming definite and solid. The lights were too bright, and the low, anguished muttering of the man in the trucker's cap was grating on him.

Halil slouched forward in the booth, careful to keep himself out of the sight of the men gathering in the parking lot. He aimed the heavy gun at the man and glared. 'Be quiet,' he said thickly, and the trucker fell silent.

The cook was crouching next to the collapsed body of the black policeman. He looked up at Halil with kind eyes. 'Son,' he began, 'This man needs a doctor. You understand?'

'He's gonna die,' said the woman sat across in another booth. 'We're *all* gonna die.'

She is right. Halil flinched as an eddy of pain crackled through his flesh. With the drug fading, the pulse of needle-sharp agony returned.

What have you done? The voice in his head sounded like his father's. *You know this is wrong. Stop it now.* But Halil couldn't be sure, because he couldn't remember exactly how his father sounded. It was too distant in his memory. Halil screwed his eyes shut and tried to remember the faces of his parents, but they were hazy shadows. Tears burned on his cheeks.

There was a rattle of metal. Halil's eyes snapped open and he raised the patrolman's handgun as three figures appeared at the diner's door. A white man with fair hair and tired eyes came in first, a dark-skinned woman close behind. Both of them had guns, but they were keeping them low. The third person was an Oriental man in a high-visibility jacket, cradling a heavy pack in his hands.

'Go away!' Halil shouted, and the effort made him wince.

'We're here to help,' said the woman. 'Just let these people go.'

Halil's thumb found the cocking hammer of the gun and pulled it back. 'You can't help,' he breathed.

Lucy's FBI badge cut through any questions the local cops had, and Marc surmised from the expressions of the senior deputy on site that he was only too happy to step back and let a Federal Agent shoulder the situation. He heard the men outside talking, rumours already blooming as to the origins of the hostage-taker. It was a sad fact that one look at the youth's face immediately sent people running toward the idea that he could be a terrorist. That would be proven right unless Marc and Lucy could get in the middle of this and stop things from escalating.

He pulled one of the paramedics away from the ambulance, a serious-looking guy with the name *Chang* on his jacket. Lucy had him gather up his medical kit, and with the local cops covering them, guns drawn across the hoods of their patrol cruisers, they warily entered Gina's Place.

The first thing Marc saw was the youth and the injured cop on the floor. The policeman's chest fluttered in shallow breaths, and blood streaked the tiles where he lay. The cop's gun was big in the fist of the skinny teenager, and the youth's eyes were wide and watery. Marc tried to guess his age – eighteen, nineteen at the most? – and gauged the fear and panic in his expression.

He was the same young man Marc had seen on the dockyard video, the one who had failed to make a break for it. There were bruises on his neck and face from where Omar Khadir had knocked him down.

Marc glanced at Lucy and she gave him a nod of agreement. She saw it too. He stepped forward and halted at the far end of the counter. He turned the Glock in his hand and put it down on the bar. 'No gun,' he said. 'We only want to talk.' Marc maintained steady eye contact with the youth, keeping his posture neutral. He worked to maintain an even tone of voice. 'We know all about you. We want to help. Nobody else has to get hurt.'

He saw the questions in the young man's expression, saw the sweat beading across his brow. 'Too late,' he replied, sniffing.

'Hope not.' A dozen different approaches had passed through Marc's thoughts before they stepped through the door. It would have been simple enough for Lucy to commandeer a rifle and take out the kid from range, or even now put him down from ten meters away with a single shot from her pistol. She was capable of it; Marc knew that. He had considered using a tazer to bring the youth down alive, but they had no idea of what kind of trigger mechanism the body bomb used. Was it internal or external? Remote or timer? *Too many questions,* he told himself, *not enough time.*

Marc took another couple of steps, ignoring the trembling muzzle of the big Smith & Wesson revolver in the youth's hand. He pointed at the police officer. 'We're going to take this man away and in return, I'm going to stay here with you.'

He got a weak, defeated nod in return, and Marc knew then that the teenager's heart wasn't in this.

'Go!' Lucy gave the paramedic a shove and he came forward, shooting looks at the youth and then at the cop.

'I need help to move him,' said Chang.

The man in the trucker cap vaulted off his chair in his eagerness to assist, sensing the opportunity for escape. 'I got it!'

Between them, the trucker and the paramedic gathered up the patrolman and carried him out. Marc watched them go, pausing to give the old cook and the waitress a reassuring nod.

Lucy holstered her gun and held out a hand. She said something in Arabic, all soft and liquid tones, and the youth replied in kind, kneading the grip of the gun.

'Well, damn,' muttered the waitress. 'He *ain't* Mexican.'

Marc only recognized one word in the young man's response, but it was enough. A name; *Khadir*.

'He wants to know if you-know-who sent us,' said Lucy quietly.

'They left him here,' Marc said, thinking out loud.

'I . . .' The youth swallowed hard and licked his lips. 'I am being punished.' He was going to say more, but then Marc saw the colour drain from his cheeks and the youth twitched in pain, doubling over across the table before him. The gun thudded down, momentarily forgotten in his agony.

Lucy saw the opportunity and shot a look at the other hostages. 'You two, get to safety.'

'Amen to that,' said the waitress, and she pulled on the cook's arm to lead him away.

'He gonna be okay?' said the older man, his brows knitting.

'Just go!' Lucy snapped, and propelled both of them toward the exit.

Marc came as close as he dared. He saw the young man's hands pulling at the thin material of his top, revealing a t-shirt beneath that was mottled brown with dried bloodstains. Rosy, distended flesh poked out over the belt loop of his jeans, and the purple-black lines of thick, fresh scars were clearly visible. Ignoring the gun, the youth clutched at a water glass and drained it.

A chill ran through Marc's veins. The repulsive consequence of what they had found in the *Santa Cruz*'s makeshift operating theatre had only been a possibility until this moment. Here was real evidence of it, sitting across from him. Waiting to die.

Now it was just the three of them, Lucy spoke again in Arabic, and again Marc picked out another word: *Shahiden*.

The youth shook his head. 'No. I don't want to die.' He rubbed tears from his eyes. 'Please.' He looked at Marc and Lucy, imploring them. 'Make it stop.'

Marc slipped his Rubicon-issue smartphone from his pocket and tabbed through the function tabs. Kara had not exaggerated when she talked about the device's capabilities. He quickly found what he was looking for, and activated the phone's signal sniffer. A scanning antenna sampled the invisible wavelengths around them, looking for active wireless transmissions.

Lucy studied the young man's face. 'Tell me your name.'

'Halil,' he managed.

'*Huh*.' Lucy glanced at Marc. 'Same name as the tag scrawled on the wall in the orphanage.' She pointed. 'This is him? What are the odds?'

Marc blinked. He had forgotten all about the bit of graffiti in the abandoned building. 'We were there,' he told Halil. 'At *Yeni Gün*. We saw it. The barracks where they kept you, the tent . . .'

The youth nodded. 'Hate that place.'

'It's gone now. Destroyed.'

Halil managed a brittle, defiant smile. '*Good*.' In the next second, he moaned as pain lanced through him.

Marc's attention was pulled back to the device in his hand. A radar-screen illuminated with pings from the cellular phones and police band radios clustered outside, the diner's card reader and a single encrypted ghost indicator that he assumed was Lucy's handset. The only other wireless node within range was close – a signal with the designation 'Seven'. His mouth went dry. He gestured at the youth. 'Halil, I need you to empty your pockets.'

He did as was asked, piling up coins and paper tissues on the table next to the revolver.

'Do you have one of these?' Marc showed him the phone. He got a shake of the head in return, and Marc looked away to find Lucy staring right at him. She didn't need to ask him the question. 'It's in him. It's *live*,' he said.

Lucy couldn't look away from Marc, because she knew that if she did, she would see the raw terror on the face of the teenager in the booth. She would see it and then she would be forced to make one of the choices that her life often demanded of her. A question of balancing life for life, of ending one so that others could go on.

The difference here was that Lucy Keyes had never once laid her crosshairs on someone innocent, and she knew instinctively that Halil was not just some murderous teen jihadi who had got cold feet at the last moment. She knew a victim when she saw one, and in that moment she hated Omar Khadir more than anyone in the world.

Would it be a mercy just to shoot Halil now, put him out of his misery and evacuate the diner? Pull back and wait for the inevitable detonation? She shook off the question with a jerk of her head.

An icy calm settled on her. 'Okay,' she began. 'This is what we are going to do. I'm going to find that medic, and we're going to get that fucked-up shit out of the kid.'

Marc's eyes narrowed. 'Is that even possible? He needs to be taken to a hospital, we have to get an air ambulance or–' He trailed off, and she saw that his thoughts were already catching up with his words. If the device Halil carried went off inside a moving vehicle on the highway, aboard a helicopter or even inside a hospital, the results would be unthinkable. 'Oh man.'

'We can spend time talking about it, or spend time doing it,' she told him. Lucy thought about what he had said as he climbed out of the car. Like it or not, they were committed here, and they had to follow it to the end.

'Okay,' he agreed, but Lucy didn't wait around to hear Marc say it.

She pushed out of the door and sprinted across the parking lot, the assembled police officers raising their guns with wary expressions on their faces. She scanned around and found Chang at the ambulance's tailgate. Inside, Deke the patrolman was being treated by another paramedic.

He saw her coming and nodded at the cop. 'He'll be fine. Minor concussion. We'll take him to County General just to be sure, and–'

'Don't care,' she broke in. 'Question. Can you open people up as well as close them?'

Chang's expression became one of confusion. 'I'm . . . not a doctor.'

Lucy grabbed his arm. 'You know what? Doesn't matter, you're close enough. Grab your gear and come with me, double-time.'

'Agent Reese?' The senior deputy was approaching. 'Ma'am, what the heck is going on in there? Y'know, I contacted dispatch and they don't know anything about any Federal–'

'We're containing it.' She gave him a sharp look, cutting off the sentence before he had time to voice it. 'And I need you to move the perimeter back one hundred yards, like *right fucking now*!' Lucy barked the last words with such force that the cops were still reeling from them when she set off back toward Gina's, the paramedic jogging to keep up with her.

When it was just the two of them alone in the diner, Halil sagged back into the booth and took panting breaths. Marc realized he had been trying not to show weakness in front of the others, but now the youth had reached the end of his ability to pretend. 'I am going to die?'

'Not if I can help it.' Marc reached over and picked up the discarded revolver. Halil made no attempt to stop him, so Marc put it aside on the bar and settled directly across from the younger man. 'I need you to trust me, Halil,' he went on. 'Do you know what they did to you?'

'They told me I would be a warrior,' he gasped. 'The commander said we would take revenge on the people who made us orphans.'

'That what you want?' Marc stole a glance at his watch, and clamped his hands together. His palms were sweating.

Halil shook his head and winced. 'My father . . . A teacher. My mother . . . They were both kind. They would be sad to see me now.'

'You tried to run.' Halil's head snapped up as Marc said the words. 'It's okay, mate. I saw it. You wanted to get away, but Khadir wouldn't let you.' He tapped the side of his face, in the place where Halil had a bruise. 'Is that why you're here?'

A nod. 'He said we would be abandoned if we did not show courage.' Halil's eyes glistened with tears. 'I . . . have no courage.' He looked up at Marc, pleading. 'I want this to be over.'

'You seem strong enough to me. What can you tell me about the . . . ?' Marc indicated his belly.

Halil looked away. 'I don't know what they did to us. It is making me sicken.'

'We can help,' Marc told him. 'But it won't be easy. It will hurt. A lot.'

The youth's head bobbed slowly. 'I do not want to be a warrior anymore.'

'And the others . . . what about them? What about Khadir?'

Fresh tears rolled down Halil's face. 'The bus. On the road, going that way.' He made a feeble wave in a southerly direction, then screwed his eyes up, scowling. 'I heard the American speak. The driver. He told the commander the names.'

'*Names*?' Marc seized on the word. 'Halil, *what names*? It's important you remember.'

'Will-Ard,' he said, sounding it out. 'Per-Shing. Perhaps they are other men.'

The words meant nothing to Marc without some kind of context, and he filed them away to consider later as Lucy came back into the diner with the paramedic. *If there* is *a later*, he told himself.

Marc went to the other man before he could get too close. He nodded toward Lucy. 'She fill you in?'

'Not really,' said Chang. 'Look, what's this all about?'

'Here's the thing,' Marc replied, taking a deep breath. 'That lad over there has something surgically implanted inside him, and you need to get it out. We can't move him. We have to do it here. We have to do it *now*.'

'Wh-what happened to your accent . . . ?' The paramedic's eyes widened.

'You are going to help us. Because you know that kid needs you.' Marc let his hand drop to the nearby pistol. 'And because I will hold this to your head if you don't.' The words came from some calm, cold place in the centre of Marc's thoughts. Chang saw the unblinking certainty in his eyes and nodded.

'Okay.' He swallowed hard. 'Help me get him up.'

Halil moaned as they manoeuvred him on top of a long table, resting him on a layer of tablecloths, a bunched-up apron for a pillow. Chang produced a pair of emergency scissors and sliced cleanly down the length of the youth's shirt, to reveal his swollen belly beneath.

To his credit, the paramedic didn't baulk at the sight of the dark, gummy sutures and unhealed scars. 'I've seen worse,' he said. 'But this . . .' He made a negative noise. 'This is shitty workmanship.'

Lucy loaded a syringe with a morphine solution and as Chang looked for a vein, Marc found Halil's hand and gripped it. His fingers were weak. 'You're going to be safe,' he said, and he tried to mean it.

'You were there,' Halil whispered, 'at the orphanage.'

'Yeah.' He saw the paramedic put the needle in and the drug discharge.

'I don't want to be sent back . . .' Halil was going to say something else, but then he fell into silence.

Chang opened his medical kit. 'He's already got something in his system, I can tell by pupil dilation. Couldn't give him a full dose, don't know how it would interact. So he's going to react when I cut, which means you need to keep him steady.' He made them use astringent antibacterial wipes on their hands, then handed each of them plastic gloves and paper surgical masks to wear. Finally, Chang gave Marc a breathing ventilator – a mouthpiece with squeeze-bulb. 'You've seen these on TV, right? Keep him breathing evenly.'

Marc nodded, put the ventilator over Halil's pallid lips, and started pumping the air bulb.

The paramedic muttered something under his breath that could have been a prayer, and then he went to the sutures in Halil's belly with the bright, shining blade of a scalpel. 'Gonna cut along the lines that are already here,' he said, talking through his actions as much for himself as for them. 'They're too fresh to have healed fully. Day old at the most.' The scalpel met flesh and sank in.

Halil twitched, but they were ready for it. Marc watched with detached interest as Chang traced the lines of an inverted 'V' over Halil's belly. There was blood, but less of it than he expected. A metallic odour rose and he started to breathe through his mouth.

The paramedic muttered again, his tone angry. 'Who did this?' he said, grinding out the question through gritted teeth. 'Is this you people? It's fucking barbaric!'

'No, not us. Keep working,' Lucy told him sternly. 'We're on a clock.'

At mention of that, Marc glanced at the big analogue clock on the wall of the diner, a chrome thing with old advertising graphics suggesting it was *Always Time for a Coke*. The minute hand was coming around to the top of the hour, and he remembered how Al Sayf liked to set off their attacks in hourly increments. The Barcelona blast had been on the dot of 6 p.m.

Chang peeled back a flap of flesh with a set of forceps and Marc looked right into Halil's peritoneal cavity, a mess of wet organic shapes that looked better suited to a butcher's block. Blood tricked down and pooled on the white tablecloths. He bit down on an automatic gag response.

'You're no use if you're going to puke,' snapped the paramedic.

Marc shook his head, grotesquely fascinated. Something was wrong in there. He saw a string of objects wrapped in plastic, linked in a chain.

'What the hell is that?' Chang saw them too, and probed at the mass with a haemostat. 'Are those . . . drugs?'

'Take over.' Marc pressed the ventilator into Lucy's hands and leaned in for a closer look. He ignored Chang's complaints and steeled himself before reaching into the open cut. It was warm and slippery, and he had to force himself not to look away.

Marc's fingers pinched the edge of the plastic packet and pulled. With a wet, sucking pop, a string of five clay-like spheres, each connected to the next by thin wires, emerged from Halil's open belly. Blood dribbled off the vacuum-sealed plastic sheath surrounding the device. 'I got it,' he said, drawing in a shuddering breath. 'Ah, shit.'

He heard Lucy deflecting Chang's questions, saying something about getting Halil sewn up and *the hell out of there* – but he wasn't really listening.

Marc carried the ugly little payload into the diner's narrow kitchen. Pots and burners were still on the go, left untended after the chaos. With a sweep of his hand, he cleared a space on a cutting board and let the body bomb snake out across it. He used a water nozzle from the dishwashing sink to clean off the device, and stood back to take it in.

It was a horrible, cunning design. Each 'pod' was a clump of HMX explosive as big as a tennis ball, the silver tabs of electrical detonators buried in them. A rat's tail of wires coiled back to a small cluster of electronics that could fit in the palm of Marc's hand. Through the plastic sheath, he could make out a long-life camera battery and the stripped down workings of an old 2G-type cell phone. All of it constructed with faultless care, each soldered joint perfect, the entire bomb assembly flexible enough to fit undetected inside a human body.

He found the clock again. Less than a minute till the top of the hour.

Marc sliced the plastic sheath with a paring knife to expose the bomb's workings. There were too many detonators, too many intertwining connectors to know which line was the primary.

It wasn't a case of *red wire, blue wire*. Every wire was the same shade of black. He gripped the control unit between his thumb and forefinger, feeling a terrible sense of pressure building behind his eyes – almost a premonition of the device's unspent destructive force just seconds from being unleashed. He stared at the inert spheres of doughy matter, uncertain what to do. *Which wire to cut?*

Without thinking about it, his hand closed around the grip of a thick meat cleaver lying nearby. He brought it down on the coil of wires and severed all of them at once. The control unit skittered away, falling to the tiled floor.

As it landed, Marc heard the device sound a high-pitched beep; in the same second, the clock outside clicked as it struck 8:00am.

For long seconds, he stood still, waiting for something else to happen. When it didn't, he gathered the inert explosives and stuffed them into a take-out box. Marc bent to scoop up the control unit and saw a tiny LCD screen among the detonator components. A line of text there read *One Missed Call.*

Tension he didn't know he had been holding in burst out in a short cackling laugh. Marc marvelled at the strange calm that had descended on him in those moments, not knowing where it had come from. Somehow, his body had barricaded all the terror he should have felt for the time it took to defang the bomb. Now that was over, the dam broke and it all came rushing over him in a wave of frigid cold. Marc had to put out a hand to steady himself on a nearby stool.

'All clear,' he managed, in a cracked voice.

The paramedic was sheathing the unconscious Halil's torso in fresh bandages. Marc could smell the chemical tang of medical-grade adhesive. 'I did a quick fix,' Chang was saying to Lucy, 'but it won't last. Plus he's got an infection from whatever idiots cut him up in the first place. We don't take this kid to the ER right away, sepsis is going to rip him up.'

Lucy shot Marc a look, and he read from it what he needed to know. 'Go get a stretcher,' she told the paramedic. 'We'll follow you to the hospital.'

Chang took two steps, and then halted as he saw Marc. His eyes narrowed 'Those weren't drugs, were they?'

'You heard Agent Reese,' he replied. 'Your patient is a material witness to a Federal crime. We need him alive and well.'

'Right, yeah,' said the paramedic, and he left the diner in a rush.

Lucy turned on Marc. 'Tell me you disarmed it.'

He showed her the severed cable. 'You could call it that, I suppose.'

'Hey, whatever works.' She paused, and then did something Marc wasn't expecting. Lucy reached out and gently stroked Halil's brow. Then the moment was gone and she was looking at him again. 'Is there a back way out?' Off Marc's nod, she came forward, tossing him his pistol. 'Then let's book.'

He hesitated, glancing at Halil. Marc felt a pang of guilt at abandoning him so soon after making his promise to save him.

Lucy saw what he was thinking and went on. 'Dane. The second those locals think hard about it, they're going to figure out we're not FBI.'

'Or the Mounties,' Marc added, and he blew out a breath, knowing she was right. They could not afford to get caught up, not now, after losing so much time in pursuit of Khadir. 'Yeah. C'mon, this way.'

This time Lucy took the wheel, and in a crunching snarl of spitting gravel, she barely let Marc get the passenger side door shut before the GT-500 leapt away and out on to the highway. The car slalomed around a pair of parked State Police cruisers and over a line of crackling road flares, cresting the next hill before the cops had time to react.

Lucy pushed the accelerator pedal to the firewall, taking advantage of the clear road ahead, and the needle on the speedometer climbed steadily up the numbers. 'You need to call Delancort,' she said.

Her jaw set. She was wondering how she could justify losing their target to preserve the life of Halil. Solomon was not a callous man, but he was pragmatic. He would not easily accept the saving of one as a priority over hundreds of others.

'In a sec,' Marc replied. He dragged the battered laptop from his pack and flipped it open. 'I need to check something first . . . The kid gave me a lead.'

'About Khadir's target?'

He shook his head. 'Don't think so. It was two names. First one was 'Willard'. Ring any bells?'

'No.' She gripped the steering wheel tighter. 'Scary movie about rats.' A school bus flashed past heading in the other direction, and Lucy couldn't help but glare at it. It was empty, one of thousands of the vehicles that were out on the streets that morning, all across the country.

'Got about twenty million hits on Google . . .' Marc's hands flew across the laptop's keyboard. 'So much for that. Second one was 'Pershing'. Like the general from World War II.'

'Right, 'Black Jack' Pershing.' She remembered the name from history class in officer candidate school. 'The Army named a tank after him . . .'

'Also schools and streets and parks, so Wikipedia says.'

Lucy felt an unexpected jolt of insight that made her breath catch. They were passing a highway sign with lane indicators directing drivers towards Baltimore, Annapolis and beyond, to Washington. She hadn't visited the nation's capital in a long time, but now the Brit's words were sparking fragments of recall, making unexpected connections. 'The park,' she repeated. 'Pershing Park in DC.'

'Got it.' Marc brought up a map application and scanned the image. 'Within spitting distance of the White House. You think Al Sayf are going to mount an attack on Washington?'

She gave a grim nod. 'I think by now we know that Omar Khadir isn't the kind of terrorist who thinks small.' Lucy took a glance at Marc and saw that his attention was fixed on the screen's display. 'What? Something else?'

'You want to know what's directly across the street from Pershing Park? *The Willard Intercontinental Hotel.*' In the next second, Marc was talking into his smartphone. 'Delancort? It's Dane. Looks like the target is Washington DC. That's where Khadir is headed. I've got location intel . . . Pershing Park and the Willard Hotel on Pennsylvania Avenue.'

'*Ah.*' The other man's reply automatically issued out of the car's wireless speakers. '*That makes a very unpleasant kind of sense.*'

'How so?' demanded Lucy. Traffic was building up, forcing her to slow. She slipped the GT-500 across the lanes, looking for the road that would bypass Baltimore and get them on the direct route to DC.

'*We have been threat modelling, looking at potential targets along the road corridor we believe Khadir is using. A political assembly in Baltimore. The Aberdeen Proving Ground. The NSA facility at Fort Meade . . . And of course, Washington.*'

Marc's eyes narrowed. 'You have a potential?'

'*We may want to consider it an* actual. *The President of the United States and the First Lady will be present today at a public rally on the National Mall.*'

'That's the strip of park, runs from the Capitol Building to the Lincoln Memorial,' offered Lucy.

'Yeah,' muttered Marc. 'And full of crowds, I'll bet.'

'It's an election year,' Lucy said.

Delancort went on. '*The president will be addressing the nation on the subject of college reform and higher education. Student groups from all over America have been invited to attend.*'

'That's how he's going to get them in there,' Marc breathed. 'Teenagers. Students. Khadir can just walk them in, then set off the bombs right in the middle of the speech . . .' He trailed off. 'It'll be carnage.'

'They'd need security passes,' Lucy added, thinking out loud. 'But he'll have thought of that.'

'*How far away are you?*' said Delancort. '*The president is scheduled to go on stage in a few hours. I will contact Mister Solomon, have him see if he can use his contacts to pass on a direct warning . . .*' He didn't need to add what would happen if that failed. '*I admit I am not confident.*'

Lucy shifted up to top gear and aimed the hood of the Mustang at the feed lane, gaining speed as they went.

'We'll make it,' said Marc, tapping the disconnect.

The warehouse was like all the others in this part of Ivy City, one among many clustered around the industrial neighbourhood in the north-eastern of the American capital. It was run down and dilapidated, and from the layers of grime covering the windows, Khadir estimated that it had been standing idle for years. He walked around the silent bus parked inside the echoing building, occasionally glancing up to make sure no-one on board was thinking of getting out. One runner was more than enough.

For all this country's might and all its claims to the status of superpower, the building was proof enough of America's weakness, of its slow rot. Only a few miles away there were gleaming streets, great monuments and ornate buildings befitting a nation-state that shouted defiance to the globe, but in this place there was decrepitude and wastage, one hidden under the other.

The clarity he had found in becoming a warrior for Al Sayf showed him these truths. Khadir did not hate the people of this nation, he pitied them, just as he pitied all the other men and women and children who toiled under blood-soiled flags. They were complacent. They needed to be shocked out of their docility, to understand that their masters could not protect them. Only when *the sword* fell would they have the same clarity that he did.

He halted where Teape was lounging against a wheel arch, watching a droning news reporter on the screen of his smartphone. A well-dressed Caucasian woman was talking directly into the camera, a video feed displayed next to her showing footage of crowds gathering at the foot of the Washington Memorial. She talked about the president and his wife, about the education platform the politician's party was using as their spur for re-election. She talked about *renewal* and *success* and other uplifting topics.

Khadir gave a derisive snort, thinking of the people in this district, wondering how much of that would reach them if their current leader served a second term. It was a moot point; by tonight the president would be dead, his wife and countless others along with him.

He pulled his own smartphone from a pocket, paging to the control application for the weapons. Number Seven was dark, the timer at zero. That meant the troublesome youth had been dealt with, the device within him having fulfilled its purpose . . . But if that was so, then why was it not being reported?

Was it possible that news of the detonation was being suppressed by the authorities? Khadir doubted that. The media were untroubled with conscience in such things, and they would broadcast any incident no matter how tawdry or bloody in order to secure a greater audience share – even if what they aired were the deaths of their own.

Khadir's concerns fell silent as he caught the sound of a vehicle pulling up outside the warehouse, and he drew a Beretta 92 from a paddle holster and approached the roller gate at the front of the old building. The Italian-made pistol was the same design as the Helwan 920 he had used in his time as an officer of the Egyptian Army, and it was comfortable in its familiarity.

He peered through a gap in the gate and saw an unmarked black van roll to a halt. Khadir stiffened as figures emerged from the vehicle – two men wearing District of Colombia Metropolitan Police uniforms – but then that familiar pre-battle tension faded as a third man joined them. *Jadeed.*

He put the gun away and opened the door without waiting for them to knock. His lieutenant entered, followed by the Britisher mercenary and his Afrikaans associate. They looked oddly out of place dressed as American peace officers.

Jadeed greeted him firmly, his eyes lit with fire. 'Commander. We have secured the last items.' He offered Khadir a plastic packet. Inside were a dozen identity passes, and from them the faces of his young charges looked back up at him.

'Good work, innit?' said the Britisher. 'No-one's gonna be able to tell those have been doctored.'

Khadir allowed a nod of agreement. 'Your employers . . . Their counterfeiters work quickly.'

'I went to the forger in Georgetown myself,' Jadeed noted. 'The cover identities have completely overwritten the originals.'

'You encountered no problems securing them?'

Jadeed shook his head. 'The exchange was made without issue.' While Khadir had been driving to the rendezvous, the advance team had tracked a specifically-targeted student party to their hotel, stealing their passes and replacing them with fakes.

'That's what happens when you work with people who know what they're doing,' said Tommy. He came closer, his belligerent swagger dialling up as he advanced. 'Not like you fucking weekenders.'

Khadir missed the exact meaning of the term but not the sense of it. 'You think we are not soldiers, like you? I have worn a uniform. I have saluted and carried a gun for 'king and country'.' He said the last with a sneer. 'Our breed of war is not yours, mercenary. Do not judge what you do not understand.'

'You what?' The Britisher rocked on his heels. 'Did you just compare your toe-rags to us?' He shook his head, and Khadir sensed too late that the man had come into the room looking for a fight. 'I *understand* you have no fucking clue about how to handle operational security! I mean, just 'cause your idea of a class hit is to blow yourselves up, you don't police the little things, do you? Like making sure your boat wasn't tracked all the way from bloody Turkey!'

Khadir's moderated manner disintegrated. 'What are you talking about?'

'Someone got aboard the *Santa Cruz* after you left,' said Ellis. 'Details are sketchy, but we lost men. There was a firefight on the ship. Grunewald is dead.'

'Point is,' Tommy snarled, 'you got fleas on you. Someone here talk?' He looked around, searching for another target to vent his annoyance on.

It took Khadir a moment to process this. 'Who were these intruders? American intelligence? The British?'

'We'll find out soon enough if you don't stick to the fucking plan, Saladin. If someone's got a scent, we can't make any more mistakes. Now, if it was up to me, I'd leave you twisting in the wind, but it ain't. This is almost done and I've had enough of babysitting all your jihadi bollocks. Don't mess about, and we can all go home happy . . .' The Britisher trailed off, then nodded toward the bus. 'Well. Most of us.'

'You are afraid to die.' Khadir's gaze bored into the mercenary as he said the words. This man he had nicknamed 'Tommy' was the exemplar of his masters, the faceless rich who comprised the

Combine. They did not fight for a belief in anything larger than themselves, only for power. There was no purity to these men.

'Say that again,' Tommy hissed.

'You fear death. Perhaps you think you will go to hell for what you have done in your life. Or perhaps you believe there is nothing beyond. It is not important. All that matters is that you will never be able to understand those who sacrifice themselves for a greater good.'

Ellis rolled his eyes. 'Nice speech. Said it a lot, I bet.'

Something in the Britisher's gaze shifted, and the hooligan mask he wore slipped. Khadir wondered if he had been played for a fool. Was this man more than just the thug he seemed to be? He could not be certain.

'You don't like me 'cause I take blood money for all the shit I do,' said Tommy. 'Fuck you, pal. I know what I am. I've made my peace with it.' His voice dropped and he prodded Khadir in the chest. 'I don't like you because you're a zealot, sunshine. You don't give a squirt of piss about anything but body count. You think you're on a mission from god, you strut around like you're better than the rest of us . . . but you ain't no soldier.' Before Khadir could respond, the Britisher leaned back. 'You're not going to be doing any dying today, are ya?' He shot another look at the bus. 'That's the difference between you and me, mate.'

His anger boiled at the man's disrespectful words, and for a moment, Khadir contemplated killing them and moving on without the mercenaries. But Al Sayf needed the Combine's goodwill. As much as he loathed these empty men, the work required that he carry on this association for a little while longer.

He turned his back on them and handed his smartphone to Jadeed, who seethed silently at the Britisher's insolence. Khadir met his gaze, switching to Arabic. 'Take this and arm the weapons. Make sure each of them is ready.'

Jadeed gave a reluctant nod and took the handset. His eyebrows rose as a question formed in his mind. 'Number Seven?'

'Wastage,' Khadir told him. 'He was weak. You were correct, my friend. I should have let you execute him at the orphanage. Instead, he served another purpose.'

Jadeed accepted that. 'I want to kill the Britisher,' he said quietly. 'After. Will you grant me that?'

'After,' Khadir agreed. 'It will help us to throw some corpses to the Americans.'

TWENTY-FIVE

Marc chanced a look at the Cabot watch on his wrist and saw the minutes falling away. Every mile they travelled seemed to take an age. His fingers drummed on the sill of the GT-500's window and he stopped himself by making a fist.

'We have time,' said Lucy, without taking her eyes off the road.

'We really don't,' he shot back. 'Look, maybe I should dial 911, phone in the threat . . .' Even as he said it, the idea seemed wrong.

'Give the DC Police descriptions of Khadir and the bus, tell them a tale about kids with bombs sewn up inside them? The cops will think you're insane.' Lucy shook her head. 'The only way they're gonna take you seriously is if you give them your name, and that'll connect with whatever Interpol warrant MI6 has with your smiling face on it. You're an international fugitive, which makes it pretty unlikely anyone is going to listen to you.'

He studied her. 'So you make the call, then.'

Lucy's jaw stiffened. 'That ain't gonna happen.'

'Why?' Marc pressed, sensing that she was holding something back from him, the same vibe he'd got on the road in Turkey. 'Apart from that whole pretending-to-be-a-Federal-Agent bit back at the diner, what's stopping you from contacting someone in Washington? Someone from your Army service? Lucy, come on–'

'No.' She shut him down hard. 'Okay, you want to know why? Because I'm on a wanted list too. See, the US Army and me? We didn't exactly part on good terms.' He opened his mouth to speak, but Lucy cut him off. 'And I will not elaborate, because it's none of your goddamned business.'

'So,' he said, after a moment. 'Up to us, then.'

Lucy pulled off 13th Street and slipped the Mustang into an underground car park below a shopping mall. As the engine died, she sat there and listened to the echo of the concrete space, the growl of other cars coming and going.

She fished a pair of sunglasses from the top pocket of her jacket and put them on, flashing a look at her reflection in the rear-view to see if they concealed the new shiner she was growing. *Good enough*, she decided, and checked the loads in her Walther semi-automatic before settling it into a shoulder holster.

Marc was doing the same thing, easing back the slide on the Glock to make sure he had a bullet in the pipe.

'We'll walk and talk,' she told him, reaching for the door handle.

He jutted his chin at the car. 'We're just gonna leave the HMX we pulled out of that kid?'

'We sure as hell are not taking it with us.' She walked on, and neither of them mentioned the ever-decreasing countdown. They both understood what missing it would mean.

Marc dragged his battered daypack up and hung it over one shoulder, hunching into it as he walked. 'Should probably split up,' he said, as they approached the door out to the sidewalk. 'More chance of spotting the bus that way.'

She was going to agree, but then they emerged into the bright daylight on the corner of F Street to see a convoy of identical school buses heading in the opposite direction. 'Or not.'

In every direction, Lucy saw coaches, buses and school vehicles. More than that, the streets between Metro Center and the Federal Triangle were choked with dozens of groups of teenage students on top of the city's usual load of transient tourists and day-trippers. They moved in flocks behind harried teachers, each cluster colour-coded by college sweatshirts or fluorescent backpacks.

'Needle, meet haystack,' muttered Marc. 'Everyone and their dog has come out today.'

'Keep moving,' she told him. They crossed down to Pennsylvania Avenue, and Lucy's own threat radar went off as she saw the up-tick in the numbers of uniformed police officers. Blue saw horses were arranged to slow traffic and manage the flow of vehicles and pedestrians into channels that the DC PD could watch – and if the need arose – cut off. Trailing a group of people carrying pro-presidential placards for the rally, they turned west and Marc pointed out a striking white Beau-Arts building on the corner.

'The Willard Hotel. Little up-market for my tastes, to be honest.'

She frowned. 'It's a landmark. It could just be that. A waypoint.'

He shot her a look. 'It's also one of the tallest buildings in the area. If you're planning a strike, it's got a good view of the target zone.' He jerked his thumb over his shoulder. The temporary stage where the rally's speeches would be given was a few blocks to the east. A whole section of the National Mall, in front of the Capitol Building and its reflecting pool had been cordoned off, between 3rd and 7th Street. From the top of the Willard, an observer would have a clear line of sight over the roofs of the Internal Revenue and Legislative Affairs buildings in the so-called Federal Triangle. 'I'll check it out. You take Pershing Park across the street.'

'Or . . .' She halted, and a weight of certainty settled on her. 'Or I don't do that.' Lucy looked around at the civilians moving past them, and she could hear the sounds of a boisterous brass section, where the band of the United States Marine Corps were playing 'The Circus Bee' to the waiting crowds. She had been entertaining the possibility that the two of them could find a way to isolate the Al Sayf cell, but as she saw the people, the numbers . . . That seemed more and more like pinning their hopes on blind luck.

'This is not a time to be cryptic,' Marc told her.

Lucy shook her head. 'I mean, you were right. I *can* make a call. Get more eyes on this.' Her mind flashed back to the ugly mess of red she had seen inside that poor Arab kid's belly, the callous device and the ugly potential within it. A dozen more of those could turn this peaceful gathering into a day of hell.

'You'll be in cuffs ten seconds later.'

'Likely,' she said sharply. 'But my liberty is a small price to pay if we can flag Khadir and his soldier-boys.'

'You sure?' He actually sounded worried for her, and Lucy found that oddly touching. But she was already walking away. Now she'd committed to the choice, she felt no doubts about it.

'Get up there,' said Lucy, jabbing her finger at the Willard's ornate parapets. 'And do some of that clever shit you're good at.'

Jadeed lined up the youths in front of the school bus. They had been given tea and hot food, woken from their fitful slumber for a last meal. Khadir did not tell them it was so, of course.

Now it was just them, Khadir, his second and the American with the dead eyes and expressionless face, the one called Teape. All the others were gone, and he had not been sorry to see the arrogant Britisher leave for the observation point with the South African. The warehouse had an expectant air that reminded Khadir of a mosque in the moments before a service began.

He walked the line of young men, measuring the balance of their confidence. It was to their credit that none of them showed weakness. Cutting the boy Halil from the crop had made sure that would not happen. He had served his purpose as a lesson, and the others had learned it well.

Jadeed offered a tight nod. 'Ready for final deployment.'

He returned the nod and gestured to the American. 'Wait inside the bus.'

Teape climbed into the vehicle, indifferent to the weight of the moment taking place around him. Khadir turned his gaze on the youths. 'We are here,' he began, speaking in Arabic. 'In the heart of enemy territory. America is a great beast, asleep as we walk softly through its domains. In the past that beast has lashed out at us. But it is a foolish, imbecilic animal. Slow and ponderous. It does not see us coming, my brothers.'

He saw some of them react; he had never called them *brothers* before this moment, and they understood the consequences of being granted that status.

'Today, we will strike a blow of great force. It will sound around the world. Every enemy will recoil in its wake. You are the bringers of glory, and after today you will be undying.' He paused and brought his hands together. 'Much has been asked of you, but you have not faltered. You make Al Sayf proud, my brothers. You make *me* proud.'

The youth closest to him, the lanky teenager called Adad, looked up with shining eyes. His words fell on fertile ground, emboldening the young troop of soon-to-be *shahiden*. Khadir wondered if they really did understand the fate that was unfolding before them. It mattered little at this point. The training at the orphanage had beaten the questions out of them long ago, forged them into soldiers that would obey willingly. Al Sayf had made them anew, he reflected.

You're not going to be doing any dying today. The Britisher's mocking words came back to him as he studied their faces, and Khadir looked inside himself, searching for any spark of guilt at the plan he had set in motion. He found none.

'The strike you lead this day will eclipse all others,' he said, closing the speech with a respectful nod. 'Go to it, brothers, and take a man's revenge on those who have wronged you.' He stood by the door and bowed to them as they boarded the bus, ending with a final handshake to Jadeed.

'*Inshallah*,' said the other man. 'Nothing can stop us now, sir.'

'From your lips to heaven's ears,' Khadir replied, although he shared little belief in higher powers. 'You know what to do. Position the weapons and then disengage. We will meet again at the rendezvous, yes?'

'Paris, in five days,' agreed Jadeed. 'Then we begin our next endeavour.'

Khadir stepped away, slapping the control button to retract the roller door and allow the bus to drive away. He gave each of the teenagers who dared to meet his eyes through the window the same fatherly gaze, and then they were gone.

He waited for the sound of the engine to fade, and walked to the far corner of the warehouse, where a tarpaulin covered a Volkswagen Jetta. He threw aside the cover and climbed into the rental car, finding the keys on the seat, along with a one-way ticket on KLM's mid-morning service to Charles De Gaulle.

Khadir glanced at the clock on the Jetta's dash, then at the timer app on his smartphone. His flight would be taking off shortly before the detonations, and he could not risk missing the departure. Every aircraft out of Washington DC not already in the air would be grounded within moments of the attack, and he had no wish to be trapped in this country while their lawmen picked through the debris. He donned a wig and eyeglasses, rubbing make up into his cheeks to make his face appear lighter.

His false smile became genuine as he drove off. By the time he deplaned in France, Omar Khadir would be responsible for redrawing the world, in blood and in flames.

Marc's attire was inappropriate for the Willard's more exclusive clientele, a dark jacket of military cut over a mix of tactical gear from the night before, but rather than brave whatever hawkish concierge patrolled the lobby, he slipped down the side street and made for the service entrance.

Parked outside was a line of trucks, each bearing the logo of a different international broadcaster. Thick black cables snaked away under plastic covers, leading toward the press gallery a block distant. Inside the Willard, away from the gaze of the hotel's well-heeled guests, tech crews were setting up their equipment to broadcast the president's address live to millions of viewers.

He aimed himself at a woman exiting the building, the tag of a laminated security pass dangling from her jacket pocket, and deliberately brushed too close to her. 'Sorry!' he said, throwing a smile back at her without losing a step. She scowled and walked on, unaware that her pass was now in Marc's hand. He tucked it in his jacket collar, using the lapel to hide the picture.

He jogged across the Willard's loading bay, ignored by one of the hotel's security guards, and squeezed into a freight elevator as the door was closing.

Two men were already inside, each wearing technician's tool vests. They gave Marc a cursory glance and continued their conversation.

The younger man was in the middle of complaining about something. 'It makes work for all of us,' he was saying. 'Would be way easier if we could just use wireless.'

The other man gave a rueful, seen-it-all shrug. 'Don't mess with the government,' he said. 'You work in this town long enough, you'll realize that's rule *numero uno*.' He looked at Marc again. 'Hey. You just get in?'

Marc's pass bore the logo of BBC, so for once he could drop the accent. 'Yeah. Off the red-eye from London.'

'You look it,' said the younger man, taking in the fatigue that coloured his expression. 'There's a rack in back of the comms room . . .'

'Thanks,' Marc said, with a wan smile. 'Can't do that, though.' He shrugged. 'Got a job to do.'

That earned him a comradely nod from the techs. 'I hate it when this shit happens, man,' continued the younger one. 'Nine times outta ten it's a false alarm.'

That caught Marc's attention. 'What do you mean?'

'They tightened up security this morning,' said the other man. 'Something about an alert . . .'

'Heard it was about some ship,' said the young technician. 'In New Jersey. Got Homeland Security rattled.'

'Really?' Marc tried to seem nonchalant. The elevator clanked to a halt and the two men got off, pushing a trolley between them.

'You coming?' said the older man.

Marc shook his head. 'I'll catch you later.' The door closed again and he tapped the button that would take him to the top floor.

In his head he was sketching a map, drawing on what he had seen on his web search as they drove in. Marc believed his guess about the Willard serving as a vantage point was sound. The other options didn't synch up; it was too far away from the rally for the deployment of any other kind of weapon, too public to be an operating base for the Al Sayf attack cell. But it *was* close enough to monitor the progress of any act of terror, and just far enough away to be on the outside of the event's main security cordon. The hotel had multiple exits that spilled out in every direction, enough that any watcher could be off and away before the echo of a bomb blast had faded. That, and the fact that the comings and goings of the press corps would provide adequate cover to anyone doing anything untoward, made it an ideal choice.

The only thing he couldn't figure was exactly how the devices were going to be detonated. He kept thinking back to the screen on the makeshift cellular trigger. *One Missed Call.*

As the lift rose, Marc felt around inside his backpack and found the dead detonator. He turned it over in his fingers, scowling at it. Any cellular device could be used to send a signal to it, and with the right set up, it could be pinged through any number of networks, not just mobile or landline, but by satellite phone or voice-over-internet protocols. If he could not see through this puzzle, the death toll would be catastrophic, and it would be his fault.

A bell rang and the freight elevator deposited him on the penthouse level. One hand around the butt of the pistol buried in his jacket, Marc set off down the service corridor. It took a physical effort not to steal another glance at his watch.

For the duration of the president's rally, a stretch of Independence Avenue had been repurposed as a parking and disembarkation area alongside the Department of Agriculture building. Barriers erected to guide the buses arriving and departing funnelled each new group of students through metal detectors, before allowing them on to the mall and into the gathering throng.

Teape pulled into an off-loading area, directed to a halt by a police officer who communicated through shrill blasts on a silver whistle between her lips.

Jadeed stood up, nervous energy fluttering through him, and cast a look over the faces of his charges. 'Remember,' he began, 'do not speak if you are spoken to, do not react. You are deaf and dumb. If you are challenged, show them your identity card and move on.'

They nodded back and Jadeed paused to slip on a pair of spectacles before adjusting the tie and shirt he was now wearing. He took a light jacket and folded it over his arm. His new attire had been carefully selected to give the impression of a scholarly, unimposing man, and he felt lost in the constricting clothes. He gave Teape a meaningful look. 'Remain here.'

'Cops ain't going to let me stay long,' he replied.

'I will return soon. In the meantime, do nothing to draw attention to yourself.'

'Sure.' Teape looked away. 'Whatever you say.'

Jadeed beckoned the youths and they rose as one, following him down the steps and off the bus in an orderly line. Some of them could not help but stare, fascinated by their first close-up view of the streets of an American city.

The group was drawn into a queue and Jadeed feigned a smile as a portly woman in a uniform shirt snatched the pass he offered and peered at it. Nearby, he saw more police officers in full deployment gear, and on the far side of the barriers there were patrols moving back and forth through the crowds. Some had dogs, their sensitive snouts looking for anything hazardous. The security situation was exactly as the Combine had said it would be.

'Wayne County School for the Deaf?' said the woman. She gave the youths a sour glance, her face pinching. 'No disrespect, mister, but if your kids can't hear, how are they gonna follow the speeches?'

Jadeed showed a wide, fixed grin. 'They can read lips, ma'am,' he told her.

Raised voices distracted the woman, and she held on to Jadeed's pass rather than hand it back. He turned to see what she was looking at and stiffened.

Jadeed saw a face he recognized. An angry man with thinning brown hair was in the process of arguing with pair of police officers, standing at the head of a group of sullen-looking teenagers. The lawmen had a fan of identity passes in their hands, and they presented humourless expressions behind the mirrored lenses of wraparound sunglasses. Jadeed knew the angry man's face. He had seen it and those of the students on the passes he had stolen from the safe of an airport motel room only a day earlier. The teacher from Los Angeles was losing his patience trying to explain that *of course* his passes were in order.

The woman gave an arch sniff and dropped Jadeed's pass back into his hand. 'Move along,' she said, dismissing him so that she might take a closer interest in what was about to happen to the party from LA. 'And have a nice day.'

Marc moved through the façade behind the hotel's well-kept corridors. Here, the carpet was threadbare and the décor was purely functional. The residents of the Willard never laid eyes on these areas, the service passages that threaded through the building like veins through a body.

He spotted a doorway leading to roof access. Marc took a step toward it and hesitated, catching the faint sound of radio static at the edge of his hearing.

There was a laundry cart off to one side, as if it had been discarded in the shadows. A sense of wrongness chimed in Marc's thoughts. It seemed out of place, and he went to it, reaching out a hand to pull back the cloth draped over the top of the wheeled basket.

In the cart was the body of a man wearing a police uniform, and he was very dead. Marc stiffened, seeing a red lesion on the policeman's throat, livid like an insect bite. *A fatal injection?*

Glancing around, he saw no blood, no signs of struggle. This had been a clean kill, designed to draw no attention. The dead man's gun was still in his holster, along with the service radio clipped to his jacket. The weak sound was coming from the handheld, and Marc leaned closer to listen, holding his breath.

'*Command, station six, how copy?*' said a woman. It was a status check, a regular call to an isolated officer on watch to monitor for any security breaches.

'*Six,*' came another voice. '*All clear.*'

A pulse of static garbled the transmission and the woman spoke again. '*Please repeat?*'

'*Six. All clear.*'

Marc caught the timbre of the reply. It was identical to the first response, the same pause, the same intonation.

'*Command confirms, over.*'

He reached down to shift the body and saw the name *Dwyer* on the dead policeman's ID tab.

Drawing his pistol, Marc made for the stairs. He climbed up and put his arm to a push-bar door, shouldering it open. Light flooded over him as he emerged on to the roof of the Willard.

He came out near the edge of the building, facing Pershing Park and the city beyond. Up here, an orchard of satellite antennae had been set up to channel the feeds of the news trucks down on the street.

Behind him, Marc heard movement and turned sharply, keeping his Glock tucked out of sight behind his back. He saw another figure in the blue of a DC cop's uniform coming toward him, drawn by the creak of the door.

The man had a craggy face beneath the peaked policeman's cap, and a curious expression. It took a fraction of a second for Marc to understand what he was seeing. It was *recognition*. He heard the click of a hammer being cocked.

'Fuck me,' said the policeman, in an accent that was harsh and grating and very definitely *not* American. 'Is that you . . . ?' Morning light flashed off a gun barrel as it aimed Marc's way, and he shrank back. 'Drop the weapon!' The policeman's Sig Sauer pistol had a non-regulation silencer attached to the muzzle, one final confirmation for Marc that he had made a grave miscalculation.

Cursing inwardly, he released his grip on the Glock and let it dangle on his trigger finger. 'You . . . killed Officer Dwyer.'

'Who?' The other man advanced, keeping the gun on him. He had to be one of Grunewald's mercenaries.

'The cop in the laundry cart.'

He shrugged, as if the man's murder was meaningless. 'I guess. Toss the gun!' snarled the killer. As Marc let the pistol fall to the ground and kicked it away, an incredulous sneer broke out on his face. 'How the hell are you still alive?' he said, with an air of mild amazement. 'You're fucking lucky, that's what you are.' He angled his head, studying him. 'Don't remember me, do you? On the yacht. We had a little back and forth, *ja*?' He gestured with the pistol.

'Novakovich . . . You were on the kill team.'

'I've done in a lot of folks,' admitted the mercenary. 'Doesn't seem to take with you, though. How'd you bring down that drone, eh?'

'You saw that?'

He got a shrug in return. 'It doesn't matter. You had a good run, but you're out now, son.' The other man pointed with the silencer, in the direction of the rear of the building. 'Start walking.'

'You gonna push me off the roof?' Marc said, trying to stall. 'Not smart.'

The mercenary laughed unkindly. 'Oh, no. You're too good to be true. I got someone you gotta meet before I shoot you dead.'

Jadeed strolled as casually to one of the plastic archways that were the last gate between the outside world and the inner cordon of the rally. To most people passing through them, the arches would have seemed little different to the metal detectors that scanned the passages into any modern airport, but it was Jadeed's business to recognize such devices for what they were, to know their capabilities and sensitivities. These arches concealed full body scanners that swept those who stepped through them with an extremely high frequency radio signal, capable of penetrating layers of clothing. Anyone concealing a weapon on their person would immediately be identified.

The arches represented the last barrier between success and failure. Jadeed glanced back at the youths following him, and beckoned the teenager in front to come forward.

Adad gave him a brief, questioning look, but said nothing. 'Go on,' he told him.

Adad emptied his pockets into a tray and walked slowly through the arch. There was a chime and Jadeed craned his neck to catch a glimpse of the screen through which another police officer monitored those entering the rally.

He saw a ghost-image of Adad, rendered like a vague chalk sketch on dark paper. Nothing of the weapon he carried within his flesh showed on the display, only the lines of his body beneath the clothes he wore.

The officer tending the arch waved at Jadeed and he bobbed his head, smiling again. He hid his relief as he passed through without sounding any alerts. One by one, each of the youths followed in Adad's footsteps, and each time the scanning machine saw nothing.

A sense of calm settled on Jadeed as he led them deeper into the crowds. *We have done it! The enemy looked and did not see.*

'This way,' he told them. Jadeed slipped his smartphone from his pocket as he walked, and saw that the data and cellular indicators were dark. No signal could reach them within the cordon.

He glanced around, taking in the crowds. Somewhere nearby, a localized jamming device was blanketing the area as part of the security precautions – a measure designed to prevent the use of cell phones to trigger remote-detonated devices. Jadeed smiled thinly, thinking of the confusion that would strike the Americans when they realized their defences had been circumvented.

He beckoned the others. 'Stay with me,' said Jadeed. 'And keep away from the men with the dogs.' They moved deeper into the throng, pushing their way toward the distant stage.

Ahead of them, a dozen tall flagpoles were spread in a semicircle, and from each fluttered the Stars and Stripes. Jadeed's smiled widened as he imagined each one of them falling to the earth, wreathed in flames.

There was a second bogus policeman on the Willard's roof. He had a pair of powerful binoculars raised to his face, peering out over the buildings to the southeast.

The South African mercenary shoved Marc toward the other man with a hard push in the small of the back. 'Hey,' snarled the merc, 'Tommy, or whatever you're damn well called, look here. I brought you a present! Not as dead as you'd like, eh?'

'What are you on about?' growled the other man, in a harsh London accent that made Marc's blood turn to ice. 'Supposed to stay at your fucking post, you tosser . . .' The second man put down the binoculars and turned to see what was important enough to interrupt him. When he met Marc Dane's gaze there was the smallest flash of shock, quickly smothered by the spread of a predatory smile.

Marc was looking at a dead man. Someone who had been consumed in fire on a French dockside, lost along with Sam Green and the rest of his squad in the explosion that destroyed the *Palomino*.

Now he heard his heartbeat thundering in his ears. Marc felt a sudden sense of dislocation, as if the roof beneath his feet had unfolded and dropped him into freefall. He tried to say the name but his throat felt like it was filled with cinders.

'You . . .' began the other man, with loathing in his words. 'You never learn, do ya? Couldn't just die and be done with it. *Shit*.'

'You're alive,' Marc blurted it out, finally finding his voice. '*Nash*.'

'Surprise,' he said, with the same arrogant sneer Marc had seen a dozen times before.

TWENTY-SIX

His hard-edged face was split by a scornful grin that seemed to eclipse everything around Marc. 'What's the matter?' Iain Nash chugged with mocking laughter. 'You look like you've seen a ghost.'

He's dead. She's dead. They are all dead. The harsh truth of Nomad team's murder was the one thing he knew was undeniable among all the shifting sands of loyalty, distrust and lies. It was the single truth he had never questioned, but now he saw this man standing in front of him and it all began to crumble.

'How . . . ?' he managed, unable to frame all the questions suddenly shouting at him for answers.

'Nash . . .' said the South African. 'So not Tommy, then?'

'Iain Nash is dead,' said the other man. 'Except he ain't.' He stepped down on to the roof proper and looked Marc up and down, enjoying the moment. 'Come on then, Dane. You always thought you were so fucking smart.' He prodded Marc in the shoulder. 'Can you figure it out, you clever little sod?'

Marc's mind reeled back to that night in France, forcing himself to remember what he had witnessed from OpTeam van. The feeds from the assault team, the night vision footage from his micro-drone. 'I saw you die!' He blurted out the words, feeling giddy and sick inside.

'Did you?' Nash sniffed. 'I tell you what, let me lay it out for you. Just so I can see the look on your sorry face.' He glanced at the other man. 'I mean, after all the trouble he's been, I deserve to get something out of this, don't I? A little entertainment?' He spread his hands. 'What did you see? Think about it. What did you *really* see with your little toy box?' Nash turned his head and spat, advancing.

The other mercenary was at Marc's back, and he felt the muzzle of the silenced Sig push against his shoulder blades, cutting off any avenue of escape. 'You . . . Got off the *Palomino* before the explosion.'

'*Bra*-fucking-*vo*.' Nash clapped, slow and exaggerated. 'That's your problem, Dane. See, you lot think you got sight of the whole world through your computers and your drones and your bloody cameras.' His mocking snarl hardened, becoming fiercer, stronger. 'I got sick of you and the rest. You never get it, you don't see how it is out in the grind. You don't get shot at or pissed on or screwed over, day in and day out.' Nash's hands contracted into fists. 'The real shit every poor bastard tommy has to deal with.' He pointed two fingers toward his narrowed eyes, looming over the other man. 'You don't see that from some nice soft chair. You don't want to get any of it on you.'

In that moment, Marc's fear faded away and in its place rose a wellspring of anger, a burning resentment at the callous murder of his team-mates, at Sam Green's cruel death, at all of it. 'Fuck you, Nash,' he spat. '*Fuck you*! We were your team and you led us to the slaughter!'

'Not everyone!' he shot back, grinning. 'You survived! I mean, who thought that would happen? *You*? Last man standing?' He gave a derisive snort. 'Wouldn't sit down and die, would ya? Like a stone in my shoe, all the way here . . .'

'Rix. Bell. Marshall . . .' Their names fell from him in a litany. 'Leon and Owen . . . And Sam! You betrayed them! *Why?*' Marc shouted, putting all the fury and sorrow in him into one word. 'What was worth that?'

'Never was a team player.' Nash gave a low chuckle. 'See, I like money. I like guns. And I like blowing things up for a living. But Six is slower than a shit at the North Pole, and I get bored easy.'

'The Combine recruited you, *ja*?' offered the other merc.

'*I* went to *them*.' Nash shook his head. 'They're already in British Intelligence. *Deep*. They snapped me up, mate. Saw my skills, knew I was hungry and fed up. But they didn't like the OpTeams, nah. They don't like things they can't manage, you get me?' He glared at Marc. 'Rix, he had a big mouth, didn't he? Was looking at stuff he shouldn't have, figured out that there was a mole at the Cross. He was going to go right to the big man, and he roped in Sam and me to help him. *Idiot* . . .' Nash hesitated. 'Well. You know how that ended up. The rest were just collateral damage.'

Marc saw the pieces falling into place. With Nash thought dead along with the rest of Nomad, he was free to drop off the radar and become a direct agent for the Combine's interests. 'You wanted to wipe us out . . .' His lips thinned. 'But it was a balls-up. You missed one.' Marc jerked a thumb in his own direction.

Nash's grin cooled. 'I admit, that did not make me happy. Anyone else, I might have been impressed, but you? Got out by dumb fucking luck.' He leaned in. 'Tell me something. Did you cry about her? When you were on the run, did you shed a tear for that bitch?'

Marc started forward, the impulse to strike Nash coming from out of nowhere, but he barely got a step before the other mercenary struck him across the back of the neck. He staggered and gasped through the pain.

'Let me tell *you* something,' Nash went on, as if nothing had happened. 'Sam . . . You weren't the first place she went for her fun. You were a long way down that list.'

'Is that why you killed her?' Marc retorted. He knew that Sam Green had been with other men before him, but it had never occurred to him to look inside Nomad. Suddenly, all the veiled slights Nash had ever directed at him took on a new focus. 'Did she have enough of your macho bullshit and cut you loose?'

Something flared in Nash's eyes, and Marc was certain he had struck a nerve. For a moment, he thought that the turncoat agent was going to take him on, but instead he pointed a finger at Marc's face and the cold sneer returned. 'Women, eh? Who knows how they think? I dunno what she ever saw in you. You're a fucking wash-out. You've never had the stones to do the job. Being a clever boy don't get you far, pal. You ain't got the fucking instinct in you.' He looked away. 'I got a call, told me you were probably heading to DC. You were either gonna show up here or get yourself caught in all the shit-storm that's coming . . .' Nash glanced at his watch. '. . . in the next thirty minutes.'

'What?' Marc caught on Nash's words. 'Who called you?'

'The other one,' said the Afrikaans mercenary. 'At MI6.'

'Like I said, *in deep*. Wasn't just me who was smart enough to see the writing on the wall,' Nash explained. 'London's been tracking you. And what Six knows, so do we.' He chuckled again. 'If you'd been good at this, you might have been able to get the drop on me. But *nah*. You're too fucking weak to pull a trigger.'

Marc met Nash's gaze. 'You'd be surprised at what I'm capable of.'

'Oh.' Nash gave a slow nod, and gestured at the air. 'All this, then . . . That's been the making of you, has it? Toughened you up?' He came closer. 'Made a man of ya?' His fist came up in a fast right cross and Marc instinctively flinched back.

The blow never landed, stopping short as Nash let his hand drop and laughed at his reaction. 'Ellis,' he said, glancing at the other man. 'Make use of this prick. Waste him and stick him with that dead copper. Make it look like he did it, give the yanks the run-around.'

'What about you?'

'Time to book,' Nash replied. 'If arsehole here found us, more trouble's coming.'

'The hotel is full of Feds,' Marc snapped, seizing on the other man's words.

'Yeah, sure,' Nash sniffed, unimpressed. 'Get him out of my sight. And for fuck's sake, make sure he's dead this time.'

The South African mercenary grabbed a handful of Marc's shoulder strap, and dragged him up by his backpack, cracking him a second time across the neck with his gun. 'Walk on,' he grated, pushing him away toward the rooftop access.

The crowd was in a buoyant mood, and music was playing across the Mall, piped in through speaker stacks arranged before the stage. On video screens as big as the side of a house, a youth group from Seattle were playing a spirited take on some old jazz number, and people were clapping. The main event was close at hand, the introduction of the President of the United States and the speech that would kick off a week of education-related rallies and political events here in the nation's capital.

Lucy's federal badge had got her into the rally, but she knew that security would have already run her details, that they would be scrambling people right now to surround her and bring her in.

She saw the Michigan school bust out on the street. They were here.

Pushing aside everything else crowding her mind, she made herself think like a terrorist, scanning the crowds and seeing only targets to be destroyed. *Where would I go?*

She started moving again, plotting out optimal points of attack, and immediately one location leapt out at her. Close to the main stage, beyond a set of tall flagpoles. Good sight lines, heavy civilian concentration. Massive potential for casualties.

As she approached, a figure caught Lucy's eye. A man in a conservative suit jacket, his face half-hidden behind thick-rimmed eyeglasses. His movement drew her because he had changed direction in the middle of his stride, pivoting away from a police dog handler. The man was carefully avoiding the gaze of the cop, and in the process he allowed her to get a good look at him instead.

She knew him. A few hours earlier, aboard Solomon's jet as it crossed the Atlantic, Lucy had spent the time when she couldn't sleep poring over files that Delancort had dredged up from Rubicon's archives. This man's face had been among them, part of a list of known associates of the terrorist Omar Khadir.

Jadeed Amarah. One of Al Sayf's active soldiers, ex-military like his commander, a zealot and ruthless with it. Amarah had made a good attempt to fox any facial recognition software that might be sifting security camera feeds, the heavy glasses breaking up his profile just enough to confuse a machine, but not enough to keep a human eye from making the connection.

She glanced around. If he was here, then so were the carriers. Lucy reached for her smartphone, then realized that it would be useless inside the no-signal cell jamming zone. Amarah drifted away, melting into the crowd, and she lost sight of him. Lucy cursed and pushed her way through another knot of teenagers, ignoring their complaints as she made a bee-line for the flags.

Behind her, she heard a dog barking, but the noise was lost as the jazz players launched into the raucous, up-tempo finale of their set. She kept pushing on, scanning the faces in the crowd. A jolt of despair clutched at her chest, and Lucy felt the first stirrings of actual panic.

What if she was standing right here, still looking for him, when it happened? A string of violent detonations, bodies bursting open into fireballs. Hundreds caught in the inferno, many more scarred for life. Horrible images of carnage clouded her thoughts and it took a physical effort for her to shake them off. She chided herself. *Don't dwell, girl,* she thought. *That's not how they trained you.*

Lucy pushed the momentary lapse to the back of her mind, and in that second she saw her target. He was no more than two hundred metres distant from her, moving toward the far end of the stage. There were three youths walking close by, following in his footsteps, and her breath caught in her throat as she realized who – *and what* – they had to be.

That meant the others Al Sayf had brought to Washington were already here, already in place. Lucy moved toward Amarah, never taking her eyes off him.

Then a strong hand closed around her wrist and she spun, trying and failing to disengage. A woman and a man were crowding in on her, both of them in the basic black suits that were the uniform of the United States Secret Service.

'Ma'am, can you come with us, please?' The female agent holding her had a dark and unreadable complexion. Lucy glimpsed the tip of a stun prod in her other hand, concealed up sleeve of her jacket.

'Don't make a scene,' said the second agent, his eyes lost behind a pair of black sunglasses.

'Listen to me,' Lucy began, keeping her stance neutral to show she wasn't a threat. 'There's a high value terrorist target on site, right there.' She turned to point to where Amarah had been standing, but her heart sank as she realized he had vanished once again. 'He's here,' she insisted. 'If you just–'

'I'll put you down if you make me.' The woman was deadly serious. 'We know who you are, Keyes. How this goes next is up to you.'

Lucy's lip curled. 'You think I would just waltz in here and let you see me unless I *wanted* to? There's a threat.'

'And we're looking at it,' said the other agent. 'Lucille Keyes, you're under arrest. Now walk . . . because we won't ask again.'

'Shit.' She hesitated. If push came to shove, Lucy believed she had a fifty-fifty chance of taking down these two. But if she did, it would be right here in broad daylight with hundreds of onlookers, and reinforcements would be on her in moments, not to mention what might happen if Amarah was spooked. The smart choice was to surrender, at least for the moment, and then try to get these people to listen to her. But time was against her. 'Okay, I'm not resisting. But I need to talk to the agent in charge, and in the next ten minutes.'

'Why?' demanded the other woman.

'Because if you wait, we may not be around to *have* a conversation.'

Each footstep was marking off the distance to that last bullet. Marc could sense it waiting for him, a burning shot that would end him on this windswept rooftop, thousands of miles from home.

The injustice of it raged inside him. After coming so far, after putting a face to the pain and the anger that had driven him, Marc could not allow it to end like this. He vowed there would be no more casualties today from Al Sayf's vindictive war and the Combine's ruthless power games. *I won't let it happen.*

He walked ahead of Ellis, slouched and feigning defeat with every pace. Given all he had been through, it wasn't hard to fake it.

In front of Marc, laid across the roof, was another cable threading toward a temporary cell-band tower erected by a tech crew from TV5 Monde. *Take the chance,* he told himself. *Got nothing else to lose.*

At the last second, Marc kicked at the cable with his heel and the impact made it twitch across the ground, sidewinding like a disturbed snake. He risked that Ellis's eye would be drawn to the motion, a reflex action that would give Marc a fraction of a second to throw himself into the shadow of a ventilator cover.

He dove forward, but Ellis was quicker than he expected and the mercenary's gun coughed twice. Two rounds from the Sig Sauer hit him between the shoulders, twin punches that knocked him down.

Neither shot penetrated through the daypack hanging on his back, the thick nylon and the case of his battle-worn laptop absorbing the brunt of the force. He hit the ground and rolled, hearing Ellis curse him and come running.

The mercenary decided not to play the game and follow him around the low vent. Instead, Ellis put one foot on the lip of the obstruction and came straight up over it with a grunt of effort, panning with the silenced gun, aiming where he thought Marc would have landed.

His target wasn't there, only the damaged backpack. Then a black blur flicked up from the roof and Ellis was struck in the chest by a length of the communications cable.

Marc emerged from behind the antenna, both hands gripping the line. He pulled hard on it, making it crack like a whip. There was enough play in the cable to use it as a makeshift weapon, knocking the mercenary from his ill-chosen perch.

Ellis went down hard and lost his gun as he hit the gravel on the roofing. The Sig Sauer bounced against the lintel and landed close to the edge.

Marc lunged at the gun as Ellis scrambled to come at him, the bigger man's muscular hands snatching at air as he failed to grab the hem of his jacket.

Marc's fingers scraped the roof and pawed at the pistol. He had it in his hand as Ellis's vice-like grip closed around his ankle. The mercenary pulled hard, dragging Marc toward him, raising his fist to strike him in the gut.

Marc pulled the trigger again and again, blind-firing and letting the recoil of the weapon bring it up and across. Hot brass cartridges clattered back at him, bouncing off his face and his chest.

All but one shot missed. The round caught Ellis in the mouth and emerged through the back of his head, blowing out a wet streamer of blood, meat and tooth fragments. The mercenary managed a strangled, gurgling moan and stumbled. His ankle caught the inner edge of the lintel and Ellis toppled over.

Marc bolted to his feet, but he was too late to arrest the other man's dive. He got to the edge just as the mercenary's body landed on a taxi parked below, cratering the hood and smashing the windshield. The terrified driver spilled out on to the sidewalk and someone screamed. Marc shrank back as all eyes on the street turned to stare upward.

He scrambled away. There had to be other observers on rooftops nearby, real cops, he guessed, and while they might have missed the chug of silenced gunfire among the noise of traffic and tourists, they wouldn't ignore screams for long.

His Glock was still lying near the access door where he had dropped it, and Marc snatched at the gun. Gathering it up with his backpack, he sagged and blew out a breath. Inside the bag, his laptop was marred with two massive impact dents and it gave a sickly rattle when he shook it. He sighed and zipped the pack closed.

The next thirty minutes. Marc stole a look at his watch, checked the remaining ammunition in the silenced Sig's magazine and doubled back the way he had come.

Nash had the smartphone to his ear, scowling at the voice on the other end of the line. 'Listen,' he snapped. 'Don't get your fucking knickers in a twist, I'm dealing with your mistakes. You just do your part and–' He broke off as he heard a crash of breaking glass and the distant noise of a woman's scream. 'I'll call you back,' Nash added, and ended the conversation. Reaching inside his jacket for his pistol, his gun cleared its holster just as the first shot chopped at the ground near his feet.

Nash dove behind a skylight. He hadn't heard the report of a firearm, which meant a silenced weapon. *Which means that dozy prick Ellis is dead and Dane has his gun.* He spat in annoyance and rose up, aiming by instinct in the direction the shot had come from.

He saw his former team mate running between two air conditioning units and fired at him, rounds sparking off the metal housings. Dane fired back blindly, trying to force Nash to keep his head down, but the ex-soldier had walked through far more intense fields of fire and never flinched. Instead, he jumped to his feet and broke into a sprint.

Marc felt the Sig Sauer go dead in his hand as he slid down behind the air con unit. The pistol's breech was jammed; Marc was firing so fast that an empty brass cartridge had jammed in the ejector port. He cursed and worked the slide, flicking the casing away. The silenced Sig was almost empty, and even though Marc still had the other gun in his backpack, both weapons used different bullets and couldn't share the suppressor. If he went to the 9mm semi-automatic, firing a shot in the open would be like sending up a distress flare. Police snipers and aerial units would be on him in moments.

But then the question became moot as Iain Nash hove into view at full tilt. Marc brought up the Sig, but his hesitation had cost him vital seconds and Nash was right there, swinging a vicious haymaker that knocked him into the air con unit with an echoing clang. Marc tasted copper in his mouth and his skull rang with the impact.

'I don't believe you,' Nash was saying, almost incredulous. 'You've got to have something wrong in your head. When are you gonna learn *to run away*?'

He followed the snarling words with another one-two punch that Marc attempted to block. He lost the silenced pistol, and staggered back as Nash continued to advance.

The other man holstered his weapon. 'You should've run in France. You had the luck in London. Instead, you come back for more. But you get no more chances, shithead.' He cracked his knuckles and shook out his hands. 'I reckon I'll enjoy this . . .'

Marc pushed off and landed two lightning blows on the right side of Nash's face, pounding as hard as he could to strike at the bigger man's jaw. Nash's head rocked under each blow as it landed, but he seemed to feel nothing.

The ex-soldier's eyes widened and he lunged forward, grabbing the daypack straps across Marc's chest. With a growl of effort, he wrenched Marc off his feet and slammed him hard against the air conditioner again. Without letting go, Nash reversed his move and flung Marc back the other way, dashing him to the rooftop.

Marc hit hard and tumbled, seeing stars. He tried to scramble back, tried to get his footing, but Nash came in like a striker making a free kick and planted a heavy tactical boot in his ribs. Fire blazed across Marc's chest as the blow landed and all the air in his lungs was expelled in a coughing gasp.

'Get up.' Nash's voice seemed distant and woolly. 'Don't puss out on me.' The bigger man dragged him up from the ground and dropped another punch to knock him down again.

Marc weathered the blow and lashed out, landing a hit in the side of Nash's knee, earning a grunt of pain. In return, Nash hauled him up and shoved Marc into the door of a machine room in the middle of the hotel rooftop.

The door buckled under the weight of him and Marc stumbled inside, blinking at the dimness within. He tried to put distance between him and Nash, but the other man was still coming.

Iain Nash had trained with the Special Air Service, he had been a full-time tactical field officer for MI6. He was in a different league to Marc Dane, who was all whipcord and adrenaline. Nash was the bulldog to Marc's greyhound, conditioned for stamina and dishing out violence as well as absorbing it. *You can't beat him head on*, Marc told himself.

The machine room was a windowless concrete space above the four elevators that served the Willard Hotel's residential floors. Positioned over each shaft was a powerful electric motor with a spinning wheel that guided steel cables down through a slot in the floor to the mechanism on the top of each lift car. Banks of switching gear and a maintenance bench were the room's only other furnishings, harsh light spilling across the chamber from a single fluorescent tube overhead.

Nash followed him in, booting the door shut as he pulled at the tab on the belt that was part of his police officer disguise. 'I gotta jet,' he said to the air. 'Work to do. But I can't pass this up, can I?' He let the belt, gun, holster and all drop to the floor, then shrugged off his jacket. 'Lost count of the number of times I thought about knocking seven shades of shit out of you.' He rolled his shoulders, savouring the moment.

'Feeling's mutual . . .' Marc panted, getting unsteadily to his feet. 'Come on, then. You're not on the terraces now, you fucking thug!'

Nash raised his hands into a boxer's stance. 'You don't know me,' he retorted. 'You've never been a soldier. You sat in a poncey helicopter, you think you can talk to me like you stood a post? Piss off!'

'You're right, Nash,' Marc shrugged, backing away toward the motor gear. 'I'm *not* like you. You're just a yob who joined up because he wanted a way to hurt people!' His temper rose, and he jabbed a finger at the other man. 'Don't come out with that 'honour of the regiment' bollocks to me. You don't give a damn about Queen and Country. You're a gutless traitor!'

'Oh, you got my number.' Nash pulled a mock-sad face. 'I'm cut to the quick, me.' His expression twisted into a savage snarl. 'They let *me* down first! Salute and do the Crown's dirty work, for what? A pittance, a crap pension and an ungrateful country run by posh wankers and asylum seekers?' He shook his head. 'Fuck that noise. I shed my blood. I want my cut.'

'And the Combine will give it to you? Off the back of killing your own squad? Murdering hundreds of innocent people?'

'Who?' Nash snorted coldly. 'You think I care about them, or those civvies out there?' He jerked his thumb in the direction of the National Mall. 'You think anyone gives a toss about Khadir's crusade or a bunch of whining Yanks? All a means to an end. If it don't happen here today, it'll happen tomorrow somewhere else.' He saw the question in Marc's eyes and grinned unpleasantly. 'Yeah, you getting it now, are ya? The Combine's been at this shit for *years.* They were selling bullets to both sides in the First World War! Now they're working up trouble where and when they want it, and coining it in. Anyone on the outside of that is a fucking chump.'

'They'll be stopped.'

'What? By you?' Nash laughed. 'And whose army?'

Words failed him, and Marc went for Nash, feinting to the right and then going low to throw out a short stabbing strike to his stomach. The ex-soldier grunted in pain and grabbed at Marc, backhanding him with a glancing blow that lit sparks behind his eyes. Off-balance, Marc couldn't stop Nash from shoving him down on to one of the elevator gears.

He collided with the main motor, barely arresting his fall before his face struck the spinning edge of the gearwheel, but Nash had followed him down and he pressed his full weight into Marc's back.

Marc's hands slipped on the motor casing, the muscles in his arms bunching as he put all his effort into holding back. The stale odour of grease filled his nostrils as the wheel flashed past inches from his face. Nash's thick fingers gripped the back of Marc's head and pushed him inexorably toward the metal gears. If the rotating rim met his flesh, it would cut into him like a blunted buzz saw.

He could hear the clatter and rattle of the elevators beneath him and for long seconds, the two of them were locked in place, each resisting the other. But Marc's muscles were already trembling with effort, while all Nash had to do was keep up the relentless pressure. The bigger man was leaning in on him, marshalling all the force he could muster.

Then, with a thudding sound, the elevator directly below reached the lobby level and stopped. The spinning gearwheel clanked to a halt and Marc felt the tiniest relaxing of Nash's hand as the other man reacted. It was the only opening he would get.

With all his remaining strength, Marc threw back his shoulders and his head. The top of his skull slammed into Nash's face and Marc felt the crunch of cartilage, a split second before it was drowned out by the wave of brutal pain that swept through him.

Nash let out a guttural, animal noise, reeling back. He blinked and dragged a hand over his nose and mouth, his palm coming away wet with blood.

Marc rolled toward the workbench, across the machine room. He snatched at the first thing that looked like a weapon – a weighty adjustable spanner – and came back toward Nash, swinging it in a wide arc.

The other man backed off and grinned, showing bloody teeth. Nash beckoned Marc with both hands. 'Let's have you, then,' he grunted, pausing to cough out a glob of bloody spittle. 'I'll shove that down your throat, prick!'

Marc raised the tool like a club, but instead of advancing to attack, he struck out at the fluorescent lighting tube hanging from the machine room's ceiling. He turned his face away as the spanner shattered the tube and plunged the confined space into semidarkness with a burst of electricity.

'I will fucking gut you!' Nash bellowed, enraged and near flashblinded. He lurched toward the door where he had dumped his jacket and belt, groping for the pistol he had discarded there. He was tired of playing this game, and Nash wanted nothing more than to end Marc Dane's life as quickly and painfully as possible.

The only light in the room was now coming up in weak shafts through the cable guides. He heard footsteps scuffling across the concrete flooring, glimpsed a shadow caught in the half-light.

Nash would kill Dane here and leave the smartphone on the body, make it look like he'd been in on the attack all along and left for dead by his Al Sayf co-conspirators. He smiled in the dark as his fingers touched the metal cylinder of a big police-issue Maglite torch. It wasn't the gun, but it would do.

Nash liked the way this story was shaping up. He grabbed the flashlight and spun around, stabbing the button to drench the room in illumination. 'Surprise, you fuckwit–'

The space in front of him was empty; then from the shadows by his side, a hard nub of metal jabbed him in the temple. From the corner of his eye he saw the blurry shape of a silencer pressed to his head.

Nash was going to say something. Marc saw it in the parting of his lips, heard the swift indrawn breath.

But he had already committed to the act. Whatever thought was forming in the other man's mind never completed the journey. Marc's finger tightened on the Sig Sauer's trigger and the gun bucked in his hand.

Nash jerked back as if he had been hit in the head by a hammer. Dark blood and brain matter glittered in the edge-glow from the flashlight as it sprayed up the wall. He collapsed into the corner of the machine room, his body giving a final shuddering twitch before it became still.

Marc held the gun tightly. In the darkness he had found Nash's pistol in the folds of his jacket, and he gambled that the ex-soldier was cocky enough to carry it with the safety off and a round already chambered. Aggressive and predictable to the last, Nash had not let him down.

It didn't seem like enough.

A man Marc had thought was dead, seemingly resurrected just to spite him and now dead again by his hand, this time for certain. It wasn't enough that he had died here, out of sight of the world, his crimes still hidden.

Marc wanted Nash to be alive so he could punish him, berate him, *kill him again*. He wanted to shoot him in the belly, let him lie there and bleed out slowly and painfully.

'I should have *known* this was coming. I knew you were a bastard from the first day I saw you,' he told the corpse, tired and furious all at once. 'You murdered Sam and all you've done is die for it.' Marc aimed the gun and wavered on the edge of unloading the rest of the magazine into the dead man, out of sheer hate for him.

Instead, he got to his feet, groaning as all the bruising and contusions across his body made themselves known. Marc gathered up the police jacket, searching the pockets for more ammunition, for anything that could be useful.

The black slab of a smartphone tumbled out and clattered across the floor.

TWENTY-SEVEN

Marc left the stairwell on the ninth floor, the door crashing open with a bang that echoed down the corridor.

A businessman who had slept late and was still in his hotel-issue dressing gown almost dropped the breakfast tray he was depositing outside his room as Marc charged past. 'Hey buddy,' he called, 'where's the fire?'

'I need this,' Marc told him, snatching up the ice bucket on the tray, handing back the empty wine bottle it contained. Marc dumped the melt water through the overflow grille of a nearby ice machine, and quickly refilled it with fresh cubes. Without pausing, he stuffed the black cell phone he'd found in Nash's jacket into the ice.

The man laughed. 'That's gonna void your warranty.'

Marc didn't reply, carrying the bucket back to the stairwell. He attached a cable to a port on the bottom of the phone as frost formed the device's glassy screen.

Marc had dumped Nash's gun, the fake police jacket and the contents of his battered daypack on the stairwell's narrow metal landing, and left his wounded laptop to power up. While it was heavily ruggedized, the portable computer wasn't invulnerable and Marc glared at the screen where it had fractured from bullet damage. Much of the display was marred with black voids, as if someone had spilled ink over a sheet of paper, but a fraction of the screen still functioned and by some miracle the machine had booted. He dropped to his haunches and tapped the keyboard experimentally.

It took three tries to get a USB socket working, and he double-clicked a password hijacker program as the laptop connected to the device down the cable. Rapidly chilling the smartphone and then hitting it with the code breaker could make the device's recent memory accessible, and make it possible for Marc to sift out the key code Nash had used to lock the phone. The memory chips inside the device would retain the patterns of the code for a short period, and cooling it stopped that data from decaying too fast.

In a few seconds, the hijacker was spooling out a page of barely-readable information on the phone's settings, and among it was the vital six digits. Marc tipped out the bucket and tapped in the numbers, the ice-cold metal of the phone burning his fingers. He flicked through the menu screens; a single application was running, and he tapped it open.

There were a series of countdown timers arranged in a column, each of them on a steady decrease toward zero, each one running a few tenths of a second slower than the one above it. The top timer clocked over to fourteen minutes and falling as he watched.

Fourteen minutes from now would be just after the top of the hour, when the president would be on stage making his speech.

What he held in his hand was a trigger for Al Sayf's atrocity. Nash had doubtless kept access to the Khadir's 'weapons' for himself, in case the Combine had decided to change the scope of the plan.

Marc sat down hard on the metal stairs, and very carefully, he drew his finger over a series of tabs next to the first timer.

ARM.

SAFE.

ZERO.

He didn't want to think about what *ZERO* would do, but *SAFE* was clear enough. He could stop this now with just a keystroke.

What if it's a booby-trap? He asked himself.

Marc screwed his eyes shut and pressed the button, holding his breath, straining to listen for the sound of a detonation. But there was nothing. He opened his eyes again.

The countdown was still going, and a pop-up message had appeared. *Command Not Sent*, it read, *Unable to Connect.*

He tried again and got the same result. It couldn't be an issue of distance, and Nash's phone was showing full bars and a strong network signal. 'Bollocks!' His curse hung in the air, and he put down the device, glaring at it.

I can't do this on my own, he told himself, reaching for his own smartphone. Rubicon's New York office answered on the second ring. 'I need Delancort,' he said.

'*He's on the other line,*' said a woman's voice. '*This is Kara. I brought the car out to Jersey?*'

He nodded, remembering the Chinese girl. 'Yeah, yeah. Red jacket.' He took a breath. 'Okay, we got a situation.'

'*Are you all right?*'

'I'll manage,' he lied, the pain in his ribs throbbing with slow insistence. 'Can you reach Lucy?'

Kara hesitated, and that was enough to tell him that something was amiss. '*We're monitoring DC police bands here, and it looks like someone matching her description has been taken into custody. I'm sorry, Dane, but you probably can't count on Lucy's help right now.*'

Marc leaned away from the phone and made a snarling noise through his gritted teeth. 'Listen to me,' he began, sucking in a deep breath. 'There were two observers in the Willard Hotel.' There was no need to go into more detail than that right now – details of Iain Nash's return from the dead and the end of him could wait. 'I got a phone from one of them, and it's running a remote timer for seven, repeat *seven*, separate devices. But the abort command isn't working, I don't know how we can locate the carriers and I have no bloody idea what to do next.'

'*Dane*?' Henri Delancort's voice cut in on the line. '*Can you run a feed from the stolen phone back to us? Our team here might be able to hack it remotely.*'

'In less than fourteen minutes?' He heard the French-Canadian swear softly under his breath. 'That's what I thought. This isn't a software problem, its *hardware*. Something's stopping the abort signal from getting through to the bomb carriers.'

'*The cell jammer!*' said Kara. '*That's it!*'

'What jammer? Where?'

She launched in to a rapid-fire explanation without pausing for breath. '*The presidential motorcade has two mobile units that contain powerful short-range cellular and radio jamming systems. They can blanket up to four square city blocks with an umbrella of electronic countermeasures. That means, no cell phone signals in or out.*'

Marc nodded. He had seen similar set-ups during his time with British Intelligence. 'Okay . . .'

'*They are usually deployed when the Secret Service is on a heightened state of alert.*' added Delancort. '*And they are now, after the incident at the Port of New Jersey.*'

'Right.' Marc thought it through. 'The bombs are programmed and activated by the remote, but once they're inside the jammer radius, they can't get the abort call so nothing can stop them from going off. Al Sayf are using the Secret Service's hardware against them . . .' His mouth was dry and he licked his lips. 'So we need to kill this jammer, then. How do we do that?'

'*Short of blowing the thing up with a missile? You would have to actually pull the plug yourself,*' Kara explained.

'*Which requires access to the staging area where the motorcade vehicles are parked,*' said Delancort. '*And even if you* could *do it, the secondary mobile unit would automatically activate to cover the signal loss of the primary in a matter of seconds.*'

An unpleasant certainty settled on Marc, a gallows-walk chill that spread through him like cold fire. 'So that's what we're doing, yeah?' He heard himself say the words.

'*I'll send you an image of the vehicle so you know what to look for,*' said Kara, and he heard the clatter of her tapping at a keyboard. '*But . . . I mean . . . How are you going to get into the secure area?*'

Marc's eyes fell to the collection of items on the landing in front of him – the police jacket, the laptop, the gun, and the contents of the backpack. He reached for the press pass he had stolen on his way into the Willard, and turned it over in his fingers. 'I got an idea.'

Lucy found herself in the back of an empty K9 mobile unit. The interior of the van smelled like wet dog and in short order she had taken to breathing through her mouth.

They confiscated her gun, her phone, her watch, just about everything she had on her short of a strip-search, before binding her wrists with a zip-tie and leaving her to wait. Still, Lucy's sense of time was good, and she estimated that they were still in the green, still in with a chance of stopping the attack.

The problem was, with each minute she sat here, that margin grew thinner. Lucy began a count to ten. At eight, she was going to start kicking at the doors and screaming.

She reached five and the rear of the van opened. The two agents who had corralled her on the Mall were there, along with an older man who had the granite-hard manner of a drill sergeant. He took off his sunglasses and gave her a measuring look.

'Come to take me for a walk?' Lucy asked. 'You bring a leash?'

'That depends on how you behave.' The older man, who was clearly in command here, glanced at his subordinates. 'I'll handle this.' He climbed into the van with Lucy, closed the doors behind him and sat down opposite her.

'You got a problem,' she told him.

'Every day,' he replied. 'I'm Special Agent Rowan. You want to tell me why you're really here, Keyes? And don't waste my time with any bullshit. We ran your jacket. We confirmed your identity.'

'Jadeed Amarah. A top lieutenant of the Al Sayf terror group. He's out there right now with his finger on the actual trigger.' She leaned toward him. 'That clear enough for you, Special Agent Rowan?'

'Yeah, that's what you told my people.' He paused, running a hand through his thinning hair. Lucy guessed Rowan was in his early fifties, and by his manner she pegged him as ex-military.

'You served?' she asked, the question coming to her automatically.

He answered by unbuttoning the cuff of his shirt and pulling it back a few inches. On the inside of his forearm was a simple tattoo in black ink, the silhouette of a dagger and the Latin phrase *de oppresso liber*.

'*To liberate the oppressed*,' she translated. 'So you were SF.' It wasn't a question. The dagger was part of the sigil of the US Army's 1st Special Forces Operational Detachment, also known as Delta Force.

'Bravo Squadron,' he told her. 'Before your time in the unit.' He rolled down the sleeve again. 'I've heard of you, Lucille Keyes. I heard about what you did.'

She shook her head. 'We don't have time for this. For the record, you really *don't* know why I ended up in the Miramar stockade. You just know what they told you.'

'Why show your face?' Rowan asked her. 'I mean, you were trained better than that. You had to know we'd tag you.'

'Of course I knew!' she shot back. 'You think I wanted to give up my nice life as a federal fugitive for shits and giggles?'

'You came to warn us about a terrorist attack.'

'Yes, goddamn it.'

Rowan cocked his head. 'Or maybe you're unstable like your file says, and this is some kind of drama you're playing out.'

Lucy hesitated on the edge of letting her ill-temper slip, but instead she pulled it back. She found the calm, centred place that kept her level each time she was preparing to make a shot. She couldn't afford to miss here, either. What she said next would mean the difference between Rowan taking her seriously or locking her up and throwing away the key.

'Do I look like I'm off-balance?' she asked, her voice firm. 'I'll lay this out for you. When the president comes on stage, operatives of Al Sayf are going to detonate multiple explosive devices in the crowd, and hundreds will die.'

Rowan stole a look at his wristwatch, but said nothing.

Lucy pressed on. 'Amarah is in disguise and only I know what he looks like. You need to help me find him before he can leave the area.' She paused, marshalling her thoughts. 'Now, you've got a choice. You can do that, or we can sit here in this mobile doghouse and wait for the clock to run out. And when you hear the sound of that first explosion and the screams, you're gonna have to look me in the eye and know you wasted the chance to stop it happening.'

The agent watched her, his expression stony and unreadable, and an unpleasant possibility occurred to Lucy. *The Combine have people everywhere,* she thought. *What if this guy is in on it?* She had a sudden, horrible vision of being forced to wait out those moments until the carnage began.

But then Rowan leaned forward and she saw real doubt flicker in his eyes. 'I don't trust you. You were one of us and you broke the code. How can I believe anything you say to me?'

'I'll make you a deal,' she replied. 'Help me catch Amarah, and I'll tell you anything you want to know about me, about who I shot and how I ended up in Miramar.' Lucy swallowed, as her throat went dry. 'But just decide fast, okay?'

'Hey!' Marc called out as he jogged across the street toward a Nissan utility van parked over from the hotel. He waved to attract the driver's attention. 'Oi, mate!'

The man frowned at him over the top of a newspaper that he wasn't really reading. He had spent his coffee break observing the arrival of the paramedics scrambling to save the life of a cop who had taken an unexpected swan-dive off the top of the Willard. 'What?'

Marc waved his stolen BBC identity card at him, panting hard. The same logo was painted in large letters along the side of the van, and the vehicle carried equipment and camera gear for the News 24 crew currently covering the opening shots of the US election campaign. 'We've got a problem,' Marc told the driver. 'I just came from the ops room,' he said, pointing back at the upper floors of the Willard. 'Camera just went down on the stage, I need to get in there and fix up a replacement right away.' Marc walked around to the side of the van and pulled on the handle of a sliding door; it stayed resolutely locked.

'What?' repeated the driver, irritated by the idea that he was going to be inconvenienced by some random glitch. 'Can't they use the number two rig?'

Marc banged on the door. 'Mate, come on! We're going live and they need both working cameras.'

'I'm not supposed to go back through the cordon. I don't have authorization,' insisted the other man. 'And I'm on a break,' he added.

'Fine. You want to check in?' Marc offered the driver his smartphone. 'Ring the ops desk. But make it quick.'

The driver gave him a wary look and shook his head. 'No, it's okay. I can make the call.' He reached for his own company phone sitting on the dash and tapped a speed-dial button that would connect him to the broadcaster dispatch.

Marc made a show of impatiently turning his phone over in his fingers, but what he was actually doing was keeping it as close as he could to the driver's handset. Embedded in the casing of Marc's device was a circuit that could mimic a cellular tower at close range, forcing any nearby phone attempting to connect to the greater GSM network to talk to it and not the nearest wireless node. Once spoofed, it was easy to channel the voice signal to somewhere other than the number that had been dialled, with the caller none the wiser.

'*Operations*,' said Kara Wei's voice.

'Yeah, this is van three,' began the driver. 'What's this about a blown ENG rig on the live stage?'

'That's right. There's a guy on his way down to you, is he there yet?' The driver shot Marc a look as Kara spun out the lie. '*We need to get a replacement set up ASAP. I've got the producer here chewing me a new one.*'

'Got it.' The other man beckoned to Marc, reaching down to release the door lock. 'On our way.' He cut the call, blew out a breath and irritably folded up his paper. 'All right, let's go.'

'Cheers,' Marc pulled open the sliding door and was barely into the van before it pulled away from the kerb and moved swiftly across the line of traffic.

'Be there in a minute,' called the driver, through a grille in the back of the cab.

'Right.' Plastic cases arranged in racks along the inside of the van contained all kinds of equipment required for the process of ENG – electronic news gathering – but Marc ignored them in favour of a green metal box sporting a white cross.

Flipping up the lid on the medical kit, he pawed through the contents and pulled out bandages, sterile wipes and a bottle of painkillers. He shook out some Ibuprofen tablets and swallowed them dry. The aftershocks from the beating Nash had given him were getting worse, and Marc was afraid that he might have cracked a rib.

Wincing with the sudden motion as the van turned sharply toward 3rd Street, Marc rolled up his shirt and grimaced at the sight of fresh yellow-purple bruises. He taped up his ribs, dressed the cuts and pulled down the shirt again. The van slowed as it bounced over a speed bump by the security checkpoint, and the last thing Marc did was pull the fake police jacket from his day-pack and shrug it on. He finished off the makeshift disguise with the threadbare cap that was still dirty with Turkish dust, pulling it down low to shade his face.

He heard the driver talking to the police officer at the checkpoint, and then the van nosed into a parking spot among the other media trucks.

Marc grabbed his pack and before the engine fell silent, cranked open the doors at the back of the vehicle and stepped out. He dropped down and walked quickly and purposefully away, putting as much distance as he could between himself and the BBC van before the driver realised something was up.

There were uniforms everywhere. Cops moved this way and that, all of them intent on their own duties, and now and then Marc glimpsed the green of a soldier's garb or the black attire of a Federal agent. He kept his head down, trying not to draw attention, doing nothing that might alert those around him that he didn't belong.

In preparation for the rally, everything east of 4th Street along the line of the National Mall had been cordoned off all the way down to the great reflecting pool in front of the Capitol building, forming a wide rectangular safe zone. Along 4th, between Madison and Jefferson Drives, the main stage for the rally rose up in front of giant video screens that formed a wall, concealing the staging area and tech centre that kept the spectacle running smoothly. Marc could hear the crowd on the far side of the screens clapping as the band on stage concluded their set with a racy rendition of 'Yankee Doodle'.

He felt a buzzing vibration and pulled his phone from his pocket, peering at the screen. As good as their promise, Rubicon had sent him a still image of a custom black Ford SUV. Sprouting from the roof of the vehicle were thick antennae, and various domes and pods that suggested all manner of electronic devices within. Marc turned a corner alongside a mobile generator truck and saw the exact same vehicle a hundred metres away. A Federal officer in a blue windbreaker was leaning on the bonnet, taking the opportunity to smoke a quick cigarette before the main event.

Reaching into his pack, Marc recovered the other phone. Nash's device seemed like it was heavier, cast out of lead. On the timer screen, the numbers were still dropping.

He stuffed it into his back pocket, took a deep breath, and started toward the SUV.

Finally, it was only Jadeed and the youth Adad. He guided him with a firm hand upon his back, and wrapped around the palm in loops were his *misbaha* beads. Adad had felt the lash of them on his flesh when he had disobeyed a teacher in the orphanage. That seemed like a lifetime ago, but the sense-memory of them was strong enough to remind the boy of his duty.

'Stop,' Jadeed told him, finding the optimal spot on the far end of the arc along which all the young soldiers had been arranged. He pointed at the stage. 'Look there.'

Adad nodded and did as he was told. 'I . . . am thirsty.'

'There will be time for that later,' Jadeed lied. 'Do you understand how important it is for you to be here? Remember what the commander told you.'

'I do,' Adad replied. 'I will.' He looked afraid, suddenly very young and very alone.

Jadeed's lips thinned. He had repeated these words over and again, and he was losing patience. 'Stand strong,' he snapped.

'My stomach . . .' Adad's hand went to his belly. 'I think I am becoming sickly. Like Halil.'

'No.' Jadeed shook his head. 'That will not be permitted.' Before Adad could make further complaint, he placed his hand – the hand wrapped with the beads – on his shoulder once more. 'These are your orders. Defy the enemy.' He had to raise his voice as the crowd applauded enthusiastically. 'Look at them, all around you. Cattle, docile and fat. When we reveal ourselves, they will be in awe of us. They will fear you.'

'Yes,' Adad replied, nodding slowly.

Jadeed gave a false smile. 'Soon, now. The American president is coming.' He stepped back. 'We will teach him a lesson,' he concluded, before turning on his heel and threading away through the crowd.

He did not look back to see Adad's face, just as he had not looked back to see any of the youths. If they obeyed – and after the hard discipline that had been instilled in them, he believed they would – each one would remain rooted to the place where he had been set.

Khadir had plotted it out on a tourist's map of the city months before. Jadeed recalled standing in a Parisian hotel room with him, looking at a semi-circle of red dots around a sketch of the main stage. The positions were carefully selected to maximise the potential impact of each of the implanted devices and cause the largest possible loss of life, but the grand target would be the American leader himself. If fate smiled on them this day, he too would be cut down in the firestorm that the bombs would unleash.

Jadeed would have given much to remain and watch the chaos, but he knew it would be foolish to chance being caught in the dragnet that would fall in the wake of the attack. Already, he was taking a risk just being here, but it was a necessary task that, like the supervision of the other bombings, could not be delegated to someone outside the inner circle.

The work was too important for him to risk capture, just as he was too important to serve the cause in so base a way as Adad and the other youths.

He saw no inequality in this. It was simply the manner of things. Jadeed's life would earn its full value through his continued commitment to the cause, and Adad's would be spent best dying for that same ideal.

The exit to Independence Avenue was only a few moments away, and Jadeed continued to make his way toward it, all smiles and contrite apologies as he pushed past the men and women he would soon see killed, the children he would soon see orphaned.

The Secret Service agent looked up as Marc approached him, momentarily guilty that he had been caught indulging in a vice. The two of them were around the same height, but where Marc's build was spare, the agent was dense. He had an Asian cast to his features and a fuzz of close-cut dark hair; he made to stub out the cigarette, but Marc shook his head and made the universal gesture of begging a smoke, bringing up two fingers to his lips.

The agent shrugged and reached for the packet he kept in his breast pocket. 'I should quit,' he offered, in a tone that made Marc think he had said the same words a hundred times before.

Marc quickly glanced left and right. They were not being observed. Before the agent could stop him, he stepped in close and grabbed at something on the man's belt.

'Hey!' The agent recoiled, but he was up against the SUV and he had nowhere to go. He thrust out with his hand, grabbing Marc's face and squeezing, trying to shove him away.

Semi-blinded, Marc couldn't see what he was doing, but he managed to complete his action through feel alone. His hand closed around the handle of a weapon and he jerked it free, fingers finding the push-button trigger.

The agent tried to call out, but Marc was already forcing the metal contacts of the X2 tazer into the other man's sternum. 'Sorry,' he told him, squeezing the trigger for a half-second.

'*Buuuh-*' The other man jerked with the power of the shock discharge, staggering as his muscles locked up and his body refused to obey his brain's commands. The agent's legs gave out and he collapsed toward Marc, knocking off his cap and almost dragging them both down with his dead weight. He wasn't unconscious, but he was barely there, shivering like a palsy victim.

'Take a load off, mate,' Marc offered, not unkindly, and deposited the agent on the cab step of the generator truck. Leaving him there, he sprinted back to the SUV and climbed in.

From the outside, the jammer vehicle's opaque windows made it impossible to see the interior. Now Marc was inside, he was confronted by a wall of electronic systems fitted into the compact space behind the driver's compartment, all running off a big battery unit buried in the SUV's chassis.

Monitors showed complex wave forms that he guessed were counter-frequencies for cellular signal carriers. Stacks of light-emitting diodes rose and fell in glowing streams as every kind of wireless communication within range was jammed into silence by a smothering blanket of artificially-generated military-specification white noise.

The system was cutting edge. In the Fleet Air Arm, Marc had been trained to operate and recognise the functions of military ECM systems, and in his time with MI6 he had used portable jammers on field missions – but the Secret Service rig was complex and he didn't know where to start with it. There was no big red 'off' switch, no power cord that he could pull, and no time to go looking for the manual.

He thought about taking out the Glock and unloading the gun into anything that looked important, but outside he could see his stunned victim climbing shakily to his feet, calling out in a ragged voice. Others heard the man and came running. Marc saw them pointing toward the parked SUV, their hands dropping to their weapons.

Jadeed finally passed through the crush of the bystanders, and at his back the crowd became a chorus of shouts and applause. He hid away a sneer that threatened to spread across his face as he passed a group of college students, no older than Adad and the rest of his soldiers. They were shouting at the top of their lungs, chanting the initials of their nation-state like it was a battle cry. Loutish, brash and uncouth, to Jadeed's mind they were the typically over-fed, over-entitled Americans he so detested.

He passed them by and exited through a turnstile, glancing down the street to find Teape and the school bus. He hunched forward, pulling his collar tight, and walked quickly back to the waiting vehicle.

The door was already open, and casting a last look over his shoulder, he climbed inside. 'Let's go,' he commanded. 'Take 2nd Street down to the Interstate and–'

He fell silent as he looked up and saw that the driver's seat was empty. Jadeed whirled, an angry retort forming on his lips. There was no time for the mercenary to play games, they were only minutes away from the first detonation.

'Jadeed Amarah,' said a voice he didn't recognize. 'Raise your hands.'

He turned and saw two figures in tactical gear crouching low along the aisle that led to the back of the vehicle. One of them had Teape pressed face-down into the floor, his arms cuffed behind him and a pistol in the small of his back. The second was a woman, and she aimed her gun directly at Jadeed's chest.

He feigned surprise and took a step back. Jadeed allowed the string of metal *misbaha* beads to slip from his wrist and gather in his closed hand. 'What is going on?'

'Do not take another step,' said the female agent, commanding him like a mother speaking to some errant child. 'Or I will shoot you.'

He hesitated on the brink of snarling out a curse at the female, and saw movement outside the bus. There were other agents in bullet-proof vests taking up positions around the vehicle, cutting off all avenues of escape. One of them, an older man with thinning hair, turned to speak to a younger, athletic black woman who seemed to have her wrists bound together.

'Michigan plates,' he heard the man say, nodding at the bus. 'How about that?'

'You believe me now?' asked the woman.

Inside the bus, the female agent rose and gestured with her gun. 'Hands behind your head. Turn around and walk down to the street.'

'This has all been some terrible mistake,' he insisted, obeying but moving slowly. 'I don't know who you think I am! I am a teacher!' His jaw tensed. How had they found him? Was this Khadir's doing, was the commander somehow displeased with him?

'Walk,' said the agent. 'I won't tell you again.'

He gave a shaky nod and stepped back toward the door, counting down the seconds. *I still have a chance to flee. When the moment comes.*

Someone was shouting at Marc to come out of the vehicle with his hands up, but then their words were lost in the brassy roar of a military band striking up the opening bars of 'Hail to the Chief'.

Without hesitating, Marc slammed the SUV's gears into 'drive', his hand falling to the starter button. He mashed it with his finger, but nothing happened. Marc's gaze dropped to the ignition and he belatedly realised there were no keys in it.

More people were closing around the vehicle now, other agents and cops with their pistols at the ready.

'Oh, shit . . .' He bent forward and played the last option he had. Securing his safety belt, Marc jammed the X2's sparking contacts against the metal head of the ignition cylinder and mashed the tazer's trigger over and over, sending powerful jolts of electricity directly into the sensitive innards of the starter system, overloading it.

The dials on the SUV's dashboard flickered as the engine gave a sluggish grunt, choked and then finally turned over. Now the brass band was joined by the roar of an excited crowd, and the first report of a pistol went unheard. Marc saw the blink of the bullet's discharge off to his right, but he felt the vehicle absorb the impact of the round as it cracked into the armoured glass of the windscreen.

He pressed his weight down on the accelerator pedal and the SUV lurched forward, kicking up shreds of turf.

That was all that was needed for others to open fire. Marc flinched as bullets smacked into the frame and the windows, shots that – if he had been behind conventional glass and unarmoured doors – would have ended him in seconds.

The vehicle sideswiped a police cruiser as it surged away, shouldering the car aside. Marc aimed the SUV at the gap between two plastic barriers and crashed through. The wheels skipped as he guided it over the sidewalk and straight across 3rd Street. Like a black missile, the jammer vehicle thundered away from the stage in the direction of the great domed senate building.

Police officers and federal agents scrambled to pursue it. More shots chopped at the tires, but the vehicle was equipped with run-flats that could absorb a dozen rounds and keep going.

Marc slapped at a switch on the dashboard and switched off the SUV's automatic traction control. The vehicle bounded back up off the road on the far side of the street, mowed down a temporary chain-link fence and scrambled over the grass, toward the serene mirror of the capitol reflection pool. On the far side of the water, Marc glimpsed the grand statues of Ulysses Grant and James Garfield silently observing the unfolding chaos.

He stabbed at the button that lowered the power windows and gave his seatbelt a last tug to make sure it was secure. Something sharp cracked off the door frame, and he guessed it was a high-calibre rifle round, ignored it.

With a savage right-left twist of the steering wheel, Marc forced the SUV into a skidding, swaying turn, then violently pulled it back in the opposite direction. With a high centre of gravity, the vehicle reacted poorly and rose up on two wheels. Marc felt it pass the point of balance and start to tip just as the front bounced over the concrete lip at the edge of the reflecting pool.

He lost all sense of direction as the SUV surrendered to gravity, and flipped over. Crashing through the still waters, the vehicle made one complete roll before it settled hard on the driver's side, its wheels still turning in the air.

Through the opened windows, water rushed in and washed over the sensitive electronics of the signal jammers, causing brilliant discharges as short-circuits flashed through the equipment.

His body alight with new pain from the impact shock, Marc coughed and took in a lungful of brackish water, clawing desperately at the airbag that had blown out to smother him. The ornamental pool was less than a meter deep, but it was still enough for a trapped man to drown in.

Jadeed took a step away from the school bus, and suddenly he was aware of a ripple of consternation running through the assembled law enforcement officers. Voices heavy with distortion crackled through their sat-com radios, calling out warnings across the only open channel. It was the opportunity he had been waiting for.

From the corner of his eye, he saw the female Federal Agent raise a hand to touch the plastic earpiece she wore, her brow furrowing in concern. He made his move.

Holding on to one end of the string of metal beads in his hand, he pivoted swiftly on his right foot and let the *misbaha* snap like a short whip, slashing them down the woman's face.

She cried out and reeled back as the makeshift lash cut a bloody line across her temple and cheek. Jadeed was already on her, coming in fast to loop the heavy gauge cord over her head with one hand and grab at her gun with the other. He performed the move flawlessly, a short and brutal dance as he used the beads to choke her and forced the agent's weapon into the soft flesh of her bare throat.

'*Get away*!' he bellowed, dragging the woman out of the line of sight of any rooftop snipers, into the shadow cast by the bus. 'I will strangle this stinking whore unless you drop your guns!'

'You're a class act, motherfucker.' The dark-skinned woman with the bound wrists had somehow got behind him, and he shifted, pulling tight on the beads and dragging the agent up to shield his body.

'Keyes, stay back!' called the older man, but she didn't acknowledge him.

Jadeed wanted to be in control, but he could feel that slipping away, second by second, vanishing like the ticks of the countdown clock. He let out a brittle laugh. 'You will weep,' he snarled. 'The sword will find your throats!'

The woman raised her hands in a dismissive gesture, and he saw they were strapped together with a thick plastic zip-tie. 'So says the coward who sends children to die in his place.'

His fury peaked, and in that moment all Jadeed wanted was to take a life, an American life, here on the hallowed streets of their capital city. To commit the first act of aggression this day, in Al Sayf's name.

He turned the pistol toward the dark-skinned woman, but she was already spinning, bringing up her leg in a blur of motion. The sweeping kick cracked Jadeed hard on the nerve cluster in his elbow. A shock of numbing pain ran down his gun arm, and his finger deadened on the trigger.

His prisoner joined in the assault and smashed the heel of her shoe down on his instep, breaking bone. Jadeed cried out and she slipped from his grasp, tumbling away to the sidewalk.

The woman with the bound wrists was agile despite her enforced handicap, crossing the distance to him in the blink of an eye. Her arms locked together, she sent her fists into his face as if they were propelled by a piston. Warm, wet fluid gushed from his nostrils and Jadeed choked. Her foot hooked his ankle and the world turned around him, the asphalt of the road coming up to slam into his back.

'No . . .' he managed, scrambling to get back up.

'*No*,' said the older man, coming into view, aiming down at him along the line of his sidearm. 'Where are the carriers?'

A ring of figures surrounded Jadeed, and he coughed out a snigger. If he had to surrender, it would be with hate in his eyes.

'They are already dead,' he spat.

The folding multi-tool on his belt saved Marc's life. Thumbing open the blade, he used it to slice through the jammed seatbelt holding him under the water and pushed away, scrambling around inside the overturned vehicle. His chest was filled with jagged nails, pain slashing back and forth as he moved.

Hands shaking, Marc reached up for the passenger side door and levered himself up and out. The last thing he did before rolling off the stalled SUV was to pull Nash's smartphone from his pocket, holding on to it with a white-knuckle death-grip.

Marc fell back into the water with a heavy splash. He rolled, soaked through, lolling against the side of the crashed vehicle, and brought the phone up to his face. People were calling out, figures were moving on the edge of his pain-blurred vision, but he ignored them. Their shouted commands didn't penetrate his awareness, the voices very far away, strained and alien and incomprehensible.

Time. *Was it time?* The moments seemed to pass sluggishly as he woke the smartphone with a touch and peered owlishly at the tiny screen. The seven clocks were there, one stacked on another, twenty-eight seconds on the uppermost. Now twenty-seven, then twenty-six, twenty-five . . .

The countdown was mesmerising, and his body ached so much, the effort to lift his finger and find the button like moving an impossible weight.

ARM. SAFE. ZERO.

SAFE ALL. Marc found the tab and prodded it. There were full signal bars, full connection for as long as it lasted. He grinned weakly, imagining hundreds of people on the far side of the big screens, their phones suddenly bleating into life with the unexpected arrival of dozens of stalled calls and delayed text messages.

Are You Sure? read the screen. *Yes/No?*

'I'm sure,' he slurred and tapped the button again.

Connecting . . . He held his breath. The voices were clearer now, and Marc could make out figures in dark uniforms wading through the reflecting pool toward him, an army of guns turned in his direction.

Command Sent, reported the device, and without further ceremony the seven bombs became inert, and the crowd kept clapping and the world on the far side of the giant screens rolled on regardless.

Marc didn't look up as the last ten seconds counted down. He needed to see them fall to zero, to know for certain.

But the bullet that entered his chest brought a storm of fire that shocked him out of consciousness, and Marc plunged into a drowning, chilling darkness that went on forever, the cascade of numbers shattering like glass.

TWENTY-EIGHT

The pain came in waves, soaking deep into him with each surge.

He couldn't sort any of it into a rational order, there were just the flashes of agony and the moments of sensory recall that jumbled into a mess of sound, colour and smell.

Blood and chemical cleaner-stink. Hard, bright light that prickled like needles. A horrible, drug-fogged sense of dislocation.

Marc rose up through the levels of awareness from the black, abyssal depths like a swimmer pushing toward the surface of an infinite sea. The real world gradually sketched itself in around him, starting with the feel of cotton against his body, of clothing and sheets and the steady pressure of a mattress against his back. There was noise – the soft and steady chimes of a heart monitor, the low rush of voices like distant breakers – and the faint medicinal odour he associated with sickness and death.

His eyes opened and he saw a hospital room of pale greens and cream, shadows of night-time cast through the window blinds. Marc heard a woman speak.

'He's awake. Call Langley.'

It was an effort to shift his weight, and when he did he realised he felt cold all down one side. Marc reached for the place where that burning, shrieking pain had cut into him in the reflection pool and found a wad of bandages, the outer layer dotted with tiny spots of blood.

The dark sea came up again, and for Marc the transition seemed to happen instantly. One moment it was night, and when his eyes opened again a heartbeat later, the room was filled with honey-gold morning light.

A doctor leaned away from him, and his eyes fixed on a single detail. She had a military identity tag on her white coat. 'He's all yours,' she told someone, and stepped out of the room.

Marc blinked and focused as a man came into view. He wore a dark suit and a plain tie, with the bland good looks of a mid-list television actor. The sort of person who might play the handsome husband on a soap opera.

The man put a cup of with water on the bedside table and gave Marc an appraising look. 'Welcome back, Mister Dane. How are you feeling?'

Marc realised how thirsty he was and he gulped down the water. 'Like fifty miles of bad road . . .' He managed.

'Being shot will do that,' said someone else, and Marc blinked, finding a second man standing at the back of the room. Although he was dressed similarly to his associate, this guy was more muscular. *He'd be the thug ex-boyfriend of the pretty female lead* . . .

He shook off the mental image. Marc was still a little dopey from whatever drugs had been pumped into his system, and his train of thought was in danger of running off the tracks. 'How . . . long was I out of it?'

'You've been sleeping it off for three days,' said the first man. 'I'm Cahill, and that's my colleague Durant. You have some questions to answer.'

The background tension of pain in Marc's side was returning as his body gradually woke up. He shifted position and winced. 'Where am I?'

'Walter Reed Medical Center,' said Cahill.

'Under guard,' added Durant.

Marc took this in. Walter Reed was a military hospital a few miles outside of Washington DC, and if he was there, it meant that there was a ring of Army steel surrounding him. It was likely that no-one outside would have the first clue about his location.

He studied Cahill, trying to get a handle on his situation. 'So. You lads aren't Homeland Security. I'd say CIA, at a push.'

Durant turned to look at him. 'We are the people holding your scrawny neck in our hands. That clear enough?'

Marc glanced at Cahill. 'Are you actually doing the *good cop, bad cop* thing?'

Cahill smiled slightly. 'Why mess with the classics?' He took a seat near the bed, while Durant hovered nearby. 'A lot of people want to talk to you, Marc. Can I call you Marc?' He didn't wait for him to reply. 'There's a long list of folks who you've pissed off.'

Marc settled against the headrest, catching sight of his pulse flicking up and down on the medical monitor. It was smoother than he expected, even though calm was the last thing he should have been. He chalked it up to the soporific effects of the medication and said nothing. Silence was always a powerful weapon in the push and pull of any interrogation.

'We know all about you,' Durant offered. 'We got your computer, your phones . . .'

'Nice work there, by the way,' said Cahill. 'Our tech guys are cursing a blue streak trying to break through the encryption you have on that laptop.'

'So,' continued the other agent. 'That puts us in a difficult position. You're a real problem. You and your friend Keyes.'

At the mention of Lucy's name, he tensed. 'Where is she?'

'Alive. Well. In cuffs,' snapped Durant. 'Like the convict she is.'

Marc's brow furrowed. Had he misheard? 'Convict?'

Durant nodded. 'Guess she don't talk about that much, huh? Keyes is a Federal fugitive.'

On the road from New Jersey she had talked about being on a wanted list. Marc hadn't pressed the issue, surmising that she had gone AWOL from her Army career, but Durant's manner suggested something else entirely. Before he could digest that, Cahill was talking again.

'Let's look at what we have. Marc Dane, rogue British Intelligence officer, disavowed by his own government and wanted by Interpol. Lucille Keyes, a disgraced former Delta Force sniper and escaped prisoner. Both in our custody after attempting to disrupt a major security operation involving the President of these United States.'

'*Disrupt* is not the word that I would use,' Marc managed.

Cahill went on. 'We have two dead men disguised as police officers. One is an ex-NCO in the South African Army, who apparently took the quick way down from the roof of the Willard Hotel in downtown DC. The other, shot dead at close range in the hotel maintenance room, is a man with the kind of deliberately fragmented record in the British military that usually indicates a Special Forces operator. Then there's our other two prisoners. A known criminal with ties to several private military contractors, and the other . . .' He trailed off.

'A Saudi national with a permanent spot on Homeland Security's watch list,' said Durant, his tone severe. 'An operative of the Al Sayf terror group.'

Cahill nodded. 'We're in the process of rounding up more. A group of mercenaries who entered the country illegally on a ship that docked in New Jersey. You know something about that?'

Marc could feel a steady pressure building behind his eyes, like the onset of a migraine headache. 'Did it happen?' he asked, the question falling out of him. 'The bombs, did they go off?'

'They didn't detonate,' Durant replied. 'And right now, nobody even knows they were there.'

A wave of relief washed over him. 'That's . . . good.'

Durant shook his head. 'Not for you.'

'Here's how I think it went,' said Cahill, gesturing with one hand. 'You and Keyes are on the outs, and you got recruited into this nasty little plot cooked up by Al Sayf. But you both got cold feet. You couldn't go through with it, so you turned on your pals. You wanted to make yourselves the heroes of the day.'

Marc looked away, incredulous at the agent's reading of the situation. 'What I *want* . . . is *answers*. I want Jadeed Amarah and Omar Khadir . . .' The mention of Khadir's name sent a charge through the room, as Cahill and Durant exchanged glances. 'And I didn't want anyone else to die,' Marc concluded.

'Amarah's not gonna be getting any visitors,' Durant told him. '*Ever*. He's going to a place that makes Gitmo look like Club Med, and he'll be there for a *long* time.'

'We did what we did to stop them,' Marc pressed on. 'People I care about were killed. The life I had was torn up. My family were threatened!' He summoned the strength to glare at the agents. 'That's not something I was going to let slide, you get me?'

'So out of the goodness of your hearts, you and Keyes came all the way to DC to warn us about a terror strike?' Cahill leaned in. 'Couldn't just phone it in like a concerned citizen?'

Marc shot him an acid look. 'Don't take the piss.' His jaw hardened. 'I'm not saying anything else until I see Lucy.'

Durant scowled, and at a look from Cahill, he produced a phone from his pocket and dialled a number. Marc heard another phone ring, off down the hospital corridor. 'Bring her in,' he said.

A moment later, Lucy stepped through the door. She looked more tired than he had ever seen her, but she managed a wan smile and without waiting for permission, she crossed to a chair and dropped into it. Marc couldn't miss the rigid-frame cuffs binding her wrists.

'Pardon me if I don't shake hands,' she said. Her manner softened briefly. 'You okay?'

'I'm okay,' he replied.

'Liar.'

'Yeah.' Marc rubbed at his eyes. 'The . . . carriers. What happened to them?'

'They're here,' said Lucy. 'After the rally ended, everyone went home . . . and they were still there, standing in a line. Waiting, just like Amarah told them too.'

'We detained all of the bombers,' said Cahill. 'The . . . *devices* . . . have been successfully removed and made safe by an EOD team. No fatalities, although the young men are still hospitalised.'

'What's going to happen to them?' said Marc. 'I mean, they're just teenagers, conditioned to be nothing better than a walking delivery system . . . They're not enemy combatants. They're *victims*.'

'You sure of that?' asked Durant.

'They scooped up the kid from the diner too, Halil,' added Lucy. 'I think the State Department are gonna get involved. Some of them are classed as minors under US law.'

Marc turned a hard glare on Cahill, and the agent raised an eyebrow, pre-empting his next words. 'Despite what you may have heard about my agency, we're not in the business of water-boarding children. They'll be interviewed and taken care of. The real issue at hand is you two.'

Marc glanced at Lucy. 'You told them the truth?' She didn't respond.

'I'd like to know why our agency is getting pressure from members of the Senate about your detention,' said Durant, the question coming from nowhere. 'You got friends in high places, Dane. Friends who all seem to share a connection to the same international multi-billion-dollar corporation.' He came closer. 'What's the deal with you and Rubicon? That's a question I'd *really* like answered.'

Cahill shot his colleague a look, silencing him. 'I'm going to cut to the chase. This is how things are going to go.' He stood up, and his veneer of civility faded away. 'Marc. You're going to be interrogated for every last piece of information you know about Al Sayf and their attempted bombing of the education rally. When we're done with you, you'll be extradited back to the UK where your own people want to have words.' He turned to Lucy. 'Miss Keyes. We'll make certain you go right back to the same cell you vacated at Miramar penal barracks, where you'll serve out the remainder of your sentence along with several extra years for all the other crimes you committed in the meantime.' Cahill's expression became impassive. 'If you two have any last words you want to share, now's the time.

After today, you won't see each other again. Hell, you'll be lucky if you even see daylight.'

Lucy forced that tired smile once more. 'I'm sorry, Dane.'

But Marc shook his head. '*No.*'

'No what?' said Durant.

'I mean *no, that's not how this is going to be.*' Marc leaned forward, ignoring the tightening of his still-raw wounds, meeting Cahill's gaze. 'I don't like that narrative. I got a much better one.'

Cahill was turning to leave the room. 'You don't get to dictate terms–'

'The Combine.' Marc let the name fall where it lay.

'The what?' Durant feigned ignorance.

'I told you before, don't take the piss,' Marc retorted. 'Don't pretend you never heard of them, it just makes you look stupid.' He grunted softly, the ache from the injuries putting his teeth on edge. 'If you know about Al Sayf, you know about the Combine, and if you know about them, you know they supplied hardware for a dozen different terror attacks . . .'

'That we're aware of,' Lucy added.

Cahill hesitated. 'I'm listening.'

'I'll bet the Central Intelligence Agency is as concerned as MI6 are about Combine penetration,' said Marc. 'So a file full of metadata showing locations, dates and origins of communications between Combine assets would be of great interest.'

'Dane . . .' Lucy's tone was a warning. 'What are you doing?'

'I'm changing the game.' He drew himself up. 'You're going to let us walk, Cahill. Free and clear.'

'We are?' Durant towered over Marc. 'Why the hell would we do that?'

'Let him talk,' said Cahill.

Marc went on. 'There's a remote server containing every last bit of data I pulled from the records of one Dima Novakovich . . . He was a broker for the Combine until he ended up surplus to requirements.' He met Durant's gaze. 'I put the intel there for safekeeping. I'll give you the password you need to access it.'

Durant cocked his head. 'I'm pretty sure I could beat that out of you.' He leaned in, radiating menace. 'That *bad cop* enough?'

'There are two passwords,' Marc said, holding firm. 'You won't know which one I've given you until you try it. The wrong one instantly kills the contents of the server memory and you get bugger all.' He looked away from Durant to the other man. 'Now, here's the thing. There are Combine ghost assets inside the CIA, and you know it. If you say no to my offer, I'll know you're one of them, because anyone else is going to jump at the chance to help the company clean house.'

Cahill smiled thinly. 'That's very clever.'

'It's what he's good at,' Lucy said warily. 'Even if it does get him into trouble.'

'There's a bonus, too,' Marc went on. 'I'll provide enough information on Al Sayf's attack for you lads to make it look like it was *you* who thwarted attempted mass murder. The CIA gets the glory and an excuse for all that black budget money you suck up.' He stopped, then snapped his fingers as something else occurred to him. 'I'll even throw in the reason why the Navy lost one of their drones last week, for free.'

Durant folded his arms and glared at Cahill. 'You're not seriously considering this bullshit?'

'Hypothetically speaking,' Cahill replied. 'If the agency accepted such an offer, there would be stipulations.' He paused, considering Marc. 'It's fair to say you've earned the displeasure of this nation. If you came across our radar again, there would be serious consequences.' Cahill glanced at Lucy. 'And as for you, Miss Keyes. Consider your citizenship *revoked*. All the rights and privileges you enjoy as an American will go away. You'll be stateless.'

Her expression soured. 'It's not like I was gonna get my GI pension anyhow . . .' She gave a shrug. 'Whatever. I'll manage.'

'I'm not done,' said Marc. 'There's one more thing.'

'Sure there is,' snorted Durant. 'You want a sleepover in the Lincoln bedroom too?'

'I need something from the NSA's cryptanalysis division.'

Cahill gave a short, humourless chuckle. 'Can't help you with that.'

'Yeah, you can,' Marc insisted. 'Get Durant here to apply some pressure.' He went on before the other agent could respond. 'I'm not going to be coy about it, everyone knows that the NSA is monitoring email traffic through Europe and the UK.'

'Fucking WikiLeaks . . .' said Durant under his breath.

Marc went on. 'That whole PRISM system your government swears is no big deal? The thing you're using to spy on everyone else, including your allies? I want it to work for me, just one time.'

'Why?' demanded Cahill.

'I got my own ghost to hunt,' Marc replied.

Cahill was silent for a long moment, before he spoke again. 'I'll need to make some calls.'

'No you don't,' said Lucy. 'The agency didn't send a man down here without the right kinds of clearance. You say it, it'll happen.' She looked toward Marc. 'That's if you're sure about this? Solomon–'

'He can't give me what I need,' Marc replied, never taking his eyes off the CIA agent. 'Do we have a deal?'

Lunch in the Rapier Club's elegant dining room had done little to ameliorate Donald Royce's mood, and after retreating to the library for a glass of port and a look over the day's papers, he still hadn't been able to shake the unsettled feeling that lay upon him.

He sat in a high-backed chair of old, well-maintained oxblood leather, his gaze drifting to the dance of flames in the fireplace. Outside, London had turned wet and dismal, and the other members who wandered past him smelled rain-damp and of cigars.

He tried to lose himself in the cosy, controlled space of the club. Royce wanted to pretend that he could remain here until all his problems melted away, safe in this impenetrable bastion of English tradition. Around him, the rich and the well-connected, the captains of industry, the officer class and the scions of landed gentry, all went about their business as if nothing mattered to them. Inside the oak-panelled walls of the Rapier Club's lounges, privilege made time stand still.

But it was a falsehood. On the other side of the antique windows looking out on to Mayfair, the world moved on. There were threats out there that could reach into these hallowed halls as easily as anywhere else. Royce's job was to deal with them, of course, but recent events had made that task harder than ever to accomplish.

Soon, Royce would be called up to Sir Oliver's office at Vauxhall Cross to present his final analysis of events that had begun with the sinking of the *Palomino* in Dunkirk, and ended with the disappearance of Marc Dane somewhere in the Maryland countryside a week earlier.

It was not a meeting he was looking forward to, just as it had not been a resolution that he could live with. Heads were going to roll. One thing after another had gone wrong, and now there were rumours coming across the Atlantic that the cousins were up to something.

Royce flipped over the copy of *The Times* and saw a column on the front page. A journalist in Washington was reeling off some supposition about the American president and the war on terror. He scowled at the ill-informed piece and tossed the paper aside.

'Sir?' Royce looked up to see one of the club's staff holding a small white envelope in his hand. The attendant wore black trousers and a red jacket with gold frogging, designed to mimic the look of a British Army uniform from the Crimean War. 'A message for you.'

Inside the envelope were the details of one of the club's private meeting rooms, along with a name he had not expected to see.

Royce forced a brittle smile, and gave the attendant a generous tip. He paused just long enough the throw the note into the fireplace before he made for the stairs.

The Alma Room was used for games of bridge, and while Royce never played, he had often seen other members engaged in lengthy sessions. One wall was a series of glass panels that led out on to an interior balcony, from which one could look down on the lobby to observe the comings and goings through the club's entrance. The room was broken up by pillars of pink marble between the antique card tables and overstuffed chairs.

Victor Welles was the only other occupant. As Royce entered, he rose and gave him a disagreeable look. 'Donald,' he said, without an iota of warmth. 'Here you are.'

'I thought you detested this place,' Royce replied. 'What did you say about it? *A den for old men and plotters.*'

'*Hidebound*,' Welles corrected. 'My exact words were, *a den for* hidebound *old men and plotters*. That opinion hasn't changed. Believe me, if it wasn't that my family had a hereditary membership here, I'd never darken its doors.' He gestured at the walls. 'It's because of places like this and the old boy network they foster that my job exists. Makes it impossible to keep the system honest.'

Royce went to a decanter on a nearby table and poured a glass of Macallan Ruby single malt. 'And yet, here you are.'

Welles's irritation took a turn for the worst. 'What is the point of all this? If you're going to try and influence my report on the situation with Dane, you're wasting your time. You lost him, and that's all on you.'

'You lost him first.' It was a cheap shot, but Royce couldn't help himself. He halted with the glass halfway to his lips. 'What do you want, Victor?'

The other man's annoyance mingled with confusion. 'I want you to stop playing games. Why am I here?'

Now it was Royce's turn to be puzzled. 'The note . . .'

'This note?' Welles pulled an envelope from his pocket, identical to the one that Royce had been given only moments earlier. The other man made a show of opening it, revealing the slip of paper within. In the same careful copperplate script, there was a request addressed to Victor Welles to meet here, at this time. The note signed off with Donald Royce's name.

'You asked me to come up,' Royce insisted. 'Just now.'

Welles shook his head. '*You* asked *me*. I should have refused–'

As he spoke, one of the glass panels slid aside. Part of the shadows on the balcony detached, revealing a figure dressed far too casually to meet the Rapier Club's stringent dress codes.

'You're both here,' said Marc Dane, 'because of me.'

Marc had to admit that he enjoyed the moment, the abject shock on the faces of the two men. Welles was the first to react, reaching inside his jacket, but Marc shook his head. 'Don't be stupid, Victor. This isn't a time to be jumping the gun.'

'How the hell did you get up here?' Royce demanded, with indignation. 'You're not a member!'

'I'm not,' Marc admitted, and he nodded down toward an imposing figure crossing the lobby. 'But *he* is.'

Ekko Solomon paused to look up at the balcony and tapped a finger to his brow in the sketch of a salute, before heading out into the grey downpour to a waiting limousine.

Welles moved toward the old rotary-dial telephone in the corner of the room. 'I'm calling Six. You can consider yourself under arrest, Dane.'

'Not doing that,' Marc shot back, stepping in to block his path. 'I told you right from the bloody start, I'm not responsible for what happened to Nomad. I'm not guilty.'

'Marc,' began Royce, 'we can sort this out. Come with me to the Cross. I won't allow Welles to make this some personal crusade. We'll get to the heart of things. You say you're innocent, I believe you.'

'I know you do,' Marc replied. He paused, glancing at his watch. He didn't have long. 'I wanted to come in. I tried to, before . . . But there's a traitor inside British Intelligence,' he began. 'That's obvious. It's the only explanation for my OpTeam walking right into an ambush. It's the reason I've been hunted across Europe and back. The Combine knew that Gavin Rix and Samantha Green were looking into their mole inside MI6. That's why they targeted Nomad, to remove the threat.'

'And you did a thorough job,' Welles shot back.

Marc glared at him, his temper flaring. '*Think*, you mouthy wanker! If I was the insider, why did I come back after Dunkirk?'

'Obvious,' Welles retorted, ignoring the insult. 'Play the 'troubled survivor' bit, get yourself some desk duty . . . You could parlay that into access to any number of important intelligence sources.'

'Except I wasn't *supposed* to survive,' Marc insisted. 'That's why there was an assassin waiting for me in France. How could he have known where I'd be? He was told where to go by someone on the inside.'

'I'm taking sides here,' Royce said carefully, 'but understand we only have your word for that.'

Marc glanced at him. 'So what about my capture order being suddenly reclassified as shoot-to-kill? Who did that?'

Welles scowled. 'That was an error . . .'

Marc shook his head. 'No. Someone wants me dead. And I know who.'

Silence fell across the room. It was Royce who finally broke it. 'We're listening, Marc. Tell us what you believe.'

'I'll tell you what I *know*,' he shot back. 'First; Iain Nash didn't die on the *Palomino*. He was part of the double-cross.'

'His body was found in the wreckage,' said Welles. 'The DCRI recovered it.'

'You know that for sure?' Marc eyed him. 'You saw data from a French secret service computer. What if that was put there before MI6 got to it?' He pressed on. 'The Combine recruited Nash. He set up Nomad and used the explosion to drop off the grid. In return, he got a new lease of life as their attack dog.'

'There's no proof–' Welles began, but Marc silenced him by pulling a folder from inside his jacket and tossing it on to the table.

Royce gingerly opened it and revealed a set of black-and-white photos, stark images of a corpse on an autopsy table. He recognized Nash's face and paled.

'The Americans have the body,' said Marc. 'I'm sure if you ask nicely, they might let you have it back. Or maybe not. After all, he *was* part of a plot to blow up the US president . . .'

Royce's hand went to his mouth. 'All that chatter we've been seeing from the Americans . . . The mobilizations, the rumours about some internal shake-up . . . That's because of the Combine? How does that connect to Al Sayf?'

'One uses the other,' Marc told him. 'The Combine make their money playing off the fear index. Nothing makes cash like a war does, yeah? They use Al Sayf to push up the threat by helping them build bombs, and rake in the rewards.'

Welles snatched up one of the pictures. 'And Nash, if he's responsible for Dunkirk, how did he end up like this?' The photograph showed the bloodless corpse, the ragged exit wound on the side of his head clearly visible.

'He reaped what he sowed,' Marc said grimly, his hand tensing with involuntary memory of the trigger-pull.

'All right . . .' Royce rubbed his face. 'Marc, we can use this. Come back with me. We'll open a full investigation. If Nash was a Combine mole, we can clear your name and get to the bottom of this.'

Marc nodded. 'He *was* a Combine asset,' he agreed, glancing at the Cabot again. 'He wasn't the *only* one.' He repeated what Nash had told him on the roof of the Willard Hotel, about the warning that had come from MI6.

Neither Welles nor Royce spoke as Marc continued, revealing what he had recovered from Novakovich's hard drive, the meta-data showing without doubt that someone inside Vauxhall Cross had been in communication with the broker and his Combine masters.

He felt fatigued just by the act of explaining it to them. 'Problem is, all the email traces in the world don't count for anything unless you can marry them up with a user code. Without that, you can't know who sent the messages.'

Royce's fingers rubbed his brow. 'Good God. We have a serious penetration of our operation and no clear sense of where to look . . . We have to move quickly, but carefully. Marc, do you think you can help us isolate this person? We can call on the techies at GCHQ, have them sift our email servers–'

Marc shook his head. 'No point. That data has already been wiped. The mole knows I was on to them. There won't be any leads inside our systems, not now. We're too late for that.'

Welles sniffed. 'No data means no way to track this double-agent, if he or she really does exist . . . and I'm not convinced of that. They'll have to be found the old-fashioned way.'

Royce glared at Welles. 'And your department will be in charge of the witch-hunt, as you've proven yourself so able in the past.'

Welles returned his fierce gaze with interest. 'Make your point, Donald, if you have one.'

'You've been trying to cast K Section and the OpTeams in the worst possible light since this started! You decided Dane was the culprit, and everything you've done has been to fit that assumption!' Royce pointed at him. 'You made me distrust my own men!'

'I'm doing my bloody job,' Welles shot back. 'I told you before. It's not personal, it never has been! I leave my biases at the door, that's why I am exceptionally good at my job. For every weak link I find, there are dozens more dedicated officers who are quietly cleared and commended. But you never hear about that, you only see the ones dragged to the gallows!'

There was a polite knock at the door of the Alma Room, cutting short the confrontation before either man could take it further.

'There is someone who knows the insider's name,' said Marc, and he called out. 'Come in.'

The attendant who had brought Royce his note opened the door for a tall, imposing man in an impeccable tan-coloured suit, flanked by two watchful and solemn bodyguards.

'Mister Pytor Glovkonin,' said the attendant by way of introduction, before backing out of the room to leave them to their conversation.

Glovkonin looked no different from the last time Marc had seen him; still wearing that air of casual supremacy, of being lord of all he surveyed. 'I assume there is a good reason for me being here?'

The question was addressed to Royce, and the flash of naked surprise on his face mirrored the moment Marc had stepped from the shadows.

'What . . . the hell?' muttered Welles. He knew full well who the billionaire oligarch was, and the suspicions that crowded around him.

'I sent the message,' Marc told the new arrival. 'You remember me? From Rome? We talked about that weird-looking sculpture.'

Recall flashed in Glovkonin's eyes. 'Ah. Yes. The worried man. Hello again. Tell me, was it a woman after all?'

'I think you know exactly what it was,' Marc shot back, and his tone made the bodyguards tense like dogs whose master had been threatened.

Glovkonin's gaze flicked to Royce and Welles, then away. A false smile slipped into rest on his face. 'Coming here was a mistake, and my time is very valuable. If you'll excuse me–'

Marc called out as he turned toward the door. 'The NSA tracked communications from within British Intelligence to a weapons broker named Dima Novakovich, all done under the auspices of a group who call themselves the Combine.'

Glovkonin paused, offering a shrug. 'That means nothing to me.'

'The emails came from a secure terminal at Vauxhall Cross.' Marc turned to look directly at Wells. '*Your* terminal, Victor.'

Royce came forward, as if he had been waiting for those words, his lips twisted in a snarl. 'You bastard! I was right!'

Welles gaped. 'No . . . *No*!' He recovered, his colour rising. 'I don't work for this . . . criminal!' He waved at Glovkonin.

The smile on Glovkonin's face faded. 'Watch your tongue,' he growled, 'or I'll have Misha and Gregor remove it.'

Royce prodded Welles in the chest. 'You're a bloody traitor!'

'That's what you wanted people to think,' said Marc, keeping his tone steady. From when he had seen the data provided by the Americans up to this moment, Marc had hoped that it would turn out to be wrong, that there was a mistake. His anger and his grief, so closely interwoven by everything that he had been through, pulled hard on him. He wanted to release it, to do violence, to give into it.

Instead, he looked Glovkonin in the eye and went on. 'The trail that led to Welles was misdirection. But not quite good enough. The actual login identity synchs to Donald Royce.'

Welles recoiled from the other man.

'That's wrong,' Royce insisted.

Marc shook his head. 'Royce used Iain Nash as his man in OpTeam Nomad, manipulating intelligence in line with Combine interests. And in turn, you have been running him for them, Mister Glovkonin.'

'I find spy stories amusing,' said Glovkonin, as he absently brushed a speck of lint from the cuff of his jacket, dismissing it as easily as he did the events unfolding before him. 'I'm sure some-body who did those things would be careful to ensure no evidence was left of their involvement.' He gestured to his men and walked away. 'Good day.'

The action was unconscious, instinctive, but both Marc and Welles saw the motion in Royce as he took a step after the Russian billionaire – as if he might offer him some kind of safety.

If Glovkonin saw that, he was utterly indifferent to it, and kept on walking. The door slammed shut at his back.

In the next second, Welles had the short-frame Browning pistol he was carrying beneath his jacket in one hand, and with the other he grabbed at Royce's arm. He forced the other man into a chair and held him there, boiling with cold fury. 'Donald Royce,' he snapped, biting out each word, 'you are being detained under the Prevention of Terrorism Act. You do not have to say anything, but it may harm your defence if you do not mention, when questioned, something which you later rely on in court. Anything you do say may be given in evidence.' Welles stepped back and took up the telephone, dialling quickly. 'This is Bravo Eight Four,' he said, 'Red call, this location.'

'You stupid, blind idiot,' Royce muttered. 'You don't understand.' He looked up and found his former officer looming over him. A gun was in Marc's hand.

'Make me,' said Marc, his voice loaded with hate. 'Tell me why you let them do it.'

Across the room, Welles saw the Glock semi-automatic in Marc's grip and raised his own weapon. 'Dane,' he warned.

Royce shook his head. 'You're naïve, Marc. That's your failing. And the worst thing is, on some level you know it. That's why you never pushed, never really tried to test yourself. You didn't want to step outside of your comfort zone. You were happy being the bloke in the van, weren't you? Letting all the hard choices be made by people like me–'

'Did that include killing your own crew?'

'Rix . . .' He sighed. 'He wouldn't back off. I tried to discourage him, but he was a tenacious sod. Then Green fell into his orbit and that meant everyone in Nomad was tainted. Nash was already in place . . . It had to be done.' Royce swallowed hard and looked up at Welles. 'I'm not going to give you anything, you understand that, don't you? I'm not wrong. I'm part of something that makes us stronger. It won't do for me to be dragged through the mud. Bad for the country and the ministry. I'll be discreetly retired–'

Marc pressed the pistol against Royce's temple. 'Like hell you will.'

'I'm not alone in what I know!' Royce shouted. 'The only way to keep the free world on an even keel is to hold those rabid dogs like Khadir on a chain! *Control*! We control them, we can . . . We can *manage* it.' Royce was unrepentant, and suddenly he had been freed to spill out everything he had kept secret, all the things he believed but never dared reveal. 'No-one wants chaos! No more murderers crashing airliners into buildings! So there are people who have the power to take control . . .'

'The Combine are guiding the war on terror because it makes them rich, not because they want to keep us safe!' Marc barked at him. 'What kind of twisted logic are you seeing, Royce? This is conspiracy, *treason*!' He jammed the gun into the other man's skull, forcing his head toward the table. 'It's murder!'

'Dane,' Welles repeated. 'He can't pay for what he's done if he's dead.'

At the last second, Marc whipped back the Glock and cracked Royce across the face with it, opening a cut that would leave an ugly, permanent scar. He stepped away and spat on the Alma Room's elegant carpet. At length, the gun vanished into the folds of his jacket and Marc produced an encrypted solid-state memory stick. He tossed it on to the table.

'That's everything I have, the NSA traces, the lot,' he told Welles. 'Same stuff I gave to the Americans. Show it to Talia Patel. She'll know what to do.' Marc turned to go, then halted. 'And do yourselves a favour . . . Tell GCHQ to tighten up the firewalls on everything, because the Yanks have their ear to the walls.'

'Where do you think you're going? You can't just walk away,' Welles insisted, as he made for the door. 'You're a witness. There'll be an investigation.'

'Do it without me,' Marc replied, and stepped out into the corridor.

A silver E-class Mercedes-Benz was pulling up outside as Marc stepped around the Rapier Club's top-hatted doorman and down to the pavement.

Glovkonin stood beneath an umbrella held high over his head by one of his *bratva* bodyguards, and not a single drop of rain marred his suit. The other guard was in the process of opening the car's door, and both thugs glared at Marc with unmasked enmity.

'Nice ride,' offered Marc, ignoring the rain as it soaked into his jacket. He thought about the gun in his pocket and wondered; *Could I draw it fast enough to put a shot into Glovkonin before his meat-heads did me in return?*

Even after stopping the Washington bombing, ending Nash, seeing Royce arrested and disgraced, the man standing in front of him was going to walk away. *And he's just one part of the Combine*, Marc reminded himself. *Another link in the rotten chain.*

'You're a persistent man, Mister Dane,' said Glovkonin, with a wan smile. 'That's a dangerous trait to possess.'

'You like being untouchable, yeah?' Marc replied. 'You think you've earned it. Can't deny, you're free and clear today . . .' He shrugged. 'But what about tomorrow or the day after? Sooner or later, the Combine is going to find the light on it. And you won't be able to drive away from that.'

Glovkonin gave him a last look. 'Best of luck,' he said, and vanished inside the vehicle, disappearing behind opaque armoured windows.

The Mercedes whispered away on to Grosvenor Street, blending into the traffic. Marc stood watching it, aware of another vehicle sliding to a halt beside him.

A door opened at the rear of the black Bentley Mulsanne, and Lucy Keyes peered out, scowling at the inclement weather. 'Hey,' she called. 'So I guess you need a lift.'

'You gonna drug me again?' he asked, without looking at her.

'I reckon we're past that,' she replied. 'C'mon. Get in. You'll catch your death out there.'

'Not today,' he told her.

TWENTY-NINE

He gave Malte an address in East London, and they set off through the city streets.

The rain gave everything beyond a greyed-out, unreal cast. Marc stared out of the window and imagined he was adrift in a sea of slow moving shapes, the other vehicles around him blocks of abstract colour and indistinct form.

'Can I offer you a drink, Mister Dane?' Ekko Solomon poured an amount of bourbon and nodded toward the Bentley's mini-bar.

'I'll pass,' said Marc. He took a breath and then turned to study Solomon and Lucy in the seat across from him. 'But thank you for everything you've done to help me through . . . all this.'

Solomon took a sip from his drink. 'You still do not fully trust me.' He raised his hand before Marc could venture a reply. 'I do not blame you. But it is I who should thank you. We had only part of the Combine's plan when you crossed our path. We knew of the missiles . . . Until that point, my people had been developing threat assessments based on attacks on airliners. We had no idea they would repurpose the explosive warheads as they did. If not for you, we would have been looking in the wrong place when Washington was targeted.' He shook his head. 'Rubicon failed to stop the Barcelona bombing. We were too late. But not this time.'

'You really think you can make a difference in the world,' said Marc. It wasn't a question.

'We continue to try,' Solomon gave a nod. 'And I would like you to be a part of that endeavour.'

Marc blinked. He honestly hadn't expected to hear that. 'You're . . . offering me a job?'

Lucy gave a wry smile. 'He pays pretty well. Plus you get good medical and dental.'

'Your status as an MI6 officer was revoked the moment you went on the run,' said Solomon. 'If you come to work for Rubicon, I can promise you a much higher wage and a better arena for your skills. Tracking and stopping an Al Sayf cell from committing an act of violence on American soil proves to me that you have the qualities of an excellent field agent.'

'I was just lucky,' Marc said, shaking his head.

'That's half the job,' noted Lucy.

'Rubicon's Special Conditions Division needs people who are willing to commit to what is right, Mister Dane.' Solomon put down his glass, and gestured at the city passing by. 'There are hundreds of other threats out there. Men like Glovkonin, factions like the Combine. The world cannot rely on nation-states to prosecute them. Sometimes more direct action must be taken. I would offer you the chance to bring the world some degree of justice.'

'Justice . . .' The word echoed in Marc's thoughts. 'I don't think that's what I was looking for. I was in this for revenge, payback for someone I cared about.' He saw a dark-haired woman standing on a street corner, and for one brief instant her face became Sam's. 'I think I still am,' he added.

'I know this need.' Solomon reached up to his neck and pulled out the silver chain that hung there, holding the metal piece strung upon it in his palm. 'At first, it is what I wanted. This is the trigger from the gun I used to kill a warlord. The first evil man I knew. I was only a boy, but I had a man's hate. He murdered the family that raised me. I took his life in payment, but it was not enough.' His eyes lost focus, and Marc knew Solomon was living that moment over again in his memory. 'There is always another warlord. There are always other victims who deserve to know justice.'

The car had left the main roads and it slowed as it passed down a narrow, leafy street. Marc saw black railings and red brick walls.

'I appreciate the offer,' he told Solomon. 'But I need some time to think about it.'

'Take as long as you wish.' He shook Marc's hand. 'You know where to find me. We will speak again, Mister Dane. I am certain of it.'

Marc climbed out of the Bentley and Lucy followed. The rain had passed, but the streets were still wet, the air still chilly.

She glanced up. 'Cloud's breaking. Sun's gonna come out, I think.'

'Yeah.' He paused. 'Look, Lucy. I'm sorry about how this came out . . . About what Cahill said.'

Lucy shook her head before he could go on. 'Dane, forget about it. Home isn't something I need a passport to prove. It's right here.' She tapped her chest. 'You can take the girl out of Queens, but you can't take Queens out of the girl.'

He gave a crooked smile and extended his hand. 'Thank you. For saving my life twice. Or three times. However many it was.'

'Hey, who's counting?' Her grip was firm. Then Lucy's expression became troubled. 'Listen, I never told you about prison. I should have trusted you with that.'

'No,' Marc shook his head. 'I don't give a damn about what you did or who you were before. I trust you . . . You're one of the few people I can say that about right now.' He let go and turned to walk away. 'Stay safe.'

She looked up at the brick arch and the open gate beneath. On the other side of the fence, manicured lawns ranged away, framing lines of grey headstones and age-worn statues.

Marc anticipated her question, giving her one last look over his shoulder. 'I've got to say goodbye to someone.'

Lucy's words proved correct, and as Marc walked out across the cemetery, the sun found its way out and cast the place in a weak, summery glow that brought life to the sprays of flowers left by loved ones to mark their sorrows.

He had nothing to lay on Samantha Green's grave, but somehow that didn't matter. She had never been one for bouquets and candlelight, she was the type who looked to the moment to know that he cared for her.

Sam had shared something strong and vital with him, but at the same time, it was fragile. He was afraid that if he looked too hard, if he applied too much pressure to define it, his memories of her would collapse and he would lose what had made her special.

Marc crouched and ran his hand over the top of the simple granite marker that bore her name and a heartfelt inscription. Her mother and father were still alive, although she had not spoken often about them. Sam's dad was ex-military, and he had understood the importance of what she did for the country. Marc wondered if that was any comfort to him now. He considered seeking them out, then thought better of it. Sam had lived much of her life in the shadows, and he had no right to draw that into the lives of the people she loved.

'I got him,' he told her, remembering the moment when the gun had bucked in his hand, remembering Nash's final moments. 'There's others, though . . . That might take a while.'

After a time, Marc stood up and saw someone coming his way, a serious, bearded man in a long coat.

'All right, mate?' said John Farrier. 'Sorry if I'm interrupting.'

Marc shook his head. 'Come to pay my respects.'

Farrier nodded. 'It was a nice service. Good turn-out.'

'Was Royce there?'

The other man frowned. 'Gave a speech.'

Marc tensed. 'He played us all. And he doesn't even think he was wrong.'

'Royce is done,' Farrier told him. 'Welles will bury him deep, have no doubt.'

'That'll have to be enough,' Marc replied. 'For now.' He took a breath. 'What are you doing here, John?'

'We tailed you,' he said. 'I thought you and me should have a talk.'

'You forgive me for Rome and getting you in the shit?'

Farrier waved the question away. 'Worked out all right. The old dog has asked me to take charge of K Section while we sort out this mess. Royce's arrest . . . Well, we're left with a lot of pieces to pick up. It's not just him, either. That data you dropped on us means we have to scour the house for any other rats that might be lurking in the basement.'

'The Americans will be doing the same,' Marc told him. 'The Combine are going to be on the back foot for a while. Might even force them into the open.'

'It's possible,' admitted Farrier. 'You want to come in and help?'

'Back to Six?' Before, that had been foremost on Marc's mind. But now the offer was there, out in the open, he found he couldn't reach for it. 'You're talking about reinstatement?'

'Eventually,' said the other man.

He shook his head again. 'I'll pass.'

'You sure?' Farrier came closer. 'If you're at large, you are going to make a lot of people very nervous. And I won't be able to help you.'

'They're worried I'm going to go the Full Snowden on them.'

'That's about the size of it.'

Marc's eyes flashed. 'Do you know how deep the Combine's reach goes? Can you promise me that someone won't throw me in a cell for safety's sake?' He nodded in the direction of figures loitering nearby, field officers who had accompanied his old friend out to find him.

When Farrier didn't answer, he looked back toward Sam's grave. 'I've lost a lot. That's going to stop now. I'm going to stay off the radar, find my own road. Not just for me, but for Katie and her family. I put them in harm's way and that's not going to happen again.'

Farrier accepted this with a sigh. 'Yeah. I'll keep an eye on them for you. But for fuck's sake, phone her when you have a minute. Your sister needs to know what went on, and you need to tell her.' He paused, thinking. 'Look, all this has pushed the Combine up to the premier league in terms of threat value. We're going to be actively hunting them now. When I tell you we could use you, I mean it . . . Unless, of course, you've already signed on somewhere else?'

'Not yet,' he noted. 'I'm considering all options.'

'*Rubicon*,' said Farrier, sounding out the word. 'You know where that name comes from?'

'The river in Italy,' explained Marc. 'A boundary line in the Roman Empire, Julius Caesar crossed it and provoked a civil war. 'The die has been cast', he said. *No turning back*.'

'Yeah, I saw that movie too. Your metaphorical point of no return. And that's what Rubicon is, Marc. That's who Ekko Solomon is. Because for all that man's good deeds and high ideals, he's not the noble crusader he paints himself. Solomon is a very dangerous bloke. He's got a lot of secrets trailing after him.'

'I'll bear that in mind.'

Farrier nodded once more, turning away. 'Watch your step, mate.'

Alone with the lost, Marc closed his eyes and listened to the silence.

The mansion on The Bishops Avenue in Hampstead was off a sheltered drive that had only one way in or out, and the other buildings surrounding it were a full storey lower. Pytor Glovkonin liked the way the other houses seemed to be bowing to the larger building, as if they were serfs paying fealty to a lord.

The Mercedes-Benz rolled to a halt and Glovkonin stepped out, not waiting for Gregor to open the door for him. He didn't want to admit it, but he was barely keeping his anger in check and his fury was something he didn't often unleash in front of his employees. He had learned the value of self-control and the power of correctly applied force. It was how he had become a rich man.

That, and a perfect sense of self-preservation. That ridiculous piece of theatre in the gentleman's club had been a mistake, and he chastised himself for falling for it. But it had served one important purpose, to alert him that the British were turning against him.

'Wait here,' he told his bodyguards. 'We'll be going to the airfield.' He left them and walked up the steps to the house, pushing open the thick oak door framed by a pair of faux-Doric columns.

Glovkonin had known all along that Royce was of limited value. All assets eventually became stale and unusable, but it was a pity that the Englishman had done so prematurely. Glovkonin had contingencies for every possible endgame involving the MI6 officer, designed to deflect attention away from the Combine and its organization, and now those would swing into action.

On the road from the Rapier Club, a few calls had set the wheels turning. The Gulfstream jet G-Kor kept at London City Airport was being fuelled, and there would soon be a flight plan filed to show Glovkonin and his wife had planned a trip to Monaco weeks earlier. The apartment on Saint Roman would be ready for them, and if the British security services were foolish enough to move against him, it would not be a simple matter. This was not fleeing, he told himself, merely a tactical withdrawal.

'Elena!' He called out to his wife as he ascended the staircase from the marble-tiled reception.

She didn't answer, and as he mounted the second flight of stairs, Glovkonin noticed the quiet. The house seemed strangled of sound, as if it were holding in a breath.

Glovkonin paused on the next landing and reached for a telephone that doubled as an intercom system. No tone issued from the handset, even when he tapped the key to connect him to an outside line. He reached for his cell phone. Detailed in gold plate and black glass, the phone had a dedicated hotline that could connect him instantly with his security staff – but where he should have had a full signal, there was only a blacked-out 'X'. Glovkonin knew the effect of a jamming device when he saw it.

He turned to look back down the stairs and something caught his eye, something he hadn't seen on the way up. There was an odd shadow by the sofa, just visible from where Glovkonin was standing. He craned his neck to get a better look, and it became clear that he was looking at the body of Erno, one of the other security men he had hired in Moscow. Erno had a halo of dark, arterial blood around him; it appeared that he had been shot through the throat at close range.

The reason for the silence, then. If Erno – who had been recruited out of the Russian Army's Spetznaz – was dead, then so were all the other men in the building.

Was this the British moving against him, or the Americans? It seemed unlikely. He knew their tactics; MI6 would have taken him in the car and a CIA strike would have been loud and destructive. This was someone else. Someone who *wanted* him to walk in.

Glovkonin considered his options. He could retreat back the way he had come, perhaps make it back to the car and find safety elsewhere; or he could press on to the upper floor where his rooms were situated, where Elena would be.

It was true that he was a ruthless man, and it was certainly not beyond him to consider his wife expendable if her life was weighed against his. But Glovkonin was also a proud man, and resentful of any enemy who dared to invade his home and damage his property. If someone was waiting to face him, it would be cowardice not to answer that challenge.

He continued his ascent, pausing to open a safe secreted behind a painting of Vilnius Cathedral. He quietly removed a loaded Makarov PM semi-automatic. Then, Glovkonin walked the last few steps up to the master bedroom that filled the house's upper floor.

The doors leading to the bedroom were already open, and Elena's bodyguard, a German woman named Yuta, lay slumped in a chair on the landing. Like Erno, she had been shot in the neck and bled out quickly.

Glovkonin tensed as he entered the room, the ghost of anger and the anticipation building in him at what bloody ruin he might find. He saw his wife lying on the wide bed beneath gales of cotton sheets, and he froze. At length, she gave a low, airy gasp and turned over, deep in sleep, utterly unaware of what had gone on around her.

A soft voice from behind him said 'That is far enough. Drop the gun and turn around.'

Reluctantly, Glovkonin allowed the Makarov to fall to the thick pile carpet at his feet. Hands open and held away from his sides, he turned to find a swarthy, well-dressed man sitting in the chair beside Elena's make-up mirror.

The man had the predatory glare of a lion, the chained violence of a killer in his element. The pistol in his hand was an assassin's gun, a Ruger 22/45 modified to mount a silencer.

They had never met before now, but Glovkonin knew this man and knew his capabilities. 'Omar Khadir,' he said, inclining his head in a greeting. 'This is unexpected.'

'Speak quietly,' Khadir demanded, pointing at the bed with the Ruger's barrel. 'If she wakes, I'll be forced to kill her.'

'Of course.' Glovkonin's annoyance at the invasion of his home faded, to be replaced with more pragmatic emotions. He found another chair and sat so he could look the terrorist in the eye. 'Did you leave anyone alive?'

'Only the woman. I needed a lure.'

'If you came here to murder me–'

'I am disappointed,' said Khadir. 'Assurances were made by your group. Against my better judgement, I chose to ally with the Combine to advance my work and you failed me. A meticulously planned operation, thousands of man-hours and hundreds of assets deployed . . . for nothing. Promises from you that this would succeed, all worthless.'

'Regrettable,' offered Glovkonin, as if he were assessing the result of an unsatisfactory business transaction.

Khadir went on, ignoring his words. 'All this because of your failure to deal with the British agent and the African.' He leaned forward, and his grip on the pistol never wavered. 'Because you were unable to solve this problem, the efforts of Al Sayf to strike against our targets have proven futile . . . and I am not a man to waste my time.'

'Clearly,' Glovkonin replied. He understood that whatever he said in the next few seconds would determine if his life would end in this room, his neck punctured by a .22 calibre bullet. 'You have every right to be angry. But I suggest we take this opportunity to discuss how to make certain that these sort of . . . *complications* . . . never occur again.'

Khadir raised the gun and aimed it at Glovkonin's throat. 'Speak,' he said, 'while you still can.'

Acknowledgments

It's been a *long* road for this project, and I'd be remiss if I didn't pause here to show appreciation to a few people. First, a moment to tip my hat to Ian Fleming, Robert Ludlum and Tom Clancy, three very different writers and very different men, whose works cast an enduring shadow over the thriller genre, and who were all great influences on this novel.

I would also like to thank my fellow author Ben Aaronovitch, whose enthusiasm, comradeship and dogged insistence helped bring *Nomad* to life; Professor Alison Leary and Jeff Punshon of the Royal Free Hospital for answering my medical and surgical questions; Shaun Kennedy for insights and insults; Rowland White, for being a fellow traveller and the first to show interest; Ian Peters, for Infosec 101; Evan Booth, for improvised weapons; and my agent Robert Kirby, for leading the charge.

Much love to my mother, who has always liked this kind of stuff, and my father, who taught me tradecraft; and last but never least, my eternally supportive better half Mandy.

This book was written on location in London, New York City and Norfolk.

MARC DANE RETURNS SUMMER 2017